Experimental Fusion

By

A. J. Nelson

 New Generation Publishing

-Prologue-

Awakening

The many scientists that crowded in the room looked upon the test-tube like structure quizzically.

Thick glass reflected red lights whirring, and as it passed through the liquid inside, the light refracted so that whatever inside was magnified. Electricity poured in through metal and wires, bringing what had once been just a theory to life. This was an old, expensive form of technology, and it took up much of the space in the room, but it was all this laboratory had at the moment and still fairly reliable. The control panel to regulate the functions of the Fusion machine was pressed into a corner, close by the machine so that the observer could monitor the experiment and act accordingly. The structure itself, held in place by the metal supports in the ceiling and floor, was like a great glass pillar, large enough for a full-grown man to stand in there and have room to jump about, providing they didn't stretch out their arms too wide.

Startled murmurs filled the laboratory, and more and more people came running to investigate the scene. All except for one; a man who was guided by another man's gentle arm, limping and unseeing, but still living.

"Amazing!"

"Intriguing!"

"Astonishing!"

For inside the structure was the first success of many failed experiments by the scientists of the year 2067, held in secret from the public and even the government lest word get out and the experiments all be ruined.

A boy was curled up there in the tube. He looked about five in human years, but two fluffy wings were curled about him, and resting on his head through his hair, were tiny tufts of downy feathers, supported and swaying in the movements of the liquid in which he rested.

The man who limped, supported by two crutches and his guide, hissed. What kind of mad plot had he gotten himself dragged into? The veins stood out blackly against red-tinged, inflamed flesh, half-hidden beneath black rosette markings and a small, neatly-trimmed beard on his chin.

The experiment, the aim of this laboratory was to fuse an animal with a human. The scientists had tried many species, from mice to jellyfish, but the previous tests had failed and the subjects had died. Most of them. This one was still alive, and he had been successfully fused with an owl.

It seemed that younger humans and animals made better test subjects, as the scientists' research seemed to have shown.

Now, the small, feather-covered boy was curled up as though nestled in an egg, but he was about to see life again anew. A scientist flipped a switch, and the fluid inside the test tube drained, and then the device itself opened up to let the experimental boy, nicknamed 'Moony' from his confines.

At first the experiment choked in order to breathe, and that was the only sign of life. Then a wide golden eye opened, as Moony looked up at the scientists curiously from beneath his feathered brow. The scientists looked bewildered, then slowly but surely, cheers rang out among them.

All except one.

Moony looked around, his eyes filled with intelligence, yet at the same time, complete clueless innocence. He awkwardly folded his wet, downy wings against his back and let out a hoot of confusion as though to say "What's happening?"

The scientists calmed at that, one of them kneeling to help the little boy find his feet. It was a most amusing sight, until eventually he stood, seeming pleased with himself, and bobbed his head in a most owl-like way, and gave another little hoot.

One of the scientists seemed puzzled.

"Do you think he'll remember anything?"

The scientist was rewarded with a high pitched "Hoooo!" from Moony, even if he didn't know what any of this was all about. One of the other scientists clapped a hand to her forehead.

"We erased his memory before we fused him, remember? It was the kindest thing to do…"

Several of the scientists groaned.

"Looks like that weapon's going to have to wait a bit longer..."

"Hoooo!"

The head scientist shook her head, but she was smiling, and most others, too couldn't help finding the experiment's attitude adorable.

The head scientist looked around, then beckoned and left the room, with Moony tottering after, beating his fuzzy wings and waddling unsteadily after her.

The feathery tufts on Moony's head twitched like the ears of a curious young puppy as he followed, ready for his first training mission, and an introduction to the life of a spy.

-Chapter 1-

Belonging

"Ha! I got you, Ginny!"

There was a huge commotion, pandemonium, craze. Feathers, fur, and scientists flew all over, scared to intervene in case they got their noses bitten off. The 'got your nose' trick had been role-switched and hastily forgotten, long ago. High pitched voices filled with the sweet, ripe sound of blossoming laughter bloomed in the air, and despite the commotion it seemed at first, it was soon clear that the commotion was caused by a mere game. The scientists, a good few of them still children at heart, or with their own children back home who they missed, could never resist the temptation to join in with the little experiments.

Ginny, a red-haired girl with a white streak in her hair, raced forward after Moony, wrinkled and flopped over ears bobbing. Her little claws upon pawed bare feet, clicked against the smooth floor beneath her feet, and she threw herself at the scientist whom Moony hid behind, pudgy arms failing at thin air as she collided with the young man's legs. The scientist looked momentarily worried, but her large, brown eyes betrayed that her little, singsong squeaks meant that she was happy. Moony skipped off over a tabletop, his high voice tutting and hooting.

"No tig-backs!" he reminded his friend, Ginny.

It had been several months since the first successful fusion, and, since the scientists had grasped the concept, many more successful fusions had followed Moony, whose fond nickname still stuck. None of these children were any older than twelve. Joey, a boy who boasted seemingly dull brown feathers, as of now, and arms that had become fuzzy wings like those that protruded from Moony's shoulders, was the oldest. It had been his twelfth birthday just a few days ago. All of the other experiments, unfortunately, had wanted some of the presents, too, and it became increasingly apparent that the experiments here were more like siblings than anything else, and as well as looking up to, and down upon, each other, playing together, and acting like children do, they all had their moments, and everyone at the party seemed to have wanted that same balloon. The experiment named Karasu, a seven-year-old boy who was fused with a hyperactive golden retriever puppy, was the one to eventually pop it.

Right now, the puppy-boy was at the other end of the table, slyly crunching away at something that could only be...

"HEY! Get off my lunch!"

The scientist that Ginny had collided with sprung into action, racing off to protect the remnants of his chicken sandwich from the greedy soul. Everyone stopped in their tracks to stare, distracted from their joys by the scientist's yell. Ears perked up, and eyes widened. That one scientist who had tempted Karasu snickered away to himself behind the crowds. Benny, pink eyes blinking slowly and nose wrinkling, lowered his long ears and twitched his whiskers, then pushed his glasses up his nose so that he could see better.

"This isn't going to end well..."

You didn't exactly need to be a master of physics to see that.

"Come here, boy... Give that back... Come on... Drop it!"

Karasu kept on eating, looking up at the scientist with his secret weapon; the ultimate puppy eyes. Despite this the scientist kept on edging forward, reaching out for the sandwich that Karasu had in his mouth. It was hardly a battle of wits, but just as it seemed that the scientist had triumphed, both Karasu and the scientist were startled out of getting the sandwich for themselves, at least for the moment. Two pairs of hands grabbed out for Karasu's meal, and the boy jerked out of the way rapidly as two furry bodies launched themselves for the sandwich. Obviously following Karasu's example, the twin Alsatian girls, Sally and Cassie, had come for their own try at the food. Twisting over onto his front, Karasu looked desperately around for a moment as he bounded away down the corridors on all four paws, tail between his legs.

Sally and Cassie tailed him closely, tongues lolling out and ears pricked. After these, the hungry scientist followed, yelling their names and annoyed hollers of "Bad dog!" and "Get back here!".

But not one of the three dog-children did, and there was one more thing that followed the unfortunate scientist, and his quarry, down the hallway. The sound of welcome laughter echoed forth, a different sound from every different animal and person. Despite the endless journey of everyone here, they would always be happy in some way.

Always.

***

Peeping his nose over the edge of the blanket as the scientist tucked him in, Karasu's usually bright brown eyes were red-ringed and sad. Karasu sniffled, looking up at the scientist who stood over him; the one whose lunch he'd stolen just a few hours before. If there was one thing that Karasu hated, it was being scolded. He shifted uncomfortably under his pale blue blanket, his

8

large, golden ears flopping with his movements. A wet black nose twitched and snuffled, and he lifted a furry hand to wipe his nose. The scientist dabbed at the boy's wet dog-eyes with a clean white handkerchief. It had turned out that one of the other scientists, one who always loved to taunt this one, had tempted the dog boy, knowing that he could never resist the urge to eat.

"Hey, don't be like that..." the scientist said, attempting a comforting smile to try to lift the child's spirits. "Just remember to only eat your own food, okay? What would happen if you found some food in the war or someone gave you it, and you ended up being poisoned or something?" Karasu looked down slightly to consider, but didn't reply verbally, his doggy mind seeming to have difficulty absorbing the facts. Though he understood human speech, one thing that Karasu couldn't do was speak out for himself. At least, not in a human voice.

"You need sleep, eh?" the scientist continued, pulling the blankets up to the dog's chin, and gently ruffling the boy's ears with a hand. He was only seven, after all. The scientist looked down as he felt a peculiar tickling feeling on his palm, to see Karasu gently licking him. The scientist slowly moved his hand away, leaving Karasu looking confused, and even more so as the scientist stood up and began to move towards the door of his dormitory room, which was modelled to look like a human kitchen. Karasu gave the tiniest of yelps and began to throw off his blankets to scamper after the scientist. The scientist, in response, moved forward again.

"Shh, Karasu!" The dog silenced in response to the command, and the scientist gently pushed the floppy-eared, blonde-haired boy back onto his bed. The boy snuggled in, but looked a little distressed still. So the scientist ruffled his soft, gold-furred ears, a gesture that he knew always helped the puppy to feel better. Karasu's pretty brown eyes closed for a few moments. "I'll see you in the morning, eh?"

As the scientist moved towards the door again, Karasu didn't look up again. When he looked back, he saw that Karasu had closed his large brown eyes, and laid his head down. He looked to be almost sleeping, until the scientist saw the gentle wagging of the boy's tail beneath the blankets, a movement that was hardly ever absent from the dog boy. The scientist smiled.

"Good night, Karasu…"

Then he gently shut the door behind him, the door automatically locking itself as soon as it had fizzed its way closed. The lights of Karasu's room flicked off into darkness.

Smiling to himself, the scientist looked around then quietly went to check on the other children as they slept or lay awake.

There was Joey, the boy who had been fused with a peacock. His eyes, as green as the plumage that he would someday develop, were peacefully closed. His downy brown feathers blended in with the nest that he slept in, and his feathery arms hugged his knees into his chest. He smiled and whispered to himself in his sleep, a sight that the scientist found almost saddening.

Then there was Benny, a boy who had been fused with an albino lop rabbit. He had short but soft white hair, and pink eyes, which were now opened to slits. He had huge, floppy bunny ears that were now draped over half of his face even as he slept on his back in his bed that had been built to simulate a shallow rabbit warren. He slept soundly, and unlike Joey, made not a whisper, with only several kicks of his muscular rabbit feet and twitches of his bobby little tail to show that there were indeed dreams flowing through his mind in a river.

Next, the scientist checked on Sally and Cassie, the

Alsatian puppy twins. They were lying curled up in a little jumble of fur and limbs on a single dog bed, in which the blankets had been chewed and thrown. Their breathing mingled soft and sweet. They were identical twins, and had been fused at the same time, with the same animal. This was clear as it was almost impossible to tell the twins apart, save for a single bullet hole in one of Cassie's ears. Each bore the closest resemblance to the animals which they were fused with, being almost entirely Alsatian dogs, save that they moved upon two paws rather than four. They possessed short muzzles and fur over their entire bodies, and flowing brown hair that reached to their shoulders. They had tails of two plumes that were constantly wagging even as they slept, occasionally tickling the other twin's nose and making them sneeze.

Ginny came next. She was a little girl who had been fused with a guinea pig. She had hair of a deep red, and a single white streak that was shaped like a wing on the right side. She possessed sweet little ears that curled and flopped, and tiny little claws to top off her pudgy little hands. She was also, the scientist had learned, the only experiment that sucked her thumb as she slept curled up in a fat little ball. She was doing that now, her chest gently rising and falling as she slept and dreamed of crunching through juicy carrots and cabbages, rather than just the hay that she munched through from her little nest.

And then Moony. Moony was the nickname that the scientists had given him before he was even conscious after the fusion, since he was the first successful experiment; barely anyone even remembered his true name. He had fused with an eagle owl, and he had two fuzzy wings protruding from his shoulders that would one day grant him the power of silent flight. There were plumes of feathers decorating his wrists

11

like some sort of soft, yet useless, armour, and further clumps of messy, downy feathers formed a scruffy tail. He walked barefoot, for each of his toes held a wickedly sharp claw. But for now, his wings served as more of a blanket than as flight tools, and now he rested peacefully, his golden eyes almost closed, as a final yawn signalled his drifting off into the dreamworld, and he dreamt of being a fully-fledged owl hunting mice with the finest of grace.

Finally, there came the room of the strangest of friends. A young girl with a gleaming, segmented blue tail was sleeping sprawled out on a tree branch with wings that made her seem like a fairy folded against her back. Her skin was tinted slight iridescent blue, and her black hair shone with a metallic blue sheen. From her forehead emerged two twitching antennae. Emerald, as she was strangely called, had been fused with a dragonfly, and she shared her room with her closest friend, a girl wrapped up beneath her in a soft fox tail named Bethany. Though Emerald was soft and flighty, Bethany was tricky and wild, always one to convince her friend to take risks. Even if those risks went bad in the end, their friendship never waned or died, and Bethany's tricky nature was evened out by Emerald's carefulness, just as Emerald's fragile skin and bones were equalled out by Bethany's relative sturdiness; each was a perfect balance to the other. Now they were each asleep, feeling entirely safe in each other's presence.

The scientist smiled to himself, a sadness in his eyes that was, to some inexplicable. Most of the children here had been homeless before, taken in by the scientists to be experimented on because the life they might have gained would be better than the one they had lived before. Some had been orphaned in the terrible war that raged on around them; the war they were being trained for, but at the same time were oblivious to, now.

In the year of 2067, it is every country for itself. It is one against the world, all others against each other. No alliances can be formed without bloodshed, so it is best not to risk it. Few people, or even no-one remembers what started the war, back in the year 2058. Every country is working hard to develop their own secret weapons to defend themselves, and in England, that weapon is humans who were merged with animals. In early testing, the experiments failed and the subjects died. All except one. That one was Toby, and he was left with injuries that couldn't be healed even by today's technology. The damage went too deep to even attempt it.

The scientist whom had been looking after the 9 young experiments as they slept in their dorm rooms was Toby's guide. He'd lived in England since before the war had begun, but since the war began, few to no people had trusted him; it was a wonder that he'd ever managed to get a job in this laboratory at all, and that was only because he'd been the one to bring the theory to life originally. The only one here who had complete trust in him seemed to be Toby; and Toby needed to have trust to do just about anything. Perhaps the head scientist of this lab, Amanda, trusted him too, but that was debatable.

It wasn't his looks.

Really, he wasn't anything special, the scientist. Dressed in a worn chestnut shirt and old denim jeans as well as the labcoat that was typical of any scientist, the man was as average as any. His eyes were blue, his hair a gentle shade of chestnut brown. His chin and cheeks were stubbly, and his hair was, as was common for him, un-brushed. It fell down to just behind his ears, and his fringe was long enough to fall in his eyes and make him blink. He had plenty of freckles over his cheeks and nose, and his skin was as pale as could be. He was of a fairly average height and, admittedly, was a little bit lanky. Unable to socialize properly, the man had taken to the habit of only eating when he as alone, and as a result, was thin and a bit underweight. Used to keeping his head down, the man walked with a slouch and his movements were shy, wary.

Nothing overly special.

It wasn't his voice that was rarely raised.

In the laboratory, he only spoke when spoken to. His voice was soft, easy on the ears as if he constantly had to to keep himself from falling into hypnotic song, and half failed. Here, it always carried a daydreaming tone as he dreamt of a better life that he might never get to live, and tones of sadness, acceptance.

It wasn't because he was a bully, either.

He was far from used to the torment that he endured himself, but he would never inflict such pain on another. He knew how it felt, and wouldn't hurt another as they had hurt him. In addition to making himself as bad as them, it would probably also get him fired. He would never be able to get away with what they did.

No.

It was because...

Lost in thought, the young man stared wistfully down at the ground that lay before him as he walked. He was jerked back to his senses as he heard jeering laughter.

"Hey, look, it's the American guy!" snickered one. The scientist flinched, and wished that they'd keep their opinions to themselves like most people would. He didn't understand why the simple fact of where he was born was so important, not now. He'd lived in England since he was 15!

"Who, Danny? I'm surprised they haven't kicked

14

him off the project yet... Isn't he meant to be with Toby?"

The scientist, Danny, as was his name, felt his cheeks burning in shame, but he clenched his hands into fists and, as usual, tried to shrug it off.

"Toby's asleep..." He muttered through gritted teeth, making his way forward.

"Permanently?" chimed in one of the other scientists, grinning roguishly.

Danny halted and whipped around, chestnut hair beginning to stand on end, but he said nothing, clamping his lips shut over his clenched teeth. His knuckles were beginning to turn white with anger, but Danny fought to keep the poisonous emotion locked in, refusing to let it show. He wasn't one to give in to torment. But still, he felt the others' words burning like hot knives in his mind, and he twitched his head to rid his mind of any foul thoughts that might cross it.

Taking a deep breath, he calmed, and turned away, saying no more. Then he slowly began to walk away, towards his own dormitory room, heard the voices beginning to fade away behind him. The lab here had its own set of rooms for those who wanted to stay to work late, or early, on projects or new weapons. Danny had nowhere else to go, so he was grateful for the shelter that this place offered him. He also had to stay with Toby, who often tried to get up early out of habit despite his many disabilities. Danny knew that Toby felt a horrible regret for ever having gotten involved with this experiment, but was never allowed to leave the laboratory in case the public caught even a glimpse of him.

Another reason for the dormitory's existence was that fusing a human with an animal to create a new experiment could be a lengthy process. The children used as experiments sometimes had to be kept unconscious for two weeks at a time whilst the viral infection that was genetically modified to contain the DNA of the selected animal did its work on the bones, skull, and even skin of the young one until completion. That being said, they also needed to be kept alive and nourished throughout this time, and needed to have instant attention at hand in case something went wrong.

The process of erasing a subject's memory could take just as long and, in rare cases, be just as risky. Scientists often scoffed at this 'unneeded' process, but it would be cruel to risk skipping it entirely; Danny, of all people, knew this much too well for comfort, having spent so much time with Toby as he thought so wistfully back to the days when he was strong again.

Finally reaching his dormitory after what seemed like a lifetime of the other scientists' jeers fading into the distance, Danny sighed in exhaustion. Tonight was an early night for him, at only 5:00PM.By the ragged snores that he could hear from the bed next to his own, Danny could tell that Toby was, as he'd predicted, asleep. This encouraged him to be quiet as he slipped from one set of his daytime clothes and into one of the well-worn sets of pyjamas that he slept in, throwing his usual clothes carelessly to one side of his bed, his brown T-shirt, trousers, and lab-coat landing crinkled on the smooth tiled floor. Danny couldn't be bothered to fold them right now, so he decided to leave that until morning; he really didn't care about tidiness right now. Not that he was a tidiness fanatic, mind you.

Even though he was exhausted, Danny felt his mind reeling over and over as he lay in bed, and he winced every time he shuffled to find a more comfortable position, worried that Toby would awake. He tried to shuffle as quietly as possible, but ended up being rather unsuccessful in that endeavour. Despite this, apparently the failed experiment slept like a log, because he didn't awake once, even when one of Danny's feet knocked against the side of the bed and created a nasty clanging sound.

The last of the summer light that had managed to break through the dust-covered skylight slowly faded away as Danny watched. Eventually his eyes drifted out of focus and into that bizarre, contorted, but strangely pleasing version of reality that was his own dream world.

Despite this, though, there was a recurring question making his mind roil even in dreams, every thought that came with it causing him to feel his heart sinking further.

Do I truly belong here?

-Chapter 2-

Training Mission

There was a thick hubbub in the air by the time morning broke. All the experiments were gathered in the Entry Room, where the congregation of scientists prepared them for their latest training mission. Despite the scientists' best efforts to keep the atmosphere calm, though, there were flurries of excited barks, yips, hoots, and caws ringing out as the experiments chattered excitedly about tactics, techniques, and what they ate for tea last night, whilst Karasu moped around because his caretaker had forgotten to give him breakfast.

Joey, who, on the other hand, could be a rather apathetic and vain sort, simply sighed and muttered sideways to Moony. "I really don't get why everyone always makes such a fuss…"

But Moony wasn't truly listening, and all he did was hiss "shh!" and then burst out into excited hooting again. Despite all the kerfuffle, it was surprising to see that Danny and Toby, those who usually paid more attention to the training missions than anyone else, were both missing.

After what seemed like an age to all the hopelessly failing scientists, one of them finally managed to gain control. The head scientist, Amanda, was known throughout the laboratory for her stern temper. The effect she put on the young mutants was similar to the effect of a headmistress walking into a classroom of rowdy children, and they all fell silent immediately, looking up with pale-faced terror, waiting to see who'd done something wrong.

Sally and Cassie each gave Karasu a nudge forward

and snickered silently as they remembered his feast yesterday, and the golden retriever boy looked vaguely ill; he obviously remembered, too. Joey looked completely calm, Moony shrank down a little so that he was hidden among the taller experiments and slyly picked his nose in the shade, whilst Benny twitched his nose nervously and huddled close to Ginny, who looked tired, and confused, her hair sticking out all over the place like she'd just been electrocuted. Even Bethany had the grace to look fairly sheepish for all the tricks she'd played yesterday, and the day before that, and the day before that, and so on... Her russet tail fluffed out even as it curled around a clearly terrified Emerald.

Amanda was silent for a few moments, observing them like a strict teacher would a silent class, waiting for one of the youngsters to make one wrong move. Her slick black hair shone like the feathers of a raven under the whirring lights of the entry room, and her brown eyes were narrowed, shining blackly beneath the shadows cast by her hair. Eventually she spoke, and a flinch ran over the ranks of the nine successful experiments like an ocean wave.

"Right, you lot!" she boomed, her voice thunderous, and echoing through the room so that everyone could hear. She knew that any attitude that was more encouraging and calming before the mission start would serve to only lure the trainees into a false sense of security.

"Today's mission deserves extra caution! Your aim is to infiltrate the security and access the scientific headquarters which create the newest secret weapons of the base country!"

Despite Amanda's voice still being loudly reverberating, excited whispers broke out among the mutants again as the scientists began to snicker amongst themselves about Amanda's poor phrasing of the mission. Amanda's face visibly darkened and she shot everyone in the room an acidic look that couldn't be neutralized.

"Silence! Your aim is to break inside and take the memory device that serves as a backup for all the data. Plans, blueprints, coding- everything relating to the country's secret weapon is stored on the device, and it must be obtained at all costs. You will have exactly an hour to complete this mission! If you do not make it out of those doors by the end of the hour, then you will have failed and the mission is forfeit!"

The children exchanged worried glances as Amanda gestured to a timer set to an hour, blazing red from the screen overlooking the entry room. They had never been on a timed mission before.

"Stay hidden, stay silent, stay unnoticed, but most of all, stay in one piece. The fate of this mission, and the fate of England, depends on those things!"

Amanda pointed towards the doors that would open up into the training room, and the mission itself. Each child, with ears pricking, feathers twitching, whiskers wiggling, looked serious. Ginny began to give those telltale little squeaks that a guinea pig makes when scared.

Slowly, the doors began to creak open, and they silently waited until the image of an alleyway beyond the door had crept into view. Amanda began to count down.

"Your mission starts in…"

The children readied themselves, each looking brave, frightened, or both.

"3…"

The children began to walk forward, filing in through the doors.

"…2…"

They looked back, their eyes holding expectations beyond any hopes. The light emerging from back in the laboratory lit up each of their faces and caused their eyes to shine.

"...1..."

Some of those that had looked brave now looked frightened. Most had begun to dance on their feet as though itching to either get a move on, or jump back through those doors; like just about any child, the experiments here were notoriously impatient. The red numbers on the timer flickered. Amanda's gaze flicked to the one who operated the timer. The scientist nodded, waiting for her cue.

"...And your time starts... now!"

And then the doors back to the laboratory slammed shut, leaving them in the darkness of the alleyway.

Now there was no other way to go but forward.

***

"Danny... Wake up, you lazy oaf..." Toby's rasping voice growled as loud as he possibly could. He couldn't see Danny, of course, but he could definitely hear the man's snoring through the one ear that worked.

Toby had been awoken by the yelling of Amanda down the hall. Apparently there'd been a power blackout sometime that morning, and the emergency power supplies had focused mostly on keeping the in-fusion experiments alive, so the usual wake-up call of a small static electric shock that would awake only the selected person had failed to go off at 8:30am. Some people had woken up despite the absence and completed their daily duties, but others seemed to have taken the chance to stay sleeping. Today had been possibly the worst day for such a thing to happen; it was the day that Danny and Toby had planned to be the first ones awake in order to give the experiments special attention before their mission, but here they were, with Toby lying helplessly in bed, and Danny still fast asleep.

Toby hissed in annoyance, jet-black ears flattening back. His glazed, sickly-yellow eyes flitted about unseeingly out of habit, and the man's thick black hair began to stand on end. He certainly wasn't the most patient of people, and his failed fusion certainly hadn't improved that. The experiments had left him blind and half deaf, with stiff, numb, and almost paralysed legs that could only twitch at the best of times. With the help of his crutches, Toby's limbs could only just support his weight. To top that off, his throat and vocal chords had been warped so badly by the fusion that it pained him even to breathe, let alone speak.

His fusion had been carried out before the discovery had been made that children made better fusions than adults.

Now he possessed legs that were covered in thick, soft black fur. These limbs had little to no muscular strength any more. There were rosettes of fur all over his body, and he had a long, thick-furred tail. He had soft black hair through which panther ears poked through, constantly twitching and turning, and a heart that had even been modified to pump too strongly, giving him blood pressure problems. In addition, his body still seemed to be trying to fight off whatever was 'infecting' him, and this gave him constant inflammations and rashes all over his body. He needed crutches to get anywhere, and a guide to deal with his blindness; Danny took this role, and so far, hadn't done anything against him, nor treated Toby like he was a child. Toby held Danny with more respect than most for that, because being treated like a child was what he hated most about his new disabilities. He absolutely refused to use a wheelchair, insisting repeatedly that he still wanted independence to some extent.

Finally getting irritated and impatient, Toby strained to move, and reached out with a hand towards the sound of Danny's snoring. His fist clattered against what he assumed was the metal framework of the bed and after a grunt and a quick shake of his now-aching fist, Toby grabbed onto it, using the metal as some sort of support. Using one arm, he dragged himself a short way forward, and with the other, he grumpily fumbled for the bedside cabinet to figure out where to go.

I'm not as helpless as they think I am... He thought to himself, a surge of victory electrifying his chest. Rasping in satisfaction, Toby stubbornly moved over to the side of the bed as far as he could without falling off, and flung his hand once more in the direction of Danny. This time, his efforts were an attempt to wake his guide.

After all that work, Toby's hand hit something, but he was pretty sure that it wasn't Danny...

Toby drew his sore hand back and rubbed the knuckles with the other, then took to searching the area for his clothes, pretty sure that he'd hit the bed frame, or something equally as... well, metal. If he couldn't wake Danny, then he'd just have to go off himself. Toby would always tell himself that, given the chance, he could act independently. The way he saw it, now was his chance to shrug off that humiliating view that everyone looked upon him with. He could do anything he wanted to, whenever he wanted!

So Toby fumbled and struggled, leaning over to one side of his bed to try to find his clothes, then the other. It took a while, but eventually he managed to find where they were. Upon discovering this, Toby fought to pull them over to him, but then, in a blind hurry, slipped the hand that was supporting him and felt only empty air. Struggling to balance himself for just a moment, in an instant Toby was falling with a muffled smack onto the smooth floor.

Ever stubborn even so, Toby eventually managed to abandon his pyjamas, pull on his underwear, his shirt, and a pair of loosely fitting trousers. Feeling proud of himself as he felt about, and took hold of, the crutches that had fallen nearby, Toby began to haul himself to his feet, wanting to get out of this room before Danny awoke; he knew that the other man would likely be worried for his safety, and Toby could hear him beginning to stir even now. To Toby's experience, Danny sometimes made funny grunting noises before waking up.

So Toby hastily limped away, supporting himself with his crutches and trying his best not to crash into anything. He fell down one set of stairs and bust his lip after walking into a wall, but other than that, Toby had surprisingly few accidents. Amanda's voice had faded long ago, so the blind man could only assume that the training mission had kicked off.

Ears pricking, he broke into a faster limp, despite the searing pains that were beginning to run through his arms, and the prickling agony and yet, scary numbness, that slipped through his torso and up his neck like some sort of ghostly parasite. Still, Toby continued to limp on, bare claws scratching against the floor even as his movements became laboured and breath ragged, his heart pounding stronger and faster as his panic rose. Time after time, Toby had felt death creeping through him, and now he felt it again.

Slipping to the ground, Toby searched around for all the tablets and pills that he kept in his labcoat, and then a second later realized that he'd left his coat back in his room- he'd left in such a hurry. Dropping his head slightly, Toby wheezed out a breath, then sucked it back in.

Sitting there, struggling, Toby listened out for voices, footsteps, or anything that would tell him he could call for help, and that someone would come to help him.

He cried out...

But nobody came.

***

In the darkness of the alleyway, the young mutants huddled into a little crowd. They were stood there for a while, taking in their surroundings and not seeming overly bothered about the passing of time. They whispered in frightened voices amongst each other, over each other's voices, and then hissed over their interrupter. Eventually, they quietened down, though, their loud fear replaced by a silent panic. Karasu was the only one who seemed unmoved, and he had sauntered over to investigate the curious scents of food that were wafting from a nearby dustbin, and he was sifting through it greedily for some sort of snack.

Eventually, Joey spoke up in a hushed voice, ruffling his tufty feathers.

"I think... I think we'd better get a move on..." he whispered, looking around. Some of the others nodded then the rest hesitantly followed.

Joey slowly began to walk, feet moving slowly but silently over the cold concrete ground. There was a crashing sound, and they all whipped around to see a wagging gold tail, and Karasu nosing through the remains of the bin he'd toppled over. He didn't look guilty at all.

"Karasu!" they all hissed at once, and the dog boy bounded over on all fours with long, gold hair bobbing over his shoulders. He reeked of strawberries and cheese, and all the children leaned away from him, seemingly determined not to be 'infected' by the smell.

Joey, now determined to be the leader of this, groaned loudly and shushed them all hastily. "Follow me..." he grumbled, flicking the short cluster of tail feathers that he possessed. They all obediently trailed after in a small huddle, with Karasu doing the walk of shame behind, with tail between his legs. His dark, puppylike eyes and the way he crouched so low to the ground made him seem young and vulnerable. He whimpered softly.

Moony seemed displeased by the thought that Joey was leading, and had taken a spot behind him, seeming convinced that since he had been the first successful experiment, he should be in charge. Joey didn't seem pleased with this, but he looked just barely able to tolerate it. Each of the others looked on expectantly as they rounded a corner of the alleyway, and saw two guards staring dead ahead, each on the side of a door that seemed made of the heaviest, thickest metal imaginable.

Everyone froze instantly, and backed behind a corner so that they wouldn't be seen. Moony looked at Joey. Joey looked at Moony. Ginny and Benny began to squeak, and both their ears drooped.

"So? What's the plan?" Moony asked expectantly, the feathered tufts on his head flattening into his hair. His golden eyes gleamed dully, and they were half closed.

"You're asking me? I thought that you wanted to be the leader here!" retorted Joey.

"No, you did! You were the one who went first and tried to be all grown-up!"

"No-one else was going to, now were they? If you didn't want to be the leader, then why did you try to push in front of me?"

"I didn't! I just have better night vision, so I thought I should go help! Besides, I was walking next to you, not in front!"

"My night vision is a million times better than yours!"

"No it isn't! You're so stupid!"

Above the bickering, Bethany began to whisper into one of Emerald's ears. In the darkness, the dragonfly-girl's eyes glittered into thousands, like each pupil possessed within it a black diamond, and the fox's eyes glowed and glittered like she was possessed. The grin on her face said it all. As she whispered, Emerald's antennae drooped, and after a while, she whispered back, visibly unsettled. Her wings were twitching from her shoulders, all four of them transparent except for tiny veins running through. They shone like the finest glass.

Twitching her lips up in a grin, Bethany watched for a second as the boys continued to argue, then wordlessly tucked her thick tail into the back of her jeans. Curling her furry little toes for a second, the girl pulled the hood of the hoody that she was wearing over her head and folded her black-tipped ears against her head so that they were hidden. As she skipped out into full view of the guards, Emerald nudged Benny and whispered into one of his huge, floppy ears. The boy blinked his pink eyes a few times and then gave her a brisk nod, ears flopping. He gave a grin then hopped out into the shadows, hiding from the guards' sight quite unlike Bethany, who skipped out to greet them, a huge smile on her face. Her purpose was clear; she aimed to distract the guards for as long as she could, and give the others the chance to attack. Her tail was hidden, as was most of her fur apart from the black over her hands that could easily be dismissed as gloves. In a few seconds, Sally and Cassie followed Benny into the darkness.

Emerald peeped out from behind the corner to watch. She had chosen each child for a specific reason. Benny had back legs that were strong enough to knock out a full-grown human with a mighty kick, and Sally and Cassie each had the instincts of police dogs and when they worked together as a team, they were more confident and skilled than most. Double the power, and double the damage.

Bethany was laughing in a childish way, and the guards seemed to be trying their best to ignore her. Bethany's amber eyes danced just as she did, skipping around in circles and pestering the guards with a string of difficult questions.

"Why are you wearing that funny suit? You look like a mechanical knight!" she giggled, gesturing to the gleaming black suit that the guard wore, obviously to be able to ward off any attacks, whilst keeping in touch with inside the building itself. Benny, Sallie, and Cassie got into position, each one waiting in the shadows behind the guard. Even despite his poor eyesight, Benny could still see with the help of his glasses; he could now see exactly where he was going to hit.

"Do you just stand there all day and do nothing? That must be reeeeeaaally boring!" commented Bethany, laughing again, but still getting no reply. She could tell that she was really pushing their buttons, though. One of them had turned away from her slightly, and the other had clenched his fists. Benny, Sally and Cassie crouched, waiting for the signal from Emerald.

Emerald sucked in her breath and spread out two of her wide wings. The thin membranes flashed.

The guards both sprang into action, that strange wing's reflection both bringing paranoia to life in each of them, but that was the signal. One guard was hurled forward as Benny leaped and kicked with a powerful flex of his muscles. He bounced forward and began to heave off the helmet, before delivering another powerful kick into the centre of his forehead. Benny threw the helmet aside and thumped at the pavement with one of his back feet.

Meanwhile, Sally and Cassie had each of the man's arms in their jaws. No matter how he swung and flailed, they shook and they writhed, and they didn't let go, until they had brought him to the ground in the way that a police dog would have done. They, too, struggled to yank off his helmet, but either this man's face was fatter, or he was more stubborn. He tried to struggle back to his feet as soon as he was down, until Sally grabbed onto his neck in her jaws, and then Cassie yanked off the helmet. The man saw stars for a moment after several blows had been delivered by unsure paws to his face, and then he saw no more.

Emerald scampered out towards them, and all the others followed, with Moony's face burning with rage and a childish shame. Emerald was plucking a passage card from one of the unconscious guards, having seen a card scanner on the wall, just beside the door. However much she stretched and strained, though, Emerald couldn't reach it. Even though Moony was busy blowing up at her, Bethany noticed her friend's struggles, and quickly finished untangling her tail. Trotting over to her friend, Bethany smiled and pricked her ears, then lifted up the shorter, six-year old girl so that she could pass the card through the machine. A little green light flashed, and Moony started hurling a tantrum at them again.

"Heeeey! But I wanted to open the door, I wanted to!" he said, stamping a foot on the ground and pointing rudely at them. They all watched expectantly, but the door didn't open. Then suddenly, their stomachs all plummeted down to their waists, and they all fell silent from their chattering as an automated voice called out to them.

"Key card analysed. Please place finger."

"Seeeeee!?" insisted Moony, hooting unhappily at them all. "I tooold you that you should've listened to me!" Moony gestured to himself with his thumb, and stuck out his lower lip, folding his arms huffily, and then plopping down on the ground. "You do this, because I just wanna see what you can come up with!"

Joey sighed. "But Moony, Amanda said that we all need to work together on this!" he protested, poking Moony irritably. "And she'll probably get really, really mad if we don't!" No-one liked the thought of the head scientist getting angry, but even this didn't faze Moony.

Besides one of the unconscious guards, Ginny was squeaking loudly as she tried to pull one of the guard's gloves off. "I'm not gonna give up! Last time we failed a mission, I wasn't allowed outta my hutch for a week!" she squealed, yanking and heaving, then beginning to chew the object off. "You're being really selfish, Moony! And selfish people can't lead, and you wanted to lead earlier, remember?"

Despite Moony's hooting protests, Ginny refused to give up, and eventually managed to work the gauntlet from the guard's hand. Then she took his hand in her fat little paws and uncurled his fingers. The rest of the children joined in with her efforts, all of them seeming remotely encouraging to her, apart from the grumpy five year old that was Moony. Joey in particular seemed pleased with this effort, if only because they were proving Moony wrong.

"Please place finger."

"Heave, ho!" he called out as he Sally, Cassie, Karasu, and Bethany worked on lifting the man's back from the ground, whilst Emerald's wings whirred as she took to the air, carrying the man's arm. She pressed one of his fingers onto the sensor, antennae waving expectantly. A light flashed under the finger she'd placed, scanning the finger closely.

"Preparing fingerprint analysis."

There was a pause, and all the children held their breaths.

"Processing…"

If it had taken any longer, a few of the experiments, aside from Emerald, who was already turquoise-tinted, might have turned blue.

"Analysis complete. Access granted. Welcome back, Tom."

The children all cheered and whispered, softly, but happily amongst themselves and they all tossed the unconscious guard carelessly back to the ground besides his comrade. All the children gathered expectantly around the door as it began to slide open with a low humming sound. Though they may have hesitated before, now even Emerald was smiling, her deep eyes glimmering with happiness, and a newly emerged confidence in her voice as she finally said something for all to hear, as she was hugged closely into her best friend, Bethany.

"I… I did it…" she whispered.

And the children all cheered even louder.

***

Back in the dormitory, there was a small mumbling sound as Danny finally came to, his blue eyes blinking dazedly about him as he gave a final, waking grunt. For a while he lay there, at loathe to remove himself from the warmth of the quilts and sheets that kept him all snug and toasty warm, but it didn't take him long to realize that there was something terribly wrong. His sluggishly sleep-induced stupor made him just lie there for a while, pondering, until he sat up in his bed and took the chance to look around.

He was the very last one to awake, and everyone else had left the dormitory, leaving their quilts and pyjamas strewn all over as though they had left in a great hurry. At first, Danny wasn't overly concerned, until he remembered that it was an important training mission this morning for the young experiments. His face fell totally, the calm, if a little tired, look quickly being replaced by one of horror. Panicking inwardly, Danny looked over to Toby's bed, only to see it abandoned, as well, Toby's labcoat hung over the bottom of the bed.

Where had he gone?!

Danny's eyes widened in fright, and he threw back his quilts, hauling on his clothes with about as much grace as a stupefied dog getting itself dressed. Wherever Toby was, he was without any kind of medication that he needed, and possibly without a guide, too...

Danny wished that he could kick himself for not waking up earlier. Slinging Toby's labcoat over one forearm, Danny heard the rattle of all the pills and the brush of cardboard against fabric in the pockets of the clothing. His heart lurched. They were all still there, meaning that Toby hadn't taken out any of the boxes and decided to risk going without. Maybe he hadn't been able to find the clothing? He couldn't have forgotten it, right?

"Toby!" Danny called out, his voice ringing down the lengthy corridors and then right back towards him as though to mock him. The halls here were like endless mazes, and Danny still found himself walking in circles or into areas that he had no knowledge of even now, after working here since the experiments had begun. What if the same thing had happened to Toby?

Supposing he hadn't crashed into anything, then one could end up anywhere if they were blind, and still think that they were going the right way.

But, blind or not, no man could simply vanish.

"Toby! Where are yoooouuuu-?!" Danny cried out desperately again, panic stealing into his voice. What if Toby was already dead? If Toby's heart rate rose too much, it could become fatal, and sometimes, even though he might try so hard to make himself heard, sometimes Toby could only utter a whisper.

Searching through the halls as if his life depended on it, Danny kept on calling. The halls seemed almost deserted. Were all the scientists too absorbed in the training mission to pay any attention to the ruckus that Danny was making?

Or perhaps they thought he was overreacting. Even though he had begun his training in medicine and first aid and had almost taken a job as a doctor, Danny still tended to overreact if he didn't know what was happening, and was rather overprotective about those he cared for. In addition to that, Danny still stirred up some distrust among the people here, because he had been born in another country; a country that was now involved, like England, in the great war that shook the whole world and every ounce of human life to its very core. Sometimes, Danny didn't even feel like he was human, the way the others treated him.

That would make sense... Danny thought bitterly to himself, heading on, checking in every door, and peeking around every corner that he went through. *And then, it'd all be my fault for not being able to get there before he died...* A thrill of horror ran through Danny's stomach, and a twinge of painful shame accompanied it. *But in the end, it really would have been my fault...*

Danny swallowed, but searched desperately on. He dared not give up, and he dared not call anyone else.

After what seemed like forever, tears of desperation had begun to gather in his eyes, but he would not stop. For every positive thought that ran through his mind, a thousand more that were negative strangled the positivity from his brain in as brutal a way as any medieval torture device could.

As Danny finally began to backtrack towards where he could hear voices discussing the progress of the training mission, Danny was barely paying any attention to where he was going any more. He was afraid of what he would find at the end of his journey.

A troubled soul, clinging to life?

A dead body?

Or simply Toby, as Danny had always known him to be… Independent and strong?

There was one thing that kept on nagging him, even worse than the revelation of many months ago.

Toby trusted me, and yet… I failed…

-Chapter 3-

Secrets Kept

Laughing and whispering amongst themselves until Joey hissed at them and even Moony silenced eventually, the nine little mutants crept down the bright corridors. Occasionally, one of them would slide with soft paws on the slippery surface beneath their feet, and others would growl at them to be quiet. Even so, they whispered amongst themselves, nervous questions such as "how much time do we have left?" or "do you think I'll be fed when we get back?"

Occasionally, they would halt and ready themselves for a tussle nervously as they heard voices from beyond one of the doors. Eventually, though, all of the young experiments gathered around a door made of plated metal. They were all quivering in anticipation, Emerald's glassy wings sending little lights dancing off of the walls around them. A gold plaque engraved with blood-red writing was fixed to the door above their heads, though only Joey could read what the words said. The children all looked at him expectantly.

"It says... It says..." Joey whispered in a hushed, and frightened, voice, craning his neck in an effort to see the words better, although it was also partially an excuse to cover up his poor reading skills. Moony hooted nervously, looking around. Bethany growled softly to herself, and Ginny and Benny huddled together and squeaked amongst themselves. The three dog mutants whined softly, huddling into one another. Karasu revelled in the attention. Emerald, however, was silent once more.

"It says... Top secret..."

"This must be it!"

"Top secret?"

"Yeah, I think so..."

"Joey must be right! He can read!"

"Aren't secrets not meant to be told to people?"

"It's our job to get secrets! Let's go!"

Moony took the lead now, his golden eyes glowing with expectation. Ruffling his wings, he, and the rest of the children stepped back as Bethany held up Emerald to swipe the card that she still held in her palm, just in case it could come in useful. Seemingly lacking in as much security as the outside doors, the door slid open with a soft whirring sound.

The first thing that they noticed in this next room was that it seemed unusually empty. Mirrors were dotted around the room in odd little locations, seemingly for no reason at all. Moony's talons clicked softly, and he seemed rather confident by now, despite the fact that nothing in any training mission was ever as easy as it seemed.

Then Moony's foot seemed to hit something. At first, there was only a soft clicking sound as his claws knocked against a different part of the ground, but then something changed dramatically. There was a whirring sound that Moony couldn't hear, but some of the hearing-oriented mutants did. Bethany gave a warning little growl and grabbed Moony's shoulder with a fur-covered paw. Moony hissed. Karasu barked loudly until someone gagged him with a hand in his mouth. Sally and Cassie both growled. Benny wrinkled his nose and perked up alertly, whilst Ginny darted about in a little circle whilst giving a guinea pig's warning shree.

"What was that for?!" Moony hissed sideways at them all. But he needn't have asked. Not even a second later, lights, laser lights, came fizzing through the air like bullets fired from unseen guns, the beams bouncing from each mirror and into the sensors on another wall. There seemed no set shapes or any gaps between them; they were leaping at random. Some cut straight across the room at diagonals or even straight across, whilst others bounced from mirrors once, twice, or even three times before meeting their home.

One thing was clear, though. It would be impossible to crawl beneath the lasers, and hurdling them would be a risk not worth taking. Moony's wings were young and possessed no feathers suitable for flying, but high above them, there were tiny gaps between the mirrors, and the lasers were more evenly spaced than they were erratic.

With Karasu silenced and Ginny with her paws clamped tight over her mouth, there was an eerie silence over the mutants' ranks as they each tried to figure out what to do. Behind them, the door slid closed with a loud bang as it hit the floor, leaving them in darkness other than the deep red light that fell upon their faces from the lasers.

As the seconds passed into minutes and time ticked menacingly away in their minds, it became frighteningly clear that none of them had any idea what to do in the situation. They each cast hopeful, and then later dismayed, glances in each other's direction as they realized that everyone else had much the same thoughts as them. But nobody said anything.

In the thick of the crowd, though, Emerald was hopping up and down, trying to see what all the fuss was about. Amongst all the mutants, Emerald was the smallest and it didn't seem like, with her dragonfly genes, she was going to be growing any time soon. Flicking her ears as she was knocked into several times by the reticent dragonfly, Bethany looked to one side then picked up Emerald as she had before.

The iridescent hair of the girl gleamed a sleek shade

of purple in the light of the lasers that hung in the air like ghostly tightrope paths, walked upon by none but flecks of dust and darkness as it strained to reach the light. She looked up with wide eyes shimmering like dark diamonds, and smiled some. She said nothing, but above the whispers of her friends and siblings, she looked to the skies hidden by darkness, where webs weaved with thin threads of light stretched taut.

She opened her glassy wings and curled her tail behind her, beginning to squirm in the arms of her friend. Eventually writhing free, she clambered up onto Bethany's shoulders and wobbled unsteadily there, able to peek up around everyone's heads.

As everyone turned to watch her, Emerald placed a single finger to her lips. Her antennae peeked up and twitched at the air beyond her. Whispers hushed into silence, squeaks into sniffles. Every shuffle was turned into an echo that seemed to mock the children as they stood watching in what should have been utter silence.

Then Emerald's wings glimmered as they fanned out even in the darkness that was so thick that it seemed to almost choke you. Pausing there for only a moment, Emerald seemed like a little fairy as she stood there, balancing on the shoulders of her foxy friend with her beautiful, iridescent form shimmering a gentle shade of purple under the ghostly light of the detecting lasers that searched for their little crew of nine.

If any one of the hundreds of spearpoint lights were broken, then all would be lost.

With little care for the danger, Emerald finally took flight with a soft, broken whirring sound, as her wings met the air every split moment. Lights spun around her, and the ground away from her, and her breaths came as sharp little squeaks every moment that her energy failed with her confidence. Nonetheless, the dragonfly continued flying, avoiding the lights with the utmost of clumsy grace and zigzagging little jerks in her movements.

What a place to make her first flight...

Ducking around one laser and swerving over another, Emerald twitched herself several times and tried to hover as she tried to calculate what to do next, where to go. She was almost there now, but the closer she got, the more her fairy-like form risked breaking one of the ever-tightening lights. Twitching forward, bit by bit, the nervousness was clearly illustrated in her movements. It was then that the children below her each gasped and squeaked.

Emerald fidgeted and panicked, worrying that she'd done something wrong, and as she did, one of her wings flashed in front of a laser, the light piercing her wing like a knife would pierce soft butter with an ease as though her wing were nothing but glass. The echoing shuffles and squeaks grew louder as Emerald's wings continued to flit and flare. There came several warning bleeps and further red lights began to flash, illuminating the darkness that hung in crimson that made the lasers almost impossible to see.

Emerald fluttered forward, eyes wide as she fought to dodge the lasers and find her way. But the alarm hadn't gone off yet, not truly... The bleeping was soft, soft enough to not be noticed by any outside of this room. Was she almost there, or merely half as before? It was hard to tell. On one side, it felt like she had been amongst these lights for an eternity. But on the other, she felt only an instant had passed.

But then, disaster struck.

Below them, panicking and yelping, Karasu had leapt forward in an idiot attempt to save Emerald from this strange, bleeping warning. As soon as he did, there was a loud screeching sound like that of a high pitched foghorn. The keen-eared mutants all buried their heads in their paws and tried to get away from the awful sound, driving their noses into the smooth floor and whimpering and crying like little puppies.

Even those that didn't have such frighteningly good hearing had clamped their hands over their ears. Emerald looked as though she could be knocked out of the sky by a feather, her wings jarring and twitching as she struggled to keep herself up. Despite this, though, she struggled on, swerving around lights and then tumbling face first onto the floor beyond. Sobbing softly in shame Emerald squirmed forward and forced herself onto shaky legs. Jerking her arms up, Emerald did the only thing she could think of doing now that she was here, and slammed a single fist against a crimson button that was flashing as red as the air. Every single red light dimmed around them, and the shreeking sound faded into its echoes before they too, were swallowed up. The change left the little ones unfocused and frightened, wondering what was going to happen, and what had just happened to them.

Wobbling on their feet, face down on the floor, or sitting staring about with no clue what to do, the children didn't seem to want to go anytime soon, and had almost forgotten about the timed mission at hand. Despite this, there came the sounds of tramping footsteps that caused them to glance about at each other, panic stricken, and then race towards the frighteningly frail-looking Emerald as she teetered and looked about to fall. Bethany grabbed her wrist and, with no time for congratulations and celebrations, heaved open a door, beneath which a soft yellow light was shining, peeping through.

This one, despite being hard to get to, seemed relatively easy to open. It was almost a trick, how easy it seemed, but the mutants couldn't find it in their hearts to complain any more. Each trying to get in first, they

40

swarmed through the door, then once they were through, slammed it tight behind them.

Now they were in a wide room, containing huge computers and flashing buttons. Through each computer screen, incomprehensible codes, models of DNA, and even the blueprints for creating chips small enough to be inserted into the individual cell of a human and ordinary-sized chips to be inserted into the human or animal body were flashing across. The neatly tiled floor like what would be found on the bottom of a swimming pool was almost hidden by wires. The young mutants understood little, if not none, of what they were seeing, but simply watched in fascination.

So absorbed in the surroundings were they, that they hardly noticed the figure sitting focused on a soft office chair before the many computers, typing up the codes and theories for every one of these models, and working slowly on his cause, the weapons that would assist his country in the massive war that gripped the earth, and make up for every last bit of the trauma that he had experienced in his past.

So focused was the scientist on his work, that even as he reached with a thin, shaky hand to take a sip from the glass of water that sat on his desk, he didn't notice the experiments that had entered his domain. With an uncoordinated twitch of his hand, the glass had dropped and shattered on the floor, scattering shards all across the floor around his desk. Giving up in his endeavour, the scientist sighed, and from the way he, for a moment, slumped forward in his seat, it was clear that whoever he was, he was absolutely exhausted.

The mutants, now eyeing the device that was plugged into his computer, began to mooch forward as quietly as they could manage. Then Karasu, being the unsteady puppy that he was, tripped up. His front paws hooked around a wire that was draped over the floor,

41

scooping his feet out from under him. He landed with a nasty thud, and everyone winced.

If he hadn't noticed them before, he noticed them now. The scientist jerked upright, and then slowly stood. He seemed almost afraid to turn around, for fear of what either he, or whoever it was who had entered, might see. However much the mutants held their breath, it was already clear that they had been noticed. Slowly, the man turned around, and in a hesitant, frightened voice, spoke out.

"Wh... Who's there?"

***

From where he was lying, with hands gripping his chest in blind, uncontrollable panic, Toby's breaths were gasping and rattling up his throat, but he could hear voices from up ahead, where there was the staircase leading to the testing room. Toby's hopes rose, and his ears pricked. His heartbeat finally began to calm and despite the pain, Toby smiled, his yellow eyes wide. Feeling ahead of him with one crutch, the injured man clambered up the stairs as best he could, then as he found that there wasn't another step, he momentarily panicked and stumbled slightly.

Limping another few steps on his crutches, Toby's nose and reddened face was met by the cold metal of a door. Quivering like a leaf, Toby felt around until he found the switch that would open the door, and was eventually met by the feeling of a smooth, round surface beneath his fingertips. He pushed the button down, then limped out, expecting to hear the greeting murmurs of other scientists, shocked exclamations of "where on earth is Danny?!" and the like. Toby felt pride filling his breast at the thought. He had proven just how independent he could be.

Now would they treat him like a normal human and not like a defenceless child?

Toby's hopes rose, and he limped forward, sticking out his chin and closing his eyes, simply because he had no reason to keep them open; well, not any more. The fact that the sickly yellow pupils were visible most of the time was out of habit. He had no real reason for his glazed eyes to be open any more. Strutting forward, Toby was surprised out of strutting as he met another set of stairs. His brow furrowed in confusion. Another staircase? This couldn't be quite right...

He swallowed, but continued on, and forced a hopeful little smile onto his face. Maybe he'd just taken a wrong turn and ended up on the path to the observatory? Someone there would surely know where he'd gone wrong...

Limping forward again, Toby dragged himself up the stairs, with muffled rapping sounds as his crutches met the stony steps. Again, he felt that stomach-churning lurch as he stepped to the top of the stairs and found that he'd just passed the last step as he failed to find the next. Limping onwards, Toby's ears had perked up. He didn't have to be an utterly masterful scientist to be able to tell that there was something very wrong. He couldn't feel anything beneath his toes, no, but he could hear the crunching of gravel beneath his crutches, and the prickle of cold air on his skin.

Despite his nervousness growing with every minute, Toby kept on walking, until the ground made tapping sounds rather than crunching sounds beneath his underused limbs and his crutches. Lifting his nose finally and sniffing the cold, clear air, Toby felt as though his skin were burning with the cold. Toby wasn't aware of anywhere in the laboratory feeling like this. Despite his neverending stubbornness, Toby now felt the sharp sting of defeat as he sank down to the ground, shaking and shivering with crutches still in hand.

Lowering his head, Toby was unable to see a burning light flashing towards him, and it was his deaf side that was facing the direction of a growing rumble. His heart beginning to falter and hammer again, Toby clenched his teeth in an effort to drive back the pain, before he brought up his hands to hide his face. The unseen world around him seemed so dark, foreboding.

He'd lived here, in this town, for his whole life, and yet Toby had never felt like he'd known a place less. He was sitting here, now, unable to see where he was going. He could be metres away from the laboratory, or he could be miles, but his arms ached from the strain of dragging him so far on his crutches. And now he sat here on the cold, hard ground, lost, alone... Would Toby ever see anyone again? They'd always told him that it was dangerous for him to leave the laboratory, but Toby hadn't believed it until now.

It was only when he felt a sharp pain in his side that Toby was jolted rudely back into his senses. Thrown to one side in cold strands that he assumed was grass, Toby gave a rasping yowl, and even this tiny motion cost him a torrent of agony. "Who... Who did this...?" he hissed, vengeance in his voice, as though he thought that someone would hear him. Toby shook as he began to try to roll onto his feet, but the entire side that had been hit had gone numb. Grimacing, Toby's ears pricked as he heard the slam of a car door, and the telltale clip-clip-clop of high heels clacking against stone, sounding quite hurried, and moving in his direction.

Toby went silent, but shifted his face so that he had turned away from whoever was approaching him. Shivering in pain, Toby flattened his ears into his jet-black hair, his tail making a rustling sound as it whipped through the grass, then went limp. Reaching out, Toby tried to gather his crutches to him again, but found that the other seemed to have skittered out of his reach. There seemed to be no escaping from whoever it was that had hit him.

"What are you doing?" Toby's ears pricked up, but he said nothing. The voice that he heard was a woman's voice. It had a tint to its sound that suggested it would usually be soft and sweet, but it was a little shocking to whoever owned the voice to round a corner and drive into a man who was just sitting in the middle of the road. "Are you blind?! Why were you just sitting there like that!? -Oh! You're bleeding!"

Toby lifted his head slightly, his eyes still closed. With her question on blindness, Toby felt his spirits sinking like a stone dropped into a bottomless sea. Was he bleeding? It was only now that he felt the telltale wetness, the feel of his clothes sticking to his flesh around the area that had gone numb. He opened his sickly-yellow eyes slightly so that she could see their clouded glaze. "There's no need to rub it in..." he rasped, feebly trying to arrange his arms so that he could push himself into a sitting position. Like his wound, though, his fingers had gone numb with the cold, and they fumbled and twitched against the cold ground beneath him.

"I... I took a wrong turn... I thought I could do this on my own, but..." he said finally, before trailing off. In truth, he was glad to at least be able to talk to someone. But that someone wasn't of the laboratory, were they? His lungs were aching from his speech, but Toby was used to all these aches and pains by now. "I've been walking for... For..." Toby looked down. How long had he been walking? It felt like hours to him.

"...Ages. I just wanted a little sit down..." he told the newcomer, then fell silent to listen to the roaring of blood through the one ear that still worked. Toby heard her speaking again, but was unable to make out the words. She sounded far, far away to him. Giving a feeble jerking cough, Toby spat out a glob of what he could only assume was blood.

"...And is that a tail...?! You have patches of fur all over you, and you have weird ears, and a tail?!" Toby finally caught some of the woman's words, and he winced, remembering far too late why he wasn't allowed to leave the laboratory; the other scientists wanted to keep the entire experiment a secret from the general public.

Tensing as he realized this, Toby felt his heart sink in his chest even as a pair of hands gently took hold of his upper arms and heaved him into a more comfortable position in the way that someone would settle a child. Turning his face in the direction that he assumed the woman was, Toby flattened his ears and bared his teeth in a display that he assumed would be threatening.

"It's a long, long story and one that you shouldn't be hearing!" he told her, his voice hissing and rasping, but sounding almost desperate. The woman, by the short gasping sound that she made, seemed shocked by Toby's outburst. Even though it felt odd to be meeting someone new, Toby felt mildly ashamed. It was clear that speaking so openly to someone was an almost completely new experience for him. He hadn't been outside of the laboratory in months.

Lowering his head, Toby went silent, a mourning air beginning to radiate from his face and posture. The woman, having settled beside him on the grass aside the road, had fallen silent. Toby assumed once more, with a renewed clarity that she had been shocked by his outburst. The long and awkward silence continued for a while, before Toby tried to speak, but found that he couldn't. The physical ache of his heart was starting up

46

again, searing pains racking his chest. Toby fought not to let it show, and was rewarded by the strange woman not seeming to notice. Eventually, though, she broke the tension, and spoke out.

"So, uh... What's your name?"

"Toby. And yours?"

"Sabrina. You do realize that you're wearing your trousers inside out, and your shirt backwards, right?"

Toby winced again. He hadn't realized that... But then again, it wasn't like he didn't have an excuse. Pricking his ears slightly, Toby lifted his head again. He could feel his cheeks burning fiercely, but either Sabrina was being polite, or she didn't notice the blush. Finally plucking up the courage and gathering up his dignity again, Toby stuck out his chin and twitched.

"Can you help me get back to my... My home?" he asked vaguely, turning towards her out of politeness and habit rather than necessity. His hopes rose.

"Your... Home...?" Sabrina replied questioningly, not seeming convinced. She'd met a strange man who was blind, deaf, and paralysed... Or perhaps 'met' was a bit of an understatement, since she'd hit him with her car. A feeling of dread rose in her stomach, but whoever Toby was hadn't complained much about his injuries. She looked at him.

"Yeah, my home... I was trying to be independent, but must've taken a wrong turn in the hallways..." he told her, with a small smile on his face. "And can you help me find my crutches, too? I have this one, but I seem to have lost the other..."

There was a soft shuffling sound before Toby felt his other crutch shoved into his hand. Fumbling with the object for just a few moments, Toby was soon ready to hop to his feet, even though he was sure that his numb legs were weak and trembling and his arms were threatening to give way as soon as he stood. A lightheaded feeling stole into his brain, clouding all his remaining senses with a thick, unwelcome fog. Reaching out with a hand, Toby stumbled and tried to find something to keep himself up, but before he was able, felt firm hands grip him around the waist to hold him steady. Toby gritted his teeth against the pain.

"Ow..." he whispered, shuffling a few steps forward with the help of his crutches. "...Thanks."

Sabrina continued to support him

"Don't mention it," she said. "Now, do you have any idea where we're going?"

"I... I remember that there's a gravel path leading to it, and it's a dead end in between two fields. It's close to that old railway line, if that helps any..." Toby looked hopeful. "And you know that new road that passes by Elvet Hill? That's nearby, too!"

Sabrina laughed, and Toby was confused by the chiming sound.

"This is that new road!"

Toby felt a little relieved, but at the same time, his cheeks burned in shame. He must have walked in one giant circle! He hung his head in shame.

"Shouldn't we get you to a hospital or something first, though?" she continued, but Toby was already vigorously shaking his head.

"No... There's a few first aiders around where I live..." he replied weakly, fairly certain that Sabrina could tell that a lot of what he was saying were lies through his teeth. To Toby, though, secrecy was the key.

"You sure about that?"

"Yeah. Are you gonna take me or what?"

Toby sounded a little desperate now. He heard Sabrina sigh, but then say nothing. Toby's tail twitched in a vexed sort of way, whipping from side to side in short little twitches. But then she took Toby's arm and began to lead him. The only thing that the man could do was follow, his shaking body giving away his pain.

Eventually, after what seemed like an age, Sabrina came to a halt.

"Is this it? This hole in the ground?" she asked Toby, sounding doubtful, if a little distasteful.

"Does it have stairs leading into it?"

"Yeah, and then a door at the bottom, from what I can see..."

"Then, yep. This is it..." Toby smiled, and shuffled one crutch forward a little, looking for the empty space that hinted to the location of the first step. From what he could hear, Sabrina was still standing awkwardly beside him. He turned towards her.

"You can go now, if you want to..." he said with a smile growing on his neatly-bearded face.

"Oh? Of course! Do you want me to?"

Toby had to pause to consider. Did he? For once, Toby actually felt as though someone actually cared for him. But, it was really all about secrecy. What would the other scientists think of him even so much as going outside?

"I... Well, you don't exactly wanna... You know, see anything..." he said, feeling as though this was the worst excuse that he'd ever come up with.

"No?"

"The truth is, I'm not meant to be here... Not outside, not talking to anyone, not anything..."

Toby trailed off, then sighed and took a limping step forward, both of his useless feet flopping onto the top stair. He desperately wanted to stay and talk to Sabrina for even just a little while longer, but if he did that, then he might never see her again. But then again... Had anyone in the laboratory even noticed his absence?

"Really? Why?"

"You've seen my tail, my ears, this fur, right? I'm

49

blind, half deaf, in constant need of medication… They don't want anyone to know about me… I'm afraid… I just… I can't tell you any more than that."

Toby closed his mouth, and lowered himself down onto the next step without a word.

"Toby…?"

Toby's ears pricked in response to the sound of his name.

"Does this mean that I can't tell anyone about you?"

Toby nodded again, saying nothing, his heart sinking with his pained breaths rasping.

"Then, your secret's safe with me."

Toby turned around in surprise to Sabrina. He was beginning to smile again, a sight that lit up his darkened face.

"Thank you…" he murmured, turning his face away after a while, though the worry plagued his mind that he might fall backwards and down the rest of the flight of stairs. "Is there anything I might be able to do in return?"

"Anything?" Sabrina sounded almost amused, but there was a long pause as she thought, a pause that Toby felt weighing upon his every heartbeat. "…Because I can't think of anything, Toby."

"Then… Then would you at least come see me again, Sabrina?" Toby blurted out without even thinking. He didn't want her to leave without him being able to ask. Quivering slightly, Toby wobbled on his feet as he waited with bated breath for her answer.

"See you again? If it would make you feel better, then okay…"

"You don't have any idea how much that means to me…" Toby closed his eyes, the tension leaving him like water gushing out from a burst dam.

"When?"

"I… I'll think of something. Do you have a phone

number or, or anything? I could borrow my guide's phone!"

Toby was almost dancing with excitement now, his eyes huge and alight with expectation. He could tell, somehow, that Sabrina was smiling.

"Sure, Toby..."

He heard the unzipping of a pocket, and then the sound of a pencil scribbling hastily on paper. Toby then felt a warm hand pushing a small square of paper into one of his hands. He clung to it along with his crutches.

"I'll be waiting for your call, okay?"

Toby nodded, his bearded face spread into a bubbly grin. This feeling... Was this what it was like to be independent again? Was this how it felt to be adult and not treated like a child? Toby looked up as he heard someone dashing away, their feet crunching on the gravelly path and knew that it would be Sabrina.

"Bye!" he called, lifting a hand and waving. But she was already gone. Turning around with the help of his crutches, Toby made his struggled way down the stairs, and then began to limp towards the opening that lead back into the laboratory. He was truly exhausted from his little adventure, and to top that off, he still had to deal with the wound, and take his blood pressure pills and painkillers. But Toby wasn't too bothered. In fact, he wasn't too bothered by anything right now. And, why was that?

In fact, it was only now he noticed how far his strength had waned, and that Toby realized the true depth of his situation. Taking a mere step forward after he'd reached the bottom of the steps was too much for him, and the young man sank down tiredly onto one side, his breaths each rattling and dragging on each for an age.

With a silly smile etched onto his face, Toby didn't even seem to comprehend what was going on, or notice the abundance of sounds and scents fading. Even the ground seemed to drop away, and made Toby feel like he was floating.

Before the last hazy darkness closed in on him in every which way, Toby was able to catch one last shout that cut through even the darkest of dazes with the finest of clarity, as though he was hearing the voice through a dream.

"TOBY!"

Ah-ha-ha... thought Toby, seeming on the verge of madness. *That's me...*

Then, he drifted away and was lost into his own little world.

-Chapter 4-

The Scientist

"You have got to be kidding me, right?"

Joey stared in what seemed like absolute distaste at the man who stood before him. It might have seemed rude to anyone else, but then again, Joey was known to be quite vain.

But on the other hand, well...

The other little mutants had to admit that he had a point.

The man whom they faced didn't look particularly threatening. Quite the opposite, in fact. He was tall and rather reedy, with clothes that were well worn and very dirty, as though he hadn't bothered to change them in weeks. The shirt that had once been blue was a greenish-brown colour with all the dirt. His before-brown trousers were tattered and a patchy black. The labcoat that he wore had been ripped and neglected, covered with food stains and smears of cobwebs and dust.

There were dark shadows under his eyes, and he was wobbling, looking like he were about to fall asleep at any given moment. He looked quite malnourished, and was so thin that you could see where the bones joined his body. There was hardly any meat on him, poor fellow, and he looked dirty and shamefaced.

He had eyes that were a sickly shade of green, and hair that was a dirty blonde colour and was spiky, curly, wild, and un-brushed. The man had clearly been neglecting to shave, too, for there was a frizzy mess of facial hair around his chin and cheekbones. He peered at the mutants through a pair of wide glasses which enlarged his sickly-green eyes and made his glazed, half-seeing pupils stand out but hid a good few of the freckles and cuts across his face, resting on the bridge of the man's squashed, piggy nose.

Moony gave Joey a rough shove in the side as the other boy seemed to decide that the poor man wasn't worth it and began to stalk off.

"Who are you?" the man repeated in a frail, scared voice, fixing his sickly gaze on the little group that had just entered his domain. Only silence answered him. The man tried again, seeming to be beginning to think he was seeing things. "Hello...?"

Moony cleared his throat, and their 'opponent's' eyes snapped into focus.

"Who are you?" Moony pestered right back, ruffling his wings.

"Me?"

"Who else?"

"I'm... James... Why do you ask?"

Moony fell silent, thinking fast and shuffling his clawed feet.

"...W-well, we, um... Someone told us that you'd been working on something cool and... Um... We all, uh, wanted to come to see what it was. We just didn't expect to find someone so... Um... Um..."

James, seeming intrigued all of a sudden, was watching them intently.

Bethany, catching Moony's dilemma, stepped forward and perked up her ears, a sly look on her face.

"...Good looking! Astonishingly dashing!" she chirped, finishing off Moony's sentence with a grin and a hand to the strange scientist, who seemed oddly flattered. Did he really believe these feeble excuses?

Of course he did.

It wasn't like he'd been outside or slept properly in a month, after all.

The unfortunate fellow was now grinning in amazement, seeming proud, and happy. *Perhaps*, thought some of the young mutants, watching him with several disbelieving, several amused, and some plain disgusted faces. *He's just glad to have someone to talk to...*

"Oh! I can't believe this is happening, I can't believe what's going on, I don't believe it! I thought those other guys would never come to their senses, because they've never let anyone else in before!" squeaked the scientist, then abruptly lurched forwards and scooped up Bethany in a huge hug. The girl was taken aback and squirmed briefly, looking at Emerald and the others in clear despair, crinkling her nose in revulsion; this man smelled of sweat and old food! Some of the others snickered at her.

"So, can you show us what you're working on?" Bethany's curious, albeit a little choked, voice broke through James' happy mutterings as she gave her friends a stony glare. The man's sickly green eyes snapped onto her, and he grinned out at her, nodding his head so hard that he lost balance and went skittering over the floor towards the controls for the screens in this room. Sitting down at his desk, Bethany was relieved when James finally put her down, almost literally dropping her.

There were a series of frantic tapping sounds as James' hands skimmed over the keyboard, and he stared at the screen as though possessed. Bethany gave her head a nudging gesture towards the monitor, to where there was a small memory device plugged in, clearly to store the vital information that was needed for the mission. As James yapped in that unique voice that sounded as though he were talking with his nose plugged, Ginny scampered over to the monitor in response to Bethany's gesture, making little squeaking sounds as she went.

Joey sat back and watched, seeming offput by all the effort the others were putting into what he viewed a person not even worth looking at. But the others were busy trying to shrug off the dizzying amounts of scientific information that James was busy tanking at them ton by ton, whilst keeping the device that Ginny shoved at them hidden from James' eyes whenever he turned around to make sure that they were still interested. They all looked at him intently, not hearing a word of anything he said.

"And, all of this vital information, every little last bit of it! It's all stored on this device, here!" James finally finished, having gotten up. He was just about to point at the monitor of his computer. But even he had realized that something was a little bit off. Bending down, the man looked closely and tapped the monitor, looking for the memory device that seemed to have vanished right under his nose. In horror, the children began to edge towards the door.

"Here? Where is it?" James looked around, and searched again with shaking fingers, seeming to think it had turned invisible. Joey had finally moved, and scurried after the rest. James seemed to look at them in full now, his vision finally becoming clear. Legs shaking, the man slowly stood up, watching them through his sickly green eyes, eyes that had been blind up until now.

Joey stepped forward, holding the memory device. Vain though he was, it was clear that the boy was getting a little bit *too* cocky now. The others watched him in horror, as James' face turned sour. "Give that back, now!" he told Joey, walking forwards and holding out his hand

Joey twirled the device, but didn't give it up. "Relax!" he said, a snooty hint in his voice. "We'll take good care of it. I can see why this place needs to be so high security! You couldn't even stand up to a fly!"

James' cheeks burned, and he glowered at the boy who stood before him. If looks could kill, then this room would have been a bloodbath by now.

"We might as well just get out of here now, because there isn't anything you can do against us!"

The other children were giving Joey horrified looks. What was he doing? He'd ruin the mission!

"Oh, no, not now..." James' face was growing redder and redder by the second, both in anger and embarrassment as the realization dawned that he'd been had. He gave them all a savage grin. "If you go now then you'll miss the best part of my explanation!"

The scientist advanced like a madman slowly towards them all, quivering with rage, and chortling eerily in anticipation.

"Oh, what flattery, to visit this old thing in this old laboratory! To come to steal my life's work! I ought to be thanking you! They called me crazy... Crazy, I tell you!"

His eyes rolled about in his head, spinning and trembling as though to watch a thousand unseen insects all at once.

"But no more! This! This is the moment of truth! The first and final display of the power that I have created! A power that will throw every other country from its feet!"

The man threw back his head and laughed manically. With every breath, droplets of red sprayed into the air, and the mutant children huddled together, frightened by this sudden change. In their training missions, they had faced guns, galloped over countrysides in search of secret bases and toppled burly men that could have crushed them with a single blow, but what kind of trickery was this they now faced?

Ginny squealed loudly, and Karasu was already looking close to passing out in response to the blood that now splattered the walls and floors, flying from James' open mouth as he laughed.

"Behold!" howled James, throwing his labcoat aside so that they could see the lines of blood that had appeared along the sides of his forearms, the gleaming tips of knives quickly turning into the blades as they thrust themselves from their comfortable nests within James' flesh.

The fabric of his shirt beneath which his belly lay began to writhe and a red stain spread out from his lower chest, quickly spreading as a set of claws ripped out from his torso, followed by a thick tentacle made from rings of metal. Then another. Then another. More and more emerged until in all their savage, writhing glory there were five tentacles, tipped with thick claws made to grab and slice, rearing up like cobras and clacking their metallic bodies against one other. One emerged from just below his heart and two emerged from where his stomach had been. And the final two emerged from his sides, just beneath his ribcage. Each one shook off the shreds of James' flesh that still clung to them, and blood splattered the floor like deadly paint, poisoning the shimmering blue with its murky gore.

As the awful spectacle came to an end, James wobbled, apparently unprepared for the pain that the tentacles had wrought his body upon their emergence, but he whipped his glasses off and threw them to one side, the lenses shattering as James stubbornly remained on his feet. One tentacle whipped out, grabbing the Fragile Emerald by her torso and lifting her high, high above James and the other mutants' heads.

"Ready or not..." challenged James, as though this

was the start to nothing more than some sickening playground game. "...Here I come!"

And then James hurled Emerald downwards, and she collided with her friends as though she were a bowling ball, and the rest of them were skittles.

The only one left untoppled, Bethany raced forward to retrieve her friend, for as much as Emerald looked like a fairy, she was as fragile as one, too. When the fox-girl found the little dragonfly, Emerald was only half conscious, her eyes were wide with fright and she, as usual, said nothing, just clung tightly onto Bethany and waited for the dizziness to pass.

Looking back up at James from Emerald, Bethany's eyes were full of vengeance, and her mind was even more so, but more importantly pouring with veins of cunning, too. Karasu had ran and hid, and was whimpering and whining under James' desk as the enraged man advanced on the other mutants, away from him. Benny stamped his foot on the ground threateningly, and Ginny shree'd a battle cry in her high pitched rodent's squeal. Sally and Cassie readied themselves with tails fluffed out and curling, snarling and exchanging glances that told one another of their silent plans. Moony splayed his wings and screeched like an angry owl protecting its nest, whilst Joey hung back like a coward, lowering himself into the shadows whilst uttering a phrase that was something along the lines of "I meant to do that..." but no-one heard, or believed him.

There came the sounds of metal rasping, and those who had fallen looked up. Some were able to move out of the way whereas others found metal, warmed by the hold that James' body had placed on the tentacles as he had merged with them, pressed into their spines to pin them. The keen devices that missed drew back, arching in the air like cobras, and clacking their claws together as James waited for the next opportunity to come along. One of them slid forward like an aerial serpent, and latched itself onto the hand of Joey's that held the memory device. Joey cawed in pain, reeling backwards as he struggled to keep hold of the memory device, but the tendril hung on, its claws putting on the pressure little by little, until the blood ran down his arms.

Sally and Cassie, the twins captured by the metallic embrace, were pinned and barking at James and the tentacle that imprisoned Joey's arm. Together they were struggling to get free from the agony of the stranglehold that the tentacle had made to cut. Only Moony shot forward with a hoot, and hooked his claws under the claws that held Joey's arm, aiming to prise them apart despite the machine's strength being far beyond his. Giving up in this exploit, Moony plucked the red-stained memory device from Joey's slippery fingers instead, and the wicked machinery finally let go of Joey's arm and leered at him, with the bloodstained claws clacking and seeming almost like the bloodstained fangs of a snake.

Folding his wings, Moony retreated, then ducked as the machine struck and flashed over his head, the points of metal that were the claws designed to slice and pierce burying themselves in the wall behind him. The metal tentacle writhed and struggled to get free with the sounds of metal scraping against metal. Blood spraying from his mouth and nose with every breath and gore running down to stain his clothing, James was a sight to behold, and he was weakening, but the tentacles that he controlled were not. Whenever one of the children came close, though, he still possessed the strength to raise an arm and block an attack with the bloodstained blades in his forearms, and none of those that tried came away with anything less than a cut.

No fighter in this battle had come away any less

damaged than the next for both sides. Except, perhaps, for Karasu, who was still hiding and was now unconscious from the scent and sight of blood. Joey, who was shivering and shaking in clear shock was clearly not going to be of much use in the battle ahead as he clutched at the ruined feathers and bloodstained skin of his forearm. Moony had been captured, but, still too stubborn to give up and believing himself to be the main part of this whole mission, was dangling by one foot from one set of claws and clutching the memory device that he held in both hands. Admittedly, though, he was being swung quite violently to and fro, and his face now looked rather green compared to before.

Emerald was still out for the count, with clear blood plasma oozing from a new wound in her side, Bethany trying her best to defend her friend despite the fact that she was being bombarded by the machines from both sides. Benny was having a similar bad time, but his situation could be seen as worse, to some. His legs were kicking and flailing about and there was a tentacle embedded in his stomach. It was wriggling and moving with frighteningly clear intent, its claws occasionally protruding for a moment through Benny's skin as it searched for his heart and Benny fought against it. Eventually, with a huge heave, Benny was free, and he hopped away from the machine whilst clutching his injured stomach.

After what seemed like an age, with only scratches and bruises, Sally and Cassie were free too, and they both stood side by side in front of their friends, loyalty and strength flowing from their postures and their faces as though they were glowing. The little group was having a bad time, but that didn't mean they were beaten.

James, however, was struggling. The blood running from his seemingly mortal wounds rendered the movements made by his human body weak, and his balance fragile. Despite this, though, his metal tentacles seemed to draw strength out of nothing, and they were animated by their own will as well as every thought that flowed from James' mind. James had sank to his knees in a puddle of his own blood and rasped at his adversaries with bloodstained teeth bared threateningly.

"You think I'm.... Done for..." he hissed, then uttered a rasped, rattling laugh. Ginny dashed in to try and make a blow, but a second later was cast back, squeaking, as a metal claw flicked her away. Moony was still suspended by the ankle, and another claw was trying to prise open his fingers and take the device away. Through the blood that rushed through his head, Moony was blinking his golden eyes in an effort to stay focused, and the more the claw dug in, the tighter his pudgy little hand drew clenched.

"Don't think... I'm gonna go easy on... A couple 'o kids..." James laughed again, breaths rasping further. There was a ghastly sloshing sound as, using those infernal contraptions as support, the injured man raised himself back up onto his feet. With two tentacles busy keeping himself upright and two trying to claim Moony's prize, that meant James had only one left to spare. Glances were exchanged beneath the scientist's nose and with every exhausted smile that was raised, the children's confidence turned from nonexistence, to strands like spider's silk connecting each of them.

With her cheeks pink and red rings around her eyes, Bethany had set Emerald down safely with the unconscious Karasu and stepped forward. Rubbing her nose with the back of a furry hand, she looked up at James with vengeance in her eyes, and her russet tail fluffed out and twitched angrily from side to side. As those who were well enough to fight gathered, and Joey seemed to pluck up the few shards of his dignity from the floor, there came the sound of clanking metal and Ginny squealing hopelessly up to Moony.

"To me!" she squeaked, as the boy turned his head dazedly towards her. "To me!"

At that, Moony stirred, and jerked his hand away from the claw that made for the memory device. He tossed it towards the little guinea pig, and she lurched for it, her clawed paws grasping at the air where it fell.

But Moony had misjudged it. They could only watch in horror as it spun in the air, and was snatched by delicate talons and held there, just out of their reach. It was almost as if someone had yelled a cue, for chaos instantly erupted as every mutant pounced on James, and set up a hubbub of cries. Caws, screeches, squeaks, and hoots echoed, as James let go of Moony and the rest of them all piled onto the mad scientist. Each dug in with claws, fangs, and any other weaponry they could find. As all the chaos rang out, Bethany had broken apart from the others. Unnoticeably, she slowly scaled the tentacle that held their mission objective. Her face was covered in cuts and scratches, and if the tentacle had flexed, the metal rungs could have cut her fingers off. But she was determined.

Down below, the children had gained the upper hand. Moony's wing had been shoved into James' face, and his feathers blinded the madman, rendered him unable to move or breathe. Then Moony shrieked in pain as James, in a moment of desperation, found his mouth full of feathers and bit down, his teeth meeting the fragile, hollow bone of Moony's wing. Benny had become a flailing mass of kicking, powerful feet and floppy ears, and one of the lenses of his glasses had cracked in all the confusion, so he was flying blind as he writhed and punched. Joey had finally found his time to shine, and he was trying to heave one of the knives from James' forearms so that he couldn't block any of his siblings, his friends, from going in for the kill.

As Bethany climbed higher and higher, and ever closer to the goal, she was aware of her handholds beginning to tighten, and her ladder beginning to try to buck and shake her off. She hadn't any choice other than to cling on for dear life and hope for the best. She could see James beginning to awaken from the shock again, and the other four tentacles that emerged from his belly and sides beginning to whip about to and fro, striking at her friends like serpents with fangs outstretched. He had managed to pull his arm free from Joey, and had given the peacock boy a deep cut across the cheek for his troubles.

Bethany squeaked as she felt herself being tipped upside down by the flailing and shaking machine that she clung to, as it raged and flailed her about, then slammed itself off of the ground, sparks flying from where it hit. Bethany was half thrown off of it, so that now she was clinging on by just her arms, wrapped about the cold, bloodstained metal in a deadly embrace. Bethany bit her tongue to keep back a cry of pain as she felt the rungs tightening about her fingers as the thing flexed, putting her hand in a stranglehold that would not be easy to escape from.

Gritting her teeth, but then giving a high pitched yowl a few moments later as she was swung like a ragdoll, Bethany gasped and flattened her ears into her fluffed out russet hair, her amber eyes looking up at where she was aiming to climb. It was there, barely a meter away now... It was nothing compared to what she had already climbed. But the metal tendril, or perhaps James, hadn't noticed her then. How could she climb up if it was writhing and twisting, slamming itself off of the laboratory walls and all things worse, like it was now?

Bethany took a deep breath and held on. As it swung itself one way, Bethany was slammed into the wall, and she managed to wrap her knees about the tentacle again, securing her grip with a fiery determination that was stronger than her cramped muscles. Breathing heavily, Bethany dug her claws into the masses of wires that served as tendons beneath the writhing metal rungs that held them in one piece.

Closing her eyes, for only a moment, Bethany thought of Emerald, her best friend. She thought of the care that Emerald would receive when they got back to the laboratory, and the celebration, the rest, that would take place after this last mission. She thought of the ticking clock, her friends- no- her siblings, as they battled down there below. All were worse hurt than she was. They were less cunning and tricky, and with less agility to help them out of trouble. If she could get that device, and secure the mission's success, then she could do anything.

Time seemed to slow around her. She was no longer clinging to a writhing, bucking machine. She was climbing the tree in her dorm room, watching as Emerald danced around her, practicing her flight like a young fairy would. She could climb to the top of this tree, even as it swayed and groaned in the wind that was produced from only a single fan. So she did. She dug her claws into the bark, and looked up to where Emerald awaited her, with her eyes, those diamond eyes, watching with such joy.

This was her moment.

Bethany's lips curled up in a smile, as she reached out to take Emerald's hand, and felt beneath her fingertips the smooth plastic covering of the memory device. She secured her hold, and then let go, taking it with her down into the mass of writhing water, the people below. The memory shattered, to be replaced by cold reality. If Bethany had been aiming, then she had hit her mark.

A moment's distraction was all that Sally and Cassie needed to pounce and tear. A chilling scream was cut off from James' lungs, and he had no chance for last words, not there and then. As the battered children retreated, panting and grinning, stained with blood, they watched as their opponent's chest rose and fell, then fell silent. As they watched, a small smile crept over his dying face, his sickly-green eyes finally crystalline clear. Their smiles faded. Was he going to attack again?

But no. The machinery sank down around him, curling up into sleep like tame dogs. He'd had enough of all this. What was it for, after all? He didn't even know what they were fighting over. He opened his lips a few times, but no sound came out. At last, there was a gentle breath, a sigh, almost.

"Thank... You..." They thought that they heard James' voice, but there was no way to tell whether it was just his last breath. There was no time for sentience in the thick of war, but still, some of the children felt slightly ashamed, almost. It seemed over so quickly; despite their injuries and suffering, this man was just what they were. A victim of the war.

They couldn't dwell on it too long, though. They needed to get back. Bethany had been to retrieve emerald, and her face was cold and stony. Didn't she care at all about James' death? That was hard to tell. Perhaps all she cared about was the fact that he had hurt her friend. They all looked at her, and wordlessly began to file from the room one by one, with Sally and Cassie wiping the blood from their muzzles before they each shouldered the burden of the unconscious Karasu together.

Benny left the room last even despite his stomach

wound, and he waited for the rest to pass him before he made to close the door behind them. With the keenest ears out of all of them, though, it was only him that began to hear the rasping of metal against metal. Suspicions rising, he slowly turned around, and backed away from the door, his throat tightening in fright.

"Uh, you guys...?" he choked out, thumping one of his back feet against the ground in fright, then backing away several frightened steps, causing the others to turn and stare at him blandly.

"Don't look now, but... I think we should... We really need to... I-it's... I..."

"Spit it out, Benny!" snapped Moony from in the lead.

"Run!"

For the bloodstained machinery was still moving.

-Chapter 5-

Revelation

"Toby! What were you thinking?!"

Danny just had to keep on asking, asking and asking the same question to the blind man repeatedly, even as he carried the limp Toby towards the room where he slept. He wasn't sure what had happened to leave Toby in such a state, but Danny had to admit that he'd never seen him so happy. He was in quite a state, what with a deep gash on one side and a rip in his clothes, and Danny suspected him to have broken a rib or two. Danny had already pinned him down and forced Toby to take his medication whether he liked it or not, but even now Toby was coming back to his senses. All the while, that stupid grin had never left his face.

After what had seemed like hours of searching but was probably in actuality about half an hour judging by the mission timer, Danny had finally noticed a dangerously cold draft creeping throughout the laboratory. Suspecting the worst, he'd finally found Toby almost unconscious, lying on the stairs that led down to the laboratory. He was glad that Toby wasn't dead, of course, but things could have been better. He was clearly delirious, and kept on muttering to himself about... someone. Had Toby gone outside? What if someone had found the laboratory?

It was a rather daunting thought, but nowhere near as daunting as the thought of Toby dying. So Danny wasn't too bothered and secrecy remained the least of his worries, at the moment at least. Danny had made sure to lock the door behind him, anyway, and that was all that mattered; they'd deal with future problems as they approached, or at least, he hoped they would.

Finally dragging the door open to Toby's room with a hiss, Danny heaved Toby up into a more stable position in his arms, and set him down on the soft sheets of his bed. Toby's face turned blearily towards him and smiled stupidly again. Danny stretched his arms out above his head and sucked in his breath. He was strong compared to some, sure, but dragging a half-conscious man through half a laboratory would take its toll on anyone. He sighed out his breath then walked over to a nearby cabinet, where healing devices that inserted small metal chips to stimulate the body to repair itself were stored.

These devices caused the cells to react in a way similar to the uncontrolled division of cancerous cell, whilst keeping the growth controlled so that the mitosis would heal a person in minutes rather than creating a life-threatening situation. The devices, thankfully, had little to no adverse effect on the body, and the chip would exit the body naturally through... Ahem... 'Bodily functions' after several hours.

There was a gentle clicking sound as Danny pressed the trigger of the device, and a minute drop of blood was visible for a mere second above the larger wound where the microscopic device had just been placed. Slowly, but surely, the blood began to form a clot and scab over before his very eyes, trapping the life-giving blood inside and returning it until the wound was but a scar, minutes later, and the pink flush had returned to Toby's blood-drained cheeks.

As soon as that was done, Danny almost fell with relief as all the tenseness left his body in a rush, even a tenseness that he never knew he was holding in. Catching himself at the last moment, Danny looked up at Toby, who seemed to be on the teetering edge between being unconscious and awake.

"Toby?" Danny called hesitantly, wanting to know if he was okay. Toby's ears twitched and he opened his eyes, giving a feeble grunt. Danny gently pulled the quilts over Toby's body in an effort to warm him up. It couldn't be too good to go outside in that kind of cold, especially if you were as prone to sickness as Toby. Toby grunted again, but then his lips suddenly spread into a huge grin as if in realization, and he slowly lifted his hands up towards his face, tilting his head downwards as though to look at them, at something that he couldn't even see. Danny was curious. What was it that he was holding in that one clenched palm?

"Danny..." whispered Toby, that unerring smile still on his face. His fingers closed once more around whatever it was he had in his hand and he held it out to Danny. It was nothing more than a tiny, folded sheet of paper.

"Danny... The number, what is it?"

Danny reached out with his hand, and took the paper from Toby. He blinked several times, then unfolded it. He brought it close to his face, and he looked and looked. He turned it over again, and looked at the other side.

Nothing.

Danny felt completely clueless. What number? What was going on? It must be pretty important to Toby, if he was asking for it; Danny knew better than most how reluctant Toby was to ask for anything. It was as if he wanted everyone else to believe that he could still see. *Is Toby going mad?* He thought to himself. "Toby, can you tell me what happened?" he asked seriously.

"I... Got lost..." admitted Toby disdainfully. "Ended up outside. There was... A lady there. She helped... She helped me find my way back, Danny. She made me feel... Feel like I was human..." Toby lifted his head from the pillows then began to heave himself into a sitting position, apparently feeling well enough now to do so. Danny rushed to help him or force him to lie back down again, but Toby's words weighed heavily on his mind for a number of reasons. He didn't say anything, but he patted Toby on the shoulder encouragingly, before pushing him back down using that same shoulder. "Go on..." Danny said.

Toby seemed encouraged, and obliged. "And she gave... Me her phone number... On this little piece of paper. Wrote it down, you know?" Toby was smiling again, but now Danny understood why, at least. He'd noticed that the other scientists in the laboratory seemed to treat Toby just like they did all the other mutants in the lab; with the same degree of respect that someone would treat a child that wasn't theirs. Toby wanted nothing more than to shrug off that impression, and he'd finally found someone who had treated him the way he'd wanted to. But perhaps there was more to it than that. Danny didn't want to appear intrusive, though, so he said nothing.

"Can you read it to me?" finished Toby at last, holding out to him the little sheet of paper again. Danny looked once more down at the paper, as if him doing so would make the words appear. He watched as Toby sat back, ears pricked as he waited with excitement and expectation on his face. The expectant look on his face made him seem, despite all his wishes and efforts, like a child anyway.

Danny looked down at the little piece of paper that he now held, he folded it up again, and looked closely. He again, turned it over in his hands, and searched, looking for any sign of writing. As a child, Danny's vision had been fairly inadequate, but he had recovered. In a last desperate effort, Danny gave a dismissive mumble of "uh, need my reading glasses," and Toby

71

nodded, suspecting nothing even though Danny hardly ever used his reading glasses. Something was definitely wrong. Pulling his glasses out from a pocket of his labcoat, Danny unfolded them and placed them on the bridge of his nose. He looked again, but still, that little piece of paper in which Toby had placed all his hopes, stayed blank.

Why, then, did Danny search that little piece of paper so fiercely as he looked for signs of writing when there were none?

"Well?" asked Toby, voice high with anticipation.

Danny looked up slightly, and he felt strangely glad that he didn't have to avoid Toby's gaze.

"Toby..." murmured Danny, his voice as gentle as he could make it. He didn't want to lie to Toby, or to anyone, really. Even white lies, the unavoidable, necessary lies, were hesitant by him. Toby opened his mouth slightly, still looking hopeful. Then he closed it again, glazed yellow eyes still somehow fixed unnervingly on Danny's face; it was almost like the blind man could still see him. "Mm-hm?" he asked.

"Toby..." said Danny again, just a slight hint louder this time, preparing himself.

"There's nothing written here..."

Toby's face fell as though a dark cloud had just passed over it. "There's... What?" he asked, voice shrinking. "It... It's blank? Is there nothing there? I mean, it must have something!"

Danny nodded slowly and then stopped remembered that Toby couldn't see him. His face flushed in shame. "No, Toby... It's blank..."

"It can't not!" cried Toby, hope rapidly being replaced by despair.

"Toby... Believe me!"

Toby didn't seem to hear him. Danny saw him shrinking even further away as he digested the facts, eyes growing shiny with tears.

"But... I c-can't... You wouldn't... That means... Sabrina... She... She lied to me!" Toby's voice had risen to a shrill yowl in desperation, its hoarse tone standing out more pronounced than ever. "But she can't have!"

Danny fell silent, and gently sat down beside Toby on his bed. "Well, she did..." he said sympathetically. Contradicting directly what Danny thought he would do, Toby was silent. A few seconds passed, but still he said nothing. After a while, he just hid his face in his hands. After another few seconds, Danny found himself hearing Toby struggling to contain his sobs. Danny wished that he could do something to help.

"I thought that she cared about me... I really thought she cared..." he whispered, and Danny felt his heart tear. Tapping Toby on the shoulder so that he lifted his head, Danny took Toby into a hug, and patted his dear friend on the back. Feeling glad that he felt Toby relaxing, Danny moved his face close to Toby's good ear, so that he could hear him, and whispered.

"I care, Toby... And I always will..."

***

"It's still moving!?"

"Don't just stand there! Run!"

"Why can't we fight it!?"

"We're timed, remember! Run!"

It was with an unsteady, lurching gait that the claws sank into the slippery, bloodied floor and created deep scores in the tiled ground. The tentacles now served as support for the body of James as his head lolled uselessly, and his limbs dangled beneath the machinery that he had created. They had raised him from the ground, and were moving with their own will.

73

The children had killed the creator, but his puppet still lived on.

It only took one miss from a tendril, one that embedded claws of metal into the ground, to convince the young adventurers that they should really get moving. With sharp cries and feet blurring, they took off into the empty room within which the lasers had woven like flame strings. The lasers were gone now, but the group of trainee spies paid that no heed.

One after another, they ran. The weakest, and those carrying their friends to safety, were those that lagged behind, but the others, all running, hopping, scrabbling away in blind panic, had almost forgotten about them. Either way, they didn't look back to check to see how those behind were doing. Sally and Cassie were struggling with their heavy load but it was a wonder that, with how much Karasu ate on a daily basis, he didn't weigh more. Sally and Cassie moved as one, but no matter the unison, it was always difficult to kart along such a heavy burden and weave that into their movements. Bethany was having a little bit of a better time, because she was alone and her load was lighter, smaller, and because Bethany was so desperate to get Emerald back to health.

Behind them, the monstrous machine slid along like five serpents tied at the middle, with James' body suspended between them and the little droplets of blood dripping from him only adding to the eerie scene. It clacked, clanged and made metallic screeching sounds as its limbs clattered against each other and smashed against the walls, taking out chunks of the stone and metal as it went, for it was so desperate to get to its prey, and was hungry for the feel of flesh beneath its claws. There was no hesitation, for now, it wasn't controlled by a human mind. It was controlled by the A.I. that had been given to it upon its construction, one that told it to kill, and nothing else.

And that wasn't all. Far from matching the speed of a normal human, the machine was catching up. Many of the people who had emerged into the corridors in response to the alarm being triggered by the machine's rampaging were trampled down or ruthlessly tossed aside. With James' body swinging lifelessly from the matter that he had created from his own distraught mind, the machine gave a lurch forward. Its hideous, metallic form crashed through the door and into the darkened alleyway, sending fragments of plaster, metal, and concrete scampering forwards over the ground after those that the machine pursued. The children were panting and sobbing in fright as they sprinted with all their breaths away around the corner. Their slipping and sliding on the floor of the corridor had cost them a lot of the distance between them and the monster.

In just a few strides, it would be right beside them.

They could hear the sounds of clacking metal and screeching wires heaving the weight of the machine forward. But they were so close! They could see the welcome glow of the laboratory beyond the limits of their training mission. It was the end! They could see the timer, too, painted in a bright green that fell on each of their faces and reflected in their eyes.

00:36...

00:35...

00:34...

So close, and yet so far! There was no time to fight any more! There was a thick crash, the sound of metal screeching against stone as the monstrous entity of metal failed to whip itself around the corner and shards of glass sprayed from where it had stumbled and skidded into the next building. It shook itself free soon after, and was after them once again.

00:15...

00:14...
00:13...

But that last, single distraction was all that they needed. Moony took up the lead and leaped into the light, came skidding to a stumbling halt amongst the scientists of the laboratory. Joey soon followed, with Ginny close after, and then the injured Benny. Following after, Bethany clutched Emerald close to her chest, and Sally and Cassie carrying Karasu brought up the rear. They had one last chance to look back at their training grounds, to see the mechanical monster leering at them one last time. They were able to, once more meet the gaze of the dead James. And watch as the alleyway faded away behind everything.

As the door to the training room slammed shut, Moony saluted to James, and some of the other children looked at Moony and the fading alleyway with exhaustion in their eyes, then followed suit.

James' form scattered into pixels.

They could hear the cheers of the scientists ringing about, people applauding for all that they were worth. First aiders rushed forward to heal the injuries, so that every one of the mutants could have their moments of glory and enjoy it without pain.

Eventually, all the children shakily stood, and those who had been unconscious awoke. Karasu was gratefully receiving treats from onlookers, and greedily chased off Sally and Cassie as they hungrily tried to get in on the fun. His happiness was cut short, however, as the scientist wrapped their arms around his torso and picked him up. The little retriever-boy looked up at the scientist with trust in his eyes, whilst all the background scientists snickered; the poor newbie wasn't to know the 'dangers' concerned with giving Karasu a bath.

As the children chattered and yelled happily

amongst themselves, tails wagging and ears twitching, Joey stood apart from the rest. He had folded his feathery arms against his chest, and was silent, at least compared to normal. The entire mission had almost been doomed to failure because of him. Without his intervention, they could have gotten out without a scratch, and the war victim, James, would never have died. Did none of the others see his pain? See how wrong this was?

He swallowed softly, but didn't say a word, a melancholy cloud hanging over his mind.

But then, out of the blue, he finally began to smile. They had completed the mission! Despite that, they had done it. That was something to be happy about, right? And more so, it meant that they could do anything! The mission had been meant for stealth, but they had fought and won anyway! Joey wiped his eye with the back of a quivering hand.

They had completed the mission. And that meant that James could finally rest in peace. With this in his mind, Joey scurried after the others. Though his voice trembled as he spoke, Joey joined in with the others' conversations, and he smiled. Now nine voices sang through the air in happiness as they trotted back to their playroom, accompanied by the supervising scientist, to play and to feed.

All would be well in the end.

Of this, everyone was sure.

Even as a lone scientist emerged to speak to Amanda, prying eyes above went unnoticed.

"Ma'am, the experiment was a success. Mercury will be awakening tomorrow, at the earliest. We'll start the memory erasing process tonight."

-Chapter 6-

The Spy

It was night time now, in the laboratory. It would have been early for some, but few of the scientists and experiments alike had been able to resist the pull of warm blankets and nests. After an exhaustion-inducing training mission and hours of playing in their playroom, the experiments had gone to bed without much whining of "I'm not tired!" or "can't I have five more minutes?" as they usually would have done. Now, they were fast asleep, all of them.

Gentle hoots drifted from Moony's room intermingled with his deep breathing, and Karasu jerked in his sleep as he dreamt of chasing rabbits down holes and playing in the sea. Sally and Cassie were almost silent, and they slept in a huddle as usual, sharing the warmth of each other and a thick, faithful blanket. Benny was down sleeping in his rabbit-hole-bed again, curled up in a furry nest, and only gentle squeaking snores drifted out. Ginny was hidden in her hay, sucking on her thumb with a little smile on her face. Joey was twitching and jerking in his sleep, dreaming quaking thoughts and erratic versions of the day's events that left him in fits. But finally, Bethany and Emerald hugged each other in their sleep, glad to have each other there.

With snores drifting from the scientists' rooms, too, and without the worry of any midnight action, there was, apart from the snores, utter silence. Not a soul was moving, and not a creature stirred in the halls.

...Except for one. Sitting among the rafters, there was a woman, her body lean and lithe from years of training from the military. Sent out on a mission to find England's secret weapon, she had posed first as an afraid, shy citizen, then as a loyal worker for several companies. Now able to mimic and mock the speech patterns and movements of this land easily, she had gone unnoticed for over three years.

Now, though, having stumbled upon the laboratory by chance during an outing to get 'supplies' from the local supermarket, she was all geared up in numerous odd contraptions and seemingly thin armour made to grant her silence and protection that would make her feel almost invincible at all times; it was bullet proof and possessed a GPS function, allowing the military to track her no matter where she may go.

Lifting her masked face slightly, she sniffed then brought up her hand to cover her nose. "Ugh… she muttered, narrowing her brown eyes and grimacing. "How can these people stand to be in here…? It stinks of animals…" she swung her legs over the beam that she was sitting on, and slipped silently to the floor, pulling the helmet down over her head a little tighter. Gently, she touched a hand to her earpiece, and heard a connection buzz into audio.

"Ah, Alma… I thought we'd lost you!" came a voice from the other side of the link, the connection seeming brittle because she was underground. "Had any luck?"

"I have located the secret laboratory, sir. It's buried underground, but seems stable enough not to be destroyed easily." Alma replied cautiously, eyes flitting around to take in her surroundings. Through heat detection goggles, she could see the shapes of sleeping scientists, and in a different room, a collection of oval-shaped devices that seemed to be emanating massive heat, for there were circles of white, orange and red surrounded by the aura of green and outlines of dark blue.

"I see… So, what are your plans?"

"Tonight, I plan to simply take a map of the general structure and find out something of the planned weapons. In the following nights, I'll look for possible weak spots in the structure, and in the weapons themselves…" Alma looked around, then flitted forward like a lean, elegant spider into the room in which she could see the strange, oval devices radiating their immense heat. "From there, I'll decide my next move," she clarified.

"Good, good…" the voice on the other end of the line sounded pleased. "I'll await your call. Until next time, Alma."

Alma closed the door with the slightest touch behind her. "Over and out," she finished, tapping her earpiece with a finger so that the connection between the two speakers was broken. Looking around her for another brief moment through the heat vision goggles, there was a small click as the woman deftly switched from her heat vision goggles and to her night vision, because the room around her was pitch black.

What she could see, however, vaguely surprised her. After all she'd seen, all she'd heard of, and all the rumours of what England's secret weapon was, the truth was perhaps even stranger than all. She was in a large room, filled with several rows of strange, oval-shaped devices from which the heat had been emanating.

Only several seemed to be actually working, and the rest had their translucent lids raised, revealing a soft, spongy layering on the inside that seemed to be well suited for moulding to the shape of a person to keep them comfortable. Each was a pure white with the company name, 'Fusion', written across a blue, or Alma assumed it was blue, stripe across the middle.

Each, however, was tipped at an angle, so that the head of whoever was inside was higher than the feet. And where the head would have gone in each device, there were four tubes. One was long and thin, and was aimed to provide oxygen to the person inside through the nose or mouth, one was to fill the container with fluid in case extra support was needed, the next was to provide the person inside with nourishment, and the last was tipped with a thin needle like the ones used by doctors to give vaccinations. The machines looked new, very new. There wasn't a speck of dust or rust on any of them, and unlike older machines, they didn't make a single sound as they worked quietly on the person inside.

Moving towards the first that was active, whilst others would be horrified, Alma was quite fascinated by what she saw. Inside of the device was a child curled up. There were tubes entering his mouth and nose, and a needle pressed into the top of his shoulder, through which Alma could see a strange, red-tinted liquid passing. The boy's ears were pointed, and in his mouth, Alma could see that several of his teeth had gone. In the gaps, she could see knifelike edges of new teeth emerging. There was a thin, skinny tail wrapped around one of his legs, and this seemed half-formed, with no fur and skin so thin that one could see the bone and blood that pulsed beneath, slowly growing and forming. Thick fur had begun to sprout from his sides and Alma could assume that it was down his back, too. The boy's head was covered in bald patches, and this shed hair, like the teeth, was resting at the bottom of the container.

It would have been a gruesome sight for anyone but nonetheless, Alma wasn't particularly moved. She had seen far worse. This child was far from a mutilated body on the battlefield. Deciding that she had seen

81

enough nonetheless, Alma looked away, not wanting to see any more of these abominations. As she looked in the opposite direction, though, something else caught her eye. It was a panel absolutely covered in different buttons and sliders each controlling different variables and effects. Alma's eyes shone with a peculiar light behind her goggles. There was a small switch on one side of the board that had two small LED's on either side. No-one was looking...

Alma was sure the scientists wouldn't miss a weapon or two...

The scientists back home, anyway.

Reaching out with a finger, Alma hesitated just short of the switch. If she were to turn it off, someone would be sure to notice. She drew her gloved hand back slowly, a sly grin spreading over her face beneath the mask. With a triumphant little hum rising in her throat as she moved, Alma made her way around the back of the panel, and then pulled on the wire several times, whilst holding the panel in place. She kept at it, until she felt the wire loosening under her fingers. The rubbery coating over the metal stayed in place and betrayed nothing. With several deft twists of the wire, Alma saw the lights on each of the Fusion machines flicker, and then go out.

On the outside, the wire seemed fine. On the inside, though, it had disconnected from the machine.

She felt a meaningless twinge of shame passing through her as she watched the boy who she'd seen before beginning to shake and writhe in his confines as he was suffocated by the fluid in the machine, but that twinge was nothing compared to the sense of victory that she felt. The ice quickly consumed her heart again, and the candle of shame was extinguished in an instant. Brushing her hands against each occupied machine as she went, there was triumph on Alma's face as she silently trod back the way she came. She would report her findings later, but now was the simple matter of leaving the laboratory before someone stirred.

Slipping like a ghost from the room's confines, Alma watched warily as the door slid quietly shut behind her with a sound like that of a blade being sheathed. She broke into a hopping, silent run merely a moment later, her toes meeting the ground with only the tiniest of singsong whispers. Watching the scenery pass her by, Alma traced, with little difficulty, back the way she had come. Past all the snoring scientists she loped, her eyes darting warily from side to side as she went. Past the training room, and hopped up the stairways leading to the outdoor world.

Gently placing her palm against the button, Alma watched the door to the outside world slide open, and smiled, seeing the starry sky high above. After being stuck cramped in this smelly little place for almost all day, Alma felt like she had forgotten what fresh air tasted like. And right now, to her, it tasted almost like sugar, with the crisp autumn air and the scents of leaves and flowers mingling with the scents of the farmers' latest crop, even if this year's harvest hadn't gone that well in the end.

Alma wasn't home- to her, the danger only added to the sweetness of the scent. The possibility of adventure sent a thrill down her spine. After lying low for three years, at least, the possibility of adventure loomed like a low, dark cloud over the horizon. Alma was quite sure that hers was the most reliable forecast of anyone's.

Thoughtfully looking up at the cloudy, starry sky, Alma gave the button a fierce whack, and the door slid closed behind her once more, sealing the secrets inside. Today, it was only lucky that she'd been able to get in. A single moment of carelessness could lead to a person's demise, recalled Alma, smugly. Today was a time like that.

Tomorrow, the spy would have to look for a different way in.

Despite herself, Alma began to smile as she headed up the stairs, taking her time with every step to think, and to admire the clean English countryside.

She could see the city in which she now 'lived' in the distance, the cathedral standing out against the full Moon that drifted down behind it. The houses, resting upon the hillsides and creeping up towards her before dispersing, looked almost like a crowd of people, watching and waiting for the endless oceans of fields to consume them.

Alma had always liked a challenge.

Today's would be to find another way in, and tomorrow's would be to snare the scientists at the right place, at the right time. There would be no way out for them, not again. Slowly, Alma would wear them down until they were nothing. And then the country would be doomed, free for America to take over, for another country to fall victim to the great war.

Then Alma would return home a hero.

Walking through the breeze and distractedly watching the leaves as they whispered, Alma thought to herself, her thoughts growing ever more ambitious as time went on. Eventually, she chuckled, and shook her head.

Not now, Alma... she told herself.

There's still time...

There's still time...

And then, Alma vanished like a ghost into the midnight mist.

-Chapter 7-

Mercury

"It worked! It worked!"

Danny was awoken from his slumber rather rudely by someone shaking him for all they were worth. His body gave an involuntary jerk, and then Danny sluggishly raised his head to stare at whoever had awoken him with glazed, out-of-focus eyes. In the bed next to his, Toby was giving a meowing yawn and rubbing his eyes. He looked better rested than Danny had seen him in months, but at the same time, he looked as though he'd been tossing and turning in his sleep.

"Mmmgh?" muttered Danny with a yawn, rubbing his eyes with the back of a hand. He opened them again a second later, blinking several times to clear the glaze from the clear blue that they should have been. "Something worked...? What worked?" he asked, eventually finding the strength in his fairly-dead limbs to push himself up into a sitting position.

"The latest experiment!" the scientist told him breathlessly, a huge grin on their face. Danny had to double take, his sleep-hazed mind unable to completely process the facts at first.

"What experiment...? I thought I said not to try anything new. They told me that they wouldn't after I found out that the scientists had been dying...?"

Danny looked at him with slight fear in his eyes.

"Don't get all huffy at me, it wasn't anything big. We were just putting in the genes of more than one animal into the experiment! They'll be even more deadly from now on!"

"Who? The experiments?"

Danny finished pulling on his shirt and gave the other scientist a dirty look. He'd already made his views on experimenting without his permission rather well known throughout the laboratory. Toby, now fully awake and ready for action, had swung his legs over the side of his own bed and waited patiently for Danny to help him get dressed.

"Yeah, the experi- woah, don't give me that look. It wasn't my fault!" the scientist raised his hands defensively, and Danny gave him that look again from where he was busy buttoning up his trousers. Sighing, Danny shook his head. "No casualties, I hope?"

"Well…"

Both Danny and Toby snapped into focus, and Toby growled softly. There was a guilty tone in the scientist's voice.

"It wasn't anything to do with us. The machines all disconnected from the control panel at some point last night. The little monkey-boy, the shark-boy, lizard-girl and the dove-girl who were in the middle of fusion were lost."

"What!? Why!?"

"I've just told you, it wasn't anything to do with us! We checked all the equipment last night, and it was fine then. Sometimes these things can happen without warning!" protested the scientist.

Danny glowered at him darkly. "So, what makes you say that the experiment was a success?" he asked suspiciously.

"There was one boy left. We'd tried something new with him. He was just up to the memory erasing stage, because his fusion was completed yesterday. He's just woken up, so we, uh, want you to introduce him to the other experiments. And Toby, too, if he wants to come, of course."

Danny listened intently. He thought for a moment about declining, but then didn't. If he didn't do this, then who else would the poor kid be landed with? Danny looked sideways at Toby, then sighed. He loved all the mutants here like they were his own children, and it saddened him to see what they were put through by the other scientists sometimes. He didn't really have a choice in the matter. "Alright, I'll do it..." he said to the scientist, and was rewarded with a pleased nod.

"I'll just get Toby ready first, okay?" Danny told him, turning around towards Toby.

"Alright. Don't take too long."

***

Ugh...

The darkness is all-consuming. There are hands, pressing in on my mind like they're trying to force me into something. But my spirit is strong, and I will not submit. This pain, this prickle of my skin, it is unfamiliar. I am changing, not what I once was.

But who does that mean I used to be?

I remember, yes... I remember now.

The pride that my father felt towards me, and my mother's gentle hand, always there to guide me. Since I was young, I have been myself, and sure that nothing could take me away from home. I can remember the happy times we shared, and the laughter... My friends sometimes teased me, for the bond I shared with my parents. Said that it would be short-lived.

I didn't believe them at the time, and though the bond we shared wasn't short lived, my parents were...

I can remember it, the fires that consumed our neighbourhood, the eerie silence unbroken by the sounds of war machines that had been developed to be deadly, and silent as the night. I was 8 at the time. I had no way of understanding the full extent of the hatred that these people felt for one another but my parents had told me that they hadn't always lived in fear of the other countries. That once, they were friends, and they travelled there for holidays, to enjoy the warmth of the sun and the people. Before the war was even considered.

It seemed a crazy thought, and it still does.

As I stood hunched over the ruins of my family, I reached a single conclusion.

Ah, yes...

That conclusion... It was to fight, for my country, for my family. I would become a warrior stronger, and fiercer, than any, any man had ever been before. And I'd hunt down those who killed my family. These dreams were, to me, sweeter than any little dream I'd had as a child, for with these dreams there came pain, a bitter pain that no-one would ever feel for themselves. The pain of someone who had nothing. The pain of someone whom had lost everything but their life.

And now... now my chance has come.

I remember this now, too. I can remember a kind man asking me if this was truly what I wanted. And it was. I wanted to be a killer, a warrior, a spy. I wanted to fight for my country, and my family that would always live on inside of me, my heart, and be forever in my memories and dreams.

He had told me that I would have forgotten. He told me that that would ease the pain.

What, then, is this? What am I thinking now?

Is this just my imagination, or what? It feels too real to be just a figment, nothing more than mere thought. These bitter, bitter memories have never left. I have nothing to do now, but wait, and think. As I think, perhaps I will rot away into the darkness. Perhaps I want to.

I want to be in the darkness once more.

Truly, this is where I belong. And this is where my heart belongs.

My mind...

My heart...

My soul...

All blind...

All blind to the bittersweet memories of I, Mercury.

***

"So, this is it, then?" Danny looked at the closed machine before them. Through the translucent glass, he could see a dark shape, but it wasn't clear enough for Danny to make out many details. Toby was standing beside him, holding his hand. Danny could tell that he, too, had mixed emotions about this. He looked almost nervous, unsure of what to do.

"Yeah, this is it. Why don't you open it?" said the scientist excitedly, gesturing with his head towards the button that would open the machine. Danny wasn't sure why he found the thought somewhat frightening. Just what was it that lurked here, beneath this covering of glass and plastic?

Danny felt as though he were standing at the entrance to a cave, within which he could hear the breaths of some great beast unlike any that anyone had ever seen before. It was an unnerving thought, this. A mutant with human intelligence, more powerful than any he had worked with before. It seemed almost like ancient legends of old, where a mere peasant would accidentally unleash a beast of such power onto the land, and be condemned to punishment for their wrongdoings.

"What was he fused with?" asked Danny, stalling for a moment.

89

"Timber wolf, grizzly bear, and rattlesnake."

"Sounds dangerous…" Danny said doubtfully.

"We're hoping so!"

Danny didn't seem too happy about that thought, and he looked at the scientist pleadingly for a second, but for whatever reason, they didn't seem to notice. "Well? Get on with it!"

Danny didn't really have much other choice by now. Bending down, Danny sucked in his breath and then pushed in the button, dreading the worst as there was a soft bleeping sound. The machine's lid slowly rose up with a hissing sound. Danny couldn't help but stare dumbfounded at the mutant inside.

The boy, or what had been a boy, was almost entirely covered in black, shaggy fur, with pink skin down his belly and upon his padded feet and hands. Beneath some patches of this fur, there were odd scatterings of shiny, brown, diamond-shaped scales either alone, or in little patches. He had large, pointed ears pricking out from a tangle of brown hair that still clung to his head from when he was human. His skull had been stretched into a short muzzle that hung limply open, and huge fangs protruded from his upper and lower jaws, almost piercing the wet, twitching nose that sat there. Those were just the bear's fangs, too. Behind those, Danny could see two fleshy lumps where there was doubtless a pair of snakes' fangs sheathed. His hands were tipped with massive, demonic claws and his lithe torso was accented by thick muscles that rippled when he so much as breathed. The boy's spine was one of the few places of his body that was not covered with fur, and this was covered with those smooth scales and dappled snakeskin markings instead. These scales ran down into a thick, snake-like tail that started off almost as thick as the boy's body, then slowly tapered out, ending in a rattle and stretching so long that it was a wonder that it had fit in the machine at all. Inside his mouth, beyond the fangs, Danny could see a forked tongue flickering as the boy slowly awoke.

For a while, it seemed as though it had been a false alarm, and Danny was about to excuse himself and leave. He turned to the scientist, but just as he let out a muffled mumble of a word, the mutant's eye flicked open, and fixed right on him. The mutant's jaws snapped closed with a crack. The sudden movement caused Danny to take in a sharp breath and freeze. The eye that was fixed on him had a slit pupil like a snake's, and was a dappled and musty yellow coloured, like sand. Watching in frozen fascination, Danny instinctively stepped forward to help as the boy wriggled and tried to get free of the tail that he was tangled up in. Even if he did look almost like a demon, the boy was still just a boy, and if he didn't remember anything, then he'd probably have to re-learn to stand and to speak.

As he did so, however, the boy parted his heavily fanged muzzle and hissed at him, his forked tongue flicking out. Danny froze, and watched as the mutant blinked, with his extra eyelids flicking over his eye for an instant before his human ones. Danny swallowed, and looked up at the other scientist with a slight despair in his eyes.

"So, uh…" Danny began nervously, eyes flicking about wildly. "What's his name?"

"He called himself Mercury before. Suits him, don't you think?"

Mercury parted his jaws slightly, and blinked slowly again. His ears twitched and swivelled like radars, there was a ghastly sloshing sound as he moved his forked tongue inside his mouth, before the boy flicked it, and then awkwardly twitched the tip of his tail with a soft rattling sound. The boy was wobbling unsteadily, but

91

he stayed standing, and there was some kind of eerie knowledge in his eyes, one that none of the mutants, not even Moony, had ever possessed upon their first awakening.

Danny was getting a bad feeling just by being here, but he politely stretched out his palm towards the new mutant, getting ready to pull back his hand at the slightest sign of a bite. With him being mostly in charge of introducing new mutants to the world around them, Danny had learned the hard way that sometimes they trusted their animal instincts rather than human ones, at first. To them, Danny was probably a strange, big animal that was offering some kind of a meal in his empty hand.

Contrary to his expectations, though, Mercury pulled his muzzle back from his palm, then stared up at Danny with confusion on his face. *What are you asking of me?* His eyes seemed to say. After a moment had passed, Mercury reached up with one of his heavily clawed hands, and touched Danny's palm delicately with his fingers and the tips of his claws. A few seconds later, Mercury's other hand followed and it wasn't long before the mutant was eagerly searching Danny's hand with the curiosity of a little puppy.

After a while of awkwardly standing there as the boy searched, felt, and explored his hand in every way that he could, the furred boy seemed to lose interest. Lowering his hands, Mercury turned his muzzled face down and seemed to be looking over himself. He didn't seem at all impressed, especially when he discovered that he had a tail that was probably twice as long as he was tall, tipped with a quivering rattle. Mercury looked up at Danny as though he was dismayed, and Danny smiled encouragingly in return.

Danny looked around for the other scientist, only to see him returning with a set of clothes that were presumably for Mercury, judging by the size of them. Danny offered the clothes to Mercury, and the boy, far from being as clueless as the others had been upon fusion, nodded slightly, dully, and began to pull the clothes onto his body. Danny felt rather confused. None of the mutants had ever behaved in this way before. Perhaps the memory erasing process had been unsuccessful in some way? Perhaps there were some parts of the brain that had not been affected by the process? Was it because he had been fused with three animals rather than just one?

With shaggy black fur and the eyes of a rattlesnake, the boy made quite an intimidating sight. If he wasn't enough to frighten off any soldiers, and kill a mammoth without too much effort, then nothing would be enough. Combine that with the mutants that were already being trained and the others that would likely be created and trained in the time that it took to get the originals up to military standard, and what do you end up with?

An unstoppable force.

In short, just what England was aiming for.

The thought made Danny give a shudder, though he wasn't sure why. His mother had died in the war when he was only young, leaving him all alone in this new country that mistrusted him. Despite all that, such fighting made Danny feel violently ill. Was it because he didn't want others to suffer in the same way?

Danny jerked from his thoughts as he found himself staring into the sandy-gold eyes that belonged to Mercury. Shaking away all negative thoughts, Danny heaved a weak smile again in the boy's direction. The mutant boy's eyelids flicked again over his gleaming eyes, and his slimy tongue flicked out past the fangs that kept his maw prised open. Danny kept that forced smile on his face for a while longer, until it grew too painful to keep in place, and his smile faded back into his usual calmness.

"Well, then, Mercury!" he said, and Mercury focused again, tongue flicking and sloshing behind his fangs. "Time to meet your comrades, eh? They'll be your friends here for a long, long time to come." Mercury's throat rumbled in what Danny assumed was some kind of agreement, or perhaps an attempt to reply. "Yes?" Danny asked softly, watching Mercury intently with kind blue eyes.

Mercury made the noise again, a curious muttering snarl mixed with a growling hiss. It wasn't very clear, but Danny thought he heard words, mixed in amongst the animal sounds. The words were faint, and contorted, as though they were spoken by a ghost, but Danny, his imagination playing up, felt his mouth dry up as he heard them, his imagination fluttering in his brain like a trapped bird.

"I... Remember... Your promissssssssse..."

***

"Can't catch me, Bethany!"

"You bet I will!"

Moony and Bethany each laughed loudly as he scrambled up to the top of the climbing frame, his claws rasping as he gripped the bars of metal that made up the structure, fuzzy wings fluttering. Bethany, though she had no wings and soft paws, was agile, and she clambered up after him, hot on his tail. Though they had been tired after the mission yesterday, even the badly injured children had been healed by the technology that the laboratory had had access to. Today was one of their few days off, and with all of them well fed and well rested, they were taking the time to laugh and play together in their playroom.

Meanwhile, Joey was preening himself happily as he looked into a nearby mirror. Benny and Ginny had hidden themselves away in a little, straw filled igloo like one would find in a rabbit hutch and were giggling to themselves, as they peeped out and watched Emerald looking for them. Sally and Cassie were chasing each other around the room and barking loudly whenever they had successfully pinned one another. Karasu, who usually occupied the nearby swing made out of an old tire, was nowhere to be seen, but howls of despair and splashes could be occasionally heard, as well as the yells of an angry scientist. Earlier that morning, Karasu had apparently stolen into the men's washroom, and that hadn't ended well for anyone involved. Especially Karasu, and the poor scientist who had been tasked with giving him a bath again.

As Danny pushed open the door that lead from the Fusion room and into the young mutants' playroom, he and Mercury were greeted by laughter and a ring of excited yells and squeaks of joy. At first, they went unnoticed, but then Moony noticed Danny, and a huge grin split his face.

Though Danny faced much scorn and taunts amongst the other scientists, he was very popular among the mutants. Danny had no children of his own, but the children here all loved him, because they knew that he would often come bearing treats and praise, and would listen to them no matter what they had to say. In a way, he was like a father to them, and a few of the children even called him 'Daddy'.

"Hey, look!" yelled Moony, pointing. Almost all of the mutants looked up, except for Benny and Ginny as they continued to hide in the hay, and Karasu as his tortured howls and splashes rang out from somewhere, far away in another corner of the lab.

"It's Danny!"

Even Benny and Ginny looked up in response to that, a mop of white hair and pink eyes popping up out of the hay at first and then Ginny's twitching nose following. Emerald scampered up to Bethany and then dragged her by the hand towards the scientist. Moony practically fell from the top of the climbing frame and ran towards him with a skip in his step and tiny hoots audible. Sally and Cassie leaped up towards Danny in an effort to bombard his face with sloppy kisses. Even Joey swaggered over with some haste.

"Danny! Where have you been!"

"Me 'n Sally were looking for you yesterday, we were!"

"Feed me! Feed me! Do you have any treats?"

"Who's that, Danny? Not Toby, the other one!"

"Daddy! He's scary!"

As they all eventually, one by one, noticed the strange boy that Danny had brought with him and received all their praises from the man even if he hadn't had the time to fill his seemingly bottomless pockets with treats, an awed hush settled over the children even before Danny had begun to speak. With eyes wide, they all huddled together as Mercury flicked his tongue, and the second lids flicked slowly over his eyes. Seeing Emerald standing before him with big eyes and arms outstretched, Danny stooped a little and scooped her up with his free hand that had let go of Mercury's the moment before. Toby was being guided by the other.

The tiny, fairy-like girl shuffled in his arms, then hugged him about the neck, a fear in her eyes. She, being fused with a dragonfly, only came up to around Mercury's waist. Danny realized that Mercury was the tallest mutant that had been brought in yet, and that the little ones undoubtedly found him imposing, frightening even. Especially the youngest and the smallest of them. Whereas Joey had previously been the oldest, having recently turned twelve, this stranger was probably the oldest they could attempt a Fusion and succeed. Unnervingly, he looked around 17, though the bear genes in him might have encouraged his growth.

Benny, hiding behind Toby, squeaked and stamped his foot in what seemed to be a threatening display towards Mercury. Toby, trying to find Benny's soft, white-haired head so that he could tousle the boy's hair, accidentally poked him in the eye. Benny squeaked and ran to hide in the straw again, and Ginny followed, leaving Toby looking upset and confused.

Most of the other mutants seemed to take this as a cue to step back away from Mercury and his fiery, barren stare. Danny turned around to console Toby for a moment, and Emerald, sitting upright in his arms, watched the newcomer with her diamond eyes warily. Mercury turned towards her, after his judging stare had scanned over the group and decided that the children were not worthy of his attentiveness. Snake eyes fixed and slowly focusing, Mercury flicked his tongue at her, and didn't make a sound in response.

Emerald seemed a little encouraged by this, and she, wordlessly, reached out with a hesitant and trembling hand that shimmered with a sapphire sheen in the light. For a few seconds she slowly reached closer, a nervous fear beginning to show on her face. She gently touched Mercury on the nose, and at first, nothing seemed to happen.

Then, as she drew her arm back, Mercury gave a ferocious snap, his monstrous fangs colliding a hair's breadth from Emerald's fragile hand. She gave a shocked yelp and snatched it back. There was a yappy, shrieking roar and a russet-coloured blur raced forward, leaping up to sink black claws into the smooth scales of Mercury's back.

In response, the ferocious mutant twisted around and roared in a voice that was like a rumble from the bowels of the earth. Deep, reverberating, and hungry. Sally and Cassie quickly joined in the tussle with a fierce war cry, each one latching on to one of Mercury's legs with canine fangs gripping tightly. Cassie was kicked brutally aside, and she went tumbling across the room until she came to a halt when she hit the climbing frame with a clang. Her sister, Sally, yipped in fear and hurtled after her.

"Cassie!" she cried, dashing over. Her sister lifted a feeble paw, and then began to struggle up onto her feet.

"Sally! Look out!"

All too late, the dog realized that she had fallen into a trap. The moment she had turned her back, Mercury had been on her tail, with Bethany swinging from his shoulders like some sort of living flag, her tail fluffed out for all it was able. The next thing Cassie knew, she had been slammed against the ground and pinned down by thick black paws. As she twisted her head sideways, Cassie could see Mercury's tongue flicking, and his thick muscles bunching. Steam coiled from his nostrils, and he heaved out a breath that was like wind gushing through an ancient cavern.

With hoots and shrieks, caws and yowls, the rest of the mutants had raced forward. Every single one of them piled onto Mercury. The distressed form of Danny, running about like a headless chicken, tried to pull the fighters apart as they tussled with shrieks and wails. Even Karasu, fleeing from his bubble-covered assailant and covered with water and foam himself, found himself dragged into the fighting as Mercury leaped onto him and pinned him down with massive claws. Emerald was struggling against Danny's grip, letting out little gasps for air whenever his grip unknowingly and protectively tightened around her chest.

Soon after the fighting had ensued, the more of the scientists came running, and some froze and turned ice-white as they beheld the sight of the chaos that had taken over the usually peaceful playroom. The most confident ones lurched forward, grabbing onto one of the attacking mutants or onto Mercury to keep him from causing any more damage. If any lives were lost in this, then that would be an utter disaster...

But perhaps they would be lucky if there was only one.

With the number of struggling, flailing bodies in the room growing by the second, and the sounds of animal cries and shrieks mingling with human yells and swearing, it took a long while before some semblance of control was reached. The mutants, most with cuts and scratches, looked ashamed as they dragged their feet or were dragged towards a very stern-looking Danny. Gently, he placed Emerald on the ground, and she and Bethany met up again with joyous looks hidden behind their childish protest at the situation.

With his other hand free, Danny clutched at the arm that he'd been using to try to drag the fighters apart, and there was a crimson stain spreading out from beneath his hand, slowly tainting through the sleeve of the white coat that he wore. His usually kind blue eyes were filled with a sudden cold steel. All the mutants stared up at him with eyes that were bright and fearful. They looked at him like they had looked at Mercury before.

"Daddy...?" began Benny, hopping forward.

But Danny wasn't listening, and Benny's question fell on deaf ears that were numb with the cold. Mercury, who was being restrained by four of the strongest scientists, was struggling and snarling, covered in bite and scratch marks. Karasu limped and whimpered, seeming to be making a show of his wounds or his terror at the sight of the blood. He stared around with big puppy eyes, not seeming focused by the more pressing matters at hand.

Finally seeming to come to his senses, Danny looked around with eyes that were just barely focused on the room in front of him.

"I'm disappointed in you... All of you..." he croaked, looking at the scientists as well as the mutants. Then he turned to look solely at the mutants. "Go to your rooms... All of you." His eyes were beginning to look glazed, and he turned to the scientists even as the children set up a chorus of "that's not fair!" and "I don't want to!" with singsong voices all whining. Danny's mood seemed to turn sour. "Do it!" he yelled forcefully. "Now!"

They couldn't do anything but fall silent and obey, too shocked to do otherwise. Danny had never raised his voice at them before.

As soon as they had left, Danny looked at the scientists. "No more experiments like... Him... None! Take him to a separate training area. I don't care where!" he gasped breathlessly, his eyes wild and frantic.

The other scientists hurried to obey, and Danny just watched them. The glaze over his eyes was growing, like clouds gathering in a clear blue sky. There was foam at the corners of his mouth, and the entire arm of his that had been bitten had gone numb.

The blood that flowed from the wound didn't cease. He could feel his pulse pounding through his head in a terrifying, nauseous way. Through the daze of sounds, Danny tried to look up, but found that he could see nothing but a hazy swirl of terrifying colours and nonexistent lights in place of those he was looking for. The strength leaving his limbs, Danny felt himself falling to his knees, his hand falling away from the ring of teeth marks and twin puncture wounds that marked the centre. That hand was sticky with crimson fluid.

A commotion began to spread amongst the scientists. Their shocked murmurs rose into an almighty clamour as realization finally struck.

Their voices spun like distant echoes that Danny could hardly comprehend, and as he supported himself as best he could, it felt as though the pain was all he knew; he could barely understand any who spoke to him, or see anyone with his tired, glazed eyes.

"Agh! 'E was bitten! Get 'im to first aid, quickly!"

"That was Mercury!"

"I didn't even know that you were working on that!"

"That... Demon! That... Fiend!"

The many voices rose up into an incomprehensible, incredible buzzing hubbub that washed over poor Danny's senses like a tidal wave, overwhelming him. Sweat formed on his face, and he soon found himself hitting the ground without even knowing, even though he felt the hands of desperate scientists trying to hold him up.

"Silence!" Amanda's voice broke through the mess of tangled voices, which quickly fell silent in response to her. "Get him to the medical room, and administer the antivenin before this ends badly."

You could almost feel the glares that she sent out to them. Danny felt hands continue in their efforts to support him. The fizzing blur of lights and colours were fading into darkness even as the people's voices rose again, and Danny imagined that he could hear the gentle tap-tapping of Toby's crutches above all the voices.

Tap-tap...
Tap-tap...
Tap-tap...

It was like the ticking of a clock, or a time bomb. But to Danny, it was the comforting sound of the one person who trusted him with his life, every single day. The thought gave Danny hope.

What are they doing now? he wondered, the airy feel of floating beginning to overtake his paralysing form. Though a rather vague question at most, the thought gave Danny hope. The feeling of floating brought with it the sense of freedom.

As Danny continued to listen to the gentle tap-tap of Toby's crutches as it rang through his mind, Danny felt the hazy darkness closing in. But the thought of trust gave him hope, and that simple feeling of hope caused his heart to swell beneath his breast. With a tiny smile playing in onto his face, Danny listened to the fading echoes of Toby's crutches as his consciousness was sucked into the darkest crevasses of his mind, collapsing in onto itself. And yet the echoes continued to ring distantly, like the tiny, soothing sound of a bell, through his mind for all to hear.

-Chapter 8-

Recovery

As the minutes trundled into hours, and hours wore on into a day, fear turned into whispers among the inhabitants of the laboratory, and simple nervousness or superstition into guilty paranoia. Those who did not know Mercury's name uttered 'Bargheist', the name of a pitch-black demon dog that was said to haunt moors, graveyards, and crossroads in the dead of night. It may not have been the kindest nickname, but it certainly fit Mercury's apparently foul nature and his venomous reputation amongst the laboratory workers.

As Danny had told them to, Mercury was taken away to a room out of the way of the other little mutants, and skilled medics were issued to each of the rooms of the injured children. As these people entered the rooms, they found that most of the little mutants flinched away from them or even hid, with the bravest of them standing up to try to insist that they did nothing wrong. To this, the doctors simply smiled and shook their heads, and despite what the children had been expecting, none received severe consequences for their fighting, as most of the blame was placed on Mercury's shoulders.

Thankfully, there were few serious injuries, with the worst being a set of deep claw marks across Bethany's shoulders, staining her russet locks red until it was healed. Moony made a record-breaking fuss despite this, and seemed to think that the fact that he'd broken a claw was life threatening. He had yelled and hooted at the poor scientists so much that the scientists had taken his favourite cuddly toy, a mouse that Moony called

Hootsy, away from his nest. Apart from this, they were mostly silent. There was a deep unease gripping everyone, even Moony. The day's events were baffling to all of them.

There was no way of describing anything to the children.

Even scientists found the situation immensely puzzling, but they each, in time, came to accept that Mercury was just a difficult character to handle, and that it had been no fault of their own. But every breath seemed bated, and every little movement caused new questions to arise. Upon closer examination of the bite wound on one of Danny's forearms, the deep teeth marks turned out to have been delivered by none other than Mercury. The twin pierce wounds in the centre of the ring of pouring gouges had turned out to have come from the vicious, venom-filled fangs in Mercury's upper jaw, behind the freakishly large fangs that kept his mouth from closing.

It was only by late afternoon that the antivenin that the scientists had delivered Danny finally seemed to have had an effect. His sweating, shuddering body finally began to stir, his face creasing repeatedly into grimaces of pain. It had been too risky to give Danny the usual method of healing for the poison that surged through his veins, but unfortunately for him, the bite had yet to stop bleeding for the venom. A good few of Danny's comrades were running back and forth like headless chickens, their panic rising; snake bites were rather rare around here, especially from venomous ones. No-one knew how this would end, but most hoped that it would end well.

Apparently, Mercury's rattlesnake DNA had come from a local collector's hoard, where one of the scientists was able to take tissue samples from a live specimen. With the rattlesnake's owner's permission, of course. The scientist who had originally proposed Mercury's creation was, however, a little shifty when it came to the other animal genes in Mercury; wolf and grizzly bear. He wasn't about to reveal anything anytime soon.

As he shivered and twitched back into wakefulness, Danny's blurred vision finally hazed back into some semblance of focus as he tried to grasp what was going on around him. Toby, the closest, was sadly able to make sure that Danny was awake by, as with Benny before, reaching out to check his pulse, then accidentally poking him in the eye. Danny gave a grunting sound of "agh!" and Toby's ears perked up. "He's awake!" he rasped. It was the first time Toby had spoken all day, and as he did, Danny stirred some more.

He reached up with a groggy hand and rubbed his stinging and watery eyes.

"Uuuuungh… Ech…" he muttered, reaching out with a pathetically floppy arm towards the nearest blurred 'person' he could see, which just so happened to be the filing cabinet on the other side of his bed.

"What's… What's going on…?" he asked cluelessly, blinking back the clouded glaze of his eyes. Toby rasped again, and Danny was shut up by the feel of someone dabbing at his mouth with a damp cloth. Danny grunted in protest, but even so, the water felt welcoming. It was clean and cool, and it eased the feeling that his throat was being hewn at by icy desert winds, a rather unpleasant feeling for anyone, to say the least. His gaze gradually clearing and his foggy mind finding the water, Danny's eyelids fluttered, and his tongue curled about his lips to lap up the water in the way that a parched dog would.

Danny heard the sounds of the news that he was awake spreading, and quickly, there were more people crowding him and pressing him with questions in voices that buzzed in Danny's ears. He winced rather visibly. The buzzing echoes of the questions faded into relative silence after one last yell from someone who noticed his evident discomfort, leaving Danny to revel in his thumping headache as he eventually opened tired eyes again.

"You look hungover..." commented one of the men, and Danny looked somewhat blank as the words registered. As it did, he found himself agreeing inwardly with the scientist, but not without a touch of shame. A second later, he heard the scientist who had spoken give a pained 'ow!' and looked up to see the guy next to him slyly moving his elbow away.

"That wasn't very polite," scolded a woman's voice, sounding sympathetic. As Danny looked around with his vision finally clearing up, he found himself wondering why there were only four people in here; it had sounded like a lot more before. With a twinge of resentment he realized a moment later that no-one else in this lab cared enough about him to come, even if whatever happened had nearly killed him.

Although...

What did happen back then? Danny found himself wondering, as he racked his brains and struggled to recall. As much as he tried, though, he was able to gather up only hazy and malformed memories from before he'd fallen unconscious.

Looking up at the other scientists with clear despair in his eyes, Toby was the only one who didn't seem to catch the hint. Though his vision was now clear, Danny felt like so many other things were now murky. Three separate sets of eyes bored into him, causing him to feel a little claustrophobic, and huddle up into himself with some difficulty; it felt as if all of his limbs were made of lead. He looked about himself pleadingly, trying to meet the eyes of the other scientists.

There was a long and intricate silence, with the blood gushing through Danny's head illustrating his vision with nauseous lines that only added to his feeling of sickness.

"What's wrong?" asked one of the other scientists again, offering a bucket. "You gonna be sick?" Danny wasn't entirely sure how to answer, but he had begun to push himself unsteadily into a sitting position. "Hey, no moving! You'll hurt yourself!" she insisted, ignoring Danny's discomfort as he tried to shrug her hand from his shoulder.

"How long have I been out?" asked Danny suspiciously.

"You got bit yesterday morning, around ten, and it's four now."

"Four in the afternoon?"

"No, four in the morning!"

Danny's heart sank. It had been that long!? It would definitely explain the lack of activity around here, at least. But he wasn't any closer to his answer of what had happened.

"What happened?" he asked eventually, after what seemed like a lifetime of considering whether or not to actually ask it. His suspicions rose as the scientists exchanged wary glances.

"You said that I got bitten... What by?"

"By a... Bargheist," answered one after what seemed like an eternity.

"A bargheist?" Danny's brow furrowed. He had heard whispers of, and read about, the mythological demon that was said to haunt England's streets at night. Danny had always been a keen student when studying legends and myths that swirled in every country. Even as he aged, he had remembered most, if not all, of what he had studied and sketched out after time, scribbling repeated notes in scribbly, scrawly, spidery handwriting that had been ironically mistaken for runes once or twice.

Danny had always harboured a secret belief of such fantasies, but to hear such an utterance from one of the other scientists? To Danny, that was the unbelievable thing.

"Well, some people in the laboratory call it that, but... Er, no... Actually, it was only Mercury..." corrected one of the others. Danny felt as though something had clicked into place in his mind, but unfortunately for him, he had no idea what that meant.

"Go on..." he muttered, straining to remember.

"Mercury- it's that new mutant. Started a huge fight amongst them all. I'm not sure how it started. I think you tried to intervene. Got a taste of rattlesnake venom... More than I'd ever want to deal with."

Danny nibbled on his lower lip nervously.

He didn't remember the events as they had happened, but something about the scientists' descriptions had seemed... Familiar. He tried to remain calm, acting as if he knew what they were on about.

"Where is he now, this... Mercury?"

They exchanged glances again. Toby's tail was flicking back and forth nervously, his ears flattened and eyes half closed. Or was it just because he was tired? Come to think of it... Had Toby been awake all night, just waiting for him to wake up? Danny felt a small candle of guilt licking into existence in his heart, as well as fondness. At times, he felt like Toby was his only friend.

"We did as you said, Danny."

"What did I say?"

"You said to keep him separate from the others. I don't think you wanted him to hurt anyone."

"Oh, right... That's good, I guess..."

He spoke thoughtfully, but there was something

burdening his mind. What was it?

"Yeah, it is... better than someone else being bitten."

"So, where is he now?"

The scientist said nothing, just looked about as though trying to avoid eye contact with Danny. He subconsciously rubbed his nose with a finger, and one of the other scientists opened his mouth as though they were about to speak. The other two looked at him, and in the end, he closed his mouth and said nothing, eyes turned downwards in shame. Finally, one of them forced a tired, pleading smile.

"He's... somewhere safe."

"Where?" Danny persisted, heart beginning to thump.

Again, they said nothing for a good, long while.

"Woops, Toby! Bedtime when Danny woke up, remember?" uttered the female scientist lightheartedly, clearly trying to change the subject.

Toby rasped.

"Wha-? But I never-?!"

She interrupted him.

"And you need to take all your medication! Very important, that, you know!" she sang.

"But I already-!?"

"Whoops! Better say bye-bye to Danny now, hadn't you?" she smiled and took a hold of his arm, yanking Toby to his feet before he could even ready his crutches.

Before Toby could further react, she dragged him out of the room by the arm, irregular tapping sounds signalling Toby's passage down the corridor as he struggled to stay upright.

"Bye, Danny-!"

Danny heard Toby hoarsely yell back towards him, and Danny swallowed, at a loss for words. He almost got the chance to speak again, but the other scientists were leaving the room as well. Danny struggled to sit up.

"Where are you going?!" he called, aghast that they, the mendicants, would just leave him, even if he was alive and awake. One of the scientists came towards him, to calm him down again. They seemed strained, red-faced.

"It's not just Toby that needs his sleep! English people need theirs too, you know!" laughed the scientist at the door, his voice sounding strained. He was resting one hand on the light switch.

"Why won't you-!?"

"Shhh, you'll feel better in the morning, I promise!"

Danny's blue eyes flicked from one to the other, and his jaw dropped. His eyes seemed to be almost ablaze with shock. Was he even hearing this right? Something was definitely a bit off here, and he wasn't sure what it was. There was an uneasy feeling rising in his gut.

The scientist just beside him was fumbling through their first aid kit. Danny's gaze whipped from them to the other to the next, in turn. The one with hands buried in their first aid kit finally removed something, but Danny was too focused on the others now to notice. There was too much happening now, all at once.

All too late, he turned to stare at the one who had been struggling with their kit, and he caught sight of the glinting tip of a needle for a fraction of a second.

"Goodnight, Danny!"

There was a sharp pain in his arm, and although he struggled at first, he was unable to fight against the sedative for long.

"Wait!" he slurred out, in a final effort, his eyelids drooping. His hands and feet had gone numb, and the feeling was growing, quickly spreading. He could no longer move.

But they didn't wait. The scientists left the room, one by one. There was a tiny clicking sound, and the light was knocked out, leaving Danny lying there with nothing to do but ponder and despair in the consuming darkness until his mind was caught up as well.

Right before he passed out, a final thought flitted over Danny's glazed eyes.

What are they trying to hide from me...?

***

It is so dark in here... so cold...

The mad thrill that had surged through my body before is now nowhere to be found. I was possessed, insane back then. It was as though I had been overcome, my strong spirit consumed by a torrent of black filth.

I am bound, held sturdy by shackles supported by electrified chains. My movements are each and every one punished by the course of lightning through my veins. I can see these chains, sense their heat burning away coolly against my boiling flesh. They press coldly against my neck, my wrists, and my ankles to hold me in place, and with every pulse, my flesh goes numb once again from the sparks that race through me like playful mice that serve no purpose other than to mock me.

Utter darkness does not serve as a hindrance to me, for I can see through the darkness, and into the heat that radiates from my foes and friends. This feeling is new to me, but I will master it with time.

I have plenty of time here in this cold, dark room.

From within the dark of the void in which I am enclosed, I can hear the hiss of a rattle. The sound is eerily amusing to me, the sound of a monster going in for the kill. I heard the sound once before. Back when those traitors lead me out into the open, and then threw me into the mouths of the waiting sharks.

The sound is my battle cry.

I can remember the sound... Then the taste, that taste of salt and metal, a taste so familiar from when I had licked my own cuts and grazes as a mere child.

The taste of blood...

The sound is a signal, and the taste, a consequence. Everything is linked together in such a way, such a fate that has always seemed entwined...

Is that so?

Let's test that, shall we?

My jaws part and tongue flicks, the sound of the bloodflow gushing through my ears turning into the crash of waves on the shore. My thoughts of self-pity quickly turn into thoughts of vengeance.

They lied to me... My own country.

I fight for my family now. I do not fight for the liars, or for the war.

I will fight for vengeance alone.

With the rattle growing and snarls ending electric thrills down my spine, I tense up. Some ill-fated will of some unknown force causes my rattling to halt, my snarls to grow, my jaws to part and tongue to flick once again. My heart pounds like a trembling, ticking time bomb well buried deep, deep inside of me.

I may have been thrown here without mercy or questioning, but I know that they will not leave me here to rot forever.

I growl.

I am not alone...

There is someone there... Where did they come from?

I can sense their beating heart, their warmth. There is another heat, another life force that has joined mine, turning the cold of darkness into a warm, welcoming glow like that of a campfire, a light to lead you from the labyrinth of a tunnel.

Other than the human's heat, I do not see any light... Perhaps night has fallen already. It wouldn't surprise me. Arching my electrified spine, I pull back my lips into an ugly grimace and I try to speak in that twisted, malformed voice that has become the only one I own.

I prepare myself.

But I am stopped. I am silent, for a single finger is pressed against my fangs. There is a form standing there, dressed in slick black armour with the face unseen.

A voice, serpentine as my very form, and seductive as a summer's breeze, curls slickly through the air like a toxic mist seeping into me, immobilizing me. And I allow it to... I hang onto every word the figure speaks, letting the voice charm me, and the promise take me into its own little world of dreaming, longing.

"I can set you free... If you will allow me."

I am overcome.

***

"I'm not completely helpless!" insisted Toby for what felt to him like the hundredth time, irritably dragging his arm out of the hand of the scientist who was guiding him (or at least trying to). Toby wasn't exactly having the greatest day ever today, and that was saying the least. The scientist who led him had already forgotten to warn him about three flights of stairs, and then had hastily corrected her lack of interest when she felt him trip and fall.

"Oh, I'm sorry, Toby! There's some stairs here!"

Now Toby had learned to search cautiously ahead with a crutch as he stepped, but despite this, he was sure that he would have a bruise or two in the morning to show for his troubles. No matter how many times he spoke to her, however, she never seemed to take note that he had spoken or even seem to be listening.

Was she ignoring him?

Or did she not understand his rasping voice?

Irritated whines rising in his throat, Toby gave yet another rasp, and finally succeeded in yanking his arm away from her. "I said, I can get there myself!" he insisted.

Unfortunately for him, it only took a moment's lapse in attention to cause disaster, and Toby felt himself tumbling to the ground as he took the weight from one of the crutches that supported him.

Uttering foul oaths under his breath, Toby's ears pricked and he stared upwards into nothingness with eyes that were sickly-yellow and lifeless. If that didn't get her attention, nothing would.

"Oh, but Toby, you need a guide! You'll end up getting lost if you don't have a guide."

"I won't need one for much longer if you have to be my guide!" pointed out Toby, his voice rudely spitting as he began to fumble his crutches over the smooth floor beneath him. She chuckled darkly, her voice seeming to Toby as though she were hiding something.

"We're almost there now," she said kindly, and Toby shook his head. Perhaps he was simply imagining things. He was blind and half deaf, after all. The one thing that Toby relied on in life right now was trust. So he didn't say anything more.

Hobbling after her and feeling as if the gentle touch on his arm was a threat, Toby felt relief flooding his tired form as the scientist finally announced that they had arrived. Allowing a slow smile to creep onto his face, Toby let himself settle down into the soft sheets of his warm bed and then curl up. His ears flicked for a second as he heard the voice of the one who had acted as his guide, and Toby found himself wondering what he'd been so afraid of before.

"Aren't you gonna get changed?"

Toby shook his head, even though he was facing away from her. It wasn't much of a secret that Toby was unable to dress himself. He didn't want this stranger taking a peep at anything she shouldn't be.

"Okay, then... Remember to get as much sleep as you can... Getting up at 7 as you usually do just won't do!" Toby could imagine that she was wagging her finger as though to scold him like a little child when she spoke, but he didn't reply, and simply waited for the telltale hiss of the door sliding mechanically closed.

Smiling to himself, Toby shifted and turned over as he tried to find the most comfortable position to sleep in, and hopefully not fall out of bed in the process. Grunting to himself every so often, the male eventually found himself curled up like a cat with his tail tickling his nose. He smiled, seeming pleased with this, and began to wait for dreams to come for him.

He waited…

And waited…

And shifted some more…

Until his clawed hands were hugging his knees tightly into his chest and even after what seemed like hours, Toby was unable to sleep. What was this? He should have dropped off right away, having stayed up all night last night to wait for Danny to come around.

Toby didn't know how, but something felt wrong. Very, very wrong. It was as though the ghost of something, unexplainable by science, was haunting him, pushing him…

Was it the scientist's strange secrecy earlier, weighing down on his thoughts?

Did it really bother him that much?

Toby shifted slightly, nervously. It couldn't have been that. He'd gotten over it soon enough! Lying still again, Toby tried to settle down, to calm his heightened nerves. But the more he tried, the more anxious he got.

Eventually, Toby found himself listening.

Ears flattened and twitching every now and then as he would hear a sound, Toby began to stir more and more often as the frequency of the sounds he was hearing began to increase. *Can't anyone else hear this?* He wondered to himself, but quickly realized that, though one of his ears was deaf, the other could pick up sounds far beyond what the human ear would even know of. Sometimes it even hurt for people to whisper to him; it seemed so loud.

Now, Toby was sure that something wasn't right. These soft sounds were like the footsteps of someone who didn't want to be heard, audible only by the rasp of fabric against fabric and the slightest swish of someone with feet like a cat's, breezing over the laboratory floor or even... the rafters?

Toby's ear twitched again. There was the gentle creaking of wood as it reacted to a weight that pressed upon it. Toby's blind, glazed eyes snapped open. Who would hide in the rafters?!

...Someone who doesn't want to be seen.

An intruder perhaps?

It certainly didn't sound like any of the young ones at play. They were, from what Toby knew, all fast asleep in their beds. Besides, Toby was sure that the other scientists locked the doors to their rooms at night. The only one of those who would be able to get up onto the rafters would be Emerald, anyway, and she was barely weightless.

Moving his quilt off as quietly as he could, Toby winced as they seemed to rustle like he was stepping on dry leaves. Fumbling for his crutches and his coat,

Toby had barely even prepared himself before he was hauling himself to his feet, the bare, fur-covered appendages sliding on the floor uselessly.

Toby grimaced as the panthers' claws that tipped his toes rasped. With a mighty heave, Toby pulled himself forward a few steps at a time and forced his exhausted breaths to remain quiet. Reaching out with a shaking hand, Toby felt around for the button that would open the door, and struggled to balance for a moment with only one crutch.

As he found it, Toby listened out for any sign that there was anyone around, his one working ear twisting about, and the other flattening itself into his hair.

Then he placed his palm against the smooth, round surface and without hesitation, pushed down.

-Chapter 9-

Trickery

"...I have infiltrated the enemy lair again, sir... I obstructed the latest of their weapon creation the last time I was in here, and they still don't suspect a thing."

"Good, good... Keep up the good work, Alma."

The spy's gaze flitted about under cover of her night vision goggles.

"I will, sir."

"Do you have anything more to report on the structure of the laboratory?"

"It appears to be split into three major sections. One which handles the research and creation of new weapons, one for training the result of fusion, and one where the scientists and the weapons can go about their daily activities and live out their lives- all in the 'safety' of the laboratory."

"Interesting... It is a large laboratory, then?"

Alma nodded unconsciously, taking the time to look into the distance and back again, then inspect curiously the many doors that each lead into different rooms or the staircases that lead to deeper or closer to the surface sections of the laboratory.

"Yes, sir. I am sure that there is much of its structure that I have yet to see."

"Should I begin to arrange an attack?"

"Not yet. There's work to do, first."

Alma was beginning to hear things now and her words trailed off, focusing on a tick-ticking rasp that sounded suspiciously familiar. Alma fell silent for a while, and her face turned into a grimace as the voice on the other side of the line seemed to take offense in

118

her sudden lack of a voice.

"Alma? Speak up!"

"Shh!" she hissed, quietly standing, her voice lowering into a whisper. Whoever it was that approached halted for a second, and looked around seemingly in response to the sound of her voice. Though her boss seemed to want to protest, Alma quickly hissed a dismissal and then disconnected, not giving him the chance to say anything more.

"Someone's coming, over and out!"

Sucking in her breath, Alma looked down at the one who approached, and knew why he looked familiar right away. She cursed inwardly in her mind, but as luck would have it, this was the only one whom had come. He was blind, and Alma assumed that his ears didn't make up for that. She wasn't about to risk it, however, and slowly stood, beginning to shuffle away in a silence so deep that it was as though she was a ghost or a vapour.

It seemed that she had misjudged the blind scientist's hearing. As soon as she made a movement, his head whipped around to stare with lifeless, unseeing eyes in her direction. She saw his hair beginning to stand on end, and he limped forwards, trying to look tough through the fear that came with facing the unknown, the unseen.

"I know you're there..." he rasped, finally coming to a halt just beneath her.

Alma made no move to reply to him.

"I said, I know you're there!" Toby said again, ears flattening. He shifted his crutches apart a bit, as though in an effort to look sturdy or a little more imposing.

Still, Alma didn't reply. *If I don't answer, he might go away...* she thought hopefully to herself. But Toby was much too stubborn for that childplay.

"I can hear your breathing..." he warned. "Who are

119

you, and what are you doing here? Who were you talking to just then?"

Alma knew by now that she was cornered. She would have to con her way out of this one, just as she had conned so many people, so many times before. Toby would be no different. Putting on a sweet smile beneath her mask just to set the character in stone, Alma slipped from the beam and landed silently next to Toby.

"Toby! Oh, Toby!" she cried in that simpering sweet voice that she had used so many times before. Although her insides reviled, she wrapped her arms around Toby's shoulders.

"Huh?!" Toby seemed taken aback, but suddenly he recognized the voice. "Sabrina! It's you!" Toby's face looked simply shocked, rather than as happy as she'd first expected. Alma, with her arms taken up holding Toby down in what he would undoubtedly take as a friendly or even loving gesture, stayed where she was and didn't let down her guard.

"Toby! You recognized me!" Alma laughed joyously, knowing slyly that Toby couldn't hug her back or else he'd fall.

"What are you doing here, Sabrina?" he asked, still sounding just that little bit let down.

"I came looking for you!"

"How did you get in?"

"The door was open," lied Alma through gritted teeth, but it seemed to sit with Toby.

"So… You do want to talk to me after all!"

"Why wouldn't I? You're so sweet, and ever so strong!" she complimented him, wondering if he could hear her trickery. Perhaps he was lying, too.

"You gave me that paper, and Danny said that it was blank…" Toby's voice softened, and sounded deeply upset.

"He did? Well, he was lying to you! I know I wrote my number on there!"

"He wouldn't lie to me, I know he wouldn't!" Toby's voice trembled with what seemed like anger at the thought. Although Toby's voice was rasping and not at all loud, Alma knew that the other scientists would begin to wake soon, and it would make for a difficult situation to escape from if he was still talking to her by the time they awoke.

"Toby, anyone can lie to you..." said Alma, that soft actor's tone supporting her voice to give the illusion that she felt sorry for him. *And I'm not lying to you... Not right now...*

Toby looked down a little, as though he was wondering who to trust in this situation. She could see his hair beginning to stand on end again as his brain worked frantically, painfully. Alma reached out with a dainty hand and, as if to add insult to injury, gently began to caress one of his dappled cheeks, marked with a rosette of panther's fur.

He shivered beneath her touch, but seemed unmoved, his blind eyes each dark and sad, unseeing in more ways than just the one. Alma could sense time ticking onwards, and her brain reached a conclusion seemingly of its own accord.

"Toby..." she whispered softly, manipulatively. "Come with me."

Toby looked up. His gaze seemed to stare right through her for a while, but then slowly, Toby nodded.

"Come, then..." Alma whispered, smiling as she laid a hand on his arm to guide him.

As she lead him, Toby followed without question, and Alma almost felt pity for the poor man; he knew no better. It felt like walking a dog, and as they reached the end of the corridor, Alma gently warned Toby of the stairs with a whisper.

"Watch out for the stairs, Toby…"

He said nothing, but he heard, and began to clamber up the flight, with the clumsy step of someone blind and frail, his crutches slipping repeatedly upon unseen obstacles. His head was bowed, fixed on the ground before him, but he wasn't watching his step. All the while, Alma's hand gently rested on his arm as it clutched at the crutch that was the only reason he could still stand.

As they finally reached the top of the stairs, Alma saw him halt as the dewy grass tickled his furry toes.

"Where are we going?" he asked, his eyes unknowing of the gentle pink dawn that tinged the horizon and painted the clouds.

"You'll see," she replied calmly, her nerves easier to handle now that they were out of the tight, enclosed space of the laboratory.

Alma continued to lead him down through a quiet, overgrown path that wove through fields, until she finally reached a place where she often sat, quite a distance from the laboratory, but ironically, a quiet resting, thinking place of hers even before she had found the secretive lab. It overlooked the quiet city of Durham, the cathedral spire standing tall and proud against the sun that gently tinted the horizon and the other buildings, all so small in comparison, standing out in their own historical, dinky little way, each stone with its own story to tell.

The fields waved as the slightest of breezy chills passed over them, the grasses all becoming one like lakes of gold and green. The clouds drifted lazily across the sky, reflecting the sunlight as though they were stained glass.

"Now, sit here…" purred Alma to Toby, gently guiding him to where he could sit comfortably. "Now this… Isn't this a nice scene?" she asked, fully aware that he was blind and would never be able to see the scene of which she spoke. Toby's face seemed to fall, and he shivered as a cold chill passed over him, ruffling his mane of black hair.

"Sabrina, I..." he whispered, sounding sad. "I can't see anything..."

Alma smiled, beginning to gently shuffle through the possessions that she carried, as quietly as she could, whilst all the while, she talked to him.

"Imagine, then, Toby... Just imagine..." she told him, her voice soft as the breeze that passed over them.

"The sun is rising now, Toby... Just imagine... The way the light silhouettes that grand city there, eh? Those little cotton-clouds all pink and soft, like candyfloss... Have you ever had that, Toby?" She began to describe the scene to him, slowly drawing something from the small bag that hung from her belt.

"Candyfloss?" Toby's mouth watered at the memories, and he closed his eyes, completely absorbed in Alma's words and in his own imaginings. He could remember exploring theme parks and carnivals with his mother and his younger sister as just a small child... He could remember the laughter, the smiles, and best of all, the sight!

"I... I remember that..." he murmured, voice breaking. Alma could see that his eyes were beginning to water. There was a small click as she readied what she held, and she looked up to check on Toby, but he didn't seem to have heard. "Oh, Toby... Don't we all remember that?" she said tenderly.

"Imagine now... The breeze is making the grass blow in waves, like little ripples on a lake surface on a completely clear day. It's so beautiful... The flowers, all of them... They look like they're dancing. I can see a pair of butterflies, now, Toby!"

Alma wrapped an arm around Toby's shoulders and

123

watched the little insects as they chased each other. Toby's watering eyes were beginning to overflow now, but his delicate smile had grown into a grin that was filled with longing, and joy; it was as if he were a child again. It was as if he were no longer blind. "Butterflies!" he sniffed, pawing at his eyes with the back of a fumbling hand. "I... I don't think I've seen any of those in y-years!"

Alma was beginning to feel some strange tug at her heart now. Toby was crying! He believed every word she told him, drinking in the poison as if it were a delicacy consumed only by kings.

"No... That's why this morning is so special, Toby..." said Alma, fighting to keep a break from her own voice now. This felt wrong... so wrong.

"Sabrina! Tell me more?" begged Toby, turning towards her and grinning now like an ecstatic child, even though he couldn't see anything.

"Alright, Toby..." she said, slowly raising a hand that held the device. It was an old, crudely-made thing, and it went against what one would expect to be carried by someone completely clad in hi-tech spy gadgets. But that was the point.

"I'll tell you more... It's getting brighter now... I can see the sun beginning to shine..." commentated Alma, her hand still trembling. For a moment she hesitated, but then she raised her hand further, taking the final step.

"Goodnight, Toby..." she whispered.

Toby began to turn his head in confusion, only to feel cold metal against his skin as Alma pressed the gun into the back of his head, where the spine connected to the skull.

He didn't need to scream. His eyes opened wide and he began to open his mouth, but Alma pressed a finger to his lips.

"Goodnight…" she repeated, saying the word as if it were an order. But it wasn't just an order for Toby; it was for herself, as well.

Then Alma tightened her finger on the trigger.

***

Danny finally awoke with a jerk, his body tensing up. His face and forehead were slick with sweat, and though his sleep may have seemed restful to the outside viewer, Danny's mind had been plagued by nightmares throughout his unconsciousness, steadily getting worse as the sedative wore off with the hours. It seemed to be late afternoon now, and despite his restless sleep, he did, in fact, feel a bit better than he had earlier in the day when he'd first regained consciousness.

But then there was the matter of what had finally awoken him. What had?

The laboratory seemed eerily silent to him, devoid of the usual hustle and bustle that accompanied the daily activities of the scientists as they tended to the young trainees, or came up with new experiments and theories. Today, though, there was nothing. Turning over onto his side, Danny looked blearily at the digital clock that blinked its red little numbers at him from on the bedside cabinet.

8:00AM? His eyebrows rose up in surprise and were hidden in the fringe of his un-brushed hair. *Crikey… I slept longer than I thought I would have…*

Danny sank back down onto the pillows and closed his eyes once again. Smiling a little to himself, he tried to let himself relax and drift off to sleep, knowing that the majority of the lab would expect him to be still asleep, anyway. But there was still the troubling matter of the past night's, or morning's, events. The smile faded from the scientist's stubbly face, and his blue eyes opened slightly as he finally remembered everything.

Blinking the sleepy glaze from his eyes, Danny sat up in bed, and swung his legs so that they dangled over the floor. His feet felt as though they were asleep at first as he rested them against the floor, but he stood up unsteadily. Splaying out his arms a moment later in an effort to balance himself, Danny took several shaky steps forward, then rested against the nearest wall, supporting himself with his good arm. The other one ached dully as though in protest, and this ache would grow into a sharp stab whenever he moved it, before a thrill of pins and needles would prickle through the appendage as he stilled.

Busied trying to find his feet on the cold floor beneath him, Danny looked up sharply as a sudden, blaring siren filled the air. A red light on the wall blazed and flashed like the light on top of an ambulance, and the shrieking warning filled the air with panic and Danny's mind with confusion.

What's going on?! Danny wondered, the panicking, frightening siren causing his blood to run cold. That was the emergency alarm, used only when the greatest needs arose. It was a signal to get out of the laboratory at all costs. Something had gone wrong.

Seeming to find his feet all at once in the sudden fright and almost losing his balance because of it, Danny slammed his fist against the button that opened the door, and felt as though it hissed open in slow motion. Grabbing his labcoat from a nearby hook, Danny threw his arms through the sleeves, then dived out of the door as soon as there was room for him.

Instantly, he wished he hadn't.

For in the hallway, there was a lump of blackness darker than the deepest of nights, hunched in the shadows as though it were watching, waiting for

126

something. It looked like a gigantic, pitch black dog. Yellow fangs had prised open its mouth to give the impression that it was grinning at the thought of the terror to come. Two sandy-gold eyes stared evilly at a single scientist who was bravely trying to face the beast, slowly backing away a distance away from Danny.

As he watched, the creature began to advance, slowly at first, but then breaking into a sprint that caused its thick muscles to ripple.

At the last second, the brave scientist finally changed her mind and turned to run. Danny's blue eyes met her brown ones for the slightest of moments, and for a second, Danny saw relief, and even joy, in those eyes. The scientist had almost reached him, and Danny reached out with a hand to try to pull the woman from the jaws of the beast.

Time seemed to slow.

Every detail, every flicker of fear was visible across the other scientist's face for a brief second, as it seemed like the fleeing woman was going to escape narrowly from those jaws of death. Every ripple that passed over Bargheist's powerful muscles as he tensed, then leaped with his massive claws outstretched and snake's fangs unsheathed. Every detail was visible to Danny's naked eye. He was moving at a pace that no man or woman would ever be able to match.

"Look out!" yelled Danny, his voice seeming to drag on for an age.

But it was already too late.

She gave a cry as thick claws sank into her sides to drag her back, away from what had seemed like a tiny drop of relief in an endless, bottomless sea of pure and utter despair. Danny grabbed her hands in his, and, with fear making his muscles thicken out, tried to drag the scientist from the jaws of the beast.

It was like a deadly game of tug-o-war.

Danny hardly stood a chance; he was only human, and yet he was up against the strength of a bear. But despite this, he refused to let go. The horrified gaze of the poor human in Mercury's jaws compelled him, made him feel as though he were a superhero. Even though his muscles ached and his lungs felt like they were burning, Danny pulled, even though he was being dragged along with the one who he aimed to save.

Bargheist's eyes burned with anger, and he clamped his claws down harder into the scientist's flesh, his fangs sinking further into her. Danny clung on harder, feeling, no, knowing that, if he let go, then this scientist would die.

The thought spurred him on and with a final, mighty heave, there was a spray of blood, and she was free of Bargheist, the beast. Danny toppled down onto his back, and she tumbled down after him, leaving a trail of blood splatters on the smooth blue floor. Danny staggered back up onto his feet, and began to pull the injured scientist up after him. Mercury stood there silently, watching them with eyes that were full of expectation and anticipation, even a hint of sick, sadistic laughter. Opening his mouth, he let the shreds of the unfortunate woman's flesh drop to the ground, and grinned wider.

He's toying with us... realized Danny with a thrill of horror. *Like a cat with a mouse...Does he think that this is all a game?*

The scientist whom he had managed to drag from Mercury's grasp was leaning heavily on him. She seemed exhausted and was shaky and pale, but she was alive, and that was all that mattered to Danny.

Well, except for the rather pressing matter of them both getting out alive, of course.

And that wasn't as simple as it sounded. Even

though Danny let the injured scientist drape an arm over his shoulder so that he could support her as best he could, the going wasn't as quick as either of them would have liked, far from. Both of them were already panting as though they were in the middle of running a marathon even after what would have seemed, to most, like a pathetic amount of time on the run.

And all the while, the monstrous form of Bargheist skulked along like a massive spider, pulled right out of the deepest nightmares that everyone would have experienced at some point in their childhood. Bargheist was neither running nor walking, just trotting along as he waited patiently for his victims to tire before he did. The female scientist hadn't yet been pierced by the poison-filled needles that emerged from his upper jaw, but even so, her injuries were taking their steady toll, bloodloss giving way into dizziness and unsteadiness.

"Danny..." she panted, between frightened gasps for air. Danny could feel her shaking beneath his supporting arm. "I don't think I can take this much longer..."

She knows my name...

Danny could feel his own muscles tiring, and he knew that he was the same, but he tried to remain encouraging, optimistic, and as usual, calm. "We... We can make it!" he spluttered in response. "Just... Keep going... Don't lose... Hope!" He struggled to push himself on further, but Danny was aware that even he, now, was slipping on the cold floor as his limbs seemed to lose concentration. Where was everyone else? Had they all been killed?

From behind them came the rasping of claws as Mercury, seeming to get bored, picked up speed.

Danny turned to the scientist. He, in all his recklessness, seemed to have reached a decision. "Your name is... Charlie, right...?" he rasped, gulping air into his pained and tired lungs.

"That's right!" she replied, her voice hissing. "Why?"

Danny turned away slightly, his cheeks burning red, and not just with their hasty flight.

"Just… Remembered…" he rasped. "You know… I've never… Felt like I've… Had a friend… Not since the war… started."

"No…?" Charlie asked, and Danny could detect guilt in her tone.

"No…" he confirmed.

"Why are you telling me this… Now…?"

Danny couldn't resist a tiny smile as he turned towards her, his blue eyes burning fiercely, as though encouraging her meek brown ones to glow equally. To her horror, he began to slow to a halt. Mercury's claws tapped against the ground behind them.

"Because you're the first who will listen!" he said, not bothering to turn towards the approaching monster.

The staircase leading to the outdoor world was visible, only a few steps away.

Danny gently set Charlie down on the stairs, and then took several steps backwards, away from her.

"If he gets me… Promise me. Get outside, okay? I have some things to take care of in here!"

He didn't even wait for an answer, in all his muddled thoughts seeming to forget about her injury. Even if he hadn't, well… It was worth a try.

Danny whipped around, turning his back on Charlie, white coat whisking like a cape in a winter's breeze as it completed the silhouette of a knight in shining armour, something that the feeble man was far from.

"There's too much here for me to just leave it to be all eaten. I need to see if we're the only ones still alive…"

At last, Charlie seemed to understand his words.

With a new emotion, courage, in his stance and creeping into his voice, Danny hid behind a mask of confidence his fear, and strode forward. Blue met gold. Danny's eyes of courage met the eyes of the snake, the flicking tongue of the serpent.

As Mercury leapt, Danny was unprepared. For the impact of the beast's claws pressing him down was strength beyond strength, throwing him to the floor like he was a fly that could be crushed by a single movement of a barbed hand.

But at the same time, so was Mercury.

Bargheist was unprepared for any resistance.

-Chapter 10-

Escape

Meanwhile, as chaos ensued elsewhere, the young experiments all huddled close into one another, whimpering as they hid in the wreckage of their beloved playroom.

They had been waiting for what seemed like, to them, an age. They had been waiting for one of the scientists to come and lead them out. Unfortunately for them, so far, no other scientists had come since they had been attacked, and even Sally and Cassie were unable to hear any sound of human footsteps except for a distant echo, and that had been some time ago now. Most of the children had been injured in some way, with only Karasu seeming relatively unscathed, physically at least.

As the horrific scene had taken place, there had been utter chaos. Blood had spattered from the tips of Bargheist's claws and his throat bellowed and echoed with a sound so feral and wild. The trainee spies, on impulse, had thrown themselves in to protect the scientists and sort out the problem(or just for plain revenge), but some of the adults had still died, and now their bodies lay strewn about the floor, one with his throat ripped out and another one or two with pieces scattered, having been torn apart by Mercury whilst they were still alive. It was difficult to tell from the carnage how many there truly were.

In the end it was lucky that any of them were alive, let alone all of them. Even if all had suffered at Mercury's claws in some way.

Emerald was missing an antenna, and her shirt was

stained with clear blood plasma and torn at the shoulder, whilst Bethany, who tried to protect her, possessed a deep cut down her cheek. Benny was walking with a limp, one foot balancing by its toes on the ground. Ginny huddled into him, clasping her paws over a deep gash on her hip as though to hide it. Sally and Cassie both had bite marks on various limbs, whilst one of Moony's wings was twisted at an odd and painful-looking angle. Joey had a gash across his abdomen that he was making such a fuss about that the others just kept on ignoring him.

"I don't think anyone's coming..." whispered Bethany eventually, as she hugged a dazed Emerald close into her chest. The others all stared at her in horror, partially because of her speaking, and partially for the words themselves. None of them had spoken in a long while, not wanting to be found by Mercury.

Bethany's words had the same effect on Karasu as if someone had told him he wasn't going to be fed for a year. The poor puppy had felt woozy all day, and now he was whiny and frightened. No-one was going to come for them, after all this? Preposterous! The boy's brown eyes widened and teared up, and he began to whimper and cry with tiny yelping sounds for what would probably be the tenth time today. His paw-like hands clenched into little fists, and he rubbed his eyes frantically, leaving smudges of red across his cheeks.

Often, moving primarily on all fours had its disadvantages.

The other children all glared at him, and Karasu wouldn't shut up until Joey clasped the puppy boy's jaw in one hand and his forehead in the other, and snapped his mouth closed with a little tap as Karasu's canine teeth met in his mouth. The puppy-boy looked absolutely stupefied, and stared tearfully up at them all in shame.

"Be quiet, alright?" hissed Joey, his eyes blazing angrily. With his feathers matted with red and an ugly gash over his stomach, the vain boy wasn't having the best of days.

Karasu's whimpers finally dropped into silence.

Now all that was audible was the distant fizz of electricity and a soft crackling sound coming from nearby, where several wires lay exposed and flickering with twisting orange lights. The lights were a particular sight that that the little group had never seen before and thus, wouldn't recognize. The scientists, making slow progress in their training, had so far neglected to teach them about the dangers of fire.

For a couple of seconds longer, they listened with their hearts in their mouths. But Bethany's words had held within them the sting of cold reality.

Nobody came.

Karasu began to whimper again, and Moony, trying desperately to be a brave little soul despite the terror and pain, puffed out his chest and twitched his fluffy little owl tufts. Without even a whisper, he received stares and gasps of horror as he slowly shivered his way from their hiding place in the rubble, and slipped over to the climbing frame, gagging as he tried to drag his gaze away from the bodies of one or two unlucky scientists, and climbed onto the climbing frame.

One by one, some of the others followed until even the cowardly ones like Karasu, not wanting to be left alone, made their way after Moony to the climbing frame. Eventually, Moony clung to the top with his claws, wide, golden eyes scanning every nook and cranny he could see. Emerald's wings whirred as she alighted down next to him, and almost immediately lost her balance.

Nothing that would help them seemed to show up, but being children, they seemed to find some way to keep amused and optimistic.

"I spy with my little eye..." began Moony. Instantly, the watching faces brightened. "Something beginning with... Tuh!"

The mood changed instantaneously, as all the children looked for things that started with the letter T.

"Tower!"

"Tire!"

"Toys!"

"Tree!"

"What's a tree?"

"Daddy told me about them! They're green things that stick out of the ground and give us food!"

"Wow, really?!"

"That's wicked!"

"I want one!"

"I think there's one in my room!"

"Is there one in here?"

"What was it, Moony?"

"Ginny got it... toys!"

All those that got the wrong answers groaned, but they all fell silent as Benny squeaked for them to quiet down, thinking he'd heard something. Even when the moment of fear was over, an eerie quiet lingered over the children. They each shivered, even in the heat. The flickering, crackling firelight had begun to spread from where it had begun.

"We need to get out of here... because that monster might come back!"

"Do you think there's still some scientists are still okay?"

"I hope Daddy is!"

There was an uncomfortable silence. Glances were exchanged, and silent conversations were held. *What if we're the only ones left?*

What will happen to us?

Moony, his body shivering, began to kick his little legs as he tried to climb down from the top of the climbing frame without hurting himself anymore and was suspended with his legs fumbling for a foothold and fingers gripping a metal. Those who didn't usually climb looked around uncomfortably for a way down, but couldn't see one.

Sally and Cassie were the first to get down, or rather, tumble down, and were both greeted by an extraordinarily happy Karasu, who had been unable to climb even a foot away from the ground.

Benny fell and, with an ear-splitting yelp, landed on his hurt leg.

All movements froze for a moment, until they all scurried and hurried to place four paws or two feet onto the ground where they were stable. Emerald fluttered, by Bethany's word, over to the door, where she kept a lookout for any sign of trouble.

Eventually, Moony fluffed out his feathers, and they all tried to look tough and confident even as Karasu grovelled at people's feet and cried happily.

"Right…" whispered the owl boy, voice quaking. "Let's get out of here…"

***

Shivering violently as chills swept over his body, Toby's mouth had gone dry and his muscles had gone numb. He could still feel cold metal pressing into the back of his skull, and Sabrina's finger holding his lips closed, preventing him from uttering even a whisper.

Her words echoed through his mind like wind in a dark cave, on repeat, over and over, cutting like knives with every turn. *Goodnight, Toby… Goodnight…* He didn't dare move a muscle, not even to blink open or close his aching eyes.

Toby had already been told by the other scientists that he wasn't allowed to go outside. Was this why? Had the world really changed so much in the short time that he'd been kept hidden away from the outside world? The torrent of frightened terror and disbelief that swirled through Toby's foggy brain all gave way to one single emotion.

Betrayal.

He'd trusted Sabrina... And yet, for all that, he'd been rewarded with nothing but death. Toby had considered the topic a few times before, but he wasn't prepared for it to happen so suddenly...

It felt so... dark. It loomed out to him like a shadowy monster, rather than the silky blanket of peace and freedom he'd thought of it to be before. It might have been ironic, had the situation been a bit brighter. Swallowing, Toby shivered, and wondered why the killing blow had not yet come.

Is she testing me? Toby wondered to himself, feeling her finger pressing down harder against his lips, as though she sensed that he couldn't take much more of this. With his heart hammering in his chest, Toby felt pain flaring up with every heartbeat. *I don't care if she is...*

Clamping his eyes tight shut, Toby began to gather his wits about him, and flicked his tail nervously. His fingers were beginning to twitch, groping sightlessly for the grass beneath his palms. Toby didn't think he could stand this for much longer. The tension felt like it was out to get him. He just wanted it to end...

Finally, Toby could stand it no more. He lifted a hand and took hold of Sabrina's wrist, wrenching her finger away from his mouth.

"Just do it!" he yowled, closing his eyes tightly, his voice fuming. "I can't take it! Go ahead, zap me or something, but I hope you burn after this!"

Sabrina didn't respond. Toby waited with bated breath, his sickly-yellow eyes fixed on the darkness behind his closed eyelids. It felt like forever and a day, but eventually, Toby felt the cold pressure leaving the back of his head. She had lowered the gun.

Toby found this just as confusing as Sabrina having a gun in the first place. His eyes opened to slits of sickly yellow, and he turned his face to where he assumed her face was.

"Hey..." he asked suspiciously. "What are you doing-!?"

"Quiet!" Sabrina snapped, suddenly seeming short tempered. Her voice had changed. It had become, from a voice that was soft and sweet, to one that was steely and sour. Toby silenced obediently, and swallowed a terse reply. Sabrina seemed to like that. She sneered.

"You know..." she said, and Toby felt a line of cold ice against his neck. He froze. "You ain't half bad... for being so *useless*!"

Toby hissed, his pride shattered. Sabrina had struck him dead on a nerve. "Hey, you! Sabrina, or whatever your name really is...!" He felt the line of ice press down, almost choking him. A trickle of warmth ran from the wound. *Is she trying to decide which method of killing me will hurt me the most...?*

"If I'm so useless, then why waste your time here playing with me, eh?"

There was a moment of silence in response to that. Toby's blood chilled even further as a thousand different theories of what she could be thinking swarmed into his mind all at once. Toby's ears pricked up. A chiming laugh like a funeral bell ringing cut through the air. Then, out of nowhere, it cut itself off. The line of ice was replaced by a hand, as Sabrina wrapped her fingers about his neck, pressing one of her nails into the wound.

Toby felt an involuntary tear trickle down one of his cheeks and absorb into one of his furred markings. *She's not killing me, but she really does know how to make it hurt... A lot...*

"Playing? Aww, how childish..." she mocked him. Toby's ears pricked. There had been a break in her voice. *Something's not quite right, here...*

"...I'm not one to take pleasure in such gruesome affairs..." Her grip about his neck tightened, and Toby gagged. *What am I thinking? Who would do that?!*

"At least... Tell me... What I did!" choked out Toby.

"What you did? ...Nothing..." There was a pause, and Toby sucked in a tortured breath. "...You just know too much."

She finally let him go, and Toby slumped limply onto the ground, heaving in gulps of sweet air.

"Heh... pathetic, Toby."

"Not as... pathetic... as you!"

"How touching of you to say such a thing. I'm honoured," Sabrina snapped bluntly at him, seeming angry about something, to contrast with her smooth demeanour earlier. Toby clenched his jaw to keep back a sharp retort, and instead said nothing.

"Keeping silent, are you? You're smarter than I thought! Now, if you'll excuse me..." Toby heard her stand, the clinking of metal and the sound of rustling fabric accompanying her. Before Toby even felt her let go, she'd thrown him onto the cold, hard ground.

"I have some things to do at that laboratory of yours. If everything has gone according to plan, there should be a little bit of action aroused by now."

Toby's face fell.

"Aw, pet lamb, don't look like that..." Sabrina crooned. "...After all, you'll probably be frozen solid by the time I get back. Folks like you seem to have all the luck." Her voice dropped into a sinister mutter.

Toby tried to push himself onto his knees, but was unable to support himself on his those weak, quivering, numb limbs. His veins boiled, feeling like there were rivers of stone pouring through them. Toby felt about with a quivering hand for his crutches.

Sabrina noticed.

"Hm-hm-hm… You won't be needing those sticks of yours." Toby heard plastic clattering and distant grass rustle and crunch drily as Sabrina tossed his crutches away. He stared upwards, and his eyes were bright with despair.

"Don't worry, I'll be back for you…" she reassured him in a voice like the wind hissing through a dead forest. She clapped her hands together as if she'd just taken care of something fairly unpleasant, then she cracked her knuckles for effect. "…I'll make sure you get a decent burial. How many people will attend the funeral, I wonder?"

Toby heard her footsteps fading into the distance as she ran away, back the way they had come.

***

Struggling and wriggling frantically under the monster's claws, it was clear through Danny's burning eyes that things were not going as he'd planned. Bargheist's claws pressed his arms into the ground, rendering them immobile, and he was left with nothing to do but kick feebly and flex his muscles as he struggled to escape.

Bargheist sneered at him, forked tongue flicking as he searched Danny's face with a snake's sense of smell. Danny cringed as he felt the slimy thing darting across his forehead, chin, and nose. He gulped as the mutant lowered his muzzle slowly and steadily towards him, as though to savour the moments of Danny's fear.

Danny could see intelligence swirling in snaking pits of golden sand, and anger boiling like magma through Bargheist's veins as he was forced to look back into the monster's eyes. They say that the eyes are windows to the soul, and by looking into this creature's eyes, Danny felt his own soul lurching, as though Bargheist was sucking it out. There was something there... something that wasn't meant to be there.

Danny could see it, and his mouth dried up.

He could see that, beyond the longing to murder and to fight, there was a poisoning, burning agony. The experiment could still feel emotions. He knew what he was doing. And he knew the pain he was causing. Danny's heart could have stopped, right there and then, as he listened to his captor's contorted growls and snarls, twisting themselves up into matted putrefactions of words that Bargheist still knew.

He knows... How can this be? His memory... Is it...? No... It can't be...

Danny felt one of Bargheist's claws move from his shoulder, to his chest, then push up his chin so that the delicate flesh of Danny's throat lay exposed for him, just ready for blood to be spilled. All the while, Danny felt wooziness fogging his mind, as he continued to stare into Bargheist's... No... Mercury's narrowing snake eyes. He wondered what truth the legends of a dragon's hypnotic stare held... One could certainly believe it, locked here and staring into these eyes of death.

Danny felt Mercury lowering a claw to rest it upon his throat, and he swallowed. In a last frantic hope, Danny flung out an arm in desperation, jerking it free of its bonding. His hand seized Mercury's face. The man was wrenched back into focus as he heard Mercury yowl in agony. Danny's fingers had found themselves hooked into the beast's eye socket, and in response, the beast recoiled. Unable to think of anything else to do, Danny held on for a while, until Mercury wrenched himself free.

To turn around and 'fight' Mercury might have been a stupid decision, but Danny felt rather pleased with himself and moved back towards Charlie with a swagger in his step as though he had meant for that to happen, as though everything had gone just the way he'd planned. Charlie was looking quite sickly as she saw flecks of blood staining Danny's shirt from Mercury's claws and his own wounds, but she was seemingly relieved that he was still in one piece. Despite Danny's telling her to escape, it seemed as though she had been looking for a way to help her sudden new friend.

The thought almost brought a tear to Danny's eye.

Someone would be willing to do that... for him? It felt like a dream... Danny gulped back the lump in his throat, blinking himself back to his senses.

Or perhaps she just couldn't move. That was a definite possibility. It wasn't anything worth crying about, either.

Woah, have these past few years really been that bad on me?

Danny began to heave Charlie back onto her feet again, but then froze as a growl erupted behind him. Mercury was rising to his paws from the shadows again, clutching with a thick paw pad at his bloodied and watering eye. His growls were contorting and twisting again in Danny's ears, into horrific shapes and shades of voice that were incomprehensible to the human tongue. But Danny heard that voice again, that contortion of mind, emerging from the fiend's foul throat. Mercury's voice howled though his cavernous maw, and his breaths whistled and hissed like the wind through a never-ending tunnel. But Danny had heard that voice before. And he understood.

"You... You lied to me... and now... now thisssssssss? Who do you think you are...?" hissed Mercury, claws clacking as he advanced. Charlie's grip on Danny's arm tightened, and Danny backed away slowly. He'd escaped once, but... Now Mercury was *truly* angry. He wasn't going to be playing games with them this time. This time was for real. *"You will pay... You will pay for thisssssssssss..."*

There was nothing more to hang onto. They were cornered.

The sounds of Mercury's claws sounded almost like the steady ticking of a clock counting down to their doom. The flames that gathered as they hurried after him down the halls only added to that feeling of imminent destruction, their twisting lights seeming to reform into a gateway to the next life.

Click...

Click...

Click...

Mercury advanced. Both Danny and Charlie could see him opening his jaws to threateningly unsheathe and yawn wide fangs at them. His golden eyes reflected the fires that burned all around him and swept the laboratory like rivers of destruction, and the blood that streamed down his face was turned into a trickle of orange magma, steaming in the heat.

Click...

Click...

Crash!

***

With an almighty clattering sound, the young mutants finally seemed to make their move. Emerging from

143

behind a pile of rubble blocking a nearby doorway, they piled over each other, over the heaps of plaster and ablaze wires. Mercury turned at the last moment in surprise, but they were already upon him, clinging and biting and kicking.

"That's for hurting my wing!" screeched Moony, digging his claws into the thick muscle of Mercury's arm.

"And staining my feathers!" cawed Joey, giving the monstrous being punch after feeble punch to his muzzle and chest.

Karasu barked and snarled in his own response, though he, instead of attacking, seemed determined to just stand back and watch, and hurl insults at Mercury in his own doggy language. Whenever blood splattered, he would shriek and recoil and he eventually ended up hiding behind Charlie and Danny.

"You leave my daddy alone!" snapped Benny, but was easily thrown aside by Mercury's might. His glasses went skittering away over the floor, a crack suddenly marking one of the lenses.

Sally and Cassie had each sunk their fangs into one of Mercury's legs, and, ripping and snarling, they aimed to bring their victim to the ground. Their mouths were too full to utter any sort of war cry. Eventually, there was an almighty crash, and they had succeeded, although Moony was left struggling to get out from under Mercury's immense, muscled weight.

As he was brought down, even Ginny had a good go at the battle, as she scurried in and started grappling his shoulders.

Emerald hung back, a short distance away. She had sunk down with her back to a nearby wall and watched the events with tiring diamond eyes. Her wings fluttered occasionally as though she was trying to stand, but could not.

"And this! This is for Emerald!" Bethany's voice suddenly rang out above all the rest, as the fox girl threw herself into the chaos with all the might she could muster, seeming to dance on her feet as she bowled onto Mercury.

Despite the outnumbering, and the chaos, Mercury was still clearly able to fight, and he thrashed and writhed, sending Ginny skidding across the floor. The others tumbled from him as he rose back up onto his feet, red patches of flesh showing where the wounds lay dripping. After recovering, the ones who had fallen stood up and raced forward, holding hands as they made to form a barrier between Bargheist, Danny and Charlie. The wall wasn't exactly well-built, but with their chests puffed out and faces all stern, the children glowered at him in their efforts to look intimidating.

For a while, Mercury's eyes were locked onto theirs, and there was a crash from further away within the laboratory as something collapsed. The children looked around nervously as the booming sound echoed.

Still, Mercury made no move to cut them down.

"Thisssss... I will remember thissssss, too... I will remember thessssssse woundssssssss...."

They didn't even have the opportunity to shudder in revulsion at the haunting voice that they heard sliding forth from beyond the fangs of bear and snake. Before they could, Mercury had turned his back on them. His tail rattled menacingly even as it dragged along behind him. As Moony went to give chase, Bargheist broke into a run, leaping beyond consuming flames, and collapsing with his tail a burning pillar. That was the only support the ruined ceiling was holding onto, and a large chunk of the ceiling collapsed behind him, barring passage.

The children seemed to think that it was over, and their ranks began to erupt with cheers. They began to jump about, grinning and chattering to themselves. They didn't seem to understand the danger of the rising heat. Karasu chased his tail in circles around Danny's legs, until the man picked him up and called for silence.

With red cheeks and redder wounds, they all turned towards him and then ran in to receive their hugs and congratulations. "We need to get out of here, now..." he said to them seriously. Their faces fell.

"I'm not scolding you, it's just dangerous in here!" Danny hastily corrected himself, hugging Karasu close into his chest. There was a pop, and a bang, and more of the ceiling collapsed, to be followed by a thick pile of dirt and concrete. The children were starting to get wary.

"The scientists said that we're not allowed to go through that door, daddy!" pointed out Benny. The other children murmured agreements to them.

"Well, I'm not one of the others, and I care about your safety rather than this dumb experiment!"

The children gasped. They saw Charlie giving him quite a strange look. There was the far-off sound of more rubble collapsing as the laboratory began to deteriorate further in.

"No arguing- look at it like another mission!" barked Danny, beginning to get rather desperate.

He turned and began to hurry up the staircase that lead outdoors, Charlie clinging to his arm and Karasu seated happily in his other. The sounds of skippy footsteps followed him out of the wreckage, and Danny was relieved that they had followed him. They could be like sheep at times; if one came after him, they all would. As the door slid open for them, Danny heaved a sigh of relief as a blast of cold air greeted them. They all followed then as soon as they were outside, sank down onto the grass. Or, at least, Danny and Charlie did. The young mutants wanted nothing more than to explore this strange new world, and see that strange place that the adults called 'outside' for themselves.

Behind them, the door hissed closed with a whir of electricity, sealing the fire and the collapsing laboratory away for good.

The children, ignoring the way they'd come, all crowded in utter fascination, around the nearest tree, and everyone stared.

"Is that a tree?" asked Moony, awed. "It looks like those things in my bedroom!"

"It is!" squeaked Ginny.

"Can I touch it?" asked Joey, scrambling up and touching it anyway.

"Can we *eat* it?" yelped sally and Cassie, questioningly.

Danny, meanwhile, sat in the background, muttering to himself. He counted carefully the children as they squabbled and squawked amongst themselves, and he, himself, was busied by tending to Charlie's wound. It should have been given attention earlier, admittedly, but there was nothing they could do about that now.

"Benny, Bethany, Ginny, Moony, Sally, Cassie, Karasu... There's Joey..." he muttered to himself aloud as he counted them carefully. Something didn't feel quite right. He counted again. "...Six, seven... Eight?"

There should be nine...

Danny gulped, and he suddenly stood up. Taking a quick stride as he jogged over to the children, he watched the eight faces turn towards him. He counted again. ...*Seven... Eight... Nine?*

He looked over the faces. Who was missing?

It was then that he realized, and his chest choked up of breath and heartbeat.

"You guys..." he began, voice taut, knowing that the news probably wouldn't be taken well, especially by the social mutants... and even less so by Bethany.

"Where's Emerald?"

**

Emerald was exhausted. Every sound echoed in her ears, and the terrifying crashes and crackling sounds were going to her head, as much as the smoke itself. Emerald had never been in a fire before, at least not like this. She didn't remember ever seeing before those rearing stallions of pain and anger.

The smoke that clogged her lungs and blurred her eyes made her every sense spin in her mind. Covering her eyes, she sobbed as voices spun beyond her hearing, and the wound in her shoulder stained her clothes a shade or two darker as it oozed blood empty of colour other than a thin red tint. She shivered even in the overwhelming heat, and as ashes crumbled down around her from the burning walls and ceiling, Emerald struggled to stand as she heard the pattering of footsteps leading away.

"Bethany!" she cried out in desperation, her voice consumed like thin grass by the licking, bucking fires as they cantered about her, spreading their overwhelming wrath in a blazing torrent. "Bethany, I'm here!"

Emerald raced forward, and reached with a hand into the flames. The stallion bit, and Emerald recoiled with a scream, clutching at her burned hand. Stepping backwards, Emerald cried out again, tears of fright and pain streaming down her face. "Bethany! Daddy! Moony! Joey! Anyone! Please! I don't like this!"

Whipping about in the small area of fire that she had left to roam, Emerald eventually fell down onto her knees, hugging herself about the chest, and folding her wings tight against her back so that they wouldn't be burned too. Emerald stared out into the flames, tears reflecting in the pupils of those eyes that looked like one, but formed hundreds. Her iridescent flesh reflected the prickling, flicking flames that pranced and danced about her, carelessly drawing nearer and nearer.

Then Emerald saw it.

A figure in the flames.

Imposing, and yet, so welcoming. As if they were emerging through a portal that lead to and from another world entirely, the silhouette stepped forth. A woman faded into view through the twisting halos of fire that coiled around her. It was at this moment that Emerald was finally able to behold the sight of the one who stood before her, take in all the details that the fire hid from view.

The woman was dressed in a tight black suit, with green goggles that looked more suited for night vision. A wave of blonde fringe drooped out from below her helmet, and had been brushed casually over the left side of her goggles. Her chest and stomach were barred by thick pads of bullet-proof armour, and her face was mostly hidden by a black mask that was wrapped over the lower part of her face. The only skin that showed was a dainty, freckled nose. The woman wore black boots, and the heels of those looked so sharp that Emerald was sure that the wearer could puncture anything with a kick.

Emerald tried to cower away, but the flames blocked her way. Seeing the fright etched upon Emerald's face, the figure knelt before her, and gently drew a length of fabric from a satchel which looked to be made of black leather at her side.

"Come, now…" whispered the figure, wrapping the cloak about the shivering Emerald. "This will protect you from being burned any more…"

Emerald, her mind all in a flurry, wondered how long the figure had been watching her. "What's happening here? Why is it so painful?" her words stumbled out as if of their own accord. "I want to get back to my friends…"

She trembled even more violently, and tried to cower away some more, but the figure stopped her again, with a gentle hand, covered by a black leather glove.

"Shh…"

Whoever it was slowly raised her hand again, and there was a gentle click as the helmet mechanically raised the goggles from her face, revealing a small area of pale, freckled flesh, and a stunning pair of shining green eyes. Her eyes were kind, with short, fluttering eye lashes, and the mask over the woman's face lifted a little, showing Emerald that she was smiling.

The gesture seemed to almost frighten Emerald, and although she took a step forward, the tears began to flow down her face again, and she let out a gentle sob. Her one remaining antenna, and the stump of the other one drooped. Emerald felt herself gathered up into the stranger's arms. She felt her wings delicately supported by one hand about her shoulders, and the other beneath her knees.

"I'll get you out of here…" there was a mutter in her ear, and Emerald opened an eye, looking up at her saviour's face again. Her eyes were once more covered by those lifeless green goggles, hiding away the floral tone again. Emerald felt the stranger begin to move, and the lady gently pulled the fabric down over Emerald's eyes. Emerald struggled a little, the darkness seeming to revile her.

Even as she did, the stranger didn't pull back the fabric again, she just broke into a run, and Emerald felt her movements jerking erratically every now and then, causing Emerald to tense and squeak. The heat around Emerald felt a little bit more bearable, but the air was still just as suffocating. Eventually after what seemed to Emerald like forever and a day, whoever it was who held her came to a sudden halt. Emerald gave another squawk, and then realised that she was being gently lowered. Her toes touched against cool ground.

The fabric was pulled back from her head as though it was a hood, and Emerald found herself blinking in the late morning light. Her face was met by a sudden wave of cold, and she gave a shudder, pulling the cloak tight around her like it was a blanket, for it still held some of the heat of the fire. The air tasted clean, and Emerald no longer felt as though she were suffocating in the thick, humid air. She looked around, her dazed mind incomprehensive of where they were.

Her chest heaved as she filled her lungs with clean air and she coughed several times, a charred, smoky taste filling her mouth. She looked reluctant as the stranger gently removed the fireproof cloak from about her shoulders and then pressed a palm upon Emerald's wounded shoulder, a wad of cotton wool in her palm soaking up the clear blood.

Emerald tried at first to get away, until she realized that she was being helped. Tensing occasionally with the pain, she was still as she allowed the stranger to aid her. She waited long-sufferingly until the wound was safely bandaged up. "That'll have to do for now..." murmured the stranger. "I wasn't expecting to have to deal with any wounded down there."

"Why were you in there? Who are you?" asked Emerald in a small, frightened voice.

The stranger didn't answer her at first, seeming busied with trying to find a bottle of water to wash Emerald's burn.

Emerald stayed as silent as she did for a while, watching as the woman worked. But she felt frightened, and those strange goggles that she wore made Emerald feel as though she was trying to look into Emerald's mind or some childish belief like that. Emerald moved forward a little and then tugged on a bit of her taut clothing.

She turned to look at Emerald through the goggles.

"Can... Can I see your eyes again?" asked Emerald feebly.

"Of course, sweetie," murmured the woman tenderly, and then lifted a hand. There was another click as the goggles lifted gently from her face. Her green eyes once again gazed down at Emerald for a few moments and they smiled, before she turned away from Emerald and started rooting through her satchel, once again. It seemed impossible that someone could have lost something in a container that small, but she seemed to somehow manage it.

"Why were you there?" asked Emerald again.

"My husband works in the laboratory," she replied confidently, seeming to be avoiding eye contact with the young girl. "I thought I heard a ruckus, so I got all kitted up and came to look for him." Emerald nodded. Having no knowledge of the outside world, the reasoning seemed good enough for her.

"That's very nice of you..." she said, shuffling her feet as she let the lady pour cold water over her burn, even though it stung. Her arm twitched. "Why did you save me?"

"You were the first one alive I found in there."

"The first? Did you not see any big, big bad black thing?"

"Big bad black thing? What do you mean?"

"Like a giant, giant monster with lots of fur that's really scary, a-and it has scales on its tail, and these horrible yellow eyes!"

"Can't say I've seen anything like that in there, dead or alive... If it does come for us, I think you'll be safe with me."

Emerald looked confused, but at the same time rather comforted. She relaxed a little, but even so stayed silent, seeming to feel awkward about this whole situation.

Meanwhile, the woman had moved towards her again, and was offering a spoonful of sweet-smelling liquid. Emerald moved her head away a little bit suspiciously. She looked up at the woman, and her eyes were questioning.

"Honey. It'll help your throat," she explained promisingly. Emerald hesitated, then opened her mouth and swallowed the honey with some hesitation. She smacked her lips, looking up with big eyes. It didn't taste poisoned.

The woman looked at Emerald expectantly, gently reaching out with another cotton bud to start dabbing at Emerald's severed antenna. The sweet, pleasant taste lay on Emerald's tongue. She'd never tasted anything quite like it before.

"...Can I have some more?" she asked eventually, smiling hopefully.

"Of course," murmured the adult, spooning more honey into Emerald's mouth. The little girl finally seemed satisfied, and she sighed and flopped, exhausted, onto the grass beneath her, running her fingers through the cold green strands.

Emerald looked up at the woman again, then about at the land around her. "Where are we?" she asked after a while.

"Have you never been outside before, dear?"

The woman settled down next to Emerald, looking kindly at her, although she still didn't remove the mask that covered her face. "Outside?" Emerald gasped, suddenly panic-stricken. "We're not allowed outside!" She fidgeted, and stood up quickly. The woman gently took hold of Emerald's arm, and pushed her down onto the grass again, urging her to relax.

"Shush… If you'd stayed in there, you would have died."

Emerald seemed to calm down slightly, but she still hugged her knees into her chest and looked a little bit wary.

"Here, come on…" the woman patted her on the shoulder comfortingly, and Emerald flinched.

They were silent for a while, the breeze quietly washing over them.

Then finally, Emerald broke the silence.

"You never answered my question…"

"Which question, sweetie?"

"Who are you?"

"Me?" Her eyes glimmered for a moment.

"My name is Sabrina."

-Chapter 11-

Bravery

As the bashful sun began to blush the clouds and retreat back over the horizon, the little group that seemed to be made up of the only survivors had had no luck in getting Bethany to cheer up. Even Karasu (whom Danny had had to keep a few times from trying to pee up a tree, much to the snickers and childish delight of his 'siblings'), who was usually the centre of attention and the only thing needed to scoop someone out of the dumps, had had no luck. The thin hospital robes that Danny had been dressed in were now in tatters, as he'd torn off a good few strips in order to bandage the children's, and Charlie's, wounds as best he could manage.

Now Bethany leaned against a nearby tree, and her gaze was turned down to the ground. The others continued to play on without her, having decided that she was just being boring. It wasn't long to wait, though, before Danny noticed her unusual silence, and strode solemnly over to see her. He knelt down beside her, tapping the russet-haired girl gently on the shoulder.

She looked up at him, teary-eyed and sniffling. Her ears pricked for a moment, but then her face fell. It was clear to Danny that she had been hoping for him to know something more than he did. He felt guilt rising in his heart and wished that he could have done more.

"Hey…"

"Daddy…" Bethany sniffled, wiping her nose with the back of a furry hand. Her eyes were red-ringed and her cheeks looked stained with salt crystals from her tears.

"Come on... Sitting here and sulking won't do anything, will it?" Danny asked her, encouraging her to see the bright side of things. She didn't seem to be convinced by his calm attitude, and even seemed a little annoyed. She avoided looking into his eyes, swinging her tail around to pluck at a patch of damp and snotty fur. It seemed that that had served as a tissue for the past hour or so, and whilst the others had been playing, Bethany had been pulling at her tail and matting the fur together. Danny reached out with a hand to stop her from ruining the beautiful fur even more.

"Bethany?"

Bethany's eyes snapped up to look at him, and together they burned with sharp amber lights. She staggered up onto her feet, and her legs seemed wobbly. Her body was quivering with rage.

"This is all your fault!" she spat, pointing the tip of a clawed finger at Danny.

Danny flinched.

"Bethany, don't be like that," he replied calmly, well used to dealing with the tantrums of the young mutants. They seemed to like getting annoyed at the slightest of things. But this time... Somehow, it felt different. With tears pouring down her cheeks, Bethany swung at him in a moment blind rage, and Danny only just managed to step back to avoid the young fox's assault.

"How can I not be! You... You killed Emerald! You left her there! You... You monster!"

Danny gave a shudder. *She thinks that I...? I killed...?*

Bethany swung at him again, and this time Danny made no move to escape. The young girl beat at his stomach and chest with clenched, flailing fists. He looked down at her for a while. "Bethany, there wasn't anything I could do... I just focused on getting you all out alive..."

"But you didn't get us all out alive!" she shrieked, burying her face in Danny's stomach again. Danny felt eyes falling upon them from all around as the other mutants turned to watch.

Danny tried to quiet her down, even just a little, by holding his finger to his lips and bending down a little, but he was given a rough clap to the face to illustrate Bethany's point. He fell silent, his mouth frozen into a shocked 'o'.

"Bethany, she might not be dead... You can't be so determined about that... Remember that Mercury escaped. She might have found a way out with him..." his words sounded almost ludicrous even to him, too good a hope to be true.

"Liar!" she yelled, hitting him again, her tail whipping about, back and forth behind her.

"Liar, liar, liar! You saw that... that *beast*! If that horrible, burning light doesn't get 'er, then it will! You saw that monster! It won't help her!"

"Bethany, come on-!"

Bethany wasn't about to be stopped now. She struck out at him again, and this time her claws left four neat, parallel marks through Danny's clothing, which quickly bore a spreading stain of purple on the frail blue fabric. She stepped back from him, then gave a fiery glare and lifted her tail. Baring the fangs of a predator, she flattened her ears back and snarled triumphantly.

"Don't say anything else!" she spat.

"You... You're just... You're nothing more than a liar, and... And a murderer! And... And I *hate* you!" There was a venomous sense of satisfaction in her voice as she finally said those cold, heartless words. The other children all stopped and stared at her. It seemed an age before they finally began to mutter

157

amongst themselves horrified words.

"She can't say that to daddy!"

"What did she do?"

"Why?"

Bethany still stood there, staring evenly, and quaking with rage.

Danny felt as though the breath had been ripped from him. Her words bit deep, like cruel shards of ice. Several seconds passed, and he didn't even breathe. When he finally did, his breath was a little squeak of air in his throat. He opened his mouth, then closed it again. The blood from the shallow wound in his chest continued to seep into his clothing.

"...Fine..." he said eventually, his voice shaking. He turned his back on her, too hurt to say any more. "...If you really feel like that..."

He began to blunder away as though he was in a hurry, unseen thistles blurred by his tears catching on his legs as though to try to drag him back. He walked away, down the overgrown path that lead down to the city, away from the laboratory. Before he came to the open road, he shrank back, hiding behind a crumbling, old stone wall, and buried his face in his hands.

His mind felt too frozen up to do anything, his throat too clogged up to speak. Her words weighed down on his mind like lumps of lead as though to poison him, and drag him down all at once. It confused him more than anything he could ever describe, and the words rung throughout him like bells chiming with his heartbeat. In the distance, he heard the cathedral bells ring out.

Is it that late already? he wondered blearily, looking through his tears at the spires silhouetted on the horizon. His brain felt too thick to comprehend anything anymore. With his heart heavy, Danny stared, and he wondered about everything around him, everything he'd ever seen, and heard, and listened to. But most of all, he wondered about Bethany's words. He hugged his knees into his chest as a cold breeze washed over him like a purifying spring.

He wondered if those words were the truth.

She's right... he thought gloomily, wishing that he didn't have to fight the urge to cry. *I should have checked that she was there...Emerald's dead now, and it's all my fault...*

He rested his stubbly chin on his knees, his blue eyes clouding up.

If I hadn't come here, maybe none of this would have happened...

He rubbed his teary eyes with the back of a hand. Somehow, he'd stumbled upon the answer to a question that had plagued him since the start of the war.

I really don't belong here...

Oh, but how he wished that he did...

Danny buried his face in his hands once again, and felt his tears finally leaking. Sniffling quietly to himself, Danny almost didn't notice another small snuffling sound, or a twitching black nose peeking out from a tangle of tall grass. Danny eventually looked up as he heard a soft whimper, and his blue eyes met with a pair of kind, worried brown ones, beneath a tangled mop of gold hair, filled with twigs, burrs, and bramble stalks.

Danny wiped his eyes again, watching as though in fascination. The figure, whoever it was, crept closer. His plumed golden tail was drooping. One droopy ear had been turned inside out by his frantic efforts, but he either didn't notice, or didn't care. Danny stretched out his arms, and the young one clad in a suddenly rather torn jogging suit tumbled into him, dog collar jingling.

"Hello, Karasu..."

Danny hugged the dog boy close into his chest, and

Karasu nuzzled into him, tail beginning to whirl as he bundled up into Danny's arms. Karasu rested his chin on Danny's shoulder for a moment, then looked up at him with brown eyes- beautiful dog eyes that seemed to just beg for happiness. Danny was unable to resist a sad smile, and Karasu nudged his face with his wet button nose.

"Ah, Karasu... You wouldn't understand any of this..."

The dog boy watched expectantly, and then lowered his gaze. Then the dog boy reached up, and despite Danny's efforts to get away, was forced into submission as the dog boy began to lick his face with a soft pink tongue. Freed from Karasu's grasp eventually, Danny sighed as he realized that the dog boy had unintentionally left muddy paw prints all over the clothes- the tattered hospital robes- that he was wearing. This was the only form of clothing that he had.

Karasu looked down, and then leaned down slightly as though to examine the prints he'd left. For a minute, Danny thought that he was going to try to clean up the mess, but then the dog boy- a little hesitantly, admittedly- began to lap gently at the wound that had been created by Bethany's claws on his chest. Danny tensed up for a moment as the wound stung a little bit, but then he relaxed, looking confusedly down at Karasu. The boy usually hated the sight and scent of blood, but now, here he was- cleaning Danny's wounds. What had caused the sudden change?

As Karasu looked up at him again, Danny noticed that the boy was shivering, and had gone pale, but his eyes looked as though they were trying to portray a message of some sort. Danny looked deep into those cute dog-eyes, searching for some hint. Karasu gave a soft and valiant *wuff*, as though to tell Danny that he

160

was okay, and that he wasn't sick.

Finally, Danny found something in Karasu's eyes, and the message seemed to reach out for him.

Be brave... those eyes seemed to say. *Face your fears... I trust you... I know you will...*

Danny hugged Karasu close into his chest. He felt Karasu's tail thumping against him happily, as Karasu expressed his joy very clearly.

Danny felt the smile fade from his face as he finally gathered the nerve enough to look up, and looked right into the face of Charlie, standing silently and looking down at him. Danny looked back at her, then lowered his gaze in shame. He forced a weak smile, gulping down his sadness as usual, to replace it with a feeble mask of optimism.

"Charlie..." he murmured, with a soft sigh in his voice.

"Danny," she replied calmly, seating herself beside him.

Karasu squirmed in Danny's arms, seeming determined to sniff this newcomer into giving him a friendly pat or a ruffle of the ears. His tail whirred so fast, like a furry gold propeller, that it seemed a wonder to Danny that he didn't take off and go flying away across the countryside.

Danny let him squirm out of his arms and jump into Charlie's, who was quickly showered with slobbery kisses from the dog boy. It was only when Karasu calmed down that Charlie spoke again, and when she did, the situation seemed almost awkward.

"I think you did good back there..." she said, watching him. Danny grunted, shrugging his shoulders. He turned away from her, and stared off into the distance, beyond the buildings, the cathedral, the many fields and into the sky beyond. Avoiding her gaze at all costs. He didn't reply at first, but his face was enough to say what he hadn't spoken aloud.

"I know that was mean of her... But you can't really blame her."

Danny's shoulders drooped a little.

"I know..." he sighed. "And I don't..."

"You really seem attached to these kids, don't you?" she asked.

"Yeah..." admitted Danny, watching the grass as it waved to him in the life-giving breeze. "They're... They're all I have left, really..."

Charlie turned towards him, but Danny didn't look towards her. It always intimidated him, the sight of someone staring at him, like they wanted to know everything. Danny didn't usually want to talk about it; he was barely known around here, at least not by the other scientists, and perhaps that was for the best. They couldn't pry open his weaknesses, that way.

"All you have left?" as he dreaded, Charlie seemed curious. Danny pursed his lips and nodded with a soft grunting sound. He didn't want to talk about this, and he turned even further away. Karasu prodded at his back with a paw. Although the boy was mute, Danny felt certain that he somehow understood him.

"I don't want to talk about it..." he uttered, sensing that Charlie wasn't about to give in. "It's a really long story. And I'm, you know, not from around here, so it won't matter to you anyway." He sounded a little bitter.

"Oh, that's okay!" Charlie corrected herself hastily. She put a hand on his shoulder and gave it a comforting squeeze, feeling his tense muscles relax somewhat. "But maybe talking about it will make you feel better?"

Danny fell silent again. He trusted Charlie, but he'd hardly talked about anything to anyone since the war had started.

"And it will matter to me," said Charlie eventually. "Because it doesn't matter where you're from, or what.

You've already proven yourself to me."

Danny turned to look at her, and searched her face as though desperately looking for some sign that she was lying. But then he slumped slightly, and finally let all his emotions come pouring out in waves of sorrow, but at the same time, relief and gratitude.

"Thank you..." he peeped feebly, his mind finally clicking onto the truth. "Thank you so much..."

"Don't get all sappy with me, just get on with it, or you'll just make yourself more upset."

Danny looked up in surprise at her steely tone of voice. And his eyes met hers for a moment. Then he simply nodded, and sighed.

"Well, they mean so much to me... Because... Because my mom was killed in the war, when I'd first moved to England..." He gulped, and looked up at her warily.

"She wasn't! And your dad?"

"I never knew my dad..." Danny's voice had turned brittle, as though it were about to shatter at any moment.

Whatever Charlie had been expecting, it didn't seem like that had been it. She looked at him as though begging for more, and Danny felt a little perturbed by the look. He shuffled a little sideways, away, an old wound feeling as though it had opened up again. He wiped his eyes with the back of a hand, and sighed once more.

"Did you have any siblings?"

"I had a brother, but... He was killed along with my mom..." he said gruffly, voice breaking.

"That's awful..."

"That's just... War. It's people dying, and all for nothing."

"Then, why do you still work in the laboratory? Or, why did you?"

"They told me that I was going to be engineering bacteria and viruses that could help people survive even the most violent of infections and wounds. I worked with them, because I thought it would help people. They told me that if I started the basic work on the DNA-modifying properties of the bacteria, using the genes of different animals as a basis, then they'd do the rest and decide on the best efforts..." He stared straight ahead, into the memories.

"They didn't. They took the bacterium and viruses, and they changed people, and hurt them- killed them, even. Killed them with *my* work." Danny's clenched fists began to turn white with the effort of keeping his emotions under control. "They turned *my* work into a weapon, when they *knew* I wanted it to help people." He sighed deeply, closing his eyes. "I suppose I should have known something was going on, now that I think about it... I mean, they never let me see the work being tested, and none of the volunteers ever stepped out of the room again. But still... I guess... I believed everything they told me... Even though they... They..."

Charlie listened intently, afraid to interrupt. Danny was silent for a long while. When he finally spoke again, his voice was breathless with defeat.

"They used me..."

Another long silence lingered between them.

Struggling to find something more to say that wouldn't cause her to appear rude, Charlie looked down and then back up at Danny's thoughtful face. Her curiosity got the better of her. "So, how did you find out? About what they were doing, I mean."

"By Toby... I heard a commotion, and what did I find? Definitely not what I'd thought I would!" Danny clenched his fists.

"I almost quit, but it was already too late... They

had the bacteria, and they knew that it worked. To stay was the least I could do. I needed to make sure that Toby was okay after what I'd done to him... And the experiments, too. I've gotten attached to them... I dunno what's up with all this, but I know that I don't want to leave them now..."

Danny bowed his head.

"It's like an apology, of sorts... I just can't seem to get anyone to see that I mean what I say..."

Charlie squeezed his shoulder again. She had been listening intently to him the whole time. Seeing that Danny was shivering, she gently removed her labcoat and draped it over him like a blanket. He looked up at her in surprise.

"Here. You need it more than I do."

Danny sniffled, but tried to look strong. "I'm not cold!" he insisted.

"Better than a few rags," she told him, winking in an effort to lighten the mood. "Besides, you could use it for a blanket, if you're staying here for the night."

He sighed, and pulled the coat tighter around him to fight against the evening chill. Karasu moved to sit back on his haunches beside Danny, seeming to sense that the man was growing sad again.

"Hm... True..." he muttered, stroking Karasu's head with a hand.

Charlie sighed. Despite everything, Danny didn't seem to be getting any happier.

"What else do you want me to do?"

"You couldn't do anything more." Danny smiled shakily. "You're a great friend, Charlie..."

Charlie smiled back at him, avoiding his gaze for only a second.

"You too, Danny..."

He sniffed.

"And to think, just yesterday, you avoided me, and I

165

avoided everyone... We were all in one piece, and there was no crazy experiments going on involving giant hulking wolves and rattlesnakes and... Was there bear in Mercury, remind me?"

"Yeah... Grizzly bear."

She laughed weakly.

"And I was Toby's guide, and we still had a place to call home..."

"The laboratory? Home?" she laughed, as though the idea was ridiculous to her.

Danny bit his lip.

"Ha! Yeah, I guess you're right..." He fell silent for a moment, laughing nervously as he agreed almost out of instinct.

"...We have our own homes..."

-Chapter 12-

Emerald's Choice

"So, dear..." Alma waited patiently as the little girl whom she now took care of gulped down as much water as she was able from the bottle the spy had provided.

"What's your name?" The little girl took a final gulp, and finished off the lot. Small as she was, Alma wondered if the girl had a bottomless stomach to contain all that water.

"Emerald..." said the little girl, breathing deeply and licking the last traces of water from her lips. Alma raised her eyebrows, because the iridescent sheen over her skin was more a gentle shimmer of blue than green as the name implied. Alma didn't comment.

"Emerald? That's a pretty name," she complimented, and the girl looked down and blushed palely. Alma wondered if the girl was hesitant to speak to strangers. Since her panicked outbursts before, Emerald had hardly spoken to Alma at all, though she admittedly appeared more comfortable now. Emerald started twiddling with the bottle lid curiously; it seemed like she had never seen one before in her life.

Alma, blinking her green eyes, watched the little girl with a smile on her face beneath the mask to create a convincing character. At least Emerald had believed her story. Her husband worked in the laboratory and she'd gone to find him? Ha, she wished. *Children these days, eh?* It seemed as though they'd believe anything they were told.

Emerald looked up at her eventually, her two eyes glimmering into hundreds. With a little prickle of unease, Alma wondered how the girl saw her. Was her vision split into hundreds? Alma smiled as the little girl watched her, and then knelt beside her to gently dab at the tip of her injured antenna. Emerald's translucent pink blood made barely a stain on the tissue that Alma used, and the girl looked up warily.

"So, Emerald..."

Emerald watched her expectantly, her many eyes all enclosed into two all glimmered separately up at her.

"Can you tell me if any more survived?"

She was silent for a moment, and Alma wondered if she was going to skip over the question as she had done so many others. Slowly, though, the little dragonfly nodded.

"There were my friends... All my friends survived. Or my brothers and sisters, because we all have the same daddy. I think there'll be some scientists, too. Daddy was trying to get us all out, and he left me behind in there..."

She looked at Alma mournfully.

"Awww... So, they're not very good friends, are they?"

Emerald looked mortified in response to Alma's words, and she leaped to her feet, her crystal-clear wings whisking.

"I never said that! Bethany was always there! She just went to protect me, and she was dragged off before she could come back to get me!" she protested.

"Oh, dear Emerald..." whispered Alma smoothly. "That's what they all say..."

She gently reached out, and tugged on one of the girl's blue-tinted pigtails. Emerald took a step back away from her, looking horrified.

"Not me! I don't just say things! I don't lie!"

"It isn't lying if you don't know, dear..." said Alma, her tone sympathetic and manipulative.

Emerald made to protest some more, but Alma was ready for resistance. Slowly, she bent down, and then, with a quick shift, removed her mask. Her face seemed dull compared to her stunningly green eyes. Her face was youthful and ordinary, freckles dappling her nose and her chin. Her brows were curved and kindly-looking, almost sad. One side of her face was traced by a fierce scar leading down to her chin and staining her plump, red lips white where they had been cut.

"I wouldn't hide anything from you, dear..." she said tenderly, brushing several strands of dark hair back from Emerald's face. Emerald looked transfixed. She reached out, and gently stroked a finger down the scar that cleft her cheek. She was silent for a while but then she replied by brushing Alma's own blonde hair from her eyes. Alma bowed her head a little to let the young girl who, when standing, only just reached Alma's shoulders when she knelt. She was so small...

*And so, so innocent...*the woman thought to herself.

"That line... What is it?" Emerald asked, touching the scar with gentle searching fingers. "Why is it there?"

"It's a scar, dear. A lot of adults have them now. It's because of the war."

"The war?"

"Yes. It's a dark, dark time. Lots of people hurt each other, and they're all trying to be better than one another."

"I think... I think that's what we were being trained for."

"It will be. That's why you have your wings, and why the others have claws and fangs, ears too. So that they can do things that no human, like I am, can ever do."

Emerald slowly digested this new information.

"Is that why the laboratory hurt us? And the

monster?"

"Yes..."

"Are you trying to say that... That this 'war' is why my friends left me? They wouldn't do that."

"You never know, dear. Stay with me for now, okay...? You'll be safe with me."

Emerald didn't protest. She spread out her arms, and Alma, taking the hint, gathered the warm little girl into a hug. Emerald folded her wings against her back, and clung on tightly, closing her eyes to squeeze the tears from her eyes. Alma gently placed the girl back on the ground as she felt the first tear drip; she didn't want the water to damage all the expensive equipment she was wearing. Taking out her handkerchief again, Alma dabbed away the tears from Emerald's eyes.

"No tears, alright?" she murmured comfortingly. "You can come back to my house for the time being."

"Really? But, I'm not allowed close to anyone who isn't a scientist..."

"My house is in the country, dear. No-one lives near me. You can stay for a while, until we find out what's going on with your friends and stuff, 'kay?"

Emerald finally nodded.

"Alright, Sabrina... Thank you, Sabrina..."

"Aww... It's okay, sweetie. Just remember to always trust Sabrina, okay? Because I know what's best for you, and that's all I want. If I say something's dangerous, it's dangerous, and if I say it's fine, it's fine. Always listen to me, promise? I don't want you hurt before we can find your friends and your daddy, alright...?"

Emerald nodded once more. "I promise, Sabrina," she said, meekly reaching out to hold Alma's hand. Alma took Emerald's hand in her own leather-gloved hand, squeezing it comfortingly before running her fingers over Emerald's wrist.

"Now, I'm going to cloak you in that fabric again, okay? So that you don't get cold, and so that you aren't seen by anyone except me. We can't disobey the scientist's orders after they've been through so much to keep them in one piece, now can we?"

Emerald let Alma drape the armour-like blanket over her, hiding her face, and tucking up her wings all warm and snug, whilst keeping a little slack in the fabric so that she could breathe.

"Good girl..."

Alma gently picked up Emerald and cradled the girl in her arms. Emerald curled up in the fabric, her wings twitching as she tried to find a comfortable place to put them. Aside for the one she had told Emerald of, Alma had another reason for her hiding of Emerald. She didn't want the little girl to see. She wanted her place of residence to remain unknown by all. By use of trickery and manipulation, Alma would keep it that way; her way.

It was only now that she let her kind eyes be replaced by sly glimmers, the smile fading from her face. As she broke into a lean sprint, she felt Emerald squirming in her grasp. The girl was trying to see out.

"Shh, Emerald..." she whispered. "It won't be long. We wouldn't want anyone to see you, now, would we?"

"Sabrina?" whimpered Emerald, continuing to squirm, before gradually settling down in her arms. "It's really dark in here... I don't like the dark very much."

"I know, sweetie," ushered Alma, the kind tone returning into her voice. "No-one does. It won't be long now, Emerald."

This was just the opportunity she'd been waiting for.

With Emerald's trust, she would have her enemy right where she wanted them.

***

As the shadows lengthened and the evening fell into darkness, the weather grew colder. As the weather grew colder, Toby's shaky breaths grew shallower, and his trembling heartbeat grew more hesitant. He lay on his side in the grass, and the green stems tickled him like unseen little children or fairies poking at the body of a bird killed by the cat.

He could do nothing but lie there and wait, ever hopeful, for someone to come or Sabrina to return. His confused mind still didn't realize that it was all a trick. It seemed like a hallucination, almost. The last time he'd been outside, Toby had been saved by pure luck. This time, it seemed that his luck had run out.

Every breeze that washed over him brought with it a fresh wave of shivers that jerked Toby's muscles awake. Every attempt he made to twitch, to try to support himself sent Toby's hopes crashing down to the bottom again. He might be alive, but he was in no fit state to start trying to pick himself up. Even as he lay, his thoughts reeling, shame clouded his judgement over all else. So the only solution, and a pathetic one at that, was simply to lie, and wait, cry out in tortured breaths as he begged silently for death to come easily.

The image that Sabrina had given him, the image of what he could have seen, still burned in his mind. *The cathedral silhouetted against orange sky and candyfloss clouds... The fields stretching off into the distance... The butterflies...* Toby felt, against his will, tears beginning to run down his face, soaking into the furry markings on his cheeks. He shivered again in the cold. The temperature seemed to be dropping by the minute. All was silent, except for the distant cry of an owl, the sound of the wind brushing its way over the fields.

Slowly, though, there came something else. The crunching of skipping footsteps down an echoed, faraway path, the laughter of someone far beyond him. It was a little girl, dragging her father by the hand. Toby felt the cold chill of sadness creeping through him.

Family... he thought to himself, swallowing back his tears. *Oh, how I wish that my family was still here...*

Toby's thoughts trailed off into distant nothingness as the footsteps trailed away, not noticing him. Toby's sickly yellow eyes, slowly trembled, narrowed, and then finally closed beneath dark eye lashes. His jet-black hair swayed softly in a breeze.

Many memories played through his mind, from those of happiness, and the effortless joy that he'd felt as a young child, to those of the deepest sorrow. He remembered all of it... scampering after his younger sister as they'd played, with his russet hair whisked back in a breeze. His cheeks were pink with the effort of simple play. He caught up to her, and then he hugged her despite her protests. In the background, his mother and father smiled proudly to each other. And then they walked on, hand in hand, into the haze that engulfed Toby's memories. Their laughter faded into distant memories.

He remembered his last moments with his mother as she lay dying beside the bodies of his father and his younger sister, to whom Toby had never gotten to say goodbye. She'd grasped his hand, and looked up, her gaze thick with trembling tears as her blue eyes met his hazel ones. The wreckage of their home was in flames around them and his throat burned with the smoke, but Toby didn't want to leave his family behind. He had called an ambulance for them, but it was already too late, even for the day's technology to take care of. Toby remembered those same tears that ran down his cheeks

173

as he begged her not to leave him. Still, she held his hand in hers'.

"Toby..." she whispered to him, in an echoing, pleading voice. *"You mustn't... You can't give in... Please... Go... live on... for us... For all of us..."*

Ah, yes... thought Toby, a slow, sad smile breaking out on his face, to mingle with his steady tears.

I... I can remember now.

***

Charlie smiled as she watched her new companions as they tussled and squeaked at one another, hard at play as they recovered when distracted from the destruction and loss. The shock of discovering Danny's past had worn off quite a bit from Charlie, herself, by now. After all, wasn't it the pain of losing someone special that brought people together to fight or the war? It wasn't always about the country. Sometimes it was about revenge, or family, too. Of all the scientists in the laboratory, there were few without some tale of woe or scar to show for their efforts.

Charlie was one of the few who had little of a tale to tell; her family was still intact, her life was mostly normal, and her job was just that. She didn't see it as some heroic duty or means of revenge. The only reason she had become a scientist in the first place was simply, because she was good at it. Science was one of the few subjects that she had excelled at, back in school. That had been a while back, true, but in the end, it had led to the job that she enjoyed. That was before the war had started. The thought made her feel quite old; the war had started 9 years ago, and she had been 21 back when she'd taken the job as a scientist, 15 years ago. That made her 36.

Danny had mentioned somewhere along the line that

he was only 25; that would explain his recklessness, perhaps. In a way, though, he was more mature than she was. He had seen more death than she had, and that had been enough for him. He didn't want to see any more, even if it was the death of someone whom had hurt him in the past.

Charlie almost wished that she had some extravagant story to tell like the others, but she knew inwardly that the wish was immature.

Speaking of immature...

Charlie looked up, and bit her tongue to keep herself from bursting out laughing.

"Danny, what are you doing?!"

"We're playing hide and seek- shh!" hissed the man, and disappeared into the tall grass with only his blue eyes and chestnut brown mop of hair peeping out. Charlie obeyed, but had to resist the urge to laugh. She could see the other children scattering away from the tightly-closed entrance of the laboratory, giggling and whispering amongst themselves.

Joey was grumbling out his numbers from where he stood with his face pressed into a tree, as Danny had apparently already been the 'seeker' and Joey was the only one of the mutants who could count to any number, even if it was only 11.

As Joey opened his eyes with a telltale cry of "ready or not, here I come!" the hiding children all hushed, shushed and pushed each other, waiting as though scared of Joey. Joey, looking about quickly, pounced on Bethany first.

"Bethany! Found you! You're not even hiding!" proclaimed Joey triumphantly. Bethany batted him away in annoyance then folded her arms.

"I'm not playing," she said gruffly, turning away.

"But-"

"I'm not playing!"

175

She clamped her lips together and stuck her chin out at him, and that was the end of it.

Joey went off to find the others, and first found Karasu with several leaves on his head, sitting in a patch of short grass with his paws over his eyes. He was grinning widely, his tongue lolling out to one side. It seemed almost cruel to 'find' him, but Joey didn't seem to get that. Joey tapped him on the shoulder, and Karasu lifted one paw slightly so that he could peer up at Joey for a second, before clasping it back over his eye to stay hidden.

"Found you, Karasu..."

The leaf-covered boy finally lowered his paws, his huge, puppy-like eyes staring up at Joey pleadingly.

"I found you!"

Karasu finally seemed convinced, and he lowered his tail and walked shamefacedly back towards Charlie.

Joey next found Moony in the nearby tree, and then Benny and Ginny as they hid together nearby Danny. Sally and Cassie were the hardest to find, as they had gone the furthest away from the laboratory and hid around the corner. The second they heard someone coming their way they would take flight and cunningly change hiding places. They were only found when Cassie, following her sister, got her shirt snagged on the fence and got stuck.

It seemed that they had been purposely avoiding Danny, because as soon as Sally and Cassie were found, they rocketed over to where Danny was hiding and piled in, clinging and barking and cawing. Danny laughed, his voice muffled for all the squirming children who pinned him down.

"Found youuuu!" they all chimed and chanted laughingly. It took a while before they let him go, and after that, they all swarmed around his legs, laughing at each other and at their antics.

"Can we play again?" asked Moony, big eyes watching Danny expectantly.

"Yes! Again, again!" yelped the other children, cheering and jumping up. Danny rolled his eyes.

"That's enough for today..." said Danny, and groans erupted from the children's ranks as they tried to protest against Danny's logic.

"Look, look, look... We need to gather our strength from the morning. There might be some people to have survived the wreckage! If there is, we need to look through the ruins when the fire's gone down, or at least look about the outside. I mean... There's bound to be more than just us. We could easily do it, what with you guys, and all your abilities!" Danny tugged on one of Karasu's ears, and tapped his wet black nose with a finger. Karasu barked happily, looking up at Danny admiringly. "But if we want to, then we'll need to get you sleep."

The children didn't seem to be pleased with this even so, and some continued to complain for various other reasons too, such as hunger.

"We'll get food in the morning, okay? I promise. You'll feel better after a good night's sleep..."

Though still seeming reluctant as they began to settle down, the mutants eventually clustered together in a huddle of feathers, fur, and shiny eyes darting about as they whispered to one another. This entire day had been frightening to them, and now, as dusk consumed, they didn't want it to be so. Most were afraid of the dark, and cowered into the centre of the group. Those left on the outside wanted to be in the middle, where it was warmest.

Neither Danny nor Charlie thought that it would be wise to introduce them to a campfire after the distress the fire inside had caused, but what choice did they have? It was so cold out here...

Eventually, after what seemed like hours, most of the frantic children had fallen asleep, leaving Danny and Charlie seated side by side, staring off into the silent night or the hesitantly crackling fire that spat out sparks.

Charlie cleared her throat quietly, and Danny turned to look at her.

"So, you're staying here for the night, are you?" she whispered to him.

"Yeah. Too risky to leave them, and we need to have some sort of a plan before blundering into the city. The police'd have us if we did that. I just wish we'd had more warning about this…"

Danny looked down at the ground, and then winced slightly.

Charlie looked confused, and in response Danny reached beneath him, and pulled out a sharp-looking rock. He gave her an awkward smile as he tossed the offending rock that he'd been sitting on to one side.

"…Oh, but you can go home if you want," he added a moment later, as if trying to be polite, or change the subject from the fact that he'd sat on an uncomfortable stone. "Will there be anyone worrying about you?"

"Well…" Charlie sounded indecisive. "Worrying? My husband might be. I never stay the night here."

Danny looked at her. "Oh? You have a husband?" he sounded interested, but not in a bad way. He was just curious; he'd never really thought about the lives of scientists other than himself. "Do you have any children?"

"A daughter. She's called Annie." Danny looked at the mound of sleeping experiments beside them, all engulfed in the comfortable folds of sleep.

"Ah… I wish I knew how that felt."

Charlie looked down a little.

"But you do…" she said wisely.

Danny didn't reply for a while. He seemed to be thinking things over, examining her words in his mind. Then finally, he smiled, and looked up at her.

"I... I guess you're right," he said, smiling at her. His eyes glimmered in the darkness.

For another long, long while, there was silence. Then Danny whispered to Charlie again.

"So, are you going home?"

"You won't mind?"

"Of course not."

Charlie stood up, her gaze still locked intently into his.

"Are you sure?"

"Do I look unsure to you?" He smiled at her, but she could see that he was beginning to shiver. She wasn't sure if it was with nerves, or the cold, though.

She hesitated, then gave a little smile.

"Okay... I'll be back for you first thing in the morning."

She turned, and began to limp away from him, struggling to support her weight on her injured leg. As she'd moved a few meters, however, she heard Danny call her name in a hushed whisper. Charlie wondered if he'd changed his mind.

"Charlie! Charlie, wait!"

"What is it?"

"I just remembered something! I needed to say thank you."

"Thank you? What for?"

"For being the best friend I could ever ask for..."

They exchanged smiles, and Charlie, seeming taken aback by Danny's gratitude, felt guilty for leaving him by the laboratory.

"And I need to say thank you, to you, too. For saving my life... I don't know how I'll ever be able to repay you for that."

Danny smiled at her, and then he laughed quietly, the sound rare for anyone to hear. Charlie didn't think she'd ever heard him laugh before.

Eventually he calmed himself, and winked playfully at her.

"You already have."

"I have? How?"

Danny looked sincerely into her eyes. There were no lies in his.

"Just by being there," he told her, then settled, and, as though he felt he had said enough, said no more to her.

Charlie felt herself smiling. She turned, and once more began to limp away down the path.

Despite all the cheeriness and the truth in the air tonight, Danny, Charlie, and the sleeping children were kept in the dark in more than one way.

None had noticed eyes of glittering gold watching them from the shadows.

Those eyes watched the scene for a while, as though waiting for a chance to strike.

But even as Danny was left alone, the creature didn't. Instead, the eyes blinked closed, and the beast that owned them slipped away into the shadows, with a rattlesnake's tail hissing along behind it.

-Chapter 13-

Survival

With nary a whispering sound emerging as the dew-speckled grass tenderly caressed her feet, Alma emerged as a quiet shadow to meet the pink dawn that crept hazily over the horizon like a distant fog. Alma's green eyes flicked over the abandoned fields ahead of her, and she weaved her way over well-trodden paths between them, making barely a sound as she moved. The grass left her tight leather outfit shimmering with the dewy moisture.

Looking out at the city for a second, Alma grunted, and smiled. She had left Emerald with the promise that she would find her friends and bring them back, but Alma had other plans in mind, and her first step was to make sure that the blind mutant that she had left behind was truly dead. As she approached the site where she had left him, Alma hesitated for just a second as she considered what would await her.

If he was already dead, then the scent would likely have attracted scavengers... It would be a most grotesque sight.

She shuddered inwardly at the thought, but wasn't too moved; she'd bore witness to much, much worse things before. With a slight toss of her flowing blonde mane, Alma shook away the thoughts and continued moving on.

The sight that she beheld was far from what she had been expecting. But then again, Alma had prepared herself for the worst. Toby lay before her, but he was still in one piece.

Frail, pale, skeleton-like hands dug their claws into

the grass. Toby's eyes were closed, and his mouth was slightly open. His brows were un-creased and he wasn't smiling, didn't look as peaceful as a dead body might have looked. A large black spider scuttled over the back of Toby's labcoat, and Alma, repulsed, kicked it off of him.

Toby didn't move.

Alma carefully knelt down by his side, watching closely. Lifting a dainty and careful hand, she began to gently trace her finger down his fur-dappled jaw. She delicately fingered his neatly-trimmed goatee for a moment, and felt for a pulse on the tender, dappled flesh of his throat. Slowly, her hand crept up, and she ran her fingers through his soft, jet-black hair. She couldn't feel any body heat, but... Something didn't feel quite right.

Using the tip of a delicate finger, Alma gently lifted one of his eyelids, and his lifeless, sightless eye stared ahead. His eyes were the deadest part of all of him. They always had been. Alma jerked her hand back, and Toby's eye flickered closed again. An awful shudder passed over him.

Alma froze. *He's still alive?!*

She lifted her lip slightly, and looked almost amused. *Heh... He's persistent, I'll give him that.*

A feeble, rattling sigh rasped over Toby's lips, but that was the first breath that Alma had heard from him. Alma felt a short tug of pity stealing its way into her heart, but she pushed it back as she reminded herself, despite the clear pain and immobility of her prisoner, that this was the enemy...

And he knew too much.

Why was it that she had been unable to kill *him* before? Alma had killed many before. She had surprised many with her skills, and the scar on her cheek was the remainder of one such battle. It had been a lucky breakthrough on their part, but the advantage hadn't lasted very long. She had plunged a dagger into the weakest part of the skull, beneath which a vital artery pulsed. He was dead before Alma had even thrown his body carelessly to the ground.

Master of blade, shot and most of all of stealth.

That was Alma. A demon in human form, as some referred to her as. She worked as a head spy for the USA, and never before had she failed a mission that she had taken on herself. It was only the presence of a teammate that would drag her down to their level. Her methods were her own, and no-one else could use them as she did.

When she had killed before, though, Alma had been overtaken with the thrill of battle, had leaped amongst the bodies of thousands, and had been driven on by the thrill of the hunt. Her adversaries had been doomed from the start, but they leaped forward with terrible ferocity in their eyes, and they wanted to kill her.

Here, this was different. Toby was lame and unarmed, unable to even see what she was doing. He hadn't even tried to hurt her.

This place was no battlefield. This was the country, with butterflies dancing over dewy ocean waves of grassy fields and golden corn and wheat, the late-year crops almost ready for harvest. The sky above was a romantic shade of pink, with wispy candyfloss clouds decorating the sky as if they were at a funfair. Alma wondered about the thoughts that had gone through Toby's mind as she'd held the gun's barrel to the back of his head. She wondered about the thoughts that had gone through his mind as she spoke to him. He'd always looked up at her, and he'd always smiled… trusted.

This wasn't a war effort…
No.

This was what they called murder. Cold-blooded murder. She, Alma, one of the most respected people in all the US... a murderer? Using the word in conjunction with herself seemed to bring her spinning back to her senses, and she collided with her few human emotions with a crack.

The impact was strong, but Alma wouldn't cry. She couldn't cry. She just stood there, staring dumbfounded down at Toby's dying body, the last traces of heat fading from him as quickly as the heartbeat which was, for once, at a dangerously healthy pace.

She swallowed and slowly bent down towards him. Her mouth felt suddenly dry, her throat as parched as a burning desert. But there was no need to be concerned about that. Gently lifting one of Toby's hands, unhooking his fingers from the ground, Alma brushed the soil from under his claws then did the same to his other hand. That done Alma hauled his lifeless body into her arms, and he slumped against her.

He was quite heavy, but not nearly as heavy as she had been expecting. Perhaps he was underweight...

With Toby clasped in her arms, Alma was able to stagger to her feet with a grunt. Growling in concentration, Alma slowly came to terms with this strange new weight, and even when she did, she wasn't quite as silent or light footed, but still managed to travel fairly safely under cover, her feet like cat's paws on the pavement. She didn't fear being seen; not at this early hour, at least.

A short while later, Alma's arms began to get tired, so she slung Toby over one of her shoulders like he was a sack of potatoes. This, at least, freed up her legs a bit more. Alma felt fairly satisfied with herself as she broke into a quick trot, halting herself nearby the entrance to where the laboratory had been burned down. She may have spared Toby, but a mission was still a mission.

And to complete a mission, she still needed to remain unseen. What harm could Toby do to that? He couldn't even see her, let alone describe her. Gently swinging Toby into her arms again, Alma knelt down to lay him on the path, carefully resting him so that it was as though he was simply sleeping.

Stepping back for a moment to admire her handiwork, Alma was distracted by the sound of an engine nearby, and the sound of a car door hissing into place. Straightening up instantly, Alma turned, and then darted over the fence into the nearest field. With her silent footsteps fading into the breezy rustle of the grass, Alma hoped that her treachery would not affect the mission at hand…

Then, like a ghost, she vanished, unseen to the human eye.

***

Danny was given a thoroughly rude awakening by the feel of someone violently shaking him. With an awkward snort and a grunt, Danny's gaze shivered up to meet her gaze with an irritable stare. It wasn't exactly the most pleasant feeling, to be awoken by a rough shaking. His irritation faded to be replaced by fear, though, as his blurry, sleep-filled gaze focused enough for him to be able to make out that Charlie's face was filled with panic.

"What is it?" he asked worriedly, jerking himself upright.

"T-T-Toby!" gasped Charlie, hurrying so much to get her words out that she stuttered and stammered.

Danny's heartbeat quickened. "Toby?! Is he alive!?" he shot to his feet, a thousand conclusions springing mercilessly into his mind as the fog cleared all in a rush.

"He doesn't... Look very... Alive!"

"What!?"

"Come, see!"

Charlie grabbed him by the hand, and he was the one that ended up dragging her along, once he knew where they were going. The bleary gazes of sleepy mutants followed them, wondering what the fuss was about. Some got to their feet to follow, and others simply lay back down again and tried to go back to sleep.

As they reached Toby, Danny collapsed onto his knees beside the other man. Toby's eyes were closed, and he lay with his hands resting on his stomach, his head turned to one side. His tail was curled about his knees. His showing skin, far from being red and inflamed like it usually was, was ghostly pale, accented by his dark rosette spots.

Danny checked his pulse, and each beat seemed weak, and eerily further away than the last.

Danny froze, and his mask of calm utterly shattered.

"Oh, no... No, no no no... no, no, no..." he whispered, as if words alone could pull Toby back from the grave.

Toby took in a juddering breath, and his throat rasped. Danny held his breath, then, with trembling hands, began to root through Toby's coat pockets to look for the many medicines that kept him alive.

It was a feeble hope, but it was all that Danny had left.

"Ch-Charlie..." Danny uttered, voice quivering as he turned to her. His blue eyes were wide and desperate. "Water... Do you have any water? For Toby?"

Charlie nodded shakily, then Danny watched her hurry over to several shopping bags that she had dropped in her panic of finding Toby, bags that presumably held food for the mutants, some of whom watched them curiously now, whilst others simply slept through all the trauma. She pushed an overly-curious (and hungry) Karasu off of the bags, then brought them over with her, taking a water bottle in one hand then holding it out for Danny to take.

Danny snatched it from her then rubbed his eyes with a sleeved wrist as he struggled to open the lid with his slippery hands.

Swallowing, Danny managed it after what seemed like an age to him, in which he was terrified that Toby would be dead by the time he'd gotten to the water.

Quivering in both relief and terror, Danny poured some water into his open palm, and then gently dabbed it over Toby's pale face. The black-haired man twitched, just barely opening his eyes.

"Toby!" howled Danny, catching the glint of those glazed eyes. Toby juddered in shock. He didn't reply, just rasped. Danny dabbed some more water across his face, and the liquid slicked down Toby's fur.

Toby stirred a little more, his eyes closing again for a minute. He sighed then seemed to be drifting off to sleep. Danny's emotions plummeted into despair again, and he took hold of Toby's face in both hands and shook him gently. Toby's eyelids twitched, and he gave a tiny cough. His voice rasped, and this time, Danny heard not a struggled breath, but words.

"Mam..." he whispered hoarsely. "You finally... Came back..."

Danny flinched slightly, staring down at his friend as his words faded back into those rasping sighs and further inaudible mutters. *He's dreaming of his mother...* Danny thought to himself, feeling guilt beginning to steal into his heart, and sorrow. Toby had told him before of what had happened to his family.

How will we ever wake him?

Toby's lifeless form slumped back down to the ground as Danny let go. Then, opening his mouth, he gave a feeble groan. Toby's eyes flickered. Danny's fingers fumbled, and, seeing that Toby was beginning to awaken, unceremoniously shoved some medication into Toby's mouth in unthinking panic. Toby choked for a second, trying to figure out what was going on, and he spat out the pills onto the dirt, coughing violently, tail fluffing out.

Danny, realizing that he probably dived in onto that a bit too fast, laid a hand on Toby's arm to try to stop Toby from panicking. He gave Toby a rousing clap on the back to halt his jerky coughs, and Toby froze, then gave a soft whimper. He looked absolutely terrified for a while.

"Who... Who's there? What... What are you trying to do to me?"

Danny felt bad for not warning Toby of his presence. Goodness knows why Toby was out there in the first place, and Danny seemed to have momentarily forgotten that Toby hadn't been guided by him in a while.

"Toby..." he whispered, then pulled Toby into a hug. He struggled against Danny's grip, but Danny didn't always give in easily. After spending so much time worrying, it felt good to see Toby alive, even if he wasn't exactly well. "It's me... your guide!"

Toby seemed flabbergasted at first, then as he finally came to terms, grew still.

"Danny!? How did you find me?"

"How could I not find you?!"

"I... I... I thought..."

Danny quickly remembered that Toby might have felt like he'd been walking for miles, but in truth been walking in repeated circles. He was blind, and had only

188

ever been outside on his own once before.

"Forget it, Toby... Come on, I'll get your medicine ready, we wouldn't want you to die now, would we?" Danny said hastily, and there was a rattling sound as his trembling hands fumbled for some more tablets that Toby hopefully wouldn't spit out this time.

"But, Danny, I-"

Danny cut him off. "Don't be like that, Toby, come on!" he stammered, panting softly as he handled the medication beginning to panic that he might not manage. "You'll be fine!"

"I'm not-"

"Hang on a sec, Toby... You need water too, right? Charlie has water!" he panicked, stumbling and bumbling erratically over his words.

"Danny," began Charlie calmly. "I don't think you're helping-"

"Nonsense! I'm trying my hardest, see?!" Danny's face was heating up. He trembled, and gave a small cry of relief as he finally managed to get the medication from its packaging. "Ah-aha! Charlie, can you give Toby the water? Hah, here we go, Toby. No, hang on, don't take those without- oh, gone already. Well, here's the water, have that now, 'kay, down it goes. Alright, Toby, so... Uh, don't drink all of it! Oh, Charlie has more... Right-"

Toby had had enough. "Shurrup!" he yowled, spraying out a fair bit of water into Danny's face. Danny looked absolutely aghast, and sat there blinking. A few seconds later, he raised a hand to wipe the water from his face with his sleeve. Toby glared through sickly-yellow eyes.

Finally, Danny seemed to pick up on the fact that something was wrong.

"Toby...?" he began, suddenly seeming wary. "Where are your crutches?"

***

As Alma made her way through the busy city streets, she was aware of the crowd flowing around her as if she was a stone in an endless river. With her blonde hair flowing behind her, and her clothes changed out of their spy gear so that she could go without a fuss, Alma's eyes were the only hint to the icy chill that had reasserted itself in her heart.

She walked with her own careful flair, a sway that seemed to mimic that of a proud flag in the softest of breeze, or a banner as it followed its bearer like a scared little puppy into battle. She moved with purpose, her movements flowing as if with a will of their own.

The throng of people around her whirred with the sounds of voices, but Alma heard only the dull throb of the air. She had trained her ear to pick up only the conversations that were useful. Whereas others might not be able to hear themselves think, Alma could hear the thoughts carried on the voices of others, too. Without a word, Alma made her way through the crowds and stared ahead, gripping the dainty handbag at her side with a steely death-grip. Her muscles rippled lithely beneath her pink shirt and denim trousers that gripped tightly to her knees.

Her face was blank, devout of any kind of smirk or frown that might give away her intent.

She was making her way through the town centre, past the marketplace where people congregated, talking and laughing as if it was just another day, free of war. She turned, and the high heels of her boots clip-clopped up the cobbled path as she made her way up towards the Cathedral, past the well-worn Elvet Bridge. Sliding through the crowds as they began to thin, Alma turned, and slipped without a word into a dark alleyway beyond the crowds. Her footsteps echoed like the breaths of a beast, but she kept on walking, unfazed.

Her heartbeat was even and her footsteps quick, her fit form as alert as an alley cat's. With time, she reached the end of the alleyway, and emerged into an unexpected little nook in the kind and homely town. Far from making big news, the scene before her was reminiscent of a time long forgotten, back from when the war had just begun. Superstition and fear had kept this place long since abandoned.

Alma ducked under a yellow police tape, old, dusty, and neglected. She was not worried; no police had been near this place in years.

Lying before her was a vast clearing, devoid of any life. The ground was covered by a layer of dust and soot. The shaky fingers of dead bushes and stunted grasses rasped pitifully at the shattered and burned walls of abandoned houses like the claws of cats wanting to be in from the cold. There were many houses here, but none were in one piece. Old bricks and the remnants of furniture littered the place, sent skyward by explosion after explosion. As Alma passed one house, she looked inside, to see hunched figures, staring lifelessly out of the window, and up towards the sky. Alma took several steps forward.

It was all that was left of a family, and this was only one of those that remained here. The blackened grey faces stared out at her, but Alma felt no remorse. The family's bony fingers each held onto one another's' and they seemed to almost be still alive, looking out through the fragments of the charred window as if they were waiting for something. Here, they would stay like so many others, still trying to protect each other as they stared out into the cold, cold world and waited for the war to pass away.

Alma passed the family without saying a word. Why grieve for one, when there would be more, so many more, elsewhere in this fragmented little town full of death? To Alma, the dead were but things of the past. Her heart had been drawn into a pinch, and now she was cold, so cold. That winter chill forever filled her now, and it froze the grief in its tracks and rendered her strong, stronger than any sheltered child.

Alma's life was her own, and she spun it herself. She moulded masks from the personas of people she'd met before, and spun cloaks from the fabrics of lies. All to keep alive, for beneath the crudely woven silk and with mask after mask lifted off, she would be nothing. Those masks floated upon empty air, and the cloaks carried by a breath of wind.

That was how Alma saw herself. Not as a person, or even an actor. Not a spy, not a trickster, not even a soldier, doing her duties. She was nothing but an empty shell, for any warmth that had dwelt within her heart had long been extinguished, any emotion had been driven away by the blanket of lies that Alma had woven for herself through her many guises, tongues, and treacheries. Now, all she was, was a cold, cold, cold winter's breeze, drifting from country to country as the seasons passed her by.

Alma's stunningly kaleidoscopic green eyes snapped into focus as she heard a crack from inside a house that she walked by. Placing her feet apart, the woman pivoted quickly and quietly on her toes, then whisked forward. The sight that met her did neither shock her nor frighten her, and she just stared out evenly, before taking a respectful step back from the gaping crack where the door had been torn from the open walls. Alma looked through the shattered windows, and she bowed her head as she stared into two orbs of gold, and caught sight of a mouth in which massive fangs gleamed. A forked tongue flickered softly.

"Well, well, well, look who we have here... I had the feeling this was where you would be."

"Ahhh, Alma... Why do you tire yoursssssself out sssso...? Sssssssssseeking a wretched sssssssssoul such as I?"

Alma laughed coldly, and turned away from him carelessly.

"Don't waste your breath, Mercury. I know why you're here..."

She heard the breath rasping in Mercury's throat, deep, huge breaths that would come usually from the throat of a bear, or some other gigantic animal as it skulked through the unseen depths of the woods.

"You're here because this is where your family lived, eight years ago..." continued Alma, a sense of purposeful malice in her voice as she quietly played on his emotions, and what she'd heard from him.

"Don't push your luck, you..." snarled Mercury, his pitch-black hackles rising.

Alma chuckled, her eyes glinting.

"How are you liking your freedom, Mercury?" Alma changed the subject breezily, with her eyes unnervingly focused on him. She bowed her head slightly, still fixed on him as her fiery stare seemed to glitter. "Does the loneliness get to you?"

Mercury stepped from the shadows. His golden eyes were fixed angrily on her.

"You... You have no rightsssssssss to quessssssstion me on that!"

The burly mutant took a strike at her, but Alma stepped nimbly to one side, and watched his massive paw go sailing by.

"Of course I don't," Alma assured him cunningly. She took a delicate step forward. Mercury arched his back as though preparing to strike, his huge fangs parting to reveal the fleshy insides of his mouth and twin snake fangs unfurling. Then she examined her nails modestly, watching him out of the corner of her eye. "But then again... freedom of speech, and all that."

Mercury growled.

"No... Not here, you don't!"

"Who died and made you king?" Alma paused. "Oh, that's right." She glowered at him darkly, a smile curling up her lips. "...Your family did."

Mercury growled even louder.

"Now, if you'll excuse me... If you're not going to listen to my offer, then I have better things to do than talk to a half-crazed rattler."

Mercury leaped in front of her, and gave a hissing snap at her, forked tongue flicking.

"Tell me... but I Asssssssssure you. If it'ssssssssssss not worth my time, then I will kill you!"

"Good luck," said Alma bluntly then smirked lifelessly, her cold, cold eyes locked onto his.

"If you can do me one little favour, then I'll make sure you get the respect... and the freedom that you deserve."

"Go on..."

"Revenge, Mercury. Take revenge on those who promised you. And kill those who show fear."

***

I stare, stare darkly into the eyes of this persistent fiend. Who does she think she is? To follow me, follow me all this way, when all I want to do is return home. Here, it is here, and it has always been here. This is where I have lived since I was young. Eight years ago, my family was killed in the war.

How does this woman know that?

This demon woman? I have said naught but a word

194

in agreement to her plight, but she promised me freedom in return. My freedom led me home. This is freedom for me. How dare she deny that! How dare she know that which I've sought to hide.

She makes me offerings within her taunts. Her eyes are different from those of those dead humans back in the laboratory. Her eyes are fathomless, wise, unintelligible. Everything in them is distant, impossible to read. They are as green as pools of poison, and just as dark and deadly, too.

I must not falter, my step must stay strong.

It is like a battle of endurance. One of us will eventually break. And it will be her. My endurance is beyond that of any human. But for now, I must lay low.

I am Mercury, joined with the spirit of the wolf, grizzly bear, and the rattlesnake as well as my own.

And I will wait, skulk, stalk, slither through the shadows.

My time will come.

I will have my own way.

But for now, I'll lie in waiting, creeping ever closer. Through trust and through truancy, I'll manipulate.

As I slowly stand up, Alma smiles. She knows me too well. I can feel it, a jerking feeling deep in my gut.

It's a warning sign to me. But I don't show it.

Snorting in great breaths, I rise up and flex my claws. I hiss out in a voice that even I, myself, can barely understand. An indescribable voice that seems more a growl than words. But Alma understands. I can see it.

As I watch her, she turns, and begins to walk away, her feet gently clicking against the ashy ground. I watch her. She's expecting something. But she won't get it out of me. I back up several steps, then return, curling up amongst the ruins of my family. I'll leave when I'm sure that Alma is truly gone.

*I won't leave my family to rot away in the darkness.
No, not this time.*

-Chapter 14-

Stormclouds gathering

Clinging to Toby like an oversized burr, Danny asked the exhausted mutant question after question after question, even though with every answer, it was becoming increasingly clear that Toby wasn't in the mood.

"So, you're absolutely sure that it was a gun? How did she get into the laboratory in the first place? Do you think it was her who started the fire?" he pushed desperately, wanting to juice Toby of every little piece of knowledge that he had on the incident at all. "Do you want any more water, or food, or another tablet? Y-your coat's overflowing with them!"

Toby sighed in exasperation, his sickly-yellow eyes closed to the world.

"I don't know, I don't know, I don't know, and yes please!" he rasped huffily. Toby listened, his working ear pricking, as he heard Danny shuffling around in the shopping bag for what felt like the tenth time, then diving into his labcoat without a warning to get Toby's medication for him. Toby gave a tiny squeak of surprise.

"Ah, ha. Here we are, stuff, stuff, stuff, and more stuff... Bum, this one's out. Why do you keep so many empty boxes in there, Toby? It's like you hoard them or something." Danny laughed a little feverishly. Toby could tell that he was trying to brighten up the situation by making jokes that weren't even really jokes.

"O-oh, here we go. Heeeere comes the train, Toby! Ch-ch-ch-ch-woo-woo! Hey, Toby. Food here. Toby. Toby? Don't pull that face at me, dude..."

Toby laughed hoarsely.

"I suddenly feel a lot less hungry..."

"...Oh." There was a soft shuffling sound as Danny lowered his hand. Toby thought he could hear disappointment in his voice, but the half-panther didn't respond. He just turned away. There was a long, awkward silence flowed between them, with neither seeming willing to say anything. Toby felt a little guilty on the inside. Danny had tried his best, after all. But mostly, Toby was busy feeling quite sorry for himself. His ears drooped, and he curled his thick, black-furred tail around his knees.

Toby sighed. So did Danny.

"Danny?"

"Toby...?"

"I'm confused..."

"Why is that, Toby?"

Toby hesitated, twiddling with the fur on the tip of his tail. His eyes stared lifelessly into the distance.

"Why do you even bother with me? You'd probably be better off without..."

Danny silenced, seemingly to take the time to consider. Toby's heart sank. With every second that passed, it seemed to Toby that Danny was just seeing what he meant.

"I owe you, Toby. After all, I... I was the one that did this to you."

Toby whipped around, seeming startled. That wasn't what he'd been expecting to hear at all.

"You... What?"

Danny halted, and Toby settled down again, assuming that Danny had been startled by his sudden attitude.

"Toby... It's not what you think. I didn't know... At least, not until I met you. The scientists... They used me. They never showed me the experiments, or even the results. They just said that it was working, and to keep on developing it. So I did."

"How did you not know?"

There was silence. Toby frowned.

"Well?"

"Looking back, I guess I really should have guessed that something was wrong when various scientists and volunteers kept on disappearing."

Toby shrugged his shoulders stiffly, staring ahead with his blind cats' eyes. "Maybe you should have..."

Danny gave a soft, incoherent mutter. When he finally spoke, there was a break in his voice.

"There... There was one good thing that came out of it, though."

"Really...?"

"Yeah... You did."

"Me?" Toby's voice sounded disbelieving. He didn't seem to understand Danny's reasoning behind this at all.

"There was a time when you... You were the only thing that kept me going. You were the only one who trusted me, and... And that made me happy... You were like a brother to me, Toby... You were the brother that I always wanted... I'm sorry, Toby…"

Finally, Toby clicked. Though he couldn't see, finally it felt like he was seeing something as though it were actually there. What was it? It was like some age-old puzzle had just been solved, leaving Toby's mind crystal clear.

"Thank you...?" Toby tried to sound sincere, but instead, he sounded tentative, and unsure. He had no idea what was happening or how to feel. Here he was, with his guide, suddenly feeling happy, for the first time in ages. At last, Toby seemed to realize that he didn't need to be truly independent to be appreciated. People treated him like a child because he acted like one.

Toby's mouth opened slightly, but he closed it again a moment after. *Was I really that... That... Blind?*

"...Danny..."

Toby felt himself suddenly engulfed into a bear hug, Danny finally seeming to give in to the emotion.

"I'd reverse everything if I could, Toby, to make you happy again... I would. But I don't know if I'd want to... 'Cause then we'd never have met..."

It felt rather awkward here, to Toby, but Danny seemed like he was the happiest he'd ever been as he finally was able to pour out all of his emotions, and Toby could feel him quivering. He closed his mouth to keep himself from saying anything more. "Danny? Are you... Crying?"

"No... 'Course not. I'm sorry, Toby..."

"...It's alright, Danny..." Toby smiled to himself, shifting instinctively to look around as he heard high-heeled footsteps limping towards them. Danny let Toby go.

"Charlie," Toby heard Danny say. He sounded much happier, and less frantic, than he had earlier. Unfortunately, the same couldn't be said for the woman who Danny had called Charlie.

"Danny!" she sounded a bit panicked.

"What's up?"

"I brought you a change of clothes. You can't go down to town in a hospital robe."

"Eh? Down to town? I can't leave the kids and Toby!"

"Then they can come with us!" insisted Charlie. There was a rustle of papers as Charlie shoved something into Danny's arms. "Recognize it?"

"Durham attacked by supposed 'beast'? ...Oh my god."

Toby was intrigued.

"What's it say?"

"Hang on a sec, Toby. I'll read it out to you:

There have been stories of locals attacked by a so-called 'beast' or 'monster' that roams the Durham city streets at night. No previous reports or sightings have been found, save for last night's encounters, which sprung up in such amounts that the accounts are being investigated. After much examination of various reports, no photos have turned up, but the most common description is that the monster, whatever it is, possesses glaring, golden eyes, massive fangs, and in many reports, the tail of a dragon. It is said to look like a huge dog, or a werewolf, which has lead or researchers to believe that it may be something to do with stories of the goblin hound, the Bargheist, which is said to take the form of a giant black dog or a bear. Further details are being investigated, and victims of attacks are being examined for unusual symptoms and for the identity of their attacker. If you have any information on this beast or where it might have gone, then please call this number...

...That's about it for useful information. We can't let this happen!"

Toby swallowed. There was a sick feeling forming in his stomach.

"What's going on? Why is it so bad? How will you get me there?"

"This isn't just some beast, Toby- you remember that new mutant?"

"Mercury?!"

"Yeah, Mercury! It's him! He bit me, and he hurt Charlie! And the Laboratory...! He just..." Danny trailed off with a worried little squeak.

Toby was silent. He could hear, back nearby the ruins of the laboratory, the children as they played in the grass. Toby wondered if they'd ever had such a good time in their life. It felt strange, to be outside again. Danny and Charlie began to talk in hushed voices, discussing plans.

He heard Danny whisper; "but if Mercury's still alive, then that means..."

But Toby knew in his gut that something was about to turn sour.

***

Sally, Cassie, and Karasu yelped and barked happily as they chased each other around the small area that was available to them. It might not have been much to anyone else, but to them, it felt like a whole new world had just opened up. Sally and Cassie, their tongues lolling out as they tumbled over each other and through the grass, both looked back to yelp to the gold-haired boy who walloped along behind them.

"Can't catch us, Karasu!"

But the boy didn't seem to care about catching them. He was having a load of fun chasing them anyway, and to put a sudden stop to that would ruin all the fun. His tail was whirling like a propeller, and, now that he was in the outside world, then it seemed like he was trying to take off and go whistling away across the countryside.

Now *that* would be fun.

As Sally and Cassie finally broke Danny's comfort zone and bounded out onto the path, they skidded to a halt, almost tripping over Toby as he lay in the middle of the path, with Danny and Charlie standing nearby. Karasu bowled into them both, unable to stop in time. Sally and Cassie both fell like skittles onto Toby's stomach, and Karasu sat behind them, wagging his tail innocently as though he hadn't done anything wrong.

Toby gave a short gasp of shock and hissed, unable

to see what had bowled into him or why. Sally and Cassie cowered away, whimpering. Karasu snuffled friendlily at Toby's shirt and coat, as though he was expecting to find food in there somewhere, even though he'd already eaten what Charlie had brought for him.

"You're called Toby, right?" squeaked Sally and Cassie fearfully. "You're the one who poked Benny in the eye! Are you going to try to poke our eyes out, too, mister Toby?"

Toby sighed. "That... That was an accident," he said mournfully. "I didn't mean it, honest. You don't need to be scared of me..."

Sally and Cassie pawed at him, beginning to regain their confidence. "Rrf! You sound like Sally did when she had a cold!" barked Cassie. "You do! My voice went all weird!" agreed Sally, putting a paw to her throat. Their ears pricked.

Karasu, seeming to lose interest upon learning that there was no food, mooched about behind them, sniffing curiously at the ground and pawing at a small spider as it scampered over the path.

He ate it.

Then, licking his lips and pulling repulsed faces as if to rid his mouth of the strange taste, Karasu returned to sniffing about on the ground and pawing at the stones. He stuck his head in a patch of long grass and then poked his wet black nose through a gap in the fence. He looked out to the field beyond then began to squeeze his way through.

Sally and Cassie finally seemed to notice his efforts. "Oh, look, Karasu's noticed something! What is it, Karasu! Come back! Danny won't be pleased if you go missing!" they both piped up, bounding over to him. As Sally heaved the seven-year-old boy back through the fence despite his struggles, Cassie took to sniffing the ground around where Karasu had been.

"Sally, Sally!" she barked a minute later. Her cry not only attracted the attention of her sister, but the attention of Danny, Charlie, and Toby, as well.

"Cassie, Cassie!" replied Sally, bounding over to her sister. Karasu followed her, his tail wagging furiously again. He barked loudly, as if he was trying desperately to say something. "What is it? Can you smell what Karasu smelled?"

"I can smell a person!" barked Cassie, and her muzzle dropped down to investigate the ground beside her sister. "So can I! They don't smell anything like any of the scientists! They smell weird!"

They both returned to investigating.

Toby's face lit up, but he also looked slightly disappointed, as if he wished that whatever the pups smelled hadn't been there. Perhaps it had been so traumatic to him, that he wished it hadn't really happened. But having a point proven would always come with some kind of selfish streak of pride, no matter what.

"See!" Toby barked at Danny. "I told you so, I told you so, I told you so! Ha! She was here!"

Danny came jogging over to the dogs, who kept on sniffing. He looked bewildered. Danny shivered as though a cold breeze had just washed over him. His brown hair flowed slightly in a breeze.

"Who? This, Sabrina person who you were talking about?" he asked. Toby nodded, a stubborn grin painting his face. "I never doubted you for a moment, Toby."

"Sure you didn't."

All the while, Sally, Cassie and Karasu kept on sniffing. Karasu was beginning to bark at them again, his large, brown puppy eyes flashing at them in what seemed, to Danny, like a hint of desperation. "What is it, Karasu?" he asked warily, moving to pat the boy's

204

head. Karasu shied away, and pawed at the ground, then barked at him again loudly. "Shh, Karasu! You'll wake the entire city."

Karasu began to dig his claws into the ground, and didn't stop barking desperately. Getting nowhere, Karasu finally lifted his face, and gave a fairly agonized howl. Danny tensed up, but he still didn't seem to understand. Karasu had never howled before.

Trailing off, the dog-boy panted at him, then lay down and sulked on the path. Sally and Cassie were still sniffing desperately, and they didn't seem to be giving anything up. Danny's mind suddenly seemed to click onto something.

"Sally, Cassie, what are you still sniffing for?"

Karasu perked up, and jumped up onto his four paws, his round face glimmering up at them. Sally took a final, deep whiff of the scent trail, then straightened up and stared wide-eyed at Danny.

"Danny, can't you smell it?!" she yelped, and Cassie straightened up too, and barked. "Yeah, Danny, can't you?"

"Smell what? You guys, my sense of smell isn't as good as yours, I've told you time and time again..."

"We forgot!"

"So, what was it?"

"We do recognize the smell, Danny! It was in the laboratory before!"

"But it smelled different then, didn't it Cassie?"

"Yeah, yeah Sally! It did!"

"Why didn't you tell us before?!"

"We thought it was meant to be there. Otherwise, the humans would have known something."

"How is it different? Does it smell of blood or something?" Danny sounded, and looked, a trifle desperate by now.

"No, Danny! There's no blood!"

"We can smell that big, scary monster that was in the laboratory before, the one that tried to hurt you."

"Mercury? Riiight..."

"Also, also! That's not all, Danny? Right, Cassie?"

Karasu had begun to quiver and tremble with anticipation.

"What else is there?"

"We'll need to tell Bethany that she doesn't need to worry anymore! We can do that! And then maybe then she'll be nicer to you again, Danny! And then, she'll play with us too!"

"Yeah, Cassie! And she'll be happy!"

Karasu barked in agreement, and rolled over onto his back, wriggling and waving his legs in the air. Danny's gaze was absolutely fixed on the excited twins.

"What makes you think that she'll be happy again, you two...?"

Sally and Cassie hugged each other close, dancing around and around on the tips of their toes with glee. Their tails wagged, wagged, and wagged like little whirlwinds.

"The smell isn't all that strange person or the monster, Danny!"

"No! There's different smells mingled in with it, and they all make it up!"

"It's mostly just that strange person, but there's another smell there too!"

"Its faint, but we know it's there, because it is? Right, Sally?"

"Yeah, Cassie! Karasu could smell it too!"

"It's Emerald!"

"Emerald isn't dead, Danny!"

-Chapter 15-

Into The Blue

Emerald was sitting, all by herself. She was huddled into a little ball, cuddling up into the soft sheets of a blanket as though it were armour, and it was the only protection she had from the outside world, from which she huddled fearfully away. Her soft, blue-tinted toes wriggled beneath the blankets, and her wings were pressed against her back and each other.

She waited for something, as she stared out into the darkness. There were no windows in here, and Alma had turned off the light so that Emerald could sleep. Emerald hadn't mentioned to Sabrina that she was afraid of the dark. Back home in the laboratory, Bethany had served as a protection from the dark, and her best friend's soft tail fur had warded away bad dreams. But here, the blanket was the only protection Emerald had. As she curled up into it, Emerald pretended, closed her eyes and tried to con herself that this blanket was Bethany, and that Bethany would protect her, as always, from the cold.

But it was difficult. Every time she closed her eyes, she heard a noise that would snap her back into her senses with a jolt, causing her to huddle down even further into the blankets with a sob. Compared to Bethany, the blanket was cold, and it didn't breathe out comfortingly warm breaths as it slept curled up about her. Sniffling softly, Emerald pulled the blanket even tighter around her, but it didn't feel any warmer, or any softer, like the fur that she so loved to cuddle up to as she slept.

Quivering there in the darkness with her eyes

glinting in the little light that gleamed through the crack in the door, Emerald wondered how humans slept like this every night. *I wouldn't like to sleep like this every night... I wanna go home, back to Bethany, and Daddy, and the others.*

Thinking that she heard something again as another sound echoed from outside the room that Sabrina had given her, Emerald squeaked, and buried herself in the blanket again with only the tip of her feathered antenna peeping out. As soon as Emerald realized, she sucked it back into the space under the blanket with a sharp whip of her head. She didn't want to lose her other antenna.

Waiting with bated breath as she struggled to listen for more sounds, Emerald flinched and tensed as she heard another sound, and pulled the covers even tighter around herself. She heard the clop-clop of high heeled boots on the wooden floor, and she cowered down even further, holding in her breath.

Peeping out of a little peephole in the blankets, Emerald was almost blinded as the door opened, and a bright light shone on her face. She covered her eyes with her hands as though to hide, and gave a soft cry of fear.

Then, from the light, there came a soft, gentle, and familiar voice.

"Oh, Emerald, dear... What are you doing all wrapped up in there, eh? Making yourself a little den, are you?"

Emerald threw the blankets from her form all in a hurry, and her fragile, kaleidoscopic wings fluttered as she dashed over to Sabrina, her arms wrapping around and clinging to the woman as high up as she could reach. Emerald buried her face in Sabrina's clothes, her heart pounding. Tears began to gush from Emerald's eyes.

"Oh, Emerald... Were you frightened?" asked

Sabrina kindly, lifting the small girl into her arms.

Emerald hugged into Sabrina's chest, her aquamarine tail curling about Sabrina's arm. Emerald nodded, too choked up with tears to speak, and buried her face in the woman's shoulder. Her tears soaked into the woman's clothes, and her tremors were soothed only by the caress of Sabrina's fingers, and the touch of her gentle voice to Emerald's ears.

"Shhh... Come, come, Emerald..." Sabrina whispered, gently stroking the dragonfly girl's hair. "I'm back now... There's no need to be scared anymore..."

Emerald looked up, her eyes all teary and dark. Those eyes, the pupils like glistening black diamonds, locked onto Sabrina's stunningly floral eyes. For several seconds, Emerald lingered, until finally, she rested her head down on Sabrina's shoulder, and sniffed softly to herself. Her eyes closed, and Emerald finally relaxed as Sabrina began to gently rock her, back and forth.

"What were you afraid of, Emerald?" asked Sabrina softly, when Emerald seemed too have finally calmed down. Emerald was silent. Sabrina watched her, her keen eyes picking up on something.

"Oh, Emerald..." she asked softly. "Are you afraid of being alone? Or was it just the darkness, sweetie?"

Emerald stayed silent for a further few seconds more. Then, she finally spoke up, her voice a hushed whisper, as though deep inside, she were still just as scared as before. "Both..." she whispered, looking up at Sabrina. The woman looked sympathetic.

"Aw, Emerald... You know, you have nothing to fear, here... I'll always be there with you." Sabrina smiled. Emerald was glad that her face wasn't still covered by that scary mask. Delicately, Emerald reached up, and began to trace the scar on Sabrina's face with her fingers, as though she was a little fairy trying to heal the old wound.

"Always, Sabrina...?"

"Always, Emerald. You'll never have to be alone again. I promise."

Emerald paused, seeming a lot happier. Sabrina continued to smile at the girl as she carried Emerald out of the little bedroom that she'd been given to stay in.

Sabrina gently placed Emerald on the cosy couch that occupied her living room. With the heaters blasting and a warm candlelight flickering in the mostly traditional looking little setting, it felt a lot warmer, and more homey, in here. "Have you ever had hot cocoa, dear?" asked Sabrina tenderly, watching Emerald as she got herself comfortable on the sofa.

"No, Sabrina..." said Emerald politely, though she looked quite confused. "What is it?"

"It's a drink, Emerald. It helps to warm you up when you're cold, and lighten up your spirits, when you're down." Sabrina smiled, and stood up. "I'll make one for you."

Emerald nodded and smiled, her eyes glimmering. She looked eagerly up at Sabrina, and a smile lit up her face as Emerald stood and made to follow. She, having spoken quite enough before, said nothing.

Sabrina raised her eyebrows.

"Do you want to come help me, Emerald?" she asked with a smile. Emerald flashed her pretty crystalline wings, and clasped her hands together as she nodded. Sabrina stretched out her hand. Emerald grinned happily, and smiled up at Sabrina as she took her hand.

"Come on, then!" called the woman sweetly, leading Emerald after her into the hallway, and into the kitchen. Sabrina gently lifted Emerald into her arms, and placed her so that she was sitting on the tabletop. Sabrina bustled about, filling the kettle with water and twinkling brightly as she showed Emerald what she was doing. Emerald, having never really seen many aspects of normal life before, watched in fascination, nodding at every sentence Sabrina said, even when she didn't understand.

"Ah-ha! Here we go..." Sabrina approached Emerald eventually as she proudly brandished a tray laden with two mugs. Emerald sniffed. Even that rich, sweet smell that had suddenly appeared was pleasing to her. The little girl dangled her legs over the edge of the table, and reached out with both hands. Sabrina took one mug in her hand and held it out for Emerald, and Emerald took hold of the warm surface and looked astounded. She raised the mug to take a sip, but with a gentle gesture of her hand, Sabrina stopped her.

"Careful you don't burn yourself," she said with a smile. "Blowing on it will make it a bit cooler." Emerald nodded, and obediently blew away some of the steam. Her eyes widened as she watched the wisp fade into the air. Emerald smiled up at Sabrina as she finally took a sip, her glistening eyes smiling up at Sabrina. The child smiled as the warmth flowed through her body, and licked her lips as the sweetness flowed over her tongue. She gave a happy shiver.

Sabrina took a sip of her own hot chocolate, even as her own floral green eyes watched Emerald expectantly. She swallowed before speaking. "Well? How is it?" she asked gently, stroking Emerald's hair with a finger. Emerald nodded eagerly. "It... It's so nice! It's so warm, too!"

Sabrina smiled. "It's meant to be..." there was silence between them both as they contentedly gulped down their hot chocolates. Eventually, each of the mugs was completely empty, and Emerald's eyelids were drooping tiredly. Emerald snuggled up to Sabrina.

A wide yawn parted her lips.

Sabrina smiled down at her.

Emerald smiled tiredly back, before snuggling up closer and folding her wings. Sabrina held her close, and Emerald felt, for what seemed like the first time since she'd arrived here, safe.

"We'll go out and look for your friends when you wake up in the morning. Alright?"

Emerald listened. She smiled.

"Yes, Sabrina. Thank you, Sabrina..."

Just before she began to drift, Emerald thought she caught the flash of a glimmer in Sabrina's eyes.

***

"Yeeeaaaaaoooow!"

Charlie whipped about as she heard a piercing howl cut through the air.

Is that Toby...? she wondered to herself, and was quickly answered by the sight of Toby and Danny nearby. Danny had changed his clothes since before and now seemed utterly determined to bring everyone with him into town, no matter what. The children could follow. Toby couldn't.

"Yaaaaeeeeergh! Put me doooown!"

Charlie didn't think that she'd ever heard Toby be so loud. His voice was usually quiet and thoughtful, if ever he spoke at all. Toby quite rarely vocalized his thoughts with such intensity. Now, Danny was standing trying desperately to calm a struggling Toby, whom he'd slung over his shoulder. Danny's legs quivered under the weight. It was clear that people weren't on the list of objects that Danny often had to lift.

"But we agreed to this!" gasped out Danny, wobbling and teetering on his toes as he struggled to hang onto Toby.

"Not to fling me around like an old sack! Lemme go!" Toby continued to struggle, and then he began to flail his arms, whipping his tail about. Danny was soon having to deal with the new obstacle of curious puppies and bunnies and feathery toddlers, and almost tripped over them all once as he staggered.

"Stoppit, Toby, I'm gonna fall!" he called out a little desperately. Toby was too stubborn to stop, though, and it wasn't long before Danny toppled over.

Toby gave another sudden, shocked hiss as Danny landed sprawled across Toby's stomach, pinning Toby down and rendering him even less mobile than he usually would be. Danny was winded, and he lay there for a few extra moments before struggling to sit up around Toby.

Charlie couldn't help but snicker softly as the shamed, embarrassed man sulked his way over to her. She forced herself to keep a straight face, though. Charlie watched him closely as he sighed, forced a smile, and looked up at her.

"So... Do you think you could take Toby in the car? Could he... You know, stay at your house for a day or two?" he asked her. There was a feeble kind of hope in his voice. "It's not like he can walk anywhere by himself."

Charlie nodded reluctantly. He did have a point, but Charlie wasn't expecting a calm reaction from her husband and Annie if she just happened to turn up home with a newcomer in hand who wanted to stay with them for a while. Especially as that newcomer had cats' ears and a tail. That being said, how would Toby react to them?

Shaking all thoughts of foreboding from her mind, Charlie smiled. "That's fine, Danny," she finally stated, looking over at Toby, who was sprawled on his back, surrounded by some of the other young mutants. He'd finally managed to convince Ginny and Benny to hold his hands, the soft paws of the sweet little creatures clinging tightly to him.

When Charlie looked back to Danny, he was already scurrying away back to Toby in order to comfort him. She followed with the rap-tap of her heels stepping lightly across the overgrown dirt-path. Danny, having bent down to speak to Toby, was finally rewarded with the satisfaction of seeing Toby smile despite the slight forced hint behind it.

Suddenly, Charlie's mind seemed to click. She realized something. "Danny...?" she asked cautiously. "Where will you go?"

Danny looked towards her. "We'll be walking."

Charlie frowned.

"We? You and the kids?"

"Yup. It's not that far into town. You can see the cathedral from here, look!"

"What will you do if someone asks about them?" It was clear that Danny was considering getting there rather than how they would explain to people when they got there.

"I could say that we're on our way to a fancy dress party!"

"A fancy dress party with very realistic costumes, where they all hoot and yip?"

"Not all of them hoot and yip. Ginny squeaks, and Joey caws, remember?" Danny corrected her knowingly.

Charlie stared at him disbelievingly, wondering if he was really trying to make some sort of joke at a time like this. He looked deadly serious. She gave a soft, almost hopeful, snicker.

"You're bluffing, right? You can't expect people to actually believe that."

"Hey," grumbled Danny irritably. "I can get them to

act in character... Now are we going or what? I'm gonna need help putting Toby in the car."

Charlie sighed, nodding hopelessly.

"Why don't you just go in with him?"

"You can't fit eleven people in one car!"

Well, that settles it, then... thought Charlie, watching Danny disapprovingly as he began to scoop up Toby into a baby-carry, rousing slightly less complaints than before. *He does have a point...*

"Alright, let's go then!" he said eagerly. The children skipped along happily after him, and even Bethany had a spring in her step; it was clear that she was eager to find Emerald.

Toby peered off curiously into nothingness as his tail dragged along the ground when Danny moved. He looked quite heavy to carry, but Danny seemed to be managing just fine, and seemed to almost bounce up the path; the sooner they left, the sooner they could find Mercury.

Charlie walked calmly after him, before breaking into a jog to catch up.

When they reached the car, the children seemed absolutely fascinated by it. Some cowered, some went leaping right on up to tap on the windows or on the sides. Moony was already climbing up onto the roof before Danny noticed him and scolded him to come down lest he end up scratching it. Each spouted their own theories of what this mysterious thing was and why it was here.

"Is this a tree, too?"

There was a click as the doors slid open with the push of a button, and they all jumped, squeaked, and hid behind one another.

"It's going to gobble us all up!" yelped Ginny, peeping out from behind Joey.

"No it isn't... Calm down, you little things... This

thing just takes people from place to place, alright? It's nothing to be afraid of, look. It can't even move until someone's in it!" Danny assured them gently. They all peeped closer, and watched as Danny placed Toby comfortably in one of the seats. Charlie smiled, and climbed in after him, making sure that the seatbelts were nicely fastened about Toby's chest and waist.

"If you want to, I'll meet you down by the marketplace?" Danny asked. "Just make sure Toby's settled and everything first. Plus, do you have anything that Toby could use as crutches? He probably won't be too happy to just sit about all day."

Charlie thought for a minute, but couldn't think of anything that she might have.

"I... I'm sure I'll find something," she said, not wanting to dash their hopes. Danny smiled happily, seemingly put at peace thanks to that.

With a farewell grin on her face, Charlie slid closed the doors with a click and a tap of a button, and watched Danny as he gathered the ranks of experiments close to him. "Take me home," she said in a loud, clear voice, and an automated voice replied to her.

"Destination added. Home."

Electricity whirred softly and the engine purred with pleasure as the car began to move.

Charlie turned around to peer out of the window and watch the world whiz by after them, and she saw Danny, watching her as she left them behind. She saw him wave, then without a word, he turned around and began to guide the children like he had guided Toby. They followed behind him in a little huddle at the side of the road as he began to stride towards the tall spire that acted like a beacon, lighting their way to the grand city of Durham.

-Chapter 16-

Facing Fear

"So, Charlie… Who's this?"

Charlie's husband looked over Toby, the unexpected visitor, with a judgingly unimpressed eye. Toby was sprawled out in the back of her car, and, despite having been strapped in by a seatbelt, seemed to have had quite a bumpy ride. At least Charlie had agreed to do the talking for him.

"This is Toby," said Charlie, with a hint of awkwardness in her voice. "He's going to be staying with us for a while, Bailey."

Bailey's face turned into a little bit of a frown. Everything following this so-called 'disaster' was, in his eyes, taking things a bit too far. Charlie hadn't even told him what had happened! Just that there were a couple of survivors, and that they needed some looking after. He hadn't thought this was what she'd meant. Taking a soft breath, he took a hold of Charlie's arm in his hand.

"Toby," he began politely. "If you'll excuse me, I need to have a little chat with our Charlie here."

One of Toby's ears slowly, slyly turned towards him. Though his eyes were closed as though in meditation, Toby gave a soft nod in response.

Bailey smiled, and they both moved away until they both assumed they were out of earshot. Toby, however, was pretty sure that he knew better. Taking soft breaths, he focused on them, feeling a little guilty for eavesdropping, but pleased with himself all the same.

"Charlie, we can't have him stay here… There's barely any room as it is!"

"No matter what you say, there's even less room in the laboratory."

"Oh, and how many more people are going to turn up after him, eh?"

"You should consider yourself lucky. I could have brought the other nine." Charlie looked at her husband with sternness in her deep brown eyes.

"Why didn't you?"

"The others all have other places to be."

"What about Toby?"

"He's blind and crippled, and he'd only act as a hindrance to them. He wouldn't be able to stand up to whatever's running amok in the city."

Bailey searched for another excuse, but was unable to find any. Finally, he just trundled shamefacedly off back towards the car as Charlie waited for him. Suddenly though, he stopped and turned to look back towards her.

"Charlie?" he asked, sounding a little bit hesitant.

"Dear?"

"You've never really told me much about the experiments at the laboratory before…"

"Yeah…? And…?" Charlie sounded somewhat wary. "What do you want to know?"

"This… 'Toby'… person. Did he…? They…?" Bailey's voice trailed off into silence as he tried to find some way to speak his mind.

"What? Did they experiment on him?" Charlie's voice cracked a little bit and she found herself sounding sharp. Bailey flinched. Charlie made her way over, and gave him a huge hug, and a kiss on the cheek. "I'm sorry, hubby…"

Bailey grunted, and hugged her back. "It's okay. You got what I meant," he said bluntly. "So, did they?"

Charlie nodded, and finally seemed as though she was admitting the truth to herself. This truth felt like the blow of a knife.

"Yeah... He was the only survivor."

Bailey grunted again, and Charlie wondered if she was squeezing him too tightly. She let go, but Bailey kept his grip around her.

"Bailey?" She asked softly. He didn't reply, but his grey-coloured eyes turned towards her.

"Can you bring Toby inside? I'm going to need to tell our daughter that we have a visitor." Finally, Bailey let go of her. He nodded with his firm face then gave her a comfortingly warm smile. It seemed strange but, for all his flaws, and all the efforts he made to appear as tough and emotionless as he could, Bailey had a fair soft side, too. At least, towards her he did.

Charlie scurried away into the house, as Bailey slowly walked towards the car and lifted Toby from his seat. At first, Toby squirmed in protest, frightened by the lack of greeting, and the fact that he had no idea who was picking him up. His yellow eyes flashed for a moment, and he swung his tail and yowled.

"Shh-! Stop wriggling, you- er... Whatever your name is! Tommy, Tabby... Oh, Toby! That's it!" he began, sounding frustrated. "Toby, I'm not here to hurt you!"

Toby finally stopped in his relentless struggles, seeming tired out by all the effort, and turned his head so that his glazed eyes were staring right through bailey.

"You promise?" he asked harshly, voice cutting in his throat. Bailey felt a little bit sick. He sounded downright ill! He sounded terrible!

"Yeah, I promise. You're staying with us for a while. At least, until we find your family to take care of you..."

"Is that some kind of sick joke?"

Bailey fell silent. "No, no, no! Just forget I said

anything…" he grumbled, trying his best not to be intimidated by this blind man's hot-tempered attitude, or weakened by the injuries that had scarred him so long ago. Could he even still be classed as human?

The claws that gripped his sides desperately as Toby tried not to fall said otherwise. So did the two panther ears that perked from his pitch black hair and the rosette markings of fur that stood out blackly against his burning skin. The tail, the fur and those sickly yellow eyes. All of it told of some stealthy beast in the thick, thick forests. Long gone.

It was almost disgusting, but there was naught that Bailey could do but put up with it for now. After all… This man was a friend of his wife's. Or was he? Had she done that to him, all those injuries? And her words echoed thickly through his mind.

He was the only survivor…

That meant that there had been others. There had been others who had died. No, perhaps not died. They had been *killed*. But by what?

Bailey took a deep breath as he thought, but continued to carry Toby into their old, traditional house, slamming the door behind him with a nimble jerk of his foot. A frizzy-haired, blonde little girl came rushing down the stairs in response to the sound.

"Oh, Daddy! Is that the visitor?" she piped in a sweet, chiming voice, reaching out with pudgy hands. "Mammy said that he was weird. How weird is he, daddy?"

"Annie! That's not a very nice thing to say."

The little girl's hands went to her mouth, and her eyes, which were grey like Bailey's own, widened. "Oops!" she peeped. "I'm sorry, daddy!"

"Don't apologize to me, apologize to Toby!"

"To-by? Is that his name?" asked the little girl as she danced on her feet, her mop of hair bouncing along

220

with her. She craned her neck in an effort to see more than just Toby's hair. "Can I see, daddy? Does he want to see me? I'm here, Toby, you can talk to me!"

Annie waved her hand frantically, until Bailey gave her a stern look, and she squeaked again, hiding behind her hands. Toby groaned slightly. Perhaps he was getting a headache.

"Annie, he won't be able to talk to you unless you calm down, and let him sit down in the living room," Bailey told her calmly, and the child obediently hop, skipped, and jumped out of the way, her eyes round and eager.

"Thank you, Annie."

"You're welcome, Daddy!"

She twirled after Bailey as he finally emerged into the living room, and dumped Toby onto the largest couch so that he would be comfortable. Annie, seemingly not understanding the concept of 'comfortable' or even 'personal space', clambered up, and plopped herself down onto him, as though Toby was a seat. Toby tensed up, and gave a shrill yowl of pain, for the area that Annie had sat upon was a sensitive one.

"Annie!" Bailey scolded her in clear frustration, lifting the girl off of him, plonking her onto a different seat.

"You don't sit on people!"

Annie pouted angrily, shoving herself off of the couch and stamping her foot on the ground. "Daddy! That's *my* seat, and he's taking up *all* of it!"

"It's not *your* seat, Annie! Behave and be nice to Toby, or I'll send you to your room!"

Annie scowled darkly at them then scurried out of the room to try and get her mother on her side of the argument.

As that was done, Bailey turned to Toby, and

221

carefully seated himself at Toby's feet so that he wouldn't hurt him.

"Hey, friend… You okay after that?"

Toby stirred, gave a pained smile, and nodded.

"Is it making you want to have kids?"

"I wouldn't say that," said Toby politely.

"The truth?"

"It's making me feel quite comforted that I'm on my own."

"Heh… Well, you're not missing out on much, kid."

"I'm not a kid!"

"No? Wait… What?"

"I'm twenty-three!"

"You're still a kid to me!" Bailey laughed, stretched out and ruffled Toby's soft black hair. He chuckled as Toby pulled a face, then snickered softly, himself, but then Toby fell silent, the smile still sticking sadly to his face. He was silent for a while, and Bailey wondered if he was thinking. *What of?* he wondered.

"I'm sure you'll have a good time staying with us," Bailey said eventually, if only to break the uncomfortable silence that had settled like dust gathering over them.

Toby gave a small shrug and a chuckle, sickly-yellow eyes opening and fixing on the empty space before him. Eventually he bowed his head in a nod.

"I'm sure I will…"

Bailey looked up as he heard the sound of a closing door, and saw Charlie entering the room with a few metal pipes in her arms and a disgruntled Annie following after.

"What are those for?" asked Bailey.

Charlie tossed the pipes down onto the empty couch beside Toby, and they made a loud clattering sound, causing Toby's ears to twitch.

"Crutches," said Charlie breathlessly. "They'll do

for now, at least."

Toby struggled to sit up, and his eyes had begun to shine, his mood seeming to have gotten better since before. "Charlie!" he called, sounding pleasantly surprised, and quite eager. "You're a star!"

Charlie looked flattered for a second, but she shrugged off the compliment.

"Call me that when they're ready. I don't think they'll serve as proper crutches quite yet, and I have to go see how Danny and the kids are getting on."

Toby's face fell.

"When will they be ready?"

"Depends on how quick Bailey works." She turned to stare at her husband hintingly.

Bailey took the hint and gave her a sour look. "Could take a few hours…" he muttered to her.

"In which case," replied Charlie. "I'll be long gone by then."

Toby's paralysed limbs quivered as he tried to get them to work. "No! No, no, you can't go without me!" he protested. "Danny's nothing without me!"

He heard Bailey snicker.

Charlie wasn't put off.

"Toby," she began firmly, walking closer. "You'd only be a hindrance if you were there. I can take you there once it's all over and sorted out, but not straight away. Alright?"

Toby was already shaking his head, gripping at the sofa with his claws as he tried to haul himself up despite everything.

"No! I'm not gonna stand back and hear people banter on all their tales of glory afterwards when I could have been there with my guide! I'm not completely helpless, I'll show you!"

He struggled off of the chair and onto the floor, but then felt Charlie taking him by the shoulders and starting to heave him back up. The tips of his toes dragged on the ground uselessly, even as his tail and arms flailed helplessly. He struggled against her iron grip.

"Get off!" he protested.

"Not until you're back where you should be."

Their voices sounded almost malicious to Toby, as if it was their fault and theirs alone, that he couldn't do this. It was like they were somehow enjoying that fact. And yet, he wanted to do something that would be a shock to those around him. Independence didn't matter, not as long as he managed something. One tiny thing.

"No! Lemme go! I have to get out, I have to!"

No response.

Toby continued to struggle, shouting like an irritable little child as he tried to writhe his way to freedom.

"You're not listening to me!"

"You're the one not listening to *us*!"

"Oh, so now *I'm* the one in the wrong!?" Toby wailed childishly. "Let go of me!"

And this time, they did. Toby plummeted towards the floor, and smacked down on his face. He hadn't quite realized how far off of the ground he was. It was lucky that they had a carpet rather than a wooden floor, but it still hurt quite a bit.

For a while, Toby lay there, winded. Then he slowly lifted his head, and grimaced. He tried to push himself up. Onto his knees, onto his back, anything. But he couldn't. He needed help, but he just couldn't admit it. He gave a mighty heave, and strained to get up. Struggled to make any sort of a difference.

"Well?" asked Charlie impatiently. "What are you waiting for?"

"If you can get up, get up!" snapped Bailey.

Toby tried again, pressing his palms into the ground and digging in his claws. He ground his sharp teeth

224

together, and managed to shift up his chest. His tail thumped against the ground, and Toby turned around to try to use his hands to drag his legs into a more manageable position. In the end, Toby slumped back onto the ground, all in a heap.

"…Just as I thought," said Charlie.

"You're completely helpless."

**

About ten minutes into their much-longer-than-it-should-have-been journey, the heavens opened up on the little group as they made their way down to town. The children had never seen rain before in their lives and at first, it was all a game to them as they pranced and bounced and tried to catch the droplets as they fell. The novelty wore off after a while, though, and they ended up hugging into a tight little group together, whining and whinging at Danny as if he could make it stop.

They were all cold and wet and whiny, and they didn't like it one bit, oh no. Even though they wanted very much to stop and find shelter and he, too, was rather sodden, Danny was absolutely determined to get to where they needed to go before resting.

"Hup-hup! Come on, you guys! Faster we move, the quicker we'll get there!" he exclaimed cheerily, clapping his numb hands together. The experiments looked up at him and gathered together in a tight little huddle. Thunder roared and lightning flashed high above them, and the children cowered away from the baying thunderclaps and the hunting arcs of lightning that soared above the city. "There's nowhere to go but forward!"

The youngest children each gathered around him and fought with each other to hold Danny's hand. It

225

was unclear to Danny whether he should feel loved or annoyed. As they started to get a little out of control in their bickering, Danny shook some water from his hair, and bent down to call out to them over the howling winds. "Hey!" he grumbled, pulling Moony and Bethany from each other. Karasu shook water from himself, and all the muddied puddle water and car pollution spattered in Danny's face. It tasted horrible. "No fighting, okay!? We're halfway there!"

"But we've been walking for ages!" hooted Moony.

"We need to find Emerald, Too!" replied Bethany, agreeing with Danny. "So we can't stop!"

Another arc of lightning forked across the sky, and they all flinched and stared upwards as it gave its ghostly cry of thunder long after vanishing. As the echoes of thunder faded away, the children's bickering returned, and with a vengeance. Trying as he might to intervene, Danny went unheard above the pattering rain and the thunderclaps that rang out through the sky.

The argument never got to reach its conclusion, though, for as another arc of lightning shot across the sky, a figure that had skulked towards them, engulfed in shadow was lit up. It hunched there for a while, and as the lightning's blaze faded away, it faded back into the unseen. Golden eyes flashed in the darkness, once. The bickering experiments calmed, frozen in fear. Their eyes flickered around, back and forth, and everyone was afraid to turn for fear that whatever hid in the shadows before them might finally emerge.

Finally, Joey spoke, his eyes locked on the shadows

"Did... Did anyone else see that?" he asked softly, backing away, just one step.

"See what?"

"I thought I... Saw something moving...?"

"Shhh!" hissed Danny.

Sally and Cassie lifted their muzzles and began to

sniff, but all the smells were drowned out by the scent of rain.

There was silence, apart from the drumming of the rain. Slowly, Danny plucked up the courage to begin to walk forward again. The experiments began to whisper amongst themselves. The pathway slowly faded into view before them as they walked, but there was nothing else. Danny gave a hoarse, nervous laugh.

"I guess we... We were just imagining it," he comforted, seeming to relax a little bit. The thunder roared again, as though it were laughing at them all, and their foolishness. They all heaved small sighs of relief.

But then they felt it.

A feeling different to before.

It wasn't like the cold, cold rain, or the wind beating against them.

No.

This was the feeling of hot breath on their necks. The feel of being hunted, the predator bearing down, clasping cold claws about you in the darkness.

Danny whipped about, and the experiments turned. Karasu began to howl to the skies in a rarely-heard chorus of despair and fear. Sally and Cassie joined in the eerie song, and the thunder's drumming served as a deep base line for the three dogs' song. The others were paralysed, all in a quiver, as they stared up and met those eyes.

Those golden eyes that belonged to none other than Mercury.

"Mercury..." whispered Danny. Half in terror, and half in a horrified fascination.

Mercury had skulked around them, so that he was at their backs, too close for comfort. Now he was crouched, silhouetted against the lightning, his golden snake eyes gleaming with every flash. His fur was slicked down by the rain, but water still poured from the glistening scales of his back and tail. The sound of his rattle trembling mingled with the sound of the rain as it poured from the heavens. His forked tongue flicked out to taste the droplets as they fell.

Danny, finally plucking up the courage to move, walked around and planted himself in front of Mercury so that the children were behind him. "I'm not letting you touch them…" he spat, venom in his voice, a burning acid that could not be neutralized.

The experiments peered out from behind him, wanting to get in on the action, but at the same time frightened to do anything. Mercury brought back to them quite frightening memories. As one of them tried to move forward at last, Danny spread his arms, both to keep the mutants behind him, and to keep Mercury from advancing.

"So you can turn around and go, or else you'll have to face me!"

Mercury's forked tongue flicked over his moist black lips. Danny watched warily, for he could see something in his eyes, something that seemed to say "oh, goody, a main course, as well!". He knew that, when up against this hulking beast, his words sounded feeble and foolish. But he stuck to them anyway, even as Mercury advanced, just by a single step, his claws rasping on the sodden ground.

"I'm warning you!" yelled Danny over the thunder, and the sound of the pouring raindrops.

Mercury continued to creep towards him. In a quick-footed and daring move, Danny gave a short yell, and then leaped forward, punching Mercury in the nose with barely a muffled *thunk*, after which he accidentally cut himself on one of the beast's fangs. Mercury seemed a little surprised, but other than a little bit of a graze on his pride, Mercury was uninjured.

228

It seemed as though that was the last straw. With a barely audible hiss to threaten them, Mercury leaped forward, and Danny reflexively pulled back in fright. The mutant's jaws snapped shut on empty air, where Danny's hand had been a moment before.

It was then that something quite phenomenal happened.

Danny hadn't noticed Karasu edging forward beneath his arm to stand beside him before, and now, with his short teeth bared and his hair and clothes sticking to his body with the rain, Karasu stood up, his tail raised and rigid. He shot Mercury a steely cold glare, a desire to protect his friends awoken that had never been seen before in the little puppy.

He was no longer the frightened little mouse that had failed in training mission after training mission and been accused of food theft by the scientists so many times. He wasn't even the soft soul that begged for cuddles and treats from his friends, begged with eyes that none could resist.

Now it was as though his puppy soul had become a lion's soul, his personality still that of a dog's. His loyalty was unwavering, and yet his sudden, newfound courage was what spurred him on.

Karasu didn't even seem to be thinking about what he was doing. He growled, he snarled, he planted his paws further apart the more Mercury advanced. Finally, as Bargheist grew too close for comfort, Karasu leapt. Mercury towered over Karasu, and his muscles were thicker, his fangs longer, and many, many times sharper. Then there was the threat of that deadly poison that inhabited Mercury's deadly fangs.

But Karasu regarded none of that.

He, himself, snapped just as viciously as Mercury did. His small size granted him a speed that allowed him to hurl himself out of the way of Mercury's swings and snaps, all the while biting and barking and clawing at Mercury's fur and ripping at his scales.

Any time Mercury turned towards the other mutants, Karasu would be there, biting and driving Mercury back away from them with all the effort he could muster into his flailing limbs and jaws. After what seemed like forever, Karasu and Mercury had drawn some distance away from them, and they circled each other. Karasu's claws were stained with blood, and he had scratch marks over his back, arms and one across his face, all of which dripped a steadily slowing stream of crimson onto the ground, only for it to be washed away in the rain.

Mercury, though, had some small wounds of his own to worry about. On the smooth snake scales of his spine, Karasu had managed to bite deep, and there were dark drops dripping from the fur of his underbelly, as well. They were both panting, tongues lolling out, as each waited for the other to tire.

It seemed like it would be Karasu, but he wasn't finished yet.

But, then again... neither was Mercury. He had seen enough of Karasu's fighting to see that there were many flaws in his defence, but those were all shoved aside by the younger boy's evasiveness. But there was one last resort. A fatal gap, that Mercury had seen.

Even as he circled, Mercury let nothing show on his face, in his eyes, or in his fanged muzzle.

Around, and around, and around, they went. Chasing each other's tails, eyes locked.

Then, Mercury turned. He broke away, and headed straight towards the other mutants. Claws outstretched, he went for them.

Karasu followed, and he leaped, and his eyes danced in sudden despair. In a final effort, Karasu grabbed onto the flesh of Mercury's neck with his claws and sank in his short teeth. There he stayed, chewing, shaking, tearing away. Mercury briefly, in quite shocked a state, tried to blindly shake him off, but Karasu, swinging like a mad pendulum, held on tightly and continued to chew, bite and rip.

Karasu was faster than Mercury had thought, and more desperate, too.

Finally coming to his senses, Mercury reared up like a mighty stallion, his fur flying and his rattle crying. With his barbed hands, he ripped Karasu from the flesh of his neck, the younger boy tearing a chunk of flesh off with him. Mercury roared in anger and pain, then, without even thinking, bit down. His fangs sank into Karasu's tender body, and Mercury tasted blood on his tongue. He dropped down onto all fours, then shook for all he was worth. Karasu cried out in pain, struggling to get free, then going limp. Finally, Mercury gave Karasu a final whip, and hurled him. The boy went flying, not even seeming to realize what was happening to him. There was a sickening thud as Karasu hit the wooden fence positioned nearby, then he sank limply to the floor with nary a shudder, leaving stains of crimson on the wood.

Mercury watched his adversaries for a few moments more, and blood poured from his wounds onto the ground with every passing moment. Thunder still roared overhead, and lightning flashed, illuminating the grisly scene in a heavenly silver light.

As soon as one of the mutants made another move, however, Mercury stepped back. In his eyes, he'd done all he'd needed to. He was undefeated, but he couldn't fight another. Not yet. His time would come later. Slowly, Mercury backed away, then turned and retreated back up the path, the way he'd come.

Before anyone could stop him, he'd vanished into the rain-slicked shadows.

But Karasu couldn't see him any longer.
His eyes were closed.

-Chapter 17-

Responsibility

Alma was sitting alone in her 'study' room, her gaze flicking back and forth over the different monitors that she used to work, and contact home. Two soft, wireless earpieces made it almost impossible to tell that she was listening to something elsewhere, and a small stud that looked almost like a piercing on the side of her mouth was the only little microphone she wore.

Words flashed over each of the monitor screens that Alma watched, and her eyes scanned and flicked over each of them, taking in every word and absorbing it like a sponge. Soft grunts and mutters of concentration were the only real sounds she made as her hands flicked energetically over the keyboard. And yet, she seemed, for some reason, unusually tense.

Was it because of Emerald?

…No, it couldn't be.

Emerald was in the living room eating her way through a large box of sweets that Alma had given her and fiddling about with a jigsaw and some toys of different farmyard animals. From the futuristic TV screen, cute puppies and kittens chased each other about Emerald, and she watched them with glee, trying to catch the prancing little ghosts as they went on adventures and invited Emerald to join them.

She should be kept busy for a while yet.

Alma thought and thought, waited, and watched, concentrating on the numbers and codes as they flashed, typing in some of her own whenever the need arose. Eventually, she sniffed, lay back in her office chair, and wiped her nose with the back of her hand as she examined her nails casually.

I can't leave this here room until I get the call... might as well think about it for a while. So she thought, her thoughts winding over and over things that could cause this unusual lapse in concentration. As she thought, Alma hummed softly to herself, tracing the patterns of the wallpaper on the ceiling as she considered.

Finally, something seemed to stroke her. She lowered her hand back down onto her lap, and sucked at her teeth curiously.

Is that it? Hm, sounds about right, she snickered inwardly to herself. *Because I went and took that dude back to where he was meant to be, that makes me a traitor. Hm! I shoulda' just left him to die... No matter what, he'll go down with this puny lil' country anyway. It's the same everywhere.*

Cruelly considering to herself, Alma waited, and waited, thoughts of all she could have slyly done trickling in through her head. *Couldn't have killed him too violently or with high tech equipment... That would have made it obvious. Maybe I could have made it look like he got mauled by a stray dog or two...* she thought to herself, amused. *Even better, place the blame on that poor, hapless doggy who just so happens to believe every promise I make him. I'll show you true freedom, alright, you foul beastie!*

Alma tested the blade of an ancient knife on the tip of her finger. These days, only the poor used knives. The perfect excuse to use them herself. In some ways, Alma was quite an old fashioned spy. She tricked people to use them to her own devices, often used weapons that were well out of date, and she often used her own hands to muck up the enemy's security devices, rather than using hacking devices.

What's the point in overdoing it? Alma thought. *I'm*

not meant to be doing anything more than my job.

Speaking of my job...

Alma was plucked out of her thoughts and tossed back into reality as an irritating ringing sound suddenly set up through her ears.

Reaching forward, she gave the keyboard a bored sort of rap, then leaned back in her chair, resting her heels on the desktop even though a stern face appeared on the monitor above her. She stared at the figure then rolled her eyes back.

"Good afternoon, sir. It's about time you called."

"That's rather rude, Alma... Please address me with the proper respect due."

"Yes, sir."

"Any updates on progress, Alma?"

"The laboratory is destroyed, and they don't suspect a thing," mumbled Alma airily.

"Good, good. What is your next move?"

"Anything you want, sir."

"This could be the breakthrough we need, then. I think it's time to put our efforts into action, Alma."

"Which efforts do you mean, sir? I feel I've put in enough effort already.,."

"That attitude of yours isn't going to get you anywhere, Alma..."

"It got me a fair position in the war, sir, and if you don't mind me saying, I'm in my house, now. I can say whatever I want to say," she said smugly.

"You're only there because we put you there. I can take it away with a flick of my wrist..."

Alma laughed.

"Truly? You really think that you're gonna find anyone else like me? Oh, and what are you going to do with them, then, eh? Send them into enemy territory and wait, what, fifteen years to find a weakness?"

Her boss flinched. Alma leaned back calmly. "My

235

my, it seems as though I've struck a nerve..."

There was silence.

"So," she continued, heartless and calm. "My orders?"

The man on the screen cleared his throat, and puffed out his chest grandly.

"Ah, yes. Your orders."

Alma stared at him, her gaze piercing.

"You are to give England a warning. Show them the power of your home country. If there are any survivors from the laboratory, assure that they, and their research, do not survive."

Alma considered that for a few moments then nodded.

"What do you mean by... Warning?"

"I mean, to destroy something. Show them what will happen if we don't get our way. Nothing too big, nothing too important... Just leave something in wreckage. Something big enough to make the news. I don't care what it is. You were provided with all the necessary equipment at the beginning of your mission, and I trust that you didn't use them all to blow up the laboratory?"

She shook her head.

"No, not one, sir."

"Good, good."

Her boss sat back, seeming satisfied.

"I will await for your call, Alma. Then I will make my move."

"Yes, sir. Over and out."

The screen flickered then went black as she disconnected, the codes quickly fading back into view. Tapping up a few short codes with a last dance of her fingers, the soft whir of electricity trailed off and went dead, and the codes faded from the screen into darkness.

Alma stood up, her muscles rippling as she moved softly towards a nearby shelf, and, in a rather disorganized manner, began to shift through various devices and occasionally stuff one or two into her satchel. Finally, she ceased in her desperate manner, and carefully lifted an object from the very top shelf.

Whatever it was was wrapped in wires, and it sat in her hands like a warm little egg, sturdy and harmless. For now. Alma turned it over in her hands, carefully taking in the path of every wire , and then gently, as she seemed to convince herself it was safe, wrapped it up in the fabric of a soft pink scarf before placing it in the bag by her side. She smiled, her eyes glimmering.

With footsteps finally echoing, Alma left the room and carefully locked the door behind her with a soft, mechanical hiss. She travelled softly down the corridor, and peered into the living room, giving the door a soft knock before entering.

Emerald looked up at her as she entered. She was surrounded by sweet wrappers and half-chewed sweets left sitting on the floor, and the little girl held a small toy dog in each hand. The rest of the toys were arranged in a small circle on the floor, and the TV blared away. Emerald seemed happy enough. Or was it just the sugar?

Alma raised her eyebrows as Emerald leaped to her feet and stumbled over, her pretty wings whirring to keep her balanced as she gave Alma a big hug. "How are you doing, sweetie?" asked Alma kindly, ruffling her hair with a hand. Emerald grinned broadly, and gave her a thumbs-up. Alma replied with her own thumbs-up, and gave the little girl a soft pat on the back.

"Have fun?"

Emerald nodded vigorously, still hugging Alma as best as she could manage. Though Alma never would have admitted it, the sight brought a warm breeze floating over her chilled heart, so cold. This child trusted her entirely. But she, as a person, had no idea what to do in a tender situation. It was only her disguise, Sabrina, who could act it out, and still manage not to feel a thing.

Alma, seeming satisfied, bent down so that Emerald could hug her about the chest. Emerald grinned, and did just that, folding her glassy wings into her sides. Finally, Emerald opened her dancing eyes and watched Alma softly. It looked as though she were about to speak.

"Sabrina...?" asked Emerald eventually, voice soft.

"Yes, dear?" Alma replied, her voice as sickly as the smile painted on her face.

"Did you find my friends?"

Alma looked down slightly. Emerald's face began to fall.

"No, Emerald... I'm sorry. But I'll tell you what, eh?"

"What?" Emerald looked up at her hopefully.

"How about you and me go on a little trip." It was more a statement than a question.

"A trip? Where?"

"Just somewhere in the city. It can take a while to climb up, but it's all worth it. The view is spectacular. We might be able to see your friends from up there," Alma reassured her, placing a hand on Emerald's shoulder.

Emerald nodded, her sadness fading into an eager look. She would do anything to find her friends.

"Alright," Alma smiled. "The weather's pretty bad out there, so we'll need to get you all dressed up for the cold."

Alma gestured for her to follow, and she did, giving little hops and flitting forward every few steps. As they

238

reached the door, Alma could hear the rain pattering and pouring outside. She gently took from a coat hanger one of her own coats, and wrapped it around Emerald's shoulders. Emerald tried to spread her wings, but Alma stopped her. "No, sweetie," she said kindly. "We don't want anyone to see those. Or your antennae, for that matter," she said gently, placing a large bobble hat over Emerald's head, a hat that was much too big for her.

Emerald fumbled at the edge, trying to look out, and Alma lifted up the edge of the hat so that the girl could see. Emerald looked around, blinking for a few moments then smiled up at Alma, who was now pulling a pair of mittens over her hands. The woman searched for a while to try to find something to hide Emerald's segmented tail, but was unable to. Alma cursed softly to herself, then sighed, examining Emerald closely. "That'll have to do, for now," she said, pulling on her own thick coat over her shoulders, and gloves over her hands. That done she draped her handbag over one shoulder, and smiled warmly at Emerald.

As the door opened, rain poured in as if in foreshadowing, and Emerald took a step back. She looked hesitantly up at Alma, but Alma held out her hand, and the girl took it. The rain washed over them as they stepped out into the open street, and were engulfed in the storm's waters. The liquid poured down the street that lead up to the cathedral in a torrent to rival the nearby river Weir.

But as Alma expected, there was no-one around.

Everyone hid in their houses, away from the pouring rain and the lightning that lit up the streets in a daze.

And yet Alma and Emerald still walked on, together, into the rain.

The unfortunate duo trundled up towards the cathedral.

***

"Karasu!" Danny called the puppy-boy's name in a voice that spoke of despair, but Karasu's sprawled form didn't move. The rain that poured upon him washed streams of crimson from his many wounds. Mercury, though he had left only minutes before, had already vanished without a trace in humiliation and anger. His blood had already washed away in the rain.

Danny hurried over to Karasu, his movements jerky with the cold and panic. He fell to his knees beside the boy, and pressed a quivering hand to the boy's chest, but he couldn't feel anything. Still not believing, Danny lifted the child from the ground and cradled him in his arms. Ignoring the feel of warm blood against his face, Danny pressed his ear to Karasu's chest in an effort to listen to what he couldn't feel.

He felt sick with nerves, stunned beyond words, and mostly, he felt like this was all his doing. Guilt and flustered agony streamed into his chest, until it felt fit to burst. But he refused to give in. He laid a hand over Karasu's mouth and nose, trying to feel for a breath of warm air that might come. Suddenly, he felt a twitch. Danny held Karasu close into his body, and hugged tightly as though he would never let go. The boy's body juddered again then gave a whimper and a sudden, violent choke. Blood spilled out over his pale, dying lips.

"Oh, Karasu..." he whispered tearfully, not caring about the blood that now stained him. "You're alive..."

The boy was too exhausted, too pained to even give a yip. His eyes flickered, the lids opening to reveal those familiar, beautiful brown eyes that watched Danny dully for a second before they glazed over and closed once more.

"Karasu!" Danny cried out his name once more, but

the tremors that racked the boy's body were the only signs of life. Karasu was losing so much blood, and so fast...

Danny, with hands trembling, removed the coat that he wore and wrapped it around the boy's middle, where blood still gushed from the final bite mark that Mercury had delivered. That was the worst. Then, Danny took a hold of Karasu's body again and stood up on wobbly legs, clutching Karasu close even as the white coat lost its pure colour to the stain of thick blood.

"We need to get to the city, quickly," uttered Danny, striding ahead, and struggling to see through the haze of mist and rain. The children looked at each other. All were pale, cold, and shivering. But none of them even dared to argue with Danny. They just followed him, without a word.

It wasn't long, probably no more than a minute or two, before they were in sight of the city, but it felt like an eternity to Danny and to the children. Karasu's already weak heartbeats grew weaker, and grew ever farther apart, with every step they took. As they finally entered the city, Danny hugged the unconscious boy to his chest, still, but was unable to hear another breath being drawn. "F-follow me..." he whispered to the mutants, but they were already following him.

His stumbling movements and bumbling numbness seemed like a punishment, and as they stumbled into the city hall, the one building with its lights on, Danny felt even more like everything was against them. The stern-looking woman who ran the place, her grey hair all up in curls and her glasses balancing on the tip of her piggy nose, turned in surprise, and she suddenly didn't look so stern any more.

"P-please," begged Danny, voice quivering with his trembles. "H-he... he was attacked... He n-needs proper care. We've got nowhere else to go..."

It was clear, and not just by his voice, that Danny was scared out of his wits of losing Karasu. *That... That would make two of them that died because of me... or even worse...*

The owner of the city hall was about to protest. They could see it in her eyes. When did she ask to have a bunch of strangers bundle in and shove a sodden, dying child into her arms? "I don't care what you do, at the very least, keep him warm whilst I call an ambulance!" added Danny.

It was then that Karasu, seeming to sense the warmth in the tips of his claws, finally seemed to come around somewhat. His glazed eyes flickered for only a moment, and there was fear struggling with the pain in his eyes. They seemed to find the woman as she stood there, and his wet, black nose twitched. His ears drooped, and he gave a fearful, painful doggy smile, like a puppy would give when he had no idea what was going on. And he didn't. His smile spoke the truth.

His eyes, glazed and unseeing as they were, stared dead ahead for a while, not even blinking as the glaze, settled over them again. Karasu's head lolled once more into Danny's arms, and he stayed silent, not giving so much as a whimper to say that he was going to be okay.

There would be no reassurance from him.

Danny's own eyes glazed over with tears, and he looked absolutely desperate. "Please!" he cried out a final time, not even trying to stop the tears. What was the point? Trying to stop the tears was like trying to pretend that he didn't have a heart. "I'm begging you!"

"Alright, alright!" she finally said, if only to get Danny to calm down.

Danny sniffled, and held Karasu out for her to take. Karasu slumped into the warmth, and didn't move. To the lady, this was quite a scary affair. She had worked here for forty years and had met all sorts of people, but nothing had ever happened like this before. She might be holding a dead body by now…

The thought made her feel a bit woozy.

What have I set myself up for here? she mused. *But they wanted me to take care of the little thing… I can't just stand here, like a lemon!* Finally seeming to have reached a decision, the woman hobbled off for a while, and returned with a phone, but Karasu still clasped, soaked through and shivering, in her arms.

"Have you not got a blanket or anything? Even some food or something, maybe to try to bring him around?" asked Danny, fumbling for the phone in her hands. She was already shaking her head, even as Danny proved that his attention had lapsed, as he paced back and forth with the phone to his ear, yammering into it as soon as he heard an answer.

The woman looked down at Karasu as he lay dying. Even though he was now in the warmth of inside, his body was stone cold, and she wondered what this man was trying to accomplish. She didn't think that there was any hope left for Karasu. Even as she watched, though, she could see the other children settling down in a trembling little huddle a short distance away from the adult. They seemed to have finally regained some confidence, for they had begun to chatter amongst themselves. She heard one of them reassuring the others, that daddy was going to protect them, and that both Emerald and Karasu would be okay in the end. They all nodded, tired, dirty faces finally smiling as they nestled up into the warmth, reassured.

Danny paced some more, his voice stammering as he spoke into the phone, calling for an ambulance to help. Their eyes of all shades watched him, gathering in hope by the second. But also by the second, Karasu's breaths slipped away. She could no longer feel his

243

fading heartbeat. The blood that soaked into the white coat wrapped around his middle was no longer new blood. It had stopped leaking from the many wounds over his body, but it was difficult to tell whether that was because he was healing, or whether there was simply too little of it to bleed any more. Finally, Danny thanked the phone, and lowered it from his head, turning towards Karasu with half hope, half absolute terror in his eyes.

"An ambulance is coming," he panted. "It should be here in a minute or two…"

Now all they had to do was wait.

Hope.

And above all else, to pray.

-Chapter 18-

Orders and Vengeance

Panting loudly, Emerald's breaths wheezed and struggled, and each one seemed to help no better. The little girl was clinging to the hand of Sabrina, the woman who led her on up this long, spiralling staircase. Behind them, the stairs fell away into an abyss of shadows, and to look down gave an insight into just how high they'd climbed.

Any time she looked back, it felt as though the darkness was reaching out to get her, and the clashes of thunder outside were the roars of whatever it was that followed them. Every time light flashed through the odd little windows that they occasionally passed, the little dragonfly girl would flinch, and hide behind Sabrina. From distantly behind them, a choir down in the bowels of the cathedral sang their melancholy hymns of praise as an organ rumbled away its tune to guide them.

Her antenna twitching slightly, Emerald's delicate eyes with their many pupils reflected the light cast upon them in a blaze.

"Sabrina...?" she whispered, tugging on her guide's arm. The woman turned, and watched Emerald kindly. The small girl cowered slightly from her, as lightning flashed again and the woman almost appeared frightening for a moment. Emerald struggled to pluck her courage back up. "Sabrina...?" she asked again.

"Yes, Emerald?" asked Sabrina kindly. "Are your wings okay?"

Emerald nodded. To tell the truth, though, they did feel quite cramped, all hunched up together in an odd position under this coat. She wondered if the woman had even been taking any notice to her, though, as Sabrina hadn't looked her way, or said anything.

"Yeah, my wings are fine," she added after a moment, still unsure if Sabrina had seen the nod. "It's just... Are we nearly there? I'm really tired..."

Sabrina smiled at her. "Oh, dear... You should have said," she said, gently patting Emerald on the back. "We're nearly there. Look, you can see the top, just there!"

Emerald felt a lot better. She smiled and nodded.

"Do you want me to carry you these last few steps?"

"No, I'm fine now!" called Emerald, skipping up the last few steps, all in a hurry, as she felt a rush of energy in her limbs. Emerald gasped as she emerged into the room. They were in one of the cathedral towers, the windows looking out over the city, into the storm.

Emerald looked absolutely awestruck, and she pressed her face against one of the windows, her breath steaming up the glass before her as she stared out over the city.

Sabrina stepped into the room behind her, a small smile on her face. She was holding her delicate pink handbag close to her side with one hand.

"Enjoying yourself, Emerald?" she asked softly, a smile on her face.

Emerald nodded, her face beaming and eyes wide.

"I can see the tops of the houses!" she cried.

"Can you see your friends?" asked Sabrina, sounding lighthearted and cheerful, but at the same time, serious. It didn't sound like she was joking.

Emerald stared out over the town, but it was so hard to see through the rain. She shook her head, still staring out.

"No, Sabrina, I can't see anything..." she whispered in that reticent voice, sounding disappointed. There was a soft rustling sound behind her as Sabrina shuffled through her handbag, and brought out a small pair of binoculars. Sometimes old-fashioned devices were the best to use. Emerald took them from her, and then looked up, confusion in her eyes. Sabrina gently helped the girl to lift the binoculars and look through them, out onto the streets beyond the rain.

Lightning flashed, and Emerald imagined that she could see them- all of them- her friends, as they made their way through the storm. Were they looking for her? Had they even realized that she was gone? How was Bethany? The more she looked, the more questions there were. She stared out into the rain, looking for answers. She heard Sabrina moving about in the room behind her, but she didn't bother to turn and look.

Eventually, Sabrina came up behind her. She stood there for awhile, following her gaze outside. Finally, Sabrina placed a hand on Emerald's shoulder. Emerald lowered the binoculars and looked up at her shyly.

"Emerald," Sabrina began sweetly, smiling. "I could see your friends."

Emerald's heart jumped. Her eyes widened and she stared up at Sabrina. She didn't say anything, but her eyes were enough to say all that she had ever needed to.

"I was going to go get them for you... If you wanted me to."

Emerald nodded. "I want to come," she said, finally speaking. Sabrina softly shook her head.

"It's too cold out there for you, Emerald," said Sabrina. "It's nice and warm in here, Emerald. Just keep on looking outside, and I'll be back faster than you can say 'goodbye'!"

Emerald opened her mouth, about to protest, but was silenced by the touch of one of Sabrina's fingertips to her lips.

"Come on..." she whispered, smiling. "It'll be
247

quicker if it's just me to go, alright? You'll be able to see your friends quicker if I go alone..."

Emerald stared down for a while, feeling her throat begin to ache. Finally, when she looked back up with tearful eyes, she nodded.

"Aw... Don't worry, Emerald... I'll be back before you know it!" Sabrina assured her, patting the dragonfly girl's shoulder again with a hand. Then the woman turned away. Emerald watched her almost fearfully.

Sabrina turned, and disappeared down the way they had come, leaving Emerald to pick up her binoculars and watch the rain fall again.

For what felt like an age, she stared, looking for a flicker or a flash, anything that might give her hope. When anything like that ever came, it wound up being only the cruel tongues of lightning, burning.

Finally, Emerald lowered her binoculars and took one last look without, and her gaze followed a drip of water as it slipped slowly down the window. She stepped back, and, sighing, rested her aching legs as she settled down to wait. Her wings were aching, and Emerald struggled to take off the coat so that she would be free, but she couldn't figure out how to do it. So she was forced to just sit there, under the dimly glowing lights, listening to the faraway choir and the rain pattering against the outside.

She could hear nothing more, except for her very own heartbeat.

But Emerald was not scared, nor sad. There was the dull flit-flit of excitement in her heart as she waited, sitting happily, staring out at the rain and the rooftops through which glistening rivers of paths wound.

Her feet kicked softly, in a childish fidgeting motion.

Her toes brushed against a bundle of wires.

Danny was staring out into the rain, his eyes glazed over. Through his tear-blurred vision he could see a distant white shape through the rain, and he could hardly hear the person who spoke to him. Karasu's limp, lifeless body had already been carried away, stuffed into the back of the waiting ambulance. The raindrops reflected the distant blue lights and echoed the crying of a siren as it sped away now, hopelessly trying to save the life that had already been taken.

The medics were blunt, but at least they had told Danny the truth. And the truth was that Karasu had almost no chance of survival; he'd been out in the cold too long, he'd bled too much for them to be able to replace in time. If Karasu survived just a few more minutes, then they might have a chance to save him.

But the more likely ending to this tragedy was that Karasu would die on the journey there, slip out of their grasp before he even made it back to the hospital. It was as though fate's cruel claws were closing in on all that remained in Danny's life. One disaster after the next was all this seemed to lead to.

In the end, was there even a point to all this suffering?

...Ah, yes... thought Danny, burying his head in his hands. *The war...*

It felt to him that no-one even knew what the greater cause was that they were fighting for. For him, it was more a personal battle, to prove himself, and most of all to avenge his mother, his brother. Perhaps everyone else fought for their own reasons, too. But the more they killed, the more people wanted them dead, and that was the very reason how this war had lasted so long.

Now, Danny looked up from where he sat, soaked to the bone, in the rain, and he wondered why he was out here. Inside, the warmth felt strangely unwelcoming to him. Like he didn't belong there. Like he'd caused too much pain, so that the dark, the cold, and the wet was what he deserved, in the end. Just seeing the children laughing and playing amongst themselves, all designing little cards for Karasu in the hospital and learning from Joey how to spell 'get well soon', tore his heart clean into two.

At the end of the day, it was only one more loss in all the madness, one more boy who no-one but he even knew well. But to Danny, it felt like Karasu's death made the world fall apart.

Karasu was the one who messed up every mission, and made all the scientists groan and complain, though they never removed him, even if Danny had to beg them not to. He was frightened of blood and cowered from weapons. He stole food and worried about not being fed, and it was impossible to fill his belly up. The more he got, the more he wanted, or so the scientists found.

And yet...

That little boy had been the one who always laughed in his doggy way. He was the one who gambolled through life all in a hurry to explore every nook and cranny and meet everyone in the world along the way. No matter the day, the night, or the situation, Karasu could brighten any heart as he bounded up looking for hugs or sensing that something was wrong. He never complained, never spoke badly of anyone, but he understood every word you said in his own way. Sometimes he understood not the words, but the emotion behind those words, and that was what he would act upon; emotion. He'd shown how brave he could be, no matter how rare. And it was that that made him all the more special.

Getting to his feet, Danny gulped back his tears,

their crystalline forms mingling with the rain that poured down his face. He practiced a fake smile, and readied himself to step back to confront the other children. He thought that he looked somewhat convincing, but his eyes looked a little strained, and red from his tears. His cheeks were flushed, but at the same time the rest of him was a deadly pale, from the cold.

He gave up.

And yet... Finally, Danny looked up, straight forward. His blue eyes began to tremble with rage. There was no use sitting here, crying about it. There was no point in risking any more lives.

Danny didn't want any more blood to be spilled.

None but Mercury's.

It was a crazy idea, crazy to the point of seeming plausible. Danny didn't care how plausible, or how crazy, it was. He wanted this. This wasn't *the* war. This was *his* war. His own, and no-one else's. No-one else would be hurt if he could help it.

He would go on.

And he would succeed.

Alone.

Silhouetted in the flashes of lightning and blurred in the rain, Danny plodded away from the weak light that shone through the rain from behind him.

Don't worry... He told himself, and them, as though he could speak with the children through his mind. *I'll be back for you all soon...*

He turned back, considering warning them about his departure. He could no longer see the warm light that burned from where they now stayed, happy in the warmth. But no. He couldn't. If he did that, then they'd just want to come.

Danny turned away, once more, shaking his head and sending the raindrops spinning away from him, only to be quickly replaced by the storm.

With a flourish and a twirl, Danny pivoted on his heels and turned quickly. Blue eyes flashing one more time, he disappeared, the rain masking his footsteps and the thunder cheering him on.

-Chapter 19-

Extrasensory

Toby was resting, listening. Though his eyes were closed, his ear perked and swivelled, listening to the sound of the rain hammering, the thunder thrashing, and the sound of the howling wind as it raged and roared.

He had had an utterly exhausting day. His head ached and his pride stung, but no matter what he tried, he simply couldn't seem to fall asleep. Even when he started to drift off, he would quickly be brought spinning back to his senses by a crack of lightning or the sound of something being thrown against the house in the wind.

Finally, Toby had had enough.

With a strained grunt, he threw his legs over the edge of the couch that he had been sleeping on, and, without even thinking, turned his head as if to look around.

Quickly he realized the stupidity behind the gesture, and stopped, only to reach out with his hands, fumbling for the crutches that Bailey had placed beside him earlier. Toby, landed with the inability to cheer up, had simply grunted and turned away. But now, at least, he was thankful that they'd brought them. He needed some exercise. He cuddled the blanket tightly about himself as though reluctant to let it go.

Finding a grasp on the handles, it took Toby a few seconds to get used to the feel of these new crutches. Then he hauled himself up onto his feet, his toes rasping against the soft carpet. After just a few steps struggled, he stopped, remembering that he had no idea where to go.

Falling still and silent, Toby waited for what seemed like an eternity until he grew impatient, and reached out further and further with the few senses he had left. Eventually, with a thrill of excitement coursing through him, he realized that he could hear... no, almost sense, the electricity, hissing and whirring softly as it flowed through the wires in the walls, when the thunder drew silent. His ear turned, and, slowly, he began to get an image of the world around him, where the electricity was, and where it wasn't. The rain pattering against glass told him where the windows were, and he felt a soft draft blowing in on his face. Stretching out one hand, Toby inched his way forward, struggling to support himself on a single crutch.

He realized, in time, that there was a hole in the fizz of electricity. He could hear a gap in the flow. As he slowly moved towards it, Toby's breath caught as his fingertips met the feel of painted wood. He felt about, and his palm met smooth metal; a door handle. Toby's hopes rose. It was as though the world around him was finally becoming real. There were no colours, no sights, no looming illusions, but he felt as though he were finally getting somewhere.

Toby again felt the thrill of excitement in his chest, and almost forgot what he was doing. Slowly, he settled down again, and the door handle turned under his palm. The door slowly eased itself open before him with the softest of creaking sounds. Toby felt his excitement growing into anticipation as he focused on which direction carried the scent of mud and fresh air; which pathway before him would lead outside. Slowly, Toby turned.

His padded feet dragged, and he eased himself forward with both crutches. His arms ached, but he didn't care for that. Toby struggled to listen out again, and he realized that he could again hear the sound of the rain, so close, rapping again against glass. Toby felt about with a hand before him, and his hand wrapped itself about another door handle. He heard a soft click as he turned it, then the door was whipped open, not by himself, but by a violent wind. Toby felt rain spewing itself over him through the open door, and thunder cracked loudly high above him.

Shivering in the cold, Toby dragged himself from the warmth and into the wind. Grimacing as the rain stung like daggers, Toby twisted back around a moment later, and slammed the door shut behind him. With a nervous glance, Toby as aware of the door softly clicking as it locked itself behind him.

The blanket tied tightly about his shoulders and arms was the closest thing to a coat that Toby had, but Toby was convinced that it was enough. It had to be. There was no going back now. As he limped forwards, Toby felt his crutches slipping and sliding on the wet surface beneath him. He could tell that he was on a fairly steep slope, and as he stumbled unknowingly down a small step, the path became uneven but still just as firm.

Wha...? He thought to himself, at a loss as to where he might be. *Am... Am I standing on a cobbled road?*

He took a step backwards, and the back of his feet bumped against the curb. Toby slowly struggled to turn himself around, wanting to step back up onto what he assumed was the footpath. He didn't exactly want to be hit by a car. Not again. *It hurt...*

As he finally dragged himself back up, the man relaxed, despite the ever-present threat of slipping. Now that he was outside, it was a much more daunting task to try and sense where he was meant to be going. His ear pricked, and as with before, he stayed there for a while, listening. He hunched over slightly in order to pull the blanket tighter around himself with a fumbling arm.

I can't hear anything over the rain! He thought eventually, despair clouding his thoughts. The wind whistled and howled mockingly at him. *It's so... so... loud!*

Ears flicking desperately, Toby turned and strained, shaking droplets from his dappled hair and spotted face, as if it would help.

He could hear the blood beginning to rush through his ears, drowning out the sound of the rain, and he fought to get himself to calm. The higher his heartbeat rose, the less he could hear. Relying on what he'd been taught before, Toby gradually began to breathe, his breaths slowing until Toby was hardly moving.

In....

And out...

In...

And out...

His fiery heartbeat slowed, and Toby began to listen again. His eyes closing, Toby began to finally feel what he had been unable to feel before. The rain as it rushed formed within Toby's mind an image. There was a thin line close to Toby where the sound was different. There, he could hear the raindrops clapping against metal.

A... Is that a streetlamp? Toby wondered after a while. He strode forward, and the sound of water tinkling against metal grew louder.

He couldn't tell exactly how far away the streetlamp was, but it was a start. Finally, Toby stretched out a fumbling palm, and hopped himself forward hesitantly. It took a while, but his wrist eventually bumped against the freezing metal surface. *Ah!* thought Toby excitedly, patting his crutches and knuckles against the streetlamp. *I was right!*

Turning away from the streetlamp, Toby slipped away from it by a few steps. His ears twitched, trying to pick up more about the world around him. He knew what to look for, now; places where the sound of the rain ricocheted away from the ground, places where the rain didn't trickle or hit at all, or where the sound was different, like if it hit metal or window glass. But it was getting harder and harder to tell.

Toby wasn't getting any closer to solving the mystery of where he was. The air smelled polluted to him, and the welcome scent of the mud and grass, the clean countryside, was nowhere. Even the summer stink of manure was nowhere and that usually haunted the laboratory like some unwelcome and admittedly very smelly ghost at this time of year. Putting these details together, Toby quickly summed up that he was somewhere in the centre of town, whereas the laboratory had been in the countryside overlooking the city.

Toby was still pondering, when an answer came singing from the skies. A cathedral bell chimed, so close, that Toby could almost feel it vibrating the air. His ears pricked, and he listened to the sound of the bells, trying to figure it out...

Finally, it struck him like a lightning bolt. Toby, despite being blind and having no other way of being able to tell earlier, was fairly surprised that he hadn't figured it out earlier. He was on the high street, somewhere near the Elvet Bridge! He used to live near here, before he lived in the laboratory, before the disaster happened.

Toby's hopes rose. *So... That means I need to go away from the cathedral.*

He listened to the sound of the bells ringing, counting the chimes as they spoke to him. *Oh...* he thought. *So, it's 6 am? People should be starting to get*

257

up soon.

If worst came to worst, then Toby might be able to ask for directions from someone.

But he still held that same childish stubbornness as before. He wanted to be independent still. Now he understood what to do, how to move! How to... How to...

How to... See, almost.

Not see, in the true sense of the word. But he could visualise where he was! He had new knowledge of where to go, how to find his way around. Suddenly, Toby felt like he didn't need a guide. He was utterly determined to prove those scientists wrong. They had scorned and humiliated him for far too long. He'd show them that he didn't need their pity!

Turning around, Toby limped and slid, struggling to balance himself on the slippery path. Water gushed around his feet. He could hear that much. It was getting harder and harder to tell what was around him as the water levels rose, higher and higher. But Toby was quite confident in himself, by now.

Licking his pointed fangs, Toby smiled and kept on moving. He was confident that he'd get to Danny, or die trying.

As he skidded and tripped over his crutches down the bank, Toby almost fell down the curb several times, warned only of the drop as his crutch went over the edge of it, and he stumbled and almost fell. As the path finally began to even out, Toby's ears pricked.

He could hear someone coming.

Her footsteps splashed wildly through the puddles as she ran, and the rain hammered against the waterproof coat that she was wearing. Toby could hear her frantic breaths, rasping and gasping as she approached.

She didn't speak to him, or even pause as she

passed. It didn't seem like, to Toby, that she'd even given him a second glance.

How could that be?

Surely a cat-eared man limping through the rain was a sight she couldn't see every day? But then again... Toby hadn't seen anything for a while. Perhaps the woman, whoever she had been, had been in too much of a hurry to care. She did sound rather frantic. Or was it almost Halloween already, so he just looked normal?

Toby could only listen with mild surprise and wondering as her footsteps and breaths faded away into the distance. She was gone as another loud thunderclap rang through Toby's ears like the boom of an enormous drum crashing its way through the heavens.

Ears twitching, Toby felt the uncomfortable feeling of more water washing over his toes, but he carried on. The normally lively city seemed deserted compared to what he remembered from many months ago. It seemed like all human life was indoors, hiding itself away from the rain, and maybe from him, too.

He could imagine children looking fearfully out of their windows into the storm, only to see a lone figure making his slow, painful way down the street.

Toby winced slightly, shaking his head. His imagination was getting the better of him...

Returning his lifeless, unseeing gaze to the world ahead, Toby continued to concentrate. He felt his way ahead with a crutch, and strained to hear more of the world around him. He could hear solitary footsteps like those of ghosts, far away in the rain. Toby wasn't even sure if they were footsteps. Before he could tell, they had vanished again.

Sighing heavily, Toby forced himself not to panic, and he hopped ahead, still listening, still using his senses in whatever way he could. His sodden blanket now provided little protection from the cold, and the wet. His fur-covered legs felt a little warmer than the rest of him, but apart from that, those sparse rosette markings over his body weren't helping any.

Sniffing again in an effort to pick up some kind of clue, Toby breathed in a raindrop, and he sneezed violently. After a while, his nose calmed again, and Toby gave a shudder, looking about himself restlessly.

Half of him wondered why he hadn't just stayed in the warmth of the house. Why had he decided to venture out into the storm in the first place? It seemed like something a madman might do...

But the other half was too proud to settle down and submit to the taunts. That half wanted to be free. That part wanted him to see again, to develop his senses, and to truly be able to live again. This side was the one that always sought independence, the one that kept Toby alive no matter what crazy trick he and fate might pull next. The side that his mother had awakened within him. Her last words echoed in his mind.

And this side was the one that refused to let Toby settle.

With this in mind, Toby felt warmth beginning to stir in his chilled limbs. With defiance in his voice, Toby looked up at the sky, and he roared back at the thunder, in a voice that no longer spoke of pain. His eyes opened, and as they did, they flashed yellow, back up at the sickly forks of lightning that arced above them. Toby's tail cast sprays of water from it, and as it did, the pitch-black fur puffed out.

Finally, Toby lowered his head, and his lips quivered upwards into a snarling smile. He set off again, his tail swinging and his head lowered, his ears flattened into his hair. Listening, feeling, sniffing, Toby made his way forward, one step at a time.

Without the cathedral bells to guide him, Toby had unknowingly turned, and was beginning to go the wrong way.

For Toby, though, it was as though he could see again. With no knowledge of his mistaken path, Toby went on, without a care but the goal, upon which his mind was dead set.

Toby felt on top of the world.

***

"Joey, how do you spell Karasu?" Moony looked up at the peacock boy with big eyes. He was busy with a red crayon, drawing Karasu's brave battle onto the paper. The children had been absolutely fascinated by the crayons at first- it was like they'd never seen anything like it. Or paper, too, for that matter.

These new 'toys' still hadn't gotten old to the little mutants. They were absolutely determined to draw all they could whilst they still had the chance. Unfortunately, that meant they needed a *lot* of paper to please them all.

"I've already told you, Moony!" grumbled Joey, engaged in doing his own drawing of- surprise, surprise- himself. "It's Ka-ra-su!"

"Yeah, but I dunno how to spell it!" complained Moony.

"I just said!"

Moony pouted and returned to drawing. There was a short silence for a while.

Then there came an interruption, one that was probably a blessing for the poor lady that ran the town hall.

"H-help! I saw it! I saw it!" she cried, panting. Her green eyes were wide with fear and exhaustion.

Some of the children stood up. Some looked scared whilst some looked excited at the prospect of danger.

"Saw what? What was it?!" hooted Moony

excitedly, hopping from foot to foot.

"There was a g-girl! A girl, in the cathedral tower!"

Bethany jumped to her feet. She was sniffing suspiciously at the air, but the rain served as a mask for whatever she might have smelled.

"What?" she asked after a while, her amber eyes narrowed. "Who?"

"I don't know! I c-couldn't see much of her! I saw that she had antennae, though, like an insect, and that she had beautiful fairy wings, and hair that reflected like sapphires! Oh, but... But then-"

"Emerald!" Bethany was up at the strange woman in an instant interrupting her. "Why did you leave her, if you're so scared!?"

"There was something up there with her," she gasped. "A... A beast! As black as the night, it was! Bigger than any human! It was a demon, I swear! I barely got out there with my life!"

"Mercury!" exclaimed Sally and Cassie, both together. Ginny and Benny both squeaked in shock at the sound of that name. Bethany was already raring to go.

"We have to go save Emerald!" They all turned to each other, nodding vigorously. Hoots, squeaks, caws, and yips all agreed. It was only little Benny and Ginny that looked afraid. Benny pushed his glasses up his nose, and Ginny twiddled with the white lock of her hair fearfully. The other children all looked at the pair, expecting them not to want to come.

"Eeek, eek! We can't leave her! Eee!" squeaked Ginny. Benny stamped his foot against the ground in agreement.

"We've been training for this! This could be our first real mission!" he exclaimed eventually, seeming to be trying to be brave, punching the air with a tiny clenched paw.

Sally and Cassie chased each other's tails in a circle, yapping excitedly. Finally, Joey spoke up. "Fine... But you do realize that there's only seven of us now, right? I mean, Karasu's dead and Emerald's the one we're saving!"

The other children stared at him, aghast. Had Joey really just said that...!?

"Karasu's not dead!" they all clamoured in varying voices and phrases. Joey seemed unhappy, but in a way that was almost smug.

"Uh, did you not hear Danny talking to that guy outside? He said that there's literally, no chance of him surviving!"

"But he will!" The usually quite nervous Ginny spoke up in a voice that was unusually firm, one that demanded attention. "I know he will! We all do! And so do you, Joey!" she snapped commandingly.

And that was the end of that. They knew that they had things to do, and they couldn't waste any more time arguing with each other when they should be getting Emerald back from Mercury.

The woman who had begged for their help took off again, and the children all lined up behind her, like a mini military readying itself for battle. Moony and Joey went to the front, followed by Ginny and Benny, then Bethany, with Sally and Cassie bringing up the rear.

Just like old times.

As the strange, green-eyed woman ran off again, the little mutants followed, and instantly were bombarded by the rain. This time, they were too focused on keeping up to bother with complaining about the weather, even though thunder still roared frighteningly, and lightning still flashed to stun them.

With their little voices all focused on gasping for breath, the children climbed the steep and slippery slope that lead up to the cathedral, and they marvelled at the cobbled road they walked and the stone bridge they passed that they couldn't see the other side of for the rain. They climbed, and they climbed, and they couldn't see for the raindrops.

The cathedral, its immense shadow usually visible from here, didn't come out of its hiding place behind the weather. Ginny, her paws clumsy and her pudgy body not suited for fitness, kept on slipping, only to be caught by Benny, even though he kept on tripping over his own massive hind feet.

But they kept on climbing, and clambering up to the top, until at last, the ground became even. There was grass here, on either side of the path leading up to a shadow in the rain. Tombstones from ages long past were tilted at odd angles as they faded into view out of the rain, some half buried in the ground or hidden by the water that flowed around them.

As the children plodded past these relics of ancient times, they felt almost haunted. They didn't know what these stones were, but the rain made them seem so gloomy, like the shadows of people that never moved any more. And one could certainly imagine that, if they looked into the rain and, in a flash of lightning, saw nothing but the silhouette of a grave.

But they made it past them.

Finally, the woman that they had been following throughout the journey halted. She looked upwards, stared into the warm light that beckoned from the cathedral.

The children, soaked through and shivering though they were, looked up as well, and they could see that they stood in the shadow of what seemed, at first glance, to be an immense castle, first built in an age long forgotten. But far from being carved from the roughly-hewn stones that were slung together to make castle ruins, this one's intricate designs were carved into the stones itself, and the place of worship was in a condition that no ancient castle would be able to see again, not whilst it crumbled into ruins, unused.

A warm glow beckoned them from inside the aged building, but still, they felt too afraid to move a muscle.

From further on inside, a choir sang their hearts out, the eerie sound of their melodious prayers soft on the ears, but seeming almost like the echoed song of ghosts as the thunder joined in.

Finally, the woman seemed to have had enough.

"Well?" she asked. "Are you going in or not? This little girl isn't going to save herself!"

They exchanged glances. Joey stepped forward, and he seemed suspicious. "Wait... Aren't you coming?"

"Oh, no! Dear, of course I'm not! If I went in there, I think that creature would give me a heart attack! I'd just be a burden to you, my little cherubs..."

There was silence, and, following the sound of the choir and the beckoning warmth, the children stepped into the cathedral. The sound of the rain fell away behind them.

The woman watched, waited until they were inside, then she turned and scampered back the way they had come.

And the children went on, confusion in their quivering footsteps, as they went on into the darkness, the labyrinth of their first real mission.

Alone.

-Chapter 20-

Memories

My scales rasp as I slide forward through the shadows, watching the rain pour in endless waterfalls on the outside. The lightning that flares through the sky lights up these old, worn halls lit up only by candlelight shimmering from doors further on inside.

I know this place, as well as I know home.

My parents, so proud, so believing, used to bring me here to sing my heart out, and to say my prayers to a merciful ghost that never seemed to appear when you called. My ears prick, and I can hear that deep, pleading song weaving through the air as the ever-believing beg the skies for this war to end.

Ah... The memories...

I look up, and pad forward. The rainwater left in my path by the pads of my paws almost look like bloodstains in the half-light. I turn back for a moment, looking behind me at the trail that is splashed by raindrops. This path is mine. It might be... No, it is not I.

I have fallen fast since losing my human body. The dead weigh hard on one who is already burdened. It is not my claws that are stained with blood. No, not mine. I am not myself. Upon passing the door leading into the main church, I halt, and turn to look. The light falls upon my face like a heavenly glow, yet the warmth doesn't even try defrost my chilled heart. Not even close.

I look out into the room itself, and my gaze rests on the altar, surrounded by the choir of white-robed worshippers as they still sing like angels. The light shining through the Rose Window with each lightning flash casts fragments of colour onto each. People seated watch them, their faces delighted, and others, standing rather than seated, are raising their own voices to sing. A little boy, one side of his face marked by a jagged scar, one eye covered by a colourful patch, is smiling widely, his face lit up by the altar.

At last, I feel a tug at my heart.

That was once me...

I keep on watching, and as I do, the boy's small voice grows louder, standing out above all the rest. His mother, smiling tearfully at her son, raises her own voice to meet his. It is then that I realize. This boy... Where is his father? They sit apart from the rest of the crowd, those two. They look happy, as if this is the first time they have gotten be free of worry and doubt, to truly pray. I look down, once more, at my hands. I tap my immense claws together, and can almost see a red glow shimmering over them, like a curse on my eyes or on my strength.

My hands clench into tight fists, and when I look again, the boy and his mother are silent once again, to listen to the priest begin to speak. The lady's eyes still glimmer with tears, but her little boy doesn't seem to understand. He is content to whisper into her ear, a wide, wide grin lighting up his tiny face. Believing.

I strain to hear his words.

"Don't worry, mamma... Daddy will be back for us soon, won't he?"

The woman turns towards him, and nods tearfully to her son, but says nothing.

The boy, despite his mother's tears, seems convinced, and gives her another beaming grin.

"All we need to do is keep on praying, and then someday God will stop this war and everyone will be happy! Won't they, mamma?"

She nodded, and finally spoke, but her voice creaked, and cracked.

"Yes, honey... He will..."

I can feel myself shrinking. That had been me once... ever loyal and faithful, following my parents' teachings and never straying from the holy path. Over the years, less and less people had come to church to pray for peace, but I still had, with my parents always there. The thought of a higher being protecting us, all of us, gave me hope, and whenever I was sad, I would talk to things around us; I believed, that, no matter what, He would be listening to my words. I would be happy again, as soon as I knew that my worries were all in the hands of Him.

I didn't understand that beliefs could change.

Not until mine did.

It happened when I was only 8, nearly 10 years ago. Flames rushed about creaking boards and cracking roofs. Some people died as their homes collapsed down onto them. Others were burned alive, their screams drowning in the flames. For others, the debris was their end, hit by flying brickwork or boards of wood that had once held up their home. My family was lost in the fires, but I survived, protected from the shockwaves by the twin shields of distance and stone. As far as I know, I was the only survivor.

That was when God abandoned me. That was when I abandoned Him, abandoned everything. I left my entire childhood behind. I lived by stealing, and foraging the streets for little scraps that people might have left, and when these scientists found me, I wanted to abandon myself again. I wanted to forget.

Their promise was what I'd wanted most for so, so long... When it didn't happen, it felt as though something had been taken away from me. It was as though they'd promised me a heart to feel with, and then doused that heart in icy water that still couldn't melt.

But now... to see these worshippers with my own eyes. To hear their gentle prayers in chorus again was to awaken something in me that had long, long lain dormant in my heart. I begin to back away from the door, and sniffed the air with a twitching nose.

Words begin to ooze lifelessly into my mind like a curse. I move backwards, and look into one of the puddles that had been formed by rain pouring into the corridor through the windows, driven by the wind. I look into my twisted, twisted face and I feel my throat tightening up. My scales gleam dully in the light that shines from behind me, my eyes gleaming a coppery gold. All that remains of myself is the mop of brown hair that drapes into my eyes.

Is this really me?

I hear a creak as the door behind me opens, ever so slightly, and I whip around to face whoever emerges, tongue hissing out of my mouth. But for what feels like the first time, I don't attack the one who stands here before me.

It is that little boy, his good eye peeping fearfully around the door, his scarred one half hidden.

"Hello? Did you come here to worship, too?" asked the boy, his tiny voice seeming so fragile, so innocent, like fine china pottery.

I don't say anything, just stand still, feeling dumbstruck, and terrified, almost ashamed to be caught here.

But he doesn't look afraid. He looks simply curious.

"You don't need to be frightened. Anyone is welcome here!" the boy says, and he begins to edge himself around the door, almost as though he is frightened, but more like he is trying not to frighten me. I flinch.

269

"I saw your eyes through the door. I thought you might be too scared to come out." The boy takes another step forward, and I take another step back, my tail subconsciously beginning to rattle without my knowing. He halts. My tongue flicks.

Gradually, the boy stretches out a hesitant hand. I step away.

"Don't worry," the boy says, smiling. "God loves all of His creatures!"

I hang my head slightly. It's as though my childhood, many years away, has returned to laugh in my face. If He really does love us all, then why did He do this to me?

I look up at him again, only to see his hand edging closer to my face. My second eyelids flick over my eyes, clouding my vision. Then my eyes close fully. His tiny palm rests against my forehead, and I am frozen, stiffly acknowledging him.

Finally, everything is returning. Words that were drilled into my mind since I was young are coming back. Something stirs inside of me, something long, long buried by emotions, anger and grief. My eyes flit open again, my ears rest flat against my skull.

I have been disobedient.

I turned away from what I was taught was right. Not believing is one thing, but to take that further, and to hurt people?

The boy takes his hand away and reaches for mine. I still don't move. He waits there for a while, twitching his hand every so often, hopefully, every time he catches me move. Then, after what seems like forever, he sighs, and slowly lowers his hand. He starts to back away a few steps, and is about to turn away from me.

"It's okay if you don't wanna..." he says softly, in embarrassment, as though he's just been cruelly teased.

I listen. I blink. I remember now.

270

I can remember...the difference between right and wrong.

Have I gone too far? I feel a hatred for these memories, greater than my hatred for any person or creature in this world. But is it too late to reclaim myself? I look down again at my shaggy, pitch-black fur, at my thick, gleaming claws, and then at the boy as he begins to walk away.

I stretch out a hand, gently placing it on his shoulder to stop him. The boy turns around again, and he looks startled, and happy.

"Mamma is calling for me," he says, smiling at me. "I need to go soon."

I nod towards him, trying to look as though I understand. But how can I, with these eyes? I reach out with my hand, and his tiny palm rests in mine, my immense fingers seeming almost like a beartrap. But the boy is happy. He looks up. His eye meets mine and it glimmers and quivers with happiness.

After that fleeting moment, I let him go, and the boy smiles at me, before chirping a quick blessing of "He'll always watch over you!" and waving his nimble little hand. Then, with a spring in his step, the boy races away to meet his grieving mother again. I watch as she gathers him into her arms, and just before they leave, I see the boy wave to me, his pink palm outstretched and face beaming.

I turn away from the door once more, and close it behind me, feeling as though I've just been broken. I'm lost and alone, a criminal hiding away from the world. I can't seem to bear anything anymore. Just as I begin to curl up into a grieving ball, my ears twitch as I begin to hear the clicking of claws approaching. Slowly, I get to my feet, like a ghostly shadow animating. I stare at them, and I recognize those silhouettes.

My heart burns with indecision. My feelings find the

271

wounds that were inflicted upon me in times gone by. Standing there to consider my options for a few moments, I softly hiss as I slip away into the darkness away from them.

I need more time...

Grief and anger crowd back into my mind again as I fight the urge to kill. My tears stain the floor as I run, and I see myself again in those mirrors of water.

I don't know what to do...

I don't know why I'm here...

I don't know what I'm doing...

Or where I'm going...

As I slip back into the shadows, I think to myself. I wonder if this awful storm is some sort of punishment from whoever watches over us, if they do. Thunder roars in response, like a mighty voice to make me cower.

My frantic mind turns over and over, ever-repeating stories and lessons. All of them seem almost foolish, but all of them hold within them some grain of truth.

I turn, and look back, and the corridor behind me seems, at first glance, empty.

But a flicker in the back of my mind seems to think that something is watching me, waiting for me to step out of my place. I turn from left to right, struggling to see.

I cry out a challenge to the sky outside, rearing my head out into the pouring rain, not caring who hears me or who knows me, who knew me.

No matter how hard I look, there is still no-one out there to protect me.

**

There was a grin on Alma's face as she plunged through the stinging, ice cold rain as it poured, sweeping over her body as if repulsed by her. Her toes made tiny splashing sounds as she pranced through puddles and the rainwater that flowed down the bank, forming a little river through the streets.

She didn't look back even for a moment.

To look back would mean to think of what she had left behind, and this would become her downfall. The more she looked back, the more she would regret, and remember that these strangers could feel pain too. Her heart would become weak, soft. She was doing what was right; helping her country survive this onslaught that called itself a war. Alma had learned that from experience, and would be weak no more.

Thunder crashed above her again, as though the gods themselves in their cloudy thrones were applauding her for her bravery, her steel will. Alma didn't take this as a sign, though, not like others might have. If she were religious, she probably wouldn't be involved in this at all. Now, her focus was centred on destroying England's weapons and present a warning. A single warning.

Submit, or die.

Whether it succeeded or failed to scare the citizens into giving in, Alma's work in this country was done. Now all she had to do was retreat to a safe distance, and await success. And so, that was where she focused.

Then suddenly, a silhouette loomed unexpectedly out of the rain. Alma got a shock, skidding to a halt. She stopped right before them, whoever they were, staring focused, and taking several steps back as she hoped, because their back was turned, that they hadn't noticed her. But the stranger's ears twitched. He didn't turn towards her, but somehow, he knew that she was there.

He wasn't a stranger to her.

Alma stood there, frozen still, and silent. The man

before her finally turned, revealing sickly-yellow eyes, searching unseeing through the darkness ahead of him looking for a way to go.

Toby... How did he get here...?! Alma thought to herself, staring dumb-struck, her heart pounding in her chest.

"Who's there?" rasped Toby, in a voice that was deceptively strong. Alma, knowing otherwise, stayed still and silent.

"I know you're there..." he repeated, staring right through her. Ever-hopeful, Alma stayed frozen, her fingertips chilled through, her feet placed apart.

"I can hear your heartbeat," said Toby. "I can hear the rain hitting you. I heard you running up to me. There's no use trying to hide. Who are you?"

Alma took a step backwards, trying to con her way out. Toby limped a step forwards, after her.

"I... Toby..." Alma whispered finally, shuffling through her handbag in some form of desperation.

Finally, it seemed as though someone had the upper hand against her. This was what sentience could do to you; beaten by a man who was blind, half deaf, and paralysed. *Blast it...* thought Alma, but only for a moment. *I should have killed him whilst I had the chance...*

"Sabrina..." Even with her voice obscured in this rain, Toby still recognized her voice. It was almost saddening. "You... You!"

Toby's white hands gripped his makeshift crutches angrily. Alma could see his tail, black fur slicked flat in the rain, beginning to twitch back and forth.

"Yes, Toby..." Alma said, sounding bored, and yet out of her element She shifted her feet almost uncomfortably. "Sound different, don't I?"

Toby's ears flattened.

"You're a spy! You... You tricked me! I can't

274

believe you'd do such a thing!"

"I can't believe what your country would go through to make some useless 'weapon'!" Alma hissed in response, gesturing to Toby's ruined body. "And what can't you believe? What's so unbelievable? For crying out loud! This is a war! There are spies everywhere!"

Toby fell silent, breaths growling in his throat. "I'll have to report you to the police!"

"And what police are going to believe you, Toby? How will you find them? How will you get back to your guide?!"

Toby paused, tail still flicking angrily. He glared into empty space, and Alma could almost hear his brain working. Eventually, Toby's gaze turned towards the ground, his ears drooping into his hair, dripping with the rain. Toby had probably hoped that with the rain, no-one would be able to see him cry. But Alma saw it. She saw ruby tears slipping down his cheeks, leaving stains upon his skin as they went. She felt almost disgusted, but at the same time, something began to stir again.

"Toby...?" she murmured, taking a step forward. He didn't respond, but she heard the rasp of one of his crutches against the pavement as he tried to move away, but was hardly able to.

"I thought you were different..." he said, and those words stung. "For a while, I actually thought you respected... cared about me, even..." His eyes snapped into focus, and suddenly Toby swung at her. Alma felt cold metal throb into her ribcage, and, caught unaware, she was flung onto her side. There was a splash as she landed face-down in the muddy, polluted rainwater that ran down the street. She choked, and gagged, struggling to her feet once more.

Toby placed his crutch squarely back onto the ground.

275

The blow had come as quite a shock. She was hardly used to being hit like that, especially not from someone like Toby. Someone so feeble.

And yet, finally, this contact was causing her to break any personal rule that she'd told herself. It was making her think. She was used to mindless cunning, brainless stunts of agility and power. Alma had never truly thought about the consequences of her actions for a long time.

"Oof..." Alma's brain spun. She could hardly think of anything to say. "That..." she squeaked feebly, eventually sitting up. "That wasn't nice..."

Toby turned on her. "Neither was trying to kill me, was it!?" he shouted, advancing even though she was already on the ground, the breath knocked out of her.

Did he know that? Alma assumed he did. It was always foolish to underestimate a foe, and this time, it seemed that she had once more made that mistake.

Alma finally picked herself up, stumbling gracefully to her feet. She stared at Toby, her green eyes even, and unsure. She said nothing, not wanting to provoke another attack from the man whom she faced warily. His ears pricked, hearing the splashes of her footsteps, her form moving through the rain.

Her confused mind jerked and juddered as it looked for a way out, but found only more barriers that blocked her. She felt sick with the new haze of thoughts, stunned beyond words. With a shaking hand, Alma whipped a small knife from her handbag, but her hands were slippery with the rain and her sweat. She pointed the knife at Toby, struggling to keep her hand steady.

Toby, his breaths laboured and shoulders drooping, pulled himself towards her. "You won't get away... I'm fighting for my family! You won't kill me..." hissed Toby. Alma paused, gathering her strength, trying to crowd her wits about her. "I'll find... A way... I know I will!"

"I don't think so!" she snapped back, pulling the knife back slightly, subconsciously, as if she didn't want him to impale himself on the blade. It didn't seem as if he'd noticed it. "Even if you can hear, you're blind, lame, and you don't even know where you are, do you? How much do you think you can do on your own?!"

Toby halted, and tipped his head to one side slightly as if to consider her question. The seconds droned on into the lengthy pattering of the rain. Finally Toby spoke up and his voice was clear, filled with the resolve of someone who had reached a decision that once, they wouldn't have wanted to face, but now, it was a decision that they were proud of.

"I am not alone," he said. "I have my guide, and all the other little ones... The ones who're half animal, like me. They don't like me much, but... But perhaps I didn't try hard enough."

Those ruby stains down his cheeks were fast fading into the rain, but beneath the skies of roaring thunder and the blades of shrieking wind, Alma dropped the knife that had settled into its place into her palm. The blade skittered off, splashing into a small puddle on the road, where the water washed over it.

Staying still, Alma continued to listen to him, for something more.

"But above all else," Toby went on. "I have my family. They're not here anymore, but it's okay..." Toby's voice had begun to break. "Because they'll always be alive as long as I remember them. They'll always be there to guide me, as long as I want them to be..."

Finally, Alma's mind seemed to snap. Taken by complete surprise, her feelings numbed as emotion flooded back into her. Her eyes were as glazed as Toby's for a moment, and she stared upwards, her heart melting, remembering what she had locked away in fear. Her tears became one with the rain as she finally cried, and as she dropped her head, her hair fell into her eyes, and she crumpled down onto her knees.

Lost into the torrent, Alma quivered and shook, her hands covered her eyes. She felt so embarrassed, so ashamed, to be caught like this by a stranger. For her weakness to be taken advantage of in this way. She wished that she could think bitterly, regret not killing Toby whilst she had the chance, but how could she? No such feelings crossed her mind. Only the utter sorrows and agony dared stir her heart, the dull ache of memories breaking the cold replaced by an overwhelming tidal wave that she could hardly bear.

She was broken.

For the first time ever, beaten.

Kneeling there in the rain, Alma's sobs were drowned out by the sounds of the storm raging on. All the while, though, Toby stood there, and Alma couldn't see his expression. She couldn't hear him through the blood that roared through her ears, if he said anything at all.

Quivering and trembling, Alma finally plucked up the courage to look up, and her eyes were red and watering, runny nose snivelling. She looked like a child, cowering away from the dark, as if her innocence had just returned. Toby's ears were pricked forward, but he hadn't said anything to her. She couldn't tell if he was confused, or triumphant. At the thought, Alma struggled to pull the pieces of herself back together, and stood up, quivering in the rain.

"Are you trying to trick me again, Sabrina?" he asked finally, rasping voice breaking bitterly. Alma shook her head then quickly remembered that he couldn't see her. "Are you? Were you off to the laboratory again to try to kill the survivors?"

Alma shivered, and swallowed, then remembered in shattered memories that what he had assumed was partially true. She *was* trying to kill the survivors. But this time, she wasn't trying to trick Toby. She was beyond that now.

"N-no..." she uttered hoarsely, stepping back. "I wasn't..."

Toby's ears twitched towards her, his slick black hair soaking in the droplets that his ears sprayed. "Then what are you trying to do? You're not going to make me pity you..." Toby turned his face away from her. "You wouldn't pity me, if we switched places..." He closed his eyes, still listening for her movements. "The enemy would never understand..."

Alma felt her heartstrings tear in response to Toby's plucking. She wiped some moisture from her eyes again, the back of her hand only seeming to serve the purpose of splashing more rainwater into the tender green.

"I... I never asked for pity..." she whispered, voice quivering indignantly. Now it was as though she was the child, and not him. They had switched places, indeed. She felt like she should be saying more, trying to reassure him, but she couldn't. He was the enemy.

Like he had said, the enemy would never understand.

"Then why did you start to cry if you weren't attention-seeking?"

Alma felt her face grow hot. "I don't seek attention! I like to be alone!" she snapped, sidestepping to see if she could get around him. Part of her, though, was enjoying this conversation. One of her newly-unearthed treasures of emotion was loneliness, and that was the most severe of all of them. Being a spy left her alone.

She was hardly allowed to talk to anyone outside of her job, even if she was convinced that they were friendly. She had no friends. Even to argue with someone felt, to half of her newly-thawed mind, like bliss.

"Oooooh," crooned Toby mockingly. "I forgot. You're a spy, aren't you? You'll only talk to people on your side of the sea!" Alma's face burned, her hair began to stand on end. "So, who do you talk to? Your mummy, daddy, even your little brothers and sisters, or a daughter or son?" He chuckled savagely. "Must be a lot of fun to have your family still intact, isn't it?"

Alma moved forward, her shoulders stiff and face darkened into a grinning snarl, one of protective pride, and injured memories.

"I have no family!" she shot back. "They're all dead! Killed by outsiders like *you*!"

That seemed to surprise him. Toby's face went into a somewhat shocked look, his mouth slightly open, and his eyes blinking at her as he tried to think of a comeback. Finally, he grunted. "Like me? That must have been really unfortunate..."

Alma was silent, her cheeks burning brighter. She didn't say more, her lips bitten closed. "Maybe not exactly like you..." she said after a while, her mouth stiff and her voice muffled."I was really little when it happened. I was just told that they were killed by some other country in the war. There weren't any faces, just huge men clad in black suits that protected them from anything- bullets, knives, explosions, you name it... That's why I went against everyone else... I was determined..."

Toby listened silently, his own lips pursed suspiciously.

Alma closed her eyes, finally remembering, and giving in to these new emotions.

"I've never felt like this before..." she admitted

finally, feeling lost in this world, out of her place. She looked down towards her feet. "I never used to feel anything... But now..." Alma cut herself off. She buried her head in her hands, glad to finally let everything pour out, after so, so long of keeping it all bottled up. "I must be going insane..."

Toby still listened patiently, his face set in stone. As it seemed like she was about to say no more, Toby finally sighed. "My family died when I was fifteen, left me alone," he murmured, so softly that she had to strain to hear. "It's still so raw... I didn't see anyone there, just the flames, and the debris, and all the bodies. We don't even know who killed them, but..." Toby flicked his tail. "That's why I did this to myself..."

Their stories were so different, and yet so similar. Toby smiled as best he could towards her, and Alma, though he couldn't see her, smiled back.

"Sabrina..." murmured Toby softly, but she silenced him with a gentle 'shh' which he, even so, could hear through the rain. She smiled softly at him, her entire being drained of anger and protest.

"You can call me... Alma." she told him, finally accepting her own name. Trusting it to someone who should have been the enemy.

But there were no enemies here.

"Alma..." whispered Toby, smiling as he rolled the name over on his tongue. "That... that's your real name...?"

Alma nodded. "Yes... That's my real name."

Slowly, but without warning, they seemed to begin to consider. Beneath those dark and stormy skies, both Alma and Toby began to laugh. The absurdity of this situation and the similarities in both of their stories was crazy, and whether it be through insensitivity or empathy, each of them kept on laughing at themselves, and at each other, their minds numbed by the cold.

For what seemed like forever they laughed and laughed.

Eventually, they calmed, each returning in their own time to their solemn state. Each listened, waiting for the other to say something to them, even if neither of them did. Eventually, Alma sighed softly, a smile still adorning her scarred face.

Toby heard the sigh, but he couldn't see her smiling.

He assumed that the sigh was one of regret, or sadness.

"What is it?" he asked her, a sudden suspicion awakening, as it finally seemed to dawn on him that he was talking to a spy. "Do I know too much?"

"Toby, dear..." Alma whispered in a voice that was softer than silk. She took hold of both his hands even as they gripped his crutches, if just to show him that she was holding nothing that could hurt him. "You've known too much for a long time..."

Toby seemed more astounded by the fact that she was holding his hands than by what she was saying, but he still looked up with a touch of fright in his eyes. She was planning something, and he knew it.

Smiling vaguely to herself, Alma decided with an inward chuckle to give him much more to be astounded about. Using her delicate fingers, Alma unwound one of her hands from his and gently pushed up his chin so that she could look into his sightless eyes. Toby swallowed nervously, and his crutches shuffled against the pavement.

"Alma-?" he began, sounding nervous, but she cut him off with a kiss, her eyes softly closed. Toby's body tensed up, startled beyond words or resistance, but as the seconds trickled on, Toby's eyes closed too, and his form seemed to melt into Alma's warmth. Her eyelids flickered, but Alma, knowing that Toby couldn't hold her back, held him close in a hug.

Opening one of her floral green eyes just a sliver, she saw that Toby had finally closed his eyes, his ears lost in his hair.

Finally, Alma felt as though her heart was clear. Though once, she had strove so hard to freeze it, now she was glad that the ice had melted away. She understood something new now, as she stood with Toby.

The heavens still poured rainfall upon them, and lightning flashed above.

It was as though the morning had finally come for her. And above, the black skies were beginning to turn grey. In the distance, rays of light began to shine, as the end of the storm crept nearer and nearer.

But no light shone upon Toby and Alma as they kissed in the rain.

No light but that that shone from their open hearts, like beacons of hope in the darkness.

-Chapter 21-

The Cathedral

With his wings shifting and fluffy feathers ruffling, Moony's golden eyes blazed with every flash of lightning, his claws gently tapping on the stone floor of the cathedral. The arches that spanned the roof made them feel as though they were skulking through the ribcage of some massive serpentine creature.

Behind Moony, Joey plodded along, seeming to suddenly no longer want to be the leader, as at last, the seriousness of the events bore down on him. Determined to do something anyway, Joey turned towards Bethany, as she sniffled and twisted her ears about, listening for some sign of her friends.

"You smell anything...?" he whispered, doubting that she could hear anything over the immense thunderclaps that shook the cathedral. "Bethany...?" He raised his voice over the wind. Her head snapped towards him, and then she hesitantly nodded.

"Yeah," she whispered. "I can smell Emerald, and that strange lady that brought us here, but other than that, I can just smell mud..." She looked about, and kept on sniffing. Finally, her eyes snapped fully open, her amber eyes blazing. "Wait..."

All the children turned towards her, their eyes lighting up in sudden fear, and hope, all at once. Ginny squeaked. Benny's paw clutched at hers. Sally and Cassie each dropped their stances, beginning to sniff like a pair of police dogs on the prowl. Bethany sniffed again, and suddenly her gaze whipped forward.

Like a secretive, elusive spider, a heavily muscled form scuttled away into the darkness around a corner ahead of them. A pair of yellow eyes flashed and smooth scales glinted for just a second. Thick claws scrabbled against the delicate stone floor beneath them as though trying to get away. Then they were gone.

Moony flexed his claws, turning his head towards his friends so that his own golden eyes flashed.

"...Mercury!" hissed Bethany, as though they didn't already know. The very mention of the mutant's name seemed to bring an eerie hush through their ranks, and they prepared for an attack from the shadows. Seven anxious pairs of eyes peered about, remembering their last encounter.

But no attack came.

It took only a few seconds for that fact to register, and then they walked on, with ears pricked nervously and eyes focused around them as well as ahead. Sometimes it helped to have seven sets of eyes, if they could use them right. Each of the little mutants made their way forward with cautious paws pitter-pattering like the rain against the roof. All the while, they felt as though they were being followed, as though unseen eyes in the shadows were always watching them. Now that they knew for certain that Mercury was in here with them, somewhere, hiding from them, the entire quest seemed a lot more ominous.

"Which way do we go?" Moony asked Bethany softly, and she sniffed the air again. Even Moony seemed nervous, though it was difficult to tell whether it was because he didn't like to ask others for help, or whether he was genuinely afraid of failing this all-important mission. After all, he was the leader now, with Joey close behind, not even bothering to preen the ruffled brown feathers adorning him. At least not yet.

Bethany's amber eyes focused, blazing gold for a moment in a lightning flash. "The scent's getting stronger!" she whispered breathlessly, then pointed to a

285

door, just down the hallway. Hearts pounding, they headed forward, towards the door that Bethany had pointed out. As they reached it, those in the back looked around in fright, anxious to get going. Moony struggled to reach the door handle, his downy wings flaring out fearfully. Joey stepped up to help, at last, and he rested his sweating palms on the handle, before turning it, and pushing it inwards with a low, menacing creak.

The children shied away from the noise, almost as though it were a monster, looking around warily to check that no-one had heard. It was difficult to tell if anyone had. No-one came running, but then again, Mercury was an expert at drifting into the shadows. Spurred on by their victory, even if it was only momentary, the children looked ahead, through the arched corridor, and set off once more.

Once more Bethany found the opportunity to direct them.

"We're almost there! The scent trail's really clear through here! I don't think Mercury's been this way, either!" she called, voice hushed. Waves of relief washed through the ranks, and they didn't seem to add together the details of what that could mean. Joey, however, seemed to be put off. Something didn't seem quite right, here. He just couldn't place his finger on it.

Benny's large, floppy ears were tuning themselves to beyond the rain, and his soft white hair was beginning to stand on end. He wrinkled his own nose, pushed up his glasses, and clapped a hand to Ginny's mouth as his friend began to squeak. "Shh!" he hissed, then, with fear sneaking into his movements, hopped forward. The rest turned towards him, eyes wide and expectant of the worst. Benny cleared his throat, one foot stamping nervously against the floor.

"I... I can hear claws..." he whispered to them. They

all exchanged glances. As the information sunk in, some finally realized what that meant. Sally and Cassie sniffed the air, but were unable to smell what they were seeking other than the stale scent from outside.

Joey was beginning to work something out. He was only 12, but he was the only one able to read the signs, and he was the oldest one here. He began to quake. "You guys..." he whispered. They turned towards him, leaving Benny standing nervously, mouth still half open as though to speak. It was clear that he really wanted to make his point, but that he didn't want to interrupt. He squeaked softly, a quietly alarmed sound, gripping Ginny's paw in his own.

"Remember what that woman said...?" began Joey. Several shaking heads, other blank stares. "She said that... That she'd been chased out by a monster. But that was after she'd seen Emerald..." More exchanged glances. Benny and Ginny squeaked louder, as she heard it too. "And Bethany said that Mercury hasn't been in here. But Emerald has. Bethany?"

Bethany grunted at him, starting to see his point, but only vaguely. "Yeah?"

"Can you smell that lady that brought us here?"

Bethany sniffed again. She did smell someone else in here, a scent that was vaguely familiar. Finally, she nodded. "Yeah..."

"So, that means that she came here first, right? Before Mercury? And she might never have met him after all?"

Moony interrupted him. "That would mean she lied to us!" he announced, sounding as if that was the most ridiculous thing he'd ever heard. "And no-one would do that! Especially not an adult!"

"But she could have... I mean, what if-" He was cut off by utter silence. He looked slowly up, and the rest, who faced Joey, turned around, to where Joey's green gaze was now fixed. A shadow stood, hunched in the doorway, barring their way out. A deep growl echoed softly through the corridor. Lightning flashed behind Mercury, and his golden eyes were fixed.

"Where are you going?" Mercury's serpentine voice skulked through the air. It wasn't a menacing or frightening question. It sounded as normal as a question a friend would ask another friend. His voice was dull, questioningly quiet, yet still held those eerie growls and hisses that they knew so well. The children's immediate assumption was that he was trying to trick them.

With eyes wide, and voices numb, they shied away from Mercury. As they did, Mercury took a step forwards, towards them, keeping the distance between them equal. His claws clicked softly on the stone floor, and another crack of thunder rolled out above, outside. *"Where are you going?"* he repeated, his voice more demanding, this time, more menacing, less friendly. He took another few steps forward, his muscles rippling as he moved. Compared to the young, tiny forms of the children, Mercury was massive, more like an animal, and a demon, than all of them put together.

Sally and Cassie stepped forward, and it was clear by their raised tails and their crouched postures that they were ready for a fight. Their brown eyes were searching, their white teeth glistening against black lips.

"We're going to find our friend," they both uttered at once. "What are you doing here?!"

Mercury's ears flattened in response to their anger. His golden eyes blazed. He didn't seem frightened, not at all. Mercury was silent. He took another step forwards, his thick claws clacking against the stone. The children backed away further, but the more they moved away, the closer Mercury got. A single step of his seemed to equal ten strides of theirs.

He only got closer, and closer, and closer, until he was nose to nose with Sally and Cassie, his golden eyes meeting Moony's, then burning into Bethany's. Benny and Ginny squeaked in fright, their brown and red eyes wide in fear and paws still entwined together. Benny pushed his glasses up his nose, trying to make himself look less afraid through his squeaks. Mercury moved on, baring his teeth at a pale and desperate Joey as he turned away.

They froze, petrified by the stony glare that the black-furred mutant gave them as he skulked among their ranks, to numb to run, and too scared to attack lest they fall victim to the venom that flowed through Mercury's fangs.

"*I am not asssssking for much,*" he finally purred, tone cool as ice, slithering backwards so that he could see them all at once. The children, whom had been holding their breaths before, finally breathed out. Sally and Cassie began to snarl. Bethany flexed her fingers threateningly, and Moony bared his claws, the wickedly sharp tips glinting.

"*Peace,*" began Mercury. "*I only asssssk that you let me passsst...*"

Bethany stood forward, placing her feet stubbornly apart. "You'll never get to Emerald!" she snapped. The others murmured in agreement. All except Joey, who was finally taking the chance to preen his feathers with his small claws, a sure sign that he was nervous. Even Benny and Ginny were nodding, giving soft little squeaks.

Mercury glowered at them, golden eyes ablaze. "*I didn't sssssssay that I would hurt her,*" he replied.

"*I never even sssssaid that I was going towards Emerald!*"

Bethany still stood her ground, and beckoned for her friends to stand beside her, so that Mercury faced a bristling, angry wall, determined to protect Emerald. Mercury's fur, and his mop of brown hair, stood on end. His tail softly flicked, creating rattling hisses of sound. Bethany advanced. This monster had caused far too much pain for him to get away from them without punishment. Bethany pointed a finger at Mercury, and her eyes narrowed to slits. She turned to look at Sally and Cassie.

"Get him!" she yelled, no longer worried about bringing monsters out of the shadows with the noise that she made. Both of the dog mutants surged forward, well ready to avenge their beloved playmate and protect the one they were seeking.

They sank claws and fangs into the shoulders and back of the immense beast. Mercury gave a startled roar, and that was the cue of the others. Bethany's tail fluffed out and she gave a yowling, yipping war cry. Moony screeched angrily, digging in his claws. Mercury lashed out in panic, and in a moment, Ginny had gone spinning across the room to collide with the wall, only spurring the others on into more wild fits of angry attacks. It didn't take long for the sturdy, pudgy little girl to get up again, and come running back, squeaking encouragement to the others as she went.

"It's alright, you guys!" she squealed to her friends, then started to mock Mercury. "That didn't hurt at all!" she taunted in the best insult she could think of. "Kick him in the face, Benny!"

Benny took a moment to grin sideways at Ginny, then did right as she asked. Mercury reeled back as Benny's strong kick hit him squarely on the nose. Sally and Cassie, thrown off by his writhing, went for the flesh of Mercury's belly, the way he had done to Karasu. Mercury reared high up, quivering and shaking. He opened his mouth and roared at his assailants, and those two deadly needles flicked into view behind his first row of knifelike fangs.

Most of the other children, clinging to his back and sides and driving inwards with their claws, were hungry for revenge. They never let him attack, and Mercury's blood splattered the walls around them like ugly paint, staining a holy place impure. Twisting about, writhing and roaring, Mercury's claws flailed, creating deep cuts across Moony's back, ripping through the fabric of his shirt. Mercury, sensing his weakness, threw the smaller mutant aside, and he skidded off over the floor, stopping as he collided with the wall.

One by one, they fell, were tossed aside, but the most any of them were given was a cut or shallow bite. Eventually, they were scattered, and Ginny had fled to help a struggling Benny to his feet. Mercury, in the centre of all the chaos, stood alone, his blood forming a dark red puddle in his shadow. As the children picked themselves up again, one by one, off the ground, Mercury made no move to advance or attack, but with several mutters amongst themselves and exchanged glances, the children did.

Mercury watched with golden, glazed, and quite frightened, eyes. He moved his hands and heavily clawed feet apart, trying to give himself a bit more balance despite the blood gushing through his ears, and the dizziness echoing through his brain. He snarled softly, menacingly, trying to secure his own survival. But they kept on advancing. Mercury tried to take a step away, but his feet slipped in his own pool of blood, still trickling from all his tears and gashes.

With a desperate snarl, Mercury's feet slid out from under him, and his legs buckled. The demonic boy sprawled sideways. Moony stood over him, looking down on Mercury accusingly.

The rest of the children followed him, crowding expectantly around Mercury, and Moony placed a clawed foot upon Mercury's neck. Mercury's two eyelids flitted over his eyes, as he waited for the killing blow.

Countless eyes stared down at their captor, as though they were proud, or waiting. Moony's claws pressed down on Mercury's neck, and he gasped for air, his fangs red with his own blood. The children's faces were cold as stone; they had waited so long for this.

Mercury had finally been beaten.

***

"Gone? Where did they go?" Danny was staring at the lady who was meant to be looking after the young mutants. His search for Mercury had gone unsuccessfully until, cold and shivering, his labcoat completely sodden through with freezing water, he had made his slow way back to the centre of town. Now he stood watching helplessly as he realized that his trust had been misplaced.

"I've told you, they went with a lady dressed in pink, up to the cathedral. She said she'd seen a little fairy girl up in the tower, and a monster, too. I don't know what was with her, but after meeting those little things, I'm about ready to believe anything." Danny stood stiffly before her, shivering in the cold and, though he wouldn't have admitted it, with fear.

"But..." he began helplessly.

"What are you protesting for? They left without even giving me a say! Besides, you weren't even there. There's no point blaming me."

Danny's hands clenched to fists. He didn't say anything, but her words stung. *She's right*, he thought to himself, feeling sick to his stomach. *It happened because I wasn't there...*

Swallowing his guilt a moment later, the lump in

Danny's throat moved slowly, painfully down to become an ache in his heart. He forced his blue eyes to open, then he looked at the woman sternly. She had her back to him now, and had busied herself making a cup of tea. Danny wasn't sure whether it was for her or him, but he was sure that his hands were too numb to hold anything, shivering too much to avoid spilling it.

"You said they went up to the Cathedral?" he asked eventually, meeting her eyes. The sour look she gave him disarmed him, and Danny dropped his gaze in shame, droplets of water still dripping from his hair and chin. He could feel her staring at him, still. Finally, he sighed softly in relief as she spoke, glad to be free of the red-hot-glare.

"Yeah, that's what she said," the woman replied, pouring out the hot water into the mugs that she had set out. Apparently Danny looked pathetic enough to have stirred up some sympathy.

"Well, then, I'd better be going..."

The woman finally seemed to take notice. "Leaving so soon?" she asked quizzically, shuffling over to the man with two mugs of steaming tea on a tray. Danny looked up at her, hesitant to do anything. "Well? I'm not gonna be blamed for sending someone out into the storm to freeze to death. I've seen war machines attack under cover of storms like these. You'd think it'd make it too risky, but no- load of the pilots these days are perfectly trained to navigate the winds and stuff. That, and technology has come on a bit since my day!"

Danny looked up at her, anxious to be off, but he tried to pretend to be interested as he reached out to warily take a cup of tea, hungry and needy of the warmth it brought. His shaking hands gradually began to regain their feeling, and as they did, Danny felt soft pain in the intense heat. He clutched the mug close to his chest before taking a hesitant sip, and replying over

293

the irritation of his burned tongue.

"You've seen it happen?" he asked softly, looking up.

"Oh, yes, I've seen things that young'uns like you could never imagine! All in years gone by, I'm afraid. This war is just one of many."

"Oh..." was all Danny could find to say, thinking sadly back to his younger days, and the death of his mother, their home up in flames. *Why does it happen?* he wondered, taking another sip of his tea despite his protesting mouth, feeling the burning warmth filling his belly in a comforting, yet at the same time uncomfortable, way. He shifted slightly, wincing as the heat took its toll.

"How long ago did they leave?" he asked dully, rubbing his nose with the back of a sodden sleeve.

"Just a few minutes ago. Don't be in too much of a hurry, though, pet. If you went back outside in this weather, you'd freeze yourself!"

Danny hung his head, looking longingly at the pouring rain through the glass doors.

"Or do you want to freeze yourself? Oh chop, chop! At least finish your tea!"

Danny gave her a look, but obediently raised the mug to his lips and gulped it down, as though he was inhaling it rather than just drinking it. Eventually, he lowered the mug and held it out, sucking in his breath in a sigh that seemed more like him catching his breath after drinking it down all at once. A little coil of steam trickled out of his mouth as the remnants of the still-heated liquid met the air. Danny swallowed.

"Thank you..." he mumbled, looking grateful, and relieved.

"Don't get all sappy with me. If you're going to find your kids, go!" she commanded him sternly, taking the mug.

294

That was the only encouragement Danny needed. Turning away, Danny looked outside into the darkness, and he saw the cathedral, silhouetted against grey skies. *Looks like the storm's finally started to pick up...*he thought to himself, hope rising in his chest. Without looking back another glance, Danny opened the door, straightened his coat, and dashed out into the rain. His feet splashed through puddle after puddle and rain whipped like icy needles into his face as he went, but at least he knew where he was going now.

Other than the city hall, it seemed as though just about every other part of town was deserted.

Occasionally, Danny would see a window of a house gleaming its warm glow to him, or see a shopkeeper waiting hopelessly in his or her shop for customers that were too scared to brave the rain. The promise of warmth beckoned his limbs as they froze again and again, but the hope of finding the children again and perhaps confronting Mercury beckoned his heart more. Every time he saw the warmth again, he would run past, leaving the people behind to wait and wish. Stumbling up the steep bank as cold water washed around his toes, Danny looked up as he saw something illuminated in a flash of lightning.

Feeling his lungs burning and his joints crying, Danny finally slowed to a walk, breathing heavily, sucking in his breaths like he would never get another chance to taste the cool, clean air that nourished him. But still he stared ahead, for standing there were two people.

One, he didn't recognize. She had flowing blonde hair falling about her shoulders. She wore a thick pink coat padded with fur, and the side of her face that Danny could see was marked with a jagged scar. Her eyes were closed; he couldn't see what colour they were. Edging forward again, Danny felt that if he stopped completely, he would freeze in the cold and be unable to move again.

The other person was much more familiar to him. Almost uncomfortably so.

Danny could see that his long, thick black hair was slicked down, stuck to the sides of his head with the pouring rain. He clutched two crutches close to him, and these crutches the only things that stopped him from falling, his feet resting limply on the ground and providing little stability. His eyes, half closed, were a sickly shade of yellow, and his skin was dappled with odd rosettes of fur. The rounded ears of a big cat were pressed, almost hidden, in his hair.

Danny's breath caught in his throat, the air that he had been so hungrily devouring just a minute ago suddenly becoming a blockage.

"Toby?" he whispered, almost too frightened to say anything.

No response. Toby was too engrossed in the stranger.

Kissing them.

Kissing.

Danny couldn't help but stare dumbly, however rude it might be. Since when did Toby have admirers? Since when did Toby have the confidence to do anything like that? Since when did he even come outdoors? Was this that... 'Sabrina' he'd been talking about? Danny was getting a bad, bad feeling already. He cleared his throat rather loudly, and both people seemed to snap back to their senses, pulling apart and turning to stare back at him accusingly.

"Toby!" exclaimed Danny, walking forward, hoping to sound like an angry father would sound if he were scolding a child, though he probably sounded quite shocked and mildly ashamed. "What are you doing?!"

"D-Danny...?" Toby asked, as though begging it to

not be him. "I... We... Well... Uh... This is Alma?" He introduced his new 'friend'. The woman flinched and backed up a few steps, her eyes now visible to be a bright, summery green colour. She looked just as awkward as Toby and as ashamed to be caught in the act as he was.

Danny watched. He blinked, and tried to speak again, but found his throat blocked up.

"What are you even doing out here, Toby?" he asked eventually. Toby shifted his crutches, his sodden tail twitching awkwardly.

"I... I know how to get around now, Danny!"

Danny watched him closely for any signs that Toby was lying, didn't know what he was talking about.

However closely Danny watched, though, there were none. Toby shifted as though he could tell Danny was watching him. "So," said Danny eventually, sounding wary, and almost irritated. His shoulders bunched up tensely. "You left Charlie's house by yourself, not having any idea where you're going or whatnot, and went out onto the streets, and then kissed the first stranger you saw? Or, um... heard?" Guilt stole into his voice.

Toby swallowed, moving back a step, turning his blind gaze away slightly. Alma stood back, looking too ashamed to do anything. Her feet seemed frozen to the pavement. She swallowed as she saw Danny looking towards her.

"But Danny... I thought you'd be happy for me... I mean... she-... This is Sabrina, Danny!"

"The one who lied to you?" Danny's gaze was locked first on Toby, then on Alma. "Did she get a sudden name change, or what?"

Toby's cheeks burned, and Danny felt a sense of shameful pride that he'd gotten his point across to him.

Sabrina- or 'Alma' as she now called herself- had

stood stiffly all the while. In her eyes Danny could finally see some form of emotion, and that emotion was changing gradually from shame, into anger, then into a sense of calm that hid all else, a face that she seemed to have mastered. She took several steps forward, then halted before Danny. He watched her warily.

"What do you want? How do you know Toby?" she asked him, and her voice was smooth as silk, holding an accent that was eerily familiar to Danny; one that he hadn't heard in almost 10 years. "Why are you taking your anger out on him?"

"I'm his guide. And... I'm not taking my anger out on Toby... I'm just trying to protect him," he replied stubbornly, catching the manipulation in her voice, and almost feeling faltered by it. Alma took another step forward towards him.

"Protect him? From... me?"

"Yes, from you," Danny glared at her, feeling that same mistrust towards her as the other scientists seemed to always feel towards him. For once, he felt he knew how they did. But at least he had a reason to mistrust her.

Ech... he thought in disgust, watching her closely. *She's plotting something. I know it...*

"Well, clearly you haven't been listening," Alma came close to him, and held one of Danny's stubbly cheeks with a dainty palm, forcing him to look at her, so that she could see the burning anger in his eyes. "Toby trusts me," she warned, whispering into his ear, and ignoring his scalding looks. "And you wouldn't want to hurt him any more than you already have, would you?"

Danny tried to bat her away like he would an annoying insect.

She avoided him with little more than a tiny twitch, flaunting her stubborn grace and catlike reaction times.

With a smirk on her face, she continued to whisper into his ear, holding him still, before raising his hand and slowly forcing him to stroke the scar on her face. Danny stood frozen in horror, his blood boiling.

"Just remember how much the truth can hurt someone," she whispered. "Sometimes it's better to lie..." She sighed airily, stepping away from him as she gave his cheek one last brush with her fingertips.

Danny felt aghast, fear causing his heart to pound. He tried not to show his fear, though, and angrily tossed his head. "I don't have time for this," he snapped. "Toby! You're coming with me. We're going to find the children!"

Toby snapped into focus. "You lost them?" he asked, sounding fearful, and almost betrayed. "How could you lose them?"

"I went out looking for Mercury. When I got back, they'd gone on a wild goose chase to find Emerald. Long story short, now we've lost Karasu, too," Danny's voice broke. "I'm going after them. The cathedral is our first lead. I can't let any more of them get hurt... I mean, I... I don't think I could bear it if I did..."

He turned away slightly, aware of Alma staring at him intently. Suddenly he realized something. His eyes snapped open.

"Alma," he began, voice stern. "You weren't the one who took them, were you?" He watched her closely for any sign of a lie, suspicion clear in his eyes. Alma shifted her feet, seemingly taken by surprise. Her mind snapped back to its old, power-hungry self, her emotions back to null. Her accent changed once more as she flitted back into character.

"Of... Of course not," she said bluntly, lying through her teeth. But Danny had noticed her change. Toby's ears pricked in surprise.

"I thought you... What's happening?" Toby asked in

299

confusion, speaking first to Alma, then to Danny.

"Doesn't matter," huffed Danny, walking towards Toby and taking a hold of his arm. "We need to go, now."

Alma stalked up towards the silhouette of the cathedral, a few metres ahead of the two men, and then turned around to face them. Now it was her turn for her eyes to burn. When Alma wanted something, she would get it. She had never once failed in a mission, and that wasn't about to start now. Danny wasn't helpless. As much as she was a highly trained spy and he just a scientist, this wasn't like killing a helpless puppy, not like the thought of killing Toby. The ice in her heart began to slowly freeze again, whilst her blood boiled elsewhere, filling her muscles with heated power.

"Come," she said softly, looking down on them with burning eyes.

"What?" Danny looked up at her, visibly confused. "What do you want?"

"I want to prove something, scientist."

Toby, too, was looking confused. His sickly-yellow eyes drifted, and his mouth opened and closed as though he were trying to think of something to say.

"Prove what?" asked Danny, shivering not in fear, but with the cold, and with barely-contained anger.

"That Toby deserves better than you," Alma smirked wryly, and she pressed her palm into her knuckles with several satisfying cracks.

Danny frowned. Was she using some sort of flattery to try to make Toby side with her? It was difficult to tell.

"Come," Alma said again. She had dropped her stance, edging her feet apart for better balance. Danny swallowed. *What on earth is she trying to do?!*

Was this her revenge for not trusting her? Maybe she had been trustworthy, and with Danny's anger, she'd only now come back to her senses? Or maybe she pitied Toby, but loathed him? Danny's mind spun.

"I don't want a fight," Danny commented warily. "I just want to get to the cathedral…"

Toby was silent all the while, his twitching ears and flicking tail giving away his anxiety. He hadn't expected Alma to turn so easily. Had she won him over when she cried?

Was it all an act?

All of it?

Danny could read Toby's expressions like the pages of a book. Gulping fearfully again, he sucked in his breath, thinking fast on his feet.

"If we fight here, people might see us," he pointed out. "Then I could turn you in to the police."

The woman gave a short huff, and a snicker, but she didn't challenge him anymore. Danny considered it a victory. Danny took a hold of Toby's elbow, ready to be his guide once more. He looked up at Alma.

"Oh, you've never seen me fight. I could kill a hundred of your police and not be scratched!"

Danny flinched. *Overconfident, isn't she?* He wondered inwardly. "Then why do you want to fight me?"

If she was telling the truth, then he'd hardly last a second. Danny could, in his own words, 'talk the ear off a donkey' but he had never been much of a fighter. He'd studied medicine for a while before becoming a scientist so naturally, he hated to see people injured and would rather flinch and be hit himself than hit someone else. If he tried to use a knife, he'd be more likely to drop it than hit something.

But she didn't respond to his question.

"Alma…?"

"Shut up."

"But-"

301

"I said, shut up!"

"Okay, I'm shutted up..." he mumbled without thinking. Danny bit his tongue as she jabbed a sharp nail at his neck. Seemed he'd gone a bit too far.

"Looky here. If I fail this mission, I'll lose all I have. So don't you get in my way. Got it?" Danny nodded nervously, not bothering to question it.

"What if I fight you...?"

"From what I can see, you're hardly worth the effort."

Toby growled softly. "He's worth a lot more than you!"

Alma turned slowly towards him, and Danny caught a flicker across her face, as though Toby had just struck a raw nerve. Instead of her usual calm, Alma showed Toby anger. "You didn't think that a minute ago," she said.

"You've been trying from the start to get the better of me! You said that he lied to me about a little, blank piece of paper! You tried to convince me that he's like you are!"

Alma looked shocked. Then she looked at Danny, who gave her a wink and a smirk, and back at Toby. "What goes around comes back around to kick you up the butt," Danny said after some careful consideration of the consequences, and for an instant he seemed rather smug.

Toby nodded. "No matter how much it hurts somebody, the truth is worth a hundred, no, a thousand lies about power, greatness, or whatever! I don't want to know what someone wants to be! I want to know who they really are!" Toby's rasping voice was shaking. The pouring rain was beginning to fall slower, the droplets thinner and lighter. The last rumbles of thunder shook the clouds.

"Danny never lied to me." Danny turned to look at

Toby, knowing that he wouldn't be able to see the smile on his face. "That's why he was- no- is- the best brother I could ever ask for."

Toby flattened his ears, sickly-yellow eyes ablaze.

"No-one else was ever there for me. To the others, I was just an experiment." Toby's voice lowered until it was soft and sad. "A failed experiment."

Danny hung his head slightly, knowing the truth in Toby's words. "You were never a failed experiment to me, Toby," he said. Toby smiled, and Danny stepped forward to give his brother a soaking, freezing, but still somehow warm, hug. "You were you.... Toby."

Toby, his eyes closed, hugged back as best as he was able, supported by Danny as well as his crutches.

For a while, Alma stood there beside them, watching with intrigue in her eyes, and emotion that could have been... Was that longing?

Danny lifted his head slightly to try to get a better look, just to make sure. As soon as she realized that Danny was watching her, Alma whipped away. *Maybe she changed because... because I'm here. We're from the same place, but I still don't trust her...* he realized. Alma continued to stare up at the cathedral as though waiting for something. *Or maybe... maybe she was just showing off. People do that sometimes. For Toby, perhaps?*

Watching her for another moment or two, Danny turned his head away from her again, and almost instantly heard a soft swish as she turned back towards them, staring helplessly, enviously, with those floral green eyes.

Danny and Toby continued to hug, as though afraid to let go of one another.

Though she could have killed both, right then and there, Alma made not a move against either of them. In time, she turned back towards the cathedral, and

303

watched, and waited, anticipation and frustration in her eyes.

For a while she lingered there, watching and waiting. Then, she began to slowly walk away, up the bank towards the cathedral. Just before she was out of sight, Alma turned back and watched once more, but only for a few seconds. Then she turned away for a final time, and whisked into the rain like a shade. She didn't seem to run or hide anywhere, she simply vanished into the shadows, the echoes of her footsteps the only things left of her, before those vanished too.

Danny looked up, and followed her gaze to the cathedral.

-Chapter 22-

Last wishes

With ears twitching and tails flicking, each of the mutants waited with bated breath as they watched Moony, with his claws pressing into Mercury's neck, savouring every moment of Mercury's fear. Their enemy's breaths were ragged and gurgling, his chest, upon which Moony stood precariously, slowly rising and falling.

"*Pleassssse...*" rasped Mercury with difficulty, in his contorted growls, his twisted voice. "*I'm not lying... I meant you no harm!*"

Moony seemed as though he were immune to the desperation in Mercury's voice. His face was icy, unforgiving. Only Benny and Ginny seemed a little more hesitant, perhaps because their gentle, fearful natures didn't want to cause any sort of harm. They weren't predators. Not like the rest of the mutants.

Struggling to keep breathing, Mercury swallowed, then spat out a little trickle of blood to one side, feeling Moony's claws digging slightly deeper. "*P-pleassssse! Lisssssten to me!*" he rasped, snarling, and taking a chance. "*Did a woman bring you here?!*"

Moony froze. Bethany's ears pricked warily. Joey seemed to be thinking, still preening his feathers with his hands and small claws.

"How did you know?" asked Bethany, sounding indignant. She stamped her feet on the ground, tail fluffing out as she scampered over to him, to point at the mutant with a furry finger.

"Have you been spying on us?" added Moony. "Because it isn't gonna help you if you were!"

Mercury hastily gave his head a feeble, denying jerk, his slit eyes fixed on them.

"*No, no, I wasssssn't!*" he rasped.

"Then how did you know?"

"*Becaussssse... Because she sssssent me here, too,*" he rumbled.

There was a deafening silence ran through the mutants who held Mercury down at knifepoint. Mercury looked over the faces who watched so closely, and there wasn't a trace of a lie in his eyes. Only the truth, and pain.

So much pain.

Joey had finally snapped. "That's it!" he cried, jumping up and down excitedly. "She wasn't trying to help us! She lied to us! That... That...!"

"...Liar!" finished Ginny boldly. "She didn't mean good!"

Sally and Cassie's eyes widened. "The scent!" Cassie exclaimed. "Joey, I can remember the scent!"

"Yeah, Cassie!" agreed Sally, readying herself for battle, and pouncing unexpectedly on her sister. "It was the one that was in the laboratory, and it was all over Toby!"

Bethany's ears perked, her amber eyes suddenly glittering with anxiety. "Emerald! You guys! We need to find Emerald!"

Seven sets of eyes turned towards her.

"Why did she want us to come here, and Mercury? Did she want us to fight?" Joey wondered aloud, not seeming to want to be stopped by now. Mercury grunted, struggling to turn himself over, back onto his front.

Moony fell with a startled hoot into the puddle of blood, then was up on his feet again in an instant, shaking and recoiling and scattering red droplets in a disgusted fit. "Just because you said that doesn't mean

306

you can come with us!" exploded Moony angrily, hopping from foot to foot as he gestured from Joey to Mercury pointedly. "You're not our friend! And you're ugly, too!"

"*Just becaussssse you sssssaid I can't doesn't mean I can't of my own will,*" replied Mercury calmly, swishing his rattling tail, and flexing his claws. Twitching occasionally as one of his wounds caused a throb through his muscles, Mercury took several limping, testing steps forward, then turned back to focus his golden eyes.

"Which means...?" Moony asked suspiciously, wings fanning.

"*I'm coming,*" Mercury growled with finality, in a voice that was, by itself, difficult to argue with. "*Whether you want me to or not.*"

Moony narrowed his own eyes and hooted angrily. "I never said that! What makes you think you can do that?!" He stamped a foot on the ground, and some of them were about to agree, when Bethany's urgency got the better of her.

"Youse!" she called over the beginnings of the argument. "We need to find Emerald!"

Mercury nodded, shuddering, then turning away to cough out some crimson-stained saliva. "*She'ssss right. There's a funny sssssssmell around here, and I want to find out what it issss.*" The mutant's nose twitched. "*And to do that, I need to sssssave my energy. You too.*"

"Who made you the adult?" hissed Moony angrily. Mercury turned towards him, eyes starting to look a little glazed.

"*I'm eighteen,*" he said. "*I think that givesssss me at leasssssst a bit of dominion over you.*"

That didn't shut him up. However, he was kept silent by his ponderings of what the mysterious word 'dominion' meant. Some of the others were forced to consider, too.

"*Doesssssss anyone want to lead?*" Mercury asked eventually, looking with dark eyes about the ranks.

"I do!" Moony said immediately. Mercury looked about again, but as none of the others protested, neither did he.

And so, they settled into their usual formation, with Joey and Moony in the lead. Bethany, with her chest puffed out in importance, strutted along just behind Moony, guiding them every couple of steps with her nose. The rest kept a close eye on Mercury as he brought up the rear.

They were getting closer and closer to their goal; just about every one of them could feel it in their gut. A nervous excitement made the silence between them thrum. The rain, they noticed eventually, had begun to calm. A grey light shone through each window they passed, lighting their way, and causing the droplets of blood that lingered in Mercury's path to glint crimson.

The black-furred mutant kept on looking back to the trail of blood as though worried that it was some kind of monster stalking him, but then he would shake himself back to his senses, and plod on, his feet dragging more and more with every step. Still they didn't fully trust him. He was with them, but not within them. He would never be the same to them.

And after all he'd caused, Mercury found himself forgiving them, as he'd been told to so many times before. A slow, sly smile crept gradually over his glistening black lips. Had something changed, all of a sudden? Was it the brink of helplessness that made him finally stop, think, and try to feel how they did?

Perhaps it was because he couldn't fight back.

So he slunk along after them like an obedient little puppy as they began to climb gradually up the spiralling staircase. The droplets of blood that splattered the ground in Mercury's path gradually thinned, but the mutants, striding ahead on Emerald's trail, didn't notice that, even as the limping, struggling male began to lag behind.

Eventually, they heard the panting as he began to struggle to speed up, to catch them. Moony turned back for a second to see what the fuss was, then turned to Bethany not for advice on how to help Mercury, but to see if they were going the right way. Some others turned back as well, and Mercury gave a strained grunt. With most seeming to take that as a threat, none of them stepped forward to help him, and those that remained simply followed their friends' lead and walked on.

Behind them, Mercury's bleary gaze slowly sunk down to the ground as he stopped, exhausted, to catch his breath, and finally realized that thanks to his influence on their lives, these children would never turn back to help him of their own accord, or without suspicion in their eyes.

A moment later, however, they turned back to look at him again, but only because Mercury's claws had begun to scrabble frantically as he hauled himself up the staircase after them, not wanting to be left behind. Satisfied, they soon turned back to follow their leaders. Although Mercury still struggled to keep up with them, they vanished around a corner, determined to find Emerald, and Mercury heard their feet tramping away up the staircase above him, growing further and further away.

Mercury heaved himself up one last step, then stopped and waited, struggling to gather up his strength once more.

Moony, far ahead, turned back and looked at the staircase behind him, just to check to see if their enemy was still skulking along behind them. "Bethany?" he asked. "Can you smell Mercury up here?" He looked around warily again as the fox-girl sniffed.

She shook her head, and they all looked around, but Mercury had gone, fell back long ago. Moony stuck out his chin, seeming to think that they were better off without Mercury to burden them. "Good riddance!" the owl boy said loudly.

Several of his friends nodded and whispered amongst themselves, quietly agreeing with Moony's reasoning. The rest of them looked around uneasily, expecting Mercury to be hunting them down once more.

But that didn't matter anymore. Bethany's tail fluffed out excitedly, and she hopped on her feet. "I can smell her!" the girl cried in a hushed, frantic whisper. More whispers met her. "N-no, I mean, she's close now! The smell's really strong!"

Bethany raced ahead and beckoned her friends to follow her. The sound of their footsteps went skittering down through the tower and upwards. One of the last bolts of lightning lit up the sky outside, then the light faded back to grey. They all looked ahead, and saw a little girl sitting softly on a bench, her head down and her antenna drooping.

The lightning flash illuminated her, lighting up the streaks of tears on her face.

Thunder roared.

The little girl didn't seem to notice them, her soft sobs finally meeting with the ears of the listeners. Her head was buried in her hands, and her body quivered with her tears.

Loneliness.

Bethany raced forward, tears springing to her own eyes. "Emerald!" she cried, her voice breaking and suddenly hoarse. Emerald finally looked up, and her vision was clouded with tears.

"Bethany...?!" Emerald's soft voice was, for once, stunned. With her diamond-like eyes opening wide, Emerald stumbled to her feet and at first, on instinct, struggled to whir her wings. After doing this, the girl quickly realized that her wings were pinned to her sides by Sabrina's coat, and raced forward on her toes instead. "Bethany!"

The dainty little dragonfly hurled herself into Bethany's arms, and her soft sobs, previously kept to herself, grew louder. The russet-haired girl caught her, and they hugged and hugged as though they hadn't seen each other in a year. It wasn't long before Bethany, too, joined her in tears, her emotions barely contained by her grinning face. In the background, Joey, being the only relatively mature one at age 12, sniffled quietly and casually wiped his nose with the back of a hand.

"I missed you!" sobbed Emerald, clinging fast to Bethany. "I missed you so much!"

"I missed you more..." replied Bethany. "I'm so sorry for going away... I didn't... I didn't realize you were still there!" Her voice now held a tortured guilt.

"Then..." Emerald's body was racked by fresh waves of tears. "You didn't abandon me...?"

"No, Emerald..." Bethany's voice was weak and breaking. "None of us did..."

The fox-tailed girl looked back at their friends expectantly, and was greeted by the sight of some nodding, with the ones with the softest hearts coming forward to surround Emerald in a group hug. There was Benny, Ginny, Sally, Cassie and most surprisingly, Moony, all giving expectant squeaks and yips and hoots as they surrounded the pair, with Moony pushing in to hug Emerald tightest, because he always wanted to be the best in everything.

It wasn't long before the rest, overcoming their shyness, came in to join the hug and stood soaking in the warmth together, listening to the calming sound of the rain gradually pitter-pattering itself away.

Finally, as the hug broke up, many expectant eyes focused themselves on Emerald, each eager to know what had happened to her and how she had ended up here. Emerald, her red tinged eyes sparkling once more and not with tears, told them everything that she could remember, about Sabrina, and the hot chocolate, and how Sabrina had brought her here, and left her. Bethany's ears were pricked eagerly as she listened for something, but Emerald didn't mention sleeping alone and frightened, or being afraid of the dark.

Her friends listened with fascination and awe on their faces. "Hot chocolate sounds like chicken!" Moony commented. "But a drink!"

Finally Joey looked quizzical. "Wait, wasn't this 'Sabrina' lass the one who brought us up here? She told Mercury to come here too, didn't she?" he asked, after Emerald had finished her story.

He looked uneasily around at the others, but few, if not none, seemed to have gotten it. "She didn't want to come inside! Why did she bring us all here? Did she want us to be baited so that Mercury to take us out?"

They all looked at each other once more in confusion and sudden anger. Bethany, however, her mind numbed with relief at having finally found her friend, didn't seem to care.

"We've found Emerald, and that's what we came here for, right?" she asked, a smile on her face. "Now, if we just leave now, we'll be fine!" Several nods and whispers were her reply. Joey was still uneasy, though. There was an itch down the back of his neck that he couldn't quite place his finger on, an itch that told him something was wrong. "No, what if she's set a trap or something? Mercury might still be here and just waiting for a signal!"

Joey's unease, though not highly contagious, was beginning to affect the other children, the more nervous ones especially.

He looked around frantically, as if to try and find something that would prove his point. After what seemed like an age, Joey caught a glint out of the corner of his eye, and took a few steps towards it. There was something under the bench that Emerald had been seated upon.

A bundle of wires.

Joey reached forward, and gave it a gentle tug, dragging the object towards him. Taking hold with both hands as it came close enough, Joey turned it so that he could see what had caught his eye. There were numbers there, flickering from one to the next as the seconds went on. Joey gulped, blinking as his green eyes reflected the red glow.

"Writing!" piped up Moony excitedly. "What does it say, Joey?"

"Numbers," croaked Joey. "I think they're numbers..."

"What's wrong?"

Sally and Cassie trotted over, looking into the glow. "They're changing! They keep on changing!" both said together, tails wagging from side to side. "What does that mean?"

"This... I think it's a timer of some sort. But what is it counting down to?" Joey looked around, his face paling from its normal colouring, to a sickly white even in the lighting of the device that he was holding on his lap.

"A timer? What does it say, Joey?"

"It says... A minute... N-no, 58 seconds, now..."

"What does it mean?" asked Sally, she and her sister looking at each other with bewilderment and almost fear on their furry faces. "Is it bad?"

313

Moony was watching now, too. "Is this a timed mission?" he asked cleverly, feeling proud for producing such a theory.

Joey looked up at him, and gulped. "Y-yeah…" he whispered, voice hoarse. "Timed…"

Joey placed the device on the floor in front of him, and stood up in a jerky, trembling motion. He knew that something was wrong.

"We need to get out of here. Now!"

***

With despair only growing in my heart, I stare upwards at the seemingly neverending staircase that lies before me, leading me up to where I need to go. Formerly kind to have let me join them, those people had lost interest again, and left me behind, to die. I hear their voices fading away as they get further and further upwards, closer to what had led them here, and yet the distance ever widening between them and me.

And the distance, I feel, isn't just one measured in metres. The distance is also in how far the pieces of my wrenched heart have been torn. The distance between my hopes and the cold, cold dash of reality.

The rain is calming, but the thunder hasn't. In between brutal clashes, I can faintly hear over the rain, the sound of my own blood slowly dripping, removing itself from my weakening form.

Is this it, then?

How long do I have before my eyes go blind, my body senseless? The fight drains out of me like water down a plughole. Of all the ways I had expected to go, whether that be giving my life valiantly in war to save a friend, or dying old and peaceful in a home of my own, this death wasn't one of those that I had expected, or wanted.

Dying all alone, with no friends, no forgiveness, no mercy... Under the roof of a holy place, a holy place that I, Mercury, had corrupted with my own foul intent, my own foul blood.

No... I didn't want this... I don't want it.

With my ears trembling, I feel tears welling up in my eyes. This pain... This agony... It cuts me in so many ways all at once. My hands, or what is left of them, clench into fists.

Something... I have to do something. I slowly open my eyes and wince, heaving a single hand to place it on the step above me. My muscles are so heavy... They feel like they are made of lead. But I have to go on. I realize now that don't want to be loved. I don't mind if I'm not forgiven.

I just don't want to be alone.

To die all alone.

I just need to go on, to keep on fighting. As long as I keep on fighting, I am alive. I am never dying as long as my heart still beats. As long as I keep my breaths even. With another jagged breath heaving my lungs, I struggle on, again. I drag myself up.

Another step...

And another...

And another...

Each shiver takes as much effort as if I were trying to lift a car, as much pain as if someone were holding me down, spikes cutting into me with every movement. But I just want to be with someone when I die. I want to see someone's face again.

However angry, however mistrusting.

My heartbeats start to falter along with my breaths. I realize that I am starved, starved of oxygen. I'm losing too much blood. That's where the dizziness comes from, those swirling waves of nausea that threaten to pin me down, threatening to make every step I drag myself my last.

I can't stop, not now...

My eyes now fill with hope. Joy awakens my heart, as through blurred, half-blind eyes I see ahead of me an open door. I can't hear very well now, but I can hear the steady drip-drip of my blood splashing against the floor. And I can hear voices talking, voices that sound panicked. Something awakens within me. A small, tired smile creeps over my lips, but I try not to let it consume me.

Drip-drip...

Drip-drip...

Drip-drip...

I shake, and pull myself on. Step after step. I just... I have to keep going. If I'm to die, I won't be dying alone now. With the steady caress of people's voices on my ears, their faces looking down at me, I will die happy. Finally, there are no steps ahead of me. However blurred my vision is, I can see that much. I can feel it, too, with a single, shaking palm that soon drops down to the floor. I can hear my own heartbeat pounding through the almost-empty veins in my ears...

I smile, still, lying in place, and staring ahead. A haze of red light pushes back the darkness.

Fuzzy, hazed, changing red light.

I blink several times. The panic in the voices around me is rising. I don't understand. Though before, I felt only peace, now, I feel restlessness tugging on my mind, forcing me to listen to those around me.

"We need to get out of here, now!"

That was the only thing I caught, and the voice that says it sounds so awfully familiar. I struggle to catch more words then rasp out what little breath I can. "What... Is going... On...?" I rasp, and the strangers turn towards me. They look so... surprised to see me, from what I can pick up through blurred, hazy eyes.

I am still not welcome here.

I try to catch what they say, but much whips past my ears, unheard.

"...Funny light, and numbers!" That was all I caught, from a voice that sounded so much younger than the first. Still struggling to pick up something more, I raise my head, with all the strength I can muster, and sniff the air. Something smells so... familiar.

It almost smells like ashes.

It smells like death. I let my head drop to the ground again, that musty, stale scent still ripe in my memories.

Gunpowder.

The fear, the horror that courses through me causes my entire body to give a single, jarring shudder. I can't say anything more, but I know what it is now. I know.

I know.

Tears spring to my eyes. So little time... So little strength I have left. I can't... I can't do it. I don't have the strength. But I have to. It's the last thing. It's the only thing I can do. It's not just for myself, either.

It's for my family, who lived and died to protect me.

It's for these people, to whom I've caused so much pain.

It's for this city, who struggle on desperately through the war.

And it's for my country, who fight on even now, as I lie here.

The last ounces of strength finally come. I lift my hands slowly, and place them on either side of my chest. Slowly, I pick myself up from the ancient stone, my chest heaving with the struggle, and my last drops of blood pouring onto the ground. They watch me in what I assume is awe, and terror. They fear that I am going to attack them again, even in the state that I'm in.

But no.

317

I shuffle forward, past them, on my knees, my tail drags along behind me, only adding extra weight. "Please..." I whisper, and it's the only thing I can. I am by the window now, my hands, my paws resting on the window ledge, using it as support. The ever-flickering red glow bores into my vision as I turn back; it's the only thing that I can still see. The one who had held the object just one minute ago is still standing by it, and he's panicking, trying to get his friends to move.

"Give it... To me..."

At first, there is no response. They all stare, even now. Their faces aren't anything but blurred shapes, their voices fuzzy and incomprehensible. What do they think I'm going to do? I heave myself up onto legs that quiver and shake, almost buckling and dropping me, still clinging tightly to the window ledge as the only support I have. I turn again, and reach out for them.

"Pleassssse..." I beg finally. The light gets closer, and brighter, until I can finally see the device, the many wires illuminated by the glowing numbers. Feeling it slip into my palm, I dig in my claws, and give a final smile to those who stand before me.

"Thank you..." I whisper, so sincere, and so helplessly defeated.

Thank you... The words echo through my mind, sounding as though someone else had said them. I can barely recognize my own voice.

I gave them, those who I finally consider as friends, a single expression. A smile that shows them, begs them, to forgive me.

And then I turn away.

With a challenging cry I lash out, lunge forward.

Shards of glass spin around me, flashing in the rain. Cutting myself on the broken glass still left in the window frame, I lean out over empty air, then wriggle and writhe my way forwards. My second eyelids flicker

318

over my eyes, then my first. I feel weightless now, timeless as I plummet into space. I can't tell where I'm going. Whether I'm going up or down, spinning right or left.

As my life flashes before my eyes, I remember now.

I remember it all.

And now, I hold those memories close.

Those precious memories.

With my last smile drifting over my lips, I open my eyes once more, and look upwards, towards the silver-forked sky. The last things I see are numbers, emblazoned in red.

3...

2...

1...

-Chapter 23-

First Loss

Standing at the entrance to the cathedral with her lips pursed, Alma was tensed up, unusually so. Every so often, she would flick up her wrist to check her watch, then shiver and look up again, into the rain, up at the tower, as though she were waiting for something.

Her throat was dry, her mouth even drier, but still she stood, as stiff as stone, her hands clenched into fists as she watched and waited, listened, expected something to happen in the tower. The more she waited, though, the longer it seemed to take, and she realized that whenever she checked her watch, barely a minute had passed since her last checking. With a sigh, Alma lowered her wrist and went back to watching the tower.

So focused was she on the cathedral tower, that it came as quite a shock to Alma as someone, or two people, to be more exact, came up beside her, with one of them eyeing her suspiciously and the other staring straight ahead into empty space. Alma blinked up at the tower, then, without turning to look at the newcomers, she spoke.

"What are you doing here?" she asked, her voice calm, emotionless, and almost cold despite her slight inner discomfort. "I thought you two were hugging."

"We couldn't let you get away without finding out what you're up to." Danny turned to give her a look that boiled with suspicion.

Alma still didn't look at him. "What if I told you that you're too late?" she asked simply.

"I wouldn't believe you," replied Danny. "I don't

think there's such a thing as too late."

Alma wasn't sure if he was being stupid or just plain childish. What did he think he could do? Danny didn't even know what she was up to!

She snorted softly, finally turning to face them with her piercing, icy green eyes burning. Toby was looking away from her still, and whether it was in shock, or betrayal, he still hadn't said a word to her.

"You," Alma said suspiciously, pointing a finger at Toby. "Say somethin'."

"Leave Toby out of this," snapped Danny protectively. "And it's rude to point."

Alma watched him closely. "Oh yeah?" she asked softly, her voice dripping with sarcasm. "And who are you to have such authority over me?"

Her eyes glittered as Danny found no words to reply. "It's better to serve a high position in the war in your own country, than to be just a useless insect in another country... Isn't it now?" she drawled on. Danny seemed taken aback, and Alma felt a smile flickering over her face in triumph. "I know how much those other scientists put you down, don't they, sweetheart?"

Alma had begun to circle the two, stalking about them like a shark homing in for the kill. Danny watched warily, and he was turning in circles, struggling to keep her in his sights and protect Toby. She could see that his face was white, but she wasn't sure if that was from fear, or the cold.

But she knew she'd found his weak point.

"Oooh... None ever tried to stick up for you, now, did they? None tried to help, no matter how much of a fuss they made..."Alma eyed him sympathetically. "It just goes to show that you don't belong here..."

Danny took a lunge at her, his fist shaking as he swung. "No..." he stammered. "I'm not listening to

321

you."

Alma stepped away from the blow with the slightest of ease. "Was that a threat?" she asked softly, her eyes sparkling. "Would you go so far as to hit someone from your own country?"

Danny was tensed up, and Alma could tell that he was trying to be subtle as he readied himself for another swing at her. "You're not from my country," he spat. "This is my country! Here!"

He swung again, and Alma skipped out of the way. There was no way a simple scientist could stand up to a trained fighter like her. But he didn't know that. No. The thought was almost amusing... Alma chuckled softly.

"Oh, you might think that. What do I know, eh?" She anticipated another strike from the angry man.

"Nothing!" retorted Danny, swinging again, as she had expected. Alma reached out and caught his fist in her own dainty palm. She hadn't been expecting him to be quite so strong, but dealt with his strength as she would an ordinary blow; with ease.

Calmly gripping his hand in hers, Alma wouldn't leave go even as he tried to pull it away from her. He lunged once more in desperation, his free hand flailing, and winding up caught by the wrist in Alma's trap. Alma chuckled once more, refusing to leave go.

"Oh, how sweet!" she crooned mockingly, giving his arms a little tug, then a twist that made Danny struggle more so, in pain. "So clumsy! Like a wee little baby."

Ignoring his struggles, Alma kept him pinned for a while, then tossed his arms back towards him, sending him stumbling backwards and falling down onto his behind. He looked at her pathetically, rubbing his burning arm, causing Alma's chuckles to only grow louder.

"Oh, that look you give me! How can I resist!?" she cooed, as though she were talking to a child.

"You... You're a monster," there came a simple, shocked voice rasping from behind her, and Alma whipped around as though stunned, as though she had forgotten that they were not alone here. Toby limped forwards a few steps, placing his crutches carefully. Alma was about to make a sharp remark, and she opened her mouth, her face scowling then closed it again. Her face returned to burning red with shame, and she lowered her gaze, away from Toby's singing stare.

"A monster..." Toby repeated, louder this time. Danny slowly got to his feet and brushed himself off with shivering hands. Alma stared at the ground then turned towards Danny, struggling to replace her shocked expression with a vicious smile once more.

How closely the man was watching her with those blue eyes made Alma feel almost uncomfortable. She shifted her feet slightly. What could he see in her? She couldn't leave this place, no. She had to confidently give a report to her boss of her success, or of her failure. Waiting for news reports simply wasn't good enough. She had to be there first-hand. So she stayed silent, not replying to Toby, which seemed a cue for Danny to have a theory.

"Ooooh..." he said, as though he knew everything now. "This is all for Toby, isn't it! You, you..." Danny snickered childishly. "...You *love* him. Don't you?"

Alma's cheeks burned. "I... Shut it, you," she hissed, cracking her knuckles threateningly. Danny flinched and was instantly silent, as though Alma had just knocked him in the mute button. Toby wasn't about to be stopped, though.

"You didn't deny it!" he pointed out, limping forward so that he unknowingly wound up right in Alma's face. Or was he conscious of that fact?

Surprisingly, she didn't react too harshly to him, simply grunted and looked away. Danny kept himself stubbornly silent, worried that his intervention might result in something bad happening to himself or Toby.

Alma chuckled softly again, finally pulling herself together. "I didn't," she said softly, stalking away from him by a few steps, her toes as light as cat's paws. "But that doesn't mean I am at peace."

Her eyes flashed as Toby looked as though he were about to speak again, and she interrupted him. "My challenge still remains open," she purred as she cunningly changed the subject, twitching lithely. "I'll tell you what, scientist." The woman jabbed a finger into Danny's nose, and he went crosseyed trying to see what it was she'd done. "If you take my challenge, you have my respect. Knock me down, and I'll leave you both alone, and I'll tell you what's going to happen to your little bunch of pets. Sound good?"

"They're not pets!" retorted Danny indignantly, getting more worked up the longer he stayed here as he finally was whipped back to the matter at hand. "And I need to find them! We don't have time for this!" Danny grabbed Toby's arm, and pulled him towards the cathedral doors, but Alma was already standing there, blocking them.

She checked her watch, smirked, and looked up at Danny. *Just a minute more...*

"Are you going to accept my challenge, or what?" she asked. "It's tempting, isn't it?"

Danny shook his head vigorously. "No!" he stammered. "It isn't tempting! You never even told me what would happen if I lost, and I can't agree to anything if I can't save them!" Danny tried to pull Toby around Alma, giving the woman a wide berth, but the more he moved, the more she did, and the harder it would be to get around her.

"Take it or leave it," she told him. "This is the only chance you're getting."

Alma licked her lips.

"And if you win, I might even call it off!" she told him, her voice crooning and comforting, as though she was talking to a child. She was lying, of course. But he didn't know that. "They'll be alive! Oh, just think of them! So happy, cheerful..."

Danny slowly let go of Toby's arm, his hands trembling. He had no other choice. "Fine," he replied, trying to sound tough. "I'll take it... Just don't hurt me too bad, 'kay?"

Alma examined her fingernails modestly. "Oh, tut, tut, tut," she whispered, as though talking to a child about a sensitive matter, her eyes widening as if she'd witnessed a sudden revelation. "Did I forget to mention something?"

Danny's stomach plummeted. "Wha-?"

"I had my fingers crossed at that last part... Oh, and, if you lose, you die," she said simply. "And Toby comes home with me!"

Danny's face went from shock, to anger, then to utter embarrassment. "You tricked me..." he whispered. "You *are* a monster!" Danny staggered backwards as Alma, not waiting for him to finish, took a warning strike at his belly. She didn't hit him, but Danny had thrown himself off balance, and almost tripped over his own feet. Not soon to be deterred, he quickly regained himself, and charged at her with his own fists bared.

Alma dodged strike after strike, every so often offering a cryptic, taunting source of advice. "Gee," she called one time. "For a scientist, you sure don't put much into practice, do you? Clumsy, slow, not even taking advantage of your weight... Ha! Did you hear that, big guy? I called you fat!"

Though she clearly didn't have a sense of humour or accuracy, Alma's taunts and her stunts of agility were wearing Danny down, doing their job, as much as he was wearing himself down. *What is she doing!?* He wondered helplessly after a while. For apart from that first attack, Alma hadn't even threatened to attack. As he swung and struggled on, it finally became clear what she was doing.

She'd tricked him... Again!

All this jumping was just a tactic, meant to enrage him into attacking, again and again, until he became so tired that he couldn't hope to dodge or block. Yes... That was it. But it was already too late. Looking up with tired blue eyes, Danny was unable to dodge as Alma finally made her first, and final, attack.

Danny was thrown backwards, and tumbled head over heels until he landed flat on his back, winded and shocked. Eventually gathering his senses, Danny began to struggle to pick himself up again, his breaths uneasy and desperate. Before he could pick himself up, though, Danny felt a foot placed firmly on his chest to pin him down. He looked up to see Alma, and in the background, the cathedral.

As he turned his head away from her, struggling to tear his gaze away from the woman who prepared to strike, his eyes caught the glint of red light.

"What the...?" he gulped. "Is that... Mercury?"

The boy fell, followed by cascades of shimmering glass shards.

In his thick paw was something that gleamed for only a moment longer.

There was a bright flash. Flames billowed out from whatever it was Mercury held, and then the light grew so bright, that he had to close his eyes. He felt the shockwave sweep over him like a blast from an air cannon, like he'd been caught in an unexpected hurricane. Steam rose up around the explosion site as the heat made its mark, and nearby trees caught alight as the fireball went from a blazing sun to a great ball of glistening, writhing fire, like billowing snake scales wrought in black and red smoke.

Danny couldn't block his ears, and he felt as though that last clash, like the last burst of howling thunder, cracking open the sky, was breaking open his very skull. Shaken by the impact, and by thoughts of what could have happened, Danny lay there, unable to get up if he tried. The cathedral walls, though singed, were still intact and the trees were still alight.

Alma, like himself, stared, in both awe, and in dismay. Her foot, still placed firmly on Danny's chest, lingered there for a moment before Alma removed it, her challenge forgotten.

Alma took several small, hesitant steps towards the cathedral. Her hands trembled, and though none could see it through the rain, small tears had begun to stream down her face. Alma dropped her head slightly, and let her blonde locks of hair fall into her eyes. With a smile trembling slowly into view on her face, Alma sniffed softly- a failed mission.

Alma had failed.

A final blow, like a volcano bellowing its final song, erupted from inside her heart, shattering the newly-formed ice and melting the pieces once more.

This was what she needed.

What she always had needed. Her confidence broken, her pride hurt, Alma sank down onto her knees, her head down, chin resting on her chest.

"Thank goodness…" she whispered, tears streaming down her face.

Danny, standing on wobbly legs, approached her warily, with Toby beside him. "What?" asked Danny, sounding very surprised.

Alma didn't appear to hear him. She stared down at the ground, and didn't reply, or, at least, not to him. Her voice became a croak, and her shuddering shoulders slumped forwards as though they were trying to shield her.

"Thank goodness…" she whispered again, her green gaze tilting upwards, to the scorched but intact cathedral tower, once more. A genuine smile, stained with tears, traced her lips.

As she looked upwards, the last droplets of rain were there to wash away Alma's tears like the caress of a guardian angel.

Then the rain finally stopped.

-Chapter 24-

Forgiveness

His footsteps hesitant and his breaths hardly daring even to hope, to believe, Danny watched as the children came, one by one, stepping out from the dark halls of the cathedral and into the light. Danny raced forward at first, arms outstretched, determined to scoop them all into a big hug, but then he stopped just before them.

Something was wrong.

Horribly wrong.

Instead of greeting Danny like they would normally have done, they just stared up at him with eyes that were dark, tired, and sad. Their shoulders were slumped and their eyes focused on the ground ahead of them, as though afraid that something was going to suck them in.

Moony's wings were drooping, and Bethany's thick, lustrous tail dragged upon the ground behind her, with Emerald not even looking at her best friend, simply following along behind, as though she were too frightened to say anything. Benny's ears were drooping, his glasses kept on sliding down his nose, and Ginny, who, even now, held tight to his hand, was giving soft, squeaking sobs of fear, her eyes covered by her remaining paw. Sally and Cassie's tails and ears were drooping, their tongues still lolling out of one side of their muzzles. Joey's hands were clenched, and his hair and feathers were untidy and erratic, sticking out at odd angles as though he hadn't preened them in a while, which was unusual for him.

They walked slowly past Danny like some sort of funeral procession, then Danny walked ahead, after them. Upon hearing his footsteps, a few of them turned back, looking frightened and dismayed, cowering away from him as they expected to be told off. Danny watched them. Moony began to cry softly, hiding his face in his hands.

"We did it..." he sobbed. "It was us..."

Danny swallowed, having difficulty figuring out what was going on. But he kept his face looking calm and kind, knelt down softly before them so that they would feel less threatened by him. They flinched again, and Moony sobbed louder, allowing himself to be gathered into Danny's arms in a hug, his large golden eyes squeezing themselves shut.

"It's okay..." whispered Danny comfortingly. "Come on... You can tell me what happened."

"N-no..." sobbed Moony. "You won't like us anymore if we do..."

"Shhh..." Danny hugged Moony closer, and gently rocked the boy in his arms, trying to calm him down somehow. If something had frightened them like this, then it must be serious. Danny looked around, wondering if Alma had done something aside from the evident attempt of trying to blow up the Cathedral. Was that what had scared the children so?

The woman was nowhere to be found. It was as though she had simply vanished.

Trying again to calm Moony, Ginny soon crept up to him, and huddled close, followed by Benny, and Sally, and Cassie. Emerald came next, and Bethany followed, and then finally Joey clung on to Danny's comforting form.

"There..." he said. "That's better... Isn't it?" He looked down at the weeping and whimpering children, some with scratches or bite marks that could only belong to one being.

...Mercury... Did he do this to them? Danny looked

up at the sobbing children who gathered close to him.

"Can you tell me what happened?" he repeated, his voice soft and comforting. Moony looked up at him, and shook his head fearfully, then hid his face in Danny's chest again. Danny felt the boy's warm tears soaking into his shirt.

Danny sighed.

"I promise," he told them. "I've seen enough to know that I could never stop liking you. You're too special to me..."

He hugged the children close, as best that he could manage.

"You're my family... all of you. I could never abandon my family. I promise..."

Finally, Sally and Cassie broke down. Though on the outside, they were as tough as steel, as businesslike as police dogs, inside they were still just little puppies, and right now, they wanted the comfort that Danny could give.

"We did it..." sobbed Sally, clutching her sister close, as she repeated Moony's vague, sorrowful words. "It was us..."

"What do you mean?" asked Danny softly, ruffling the two dog-girls' hair with his free hand, one after the other, until they leaned in close and begged for more comfort.

"M-Mercury..." Cassie whimpered. Her sister huddled close, and the rest cringed and cowered. "We... He... He tried to make friends with us..."

The girls began to sob again.

"But... But..."

Moony gave a sorrowful hoot, burying himself in Danny's comforting hug. "We killed him! We killed Mercury!"

Ginny sobbed louder, tiny squeaks making her body tremble. "We did! And I was happy about it, and I talked to them, and wanted them to!" She turned around to hug Benny close, in case Danny brushed her away as all of them now expected him to.

But then he didn't.

He simply watched, and listened, with that look of understanding on his face that he always wore as he spoke to them.

"And he wanted to come with us, once... Then h-he stayed back, and we l-left him behind, but then he caught up to us..." Joey's voice trembled with weakness rather than pride. "I thought something was up when he came towards us, but... But I never thought he was ever trying to help us... Ever..." He sniffed.

"Then he took that thing off Joey and jumped out the window," added Moony, sniffling.

Joey nodded, rubbing his eyes with the back of a hand. "It could have been us in that bright light, there, and it could have been in the cathedral, like it was in that house in the training mission, once!"

They each sniffled and sobbed, and Danny hugged them and comforted them as best he could.

"B-but Mercury t-took it, and he did it himself..." added Moony. "Even though we attacked him, and we left him behind, and he was all covered in blood..."

They continued to sob and cry.

Danny sighed softly.

"Don't be too sad," he whispered. "We need to move on from all this. This is a war, and in war, people are going to leave us."

The children looked up at Danny with watery eyes.

"Growing up is all about learning, and getting stronger. And you can't get stronger if you don't overcome losses, like this. You need to learn from your mistakes so that you don't make them again." Danny brushed away some of the tears from the mutants' soft tear-stained faces as they turned their faces to look up at him. "So be happy, and learn! This was what Mercury wanted. For you to live! He wanted to help you, and he did, by giving his own life- for you! He did that, so what's the point in crying about it?"

They gazed up at him still, and Danny could see their soft, trusting eyes flashing in the light.

"You don't need to be hard on yourself. You did what you thought was right..." Danny finished, gently placing a hand on Moony's shoulder and looking first into his golden eyes, and then around at the rest as they looked for the comfort of a father that none of them had ever had.

Apart from Danny.

The thought warmed the man's heart, but as much as this, formed a lump in his throat.

Danny looked up at the cold midday sky, still laden with tendrils of grey clouds that drifted lazily across his field of view. It still looked heavy with rain, even though the worst of the storm had passed and was now little more than a shadow, thick and dark, in the distance.

"Come on," said Danny, to the children, standing up and lifting an exhausted, still-tearful Moony with him. "We need to find somewhere to stay for a while. Would any of you be fine with staying in the cathedral for a bit?"

They all shook their heads, for apparently the events that had occurred in the holy building had left a lasting mark on the young ones' minds.

Danny looked at the crowd of astounded people who had gathered in response to the explosion, all ready to pester, and he gave a tired grin that said 'let's discuss this in the morning'... None smiled, none laughed, but Danny didn't respond to them.

His eyelids flickered, and his sodden form was still dripping in the cold air that still brought with it promises of yet more rain. With a sigh, Danny took Toby's arm, and together they led the children away from the cathedral, all in a line. They followed with tails raised higher, and as they passed the people, they offered hesitant childish grins and quiet squeaking noises, beginning to return slowly back to their old selves.

They walked on, and on, and on into the afternoon, all the while looking for somewhere that beckoned them with a warm, warm glow. But nowhere jumped out towards them. Eventually, exhausted and defeated, they all slumped down in the shelter of a doorway, unable to go any further.

Shaking off the rain onto each other and pushing everyone out of the way as they argued over the best places to sleep, Danny sat and watched them, until one by one, they shuffled themselves off into hazy, trembling, dreamless sleep. Eventually even Toby was asleep, using his guide's chest as a warm, breathing pillow.

Danny, though, stayed awake, and he looked upwards at the sky. He couldn't sleep, for some reason; whether it be in regret for what had occurred at the cathedral, or sorrow for these children, something was causing a prickle of unease through his mind whenever he closed his eyes. Sighing softly, Danny looked over at the children again, and for a minute, thought he saw the flash of a pair of familiar, amber eyes before they quickly closed as if trying to fool him.

"Bethany…?" whispered Danny, his voice softly hushed.

No response. Her ears only softly flicked.

"Bethany…!" he repeated, a little bit louder this time.

Finally, the girl opened an eye just a sliver, seeming to be trying to check to see what he wanted without giving away that she wasn't really sleeping. The glint of her eyes in the starlight gave her away, though. Danny nodded to her then gave his head a quick twitching gesture to tell her to come to him. Bethany looked hesitant, and didn't move at first. Eventually, though, she slowly sat up, and looked at him, her ears drooping backwards in what he assumed was shame.

"Come here," whispered Danny, his voice straining to make itself heard. Bethany's ears pricked forward softly, and she slowly edged her way over to him, stepping carefully over her sleeping brothers and sisters. Swallowing anxiously, the girl twisted the soft fur of her tail in her hands, her amber eyes glowing eerily in the dark.

"Why are you still awake?" he asked her softly. Bethany continued to twist the fur of her tail in her hands, looking down at the ground, with her eyes flitting about nervously. She avoided his gaze as if it were a curse, and didn't say anything. "Bethany?"

Still, she said nothing, twisting her tail in the dark with those soft, furry hands.

Finally, she looked up at him. She opened her mouth, and her voice came out as a soft croak, almost unintelligible at first. "I just couldn't sleep..." she mourned.

Danny reached out a hand for her to hold, and the little girl simply stared at it, then shook her head and took a step back, away from him. Slowly and shamefacedly, Danny lowered his hand back down to his side.

"Bethany..." he whispered, as though he were about to say something. Then he said nothing.

"What?" croaked Bethany, her voice a soft whine that threatened to break into a sob.

"This is all because of me, isn't it?" he asked, voice dying in his throat.

Bethany looked up at him with her eyes shocked. She quickly shook her head, then considered only after. Slowly, but surely, she nodded.

Danny sighed. "I knew it..." he muttered.

Bethany hung her head slightly. "I mean, you did leave Emerald back in the laboratory, and she could have died!"

Danny covered his eyes with his hand, and breathed deeply. It took a few seconds for Bethany to realize that he was trying to force himself not to cry. As she did, her tail drooped and her ears went back.

"I never meant to..." he murmured sorrowfully. "I just... I was so focused on getting everyone else out that... That I didn't even notice she was missing. She's always so quiet..."

Bethany looked up at him, and finally inched closer.

"I know that she's your best friend... And you know, I didn't mean to do that..." The man sighed, wanting to curl up into a ball or move away from them, but knowing that doing so would disturb Toby, who finally lay peacefully asleep. "It wasn't on purpose..."

Danny shook his head and let out another long sigh.

Bethany stayed silent but took another step towards him. Slowly, she removed Danny's hand from his face, and held it close. Danny looked up with teary eyes, surprised.

"Do you... Do you still hate me, Bethany...?" he asked softly, as though he was dreading to hear her answer.

Bethany gently shook her head.

"Did you ever hate me?"

She hesitated for a while then quietly shook her head again.

Danny looked into her eyes for a while, seeking the truth.

Then he pulled her close, into a one-armed hug.

336

"I knew it…" he whispered, sounding as though he were about to cry again any moment. A broad smile adorned his face, his hands trembled with relief.

At first she stiffened, the she melted into his hug, her mind finally cleared of that consuming, guilty fog that had hung over her, unconsciously, for so long.

Finally, Danny pulled away, and his soft eyes looked into hers, holding the gentle warmth that one would feel if they were sitting with their friends about a campfire.

"Come on, sleep now," he whispered, voice warm, and his eyes kind. "You need to gather your strength again. It's been a long, stressful day."

Bethany reluctantly nodded, far from displaying the usual reluctance to go to bed. Turning away from Danny, her tail fluffed out, and she scampered back to her place amongst the others. As she settled down, Bethany looked up at Danny again, one last time. "If I'm sleeping, what will you do?" she asked.

Danny smiled softly.

"I need some time to think," he said simply.

Bethany, seeming satisfied, curled up once more, and Danny watched over her for a while, until he was sure that she had succumbed to sleep. Then he stared out into the darkness, and up at the stars once more. A smile played over his face as the minutes passed, and eventually, despite his words, Danny, too, nodded off.

And for what felt like the first time in ages, he slept peacefully.

-Epilogue-

Happiness

Today was an unusual day for the little city of Durham.

It was weeks after the incident of the warning that Alma had tried to give, and with that in mind, preparations had taken what felt like a lifetime to some, and minutes to others. But plans had come together, as plans rarely ever seem to do, and anticipation and excitement was high, every breath hanging in the air.

It was very unusual.

For one thing, it was sunny, and sunny days in England are things hard come by. Usually in winter, the clouds were laden with frost and snow, but it only snowed when you didn't want it to, then rained when you wanted it to snow. Sunny days were rare and only ever seemed to happen when every person in England was in work, or at school, or whatever. Now there was not a cloud in the sky, and the sun blazed down clear and true as if in congratulations.

And for another, there were things happening in the usually forgotten little town. Crowds and crowds had gathered, all there to congratulate a little group of people for their efforts in the war. Sunlight danced from the glimmering walls of the cathedral as it overlooked the scene from high up on its hill, restored of the ashes in the very centre of that little loop in the river that the city was built around. Cheering, crying voices made the air sing with joy, and applause made hearts swell with pride.

In the centre of the crowd, were several grinning faces, and each one was familiar, their chests adorned with glittering gold medals that the sun lit up, so it

338

seemed that each person had captured and was wearing their own sun.

The children were persistent, each pestering Danny to be lifted up so that they could see more of the crowd, and so that the crowd could see them too. Joey was the only one who didn't, and instead, he was preening and preening, desperate to look his best for the people who were admiring him.

Sally and Cassie jumped about and barked and yipped, and the crowd loved them like anyone would love a little pair of puppies that begged for attention from them. Waves of 'aww' and 'aaah' rolled out under the blue sky.

Emerald, in the meantime, shied away behind Danny as she clung to his legs, her cheeks blushing pink and her diamond eyes darting. She seemed frightened to be seen, and it was the first time she'd ever seen so many people in her life, or at least in the one that she remembered.

But then, Bethany, smiling and waving at the crowd, took Emerald's hand. The pair, best of friends, smiled at each other, then without hesitation stepped out to greet the cheers, and the many smiling faces. Emerald at first huddled into her friend, but then she began to fall into a rhythm, her wings slowly spreading out, and vibrating softly. Her feeler gently touched at Bethany's cheek, to make sure that she was still there even when Emerald wasn't looking. Then Emerald pushed from the ground, and soared out over the crowd to hear their cheers, and whoops of utter delight. Bethany watched her, with sheer pride in her eyes, and just that slight touch of envy that came with being grounded.

Moony hooted and boasted and pranced in circles whilst flaring and beating his tiny wings in pride. "Look at me!" he called out anxiously to the crowd as they watched Emerald fly, her kaleidoscopic wings casting splashes of light over the crowd, and her hair dancing turquoise in the light. "Look at meee!"

Benny and Ginny held hands and squeaked at each other, content as they went around giving soft little hugs and received treats of chocolate from the crowd. Their noses twitched at each other and they grinned and whispered shyly, always sticking close to where their friends were, and never straying far away even if it meant being petted or held.

And then there was Danny, who had never felt happier in his life.

He kept on sniffling and having to wipe his eyes with his fingers to stop anyone in the crowd from seeing his watering eyes. Finally, he felt like he truly belonged here. A gold medal sat upon his chest and beamed out sunlight, dazzling the crowd in all its glory. He no longer aroused suspicion whenever he spoke, or was teased by all who knew him relatively well.

No.

Now he stood in the midst of this cheering, calling crowd, and he was proud. Proud of all those around him. Proud of this country, and his friends. But most importantly, he was finally proud of himself. Now, Danny had never been particularly egotistic or vain, nor had he ever had a particularly high self-esteem, but that was why it was so important. He was here. And he was happy with what he had done. He was proud of who he was. And it was these people who made it so.

In the crowd, there were some people who stuck out to him like sore thumbs, yet at the same time, looked like complete strangers. They were scientists like him, the survivors of the 'accident' that had destroyed the laboratory. They were the lucky ones, who had, like Danny, gotten out alive. But unlike him and Toby, they had had homes to go to.

They had once treated him as a burden, a shame to

the laboratory.

But now, they had changed. No longer laughing or jeering at his accent or where he had come from, now they were in the crowd, looking somewhat jealous and a little bit unsettlingly sneaky, but still in the crowd. They cheered, clapped and hollered congratulations along with the rest, and tried their best to call over the little mutants to see if they were recognized, but were ignored as the other people offered treats and new friends.

Danny could have laughed. He turned to Toby, who stood beside him, and he took hold of his brother's arm.

Toby was grinning broadly. His blind eyes were flitting about instinctively and in joy as he struggled to see what was going on around him.

"Danny...?" whispered Toby hoarsely. Danny looked at him, and he smiled, baring gleaming white teeth.

"Yes?" he asked softly, knowing that Toby could hear him, even over the crowds.

"Is Alma here?" Toby replied eventually, his cheeks beginning to blush a deep, surprising shade of red.

Danny looked out into the crowd, and tried to see. Eventually, Danny caught the glint of pale, unremarkable green eyes, peeping slyly out from the crowd, before they quickly vanished again, pulling back in embarrassed shame. She wasn't meant to be here.

But she wasn't dangerous any more.

"Yes..." Danny whispered softly to Toby, as though Alma, hiding somewhere among the crowds, could hear him. "She's here."

With his ears pricked, Toby could hear the voices amassed, and hear the joy and the sounds of the people clapping, applauding him, giving him the proper respect that he deserved. He listened out for Alma, but

341

he couldn't hear her elusive voice. He wasn't disappointed, though; Toby's chest puffed out in pride, because that was just the way his mind worked. He wasn't a child anymore, and these people didn't see him as one. Toby, breathing in breaths of the clean, fresh air that he still needed to get used to, tipped his head upwards towards the sky, and then laughed in his rasping, yowling voice.

Danny looked sideways at Toby, almost wondering if Toby was alright- his laughter was quite an unnerving sound for some. But then he saw the smile that Toby's face still held, and then Danny tipped back his own head to look up towards the sky. His eyes reflected the dazzling sunlight and he felt the warmth on his face.

With his eyes closing and his lungs filling with air, Danny's chest heaved, and he began to laugh as well.

At the same time, something lurched out of the crowd, a special guest that had been promised walkies a few days ago. With a flying dog lead trailing from his red dog collar, whoever it was had broken free of a person's hold and come running at the scent of someone familiar. Brown eyes wide with excitement and stubby legs blurring, he bounded forward, and threw himself up into Danny's arms as the man laughed, bowling him roughly off his feet so that he only just caught the wriggling missile.

Danny laughed even louder.

A wet black nose pushed itself into Danny's cheek, whilst a tail blurred and whirled and blurred some more, as if the slobbering wielder was about to take off. Danny laughed, and hugged the wriggling mass close to him, careful of the masses of bandages that held him in one piece, keeping his wounds from re-opening. The mass barked, and yelped, and barked some more, fitfully licking and slurping at Danny's face, as though he'd never seen Danny before in his life and never would again.

As Danny looked up once more, and laughed once more, his joyful voice echoed and mingled with that of the crowd's.

The child he held watched him as well, and with a doggy smile on his face, the boy barked, golden ears flopping and golden hair glinting like the medals in the sun. As he listened to Danny laugh, the boy's ears pricked, and his tongue lolled out.

Hugging close with great dog-eyes that laughed in their own way, the boy's jaws parted slightly, and he seemed to laugh as well.

He looked up at all who gathered around him, and he begged with his eyes for hugs and petting, which he gratefully received with a tail that wagged at the speed of sound and licks from a soft pink tongue.

Still he did not speak and still he couldn't say a word.

But here, he didn't need any words.

Karasu's actions were enough to say everything that he needed.

I'm so glad to be alive…

***

A short while away from the gathering, from which all the happy voices cheered, a young, plump face with blonde hair falling softly into his gentle brown eye, looked out over the scene, and he marvelled at all he could see from his perch. He was resting with his chin on the windowsill, looking out at the people who scurried like little ants far below him.

Upon his face, there was a peaceful smile, and as the boy looked up, he saw the rest of his room. The walls, painted a sunny shade of blue like the sky outside, were mostly covered with posters and pictures. The posters were mostly of various animals of many different types, from bears and wolves, to posters of reptiles. Among the animals, there were posters of England flags, and posters of men dressed up and ready to go out into war, laden heavy with weapons and armour. To contrast, there were also pictures of the holy cross, like the one engraved in silver, strung about the boy's neck.

And there was one, in the middle, that he had drawn himself.

This picture was a rather poorly-drawn picture, admittedly, but it was of a man, and a boy, standing together. They were holding hands and each bore a huge, bright red smile on his face. In the picture, the boy's eyes were brown and his hair bright yellow. His father had eyes that were brown like his, and hair that was also brown. They both stood together in the picture under a sky that was bluer than the sky would ever be, on squiggles of grass that their feet only just touched. The sun, in that picture was brighter than it ever had shone and would shine again.

This was the picture that the boy focused on most. His mother was downstairs. She said that she needed to talk to his grandma, and his granddad, about something. The boy seemed to know what it was all about, but he wasn't as upset as she had seemed.

He was too innocent, too childish, to be upset.

So instead, the boy decided that he would draw once more, like he had done with the picture he had pinned up on his wall, years ago.

The boy smiled.

He was much better at drawing now. Much better than he had been back when he'd first done that picture, but still it remained a personal favourite of his.

Softly, the boy turned away from his windowsill, and trotted over to the set of drawers by his bedside cabinet. His eyes shone with happiness and pride as he drew out all his colouring pencils and a small set of paints that he kept there for special occasions. The boy staggered forward with his arms full, and dumped all the pencils and paint out on the desk, all covered with paper and unfinished drawings. When he returned again with a shining photograph, the boy carefully pushed all the pencils aside and set the photograph just out of the way, so that he could still see it. Using his hands to clear some room, the boy trundled away gain, and came back with a small sketch pad, which he laid out carefully on the table, folding over the cover so that he could rest on it.

Then the boy began to draw.

His pencils quivered and danced over the paper as he willed them, with his wrist twitching and flickering to create what he wanted and needed on his picture.

His eye searched and flicked back and forth, looking for a place to put his next piece of scenery or his next part of the picture. He drew lots of flowers, petals growing out of little central puffballs, and he drew the background; clouds. Beautiful, swirling clouds surrounding faint, white-capped mountains.

But then the boy stopped.

He decided.

He smiled.

He rubbed out the mountains, and kept only their silver peaks, rearing up out of the silver fog, far away. With a smile on his face, the boy drew two figures in the centre of the page, and filled the sky with life. Blossoms fluttered on a breeze that he drew with a soft blue pencil, and light shone down from the sky, in which there was no sun, only life and the faraway mountains. For the ground, the boy drew more squiggles; he had never really improved at drawing grass.

Then, the boy held his breath. Once more, he scurried from his room, and came back with a cup of water carefully grasped in his pudgy little hands. He placed the cup carefully on his desk, making sure that he didn't spill it. With a shivering hand, the little boy took a plate covered with paint stains out of a drawer beneath his desk, and set it carefully beside his half-finished picture. Carefully avoiding his picture, the boy squirted a small blob of paint onto the plate then daintily dipped the tip of a paintbrush into the cup of water, then into the paint.

His eyes focused and his soft face serious, the boy began to, with the most delicate of care, paint the sky a stunning shade of blue. His eye narrowed, darting occasionally from one side of the picture to the other to check that he was doing it right. With deep breaths making him tremble with concentration, the boy painted the grass with little flurries of green dashes, made the peaks and the clouds silver by doing the shadows softly grey.

Finally, as he heaved in a deep breath, the boy began to colour in the figures.

One, he coloured like an ordinary human, wearing a black army uniform. His eyes were brown, his hair a single shade lighter, a touch redder. The man had a stubbly chin and sun-browned skin, showing that he'd been away from home a lot.

The other was dramatically different.

It was darker than the shadows, with thick, shaggy fur trailing from the shoulder blades and elbows, and the backs of his knees and feet. Its eyes were golden and its teeth yellowed, large, and scary-looking, a forked tongue poking out between them. Its head was half-hidden by a mop of brown hair, and through this two pointed ears pricked. The boy continued, putting every detail into every claw, and struggling to replicate the scales that had ran down his back. Finally, the boy managed, and continued on with the tail, that long, long snake tail that he remembered so well.

The boy added a smile to the mutant's face.

With a shaking hand, the boy shone light into the eyes of his drawings, brought to life.

In the sky he painted the flowing robes and the wings of many doves touching their feathered tips together.

With tears almost forming in his eyes, the boy's smiles were neverending.

He took the drawing in both hands, and his gentle fingers trembled. Carefully, the boy carried the drawing over to his bed, and set it out carefully on the quilts, and he examined it, looking carefully for anything that seemed to him to look bad. But he was pleased.

The boy could see it, see the picture, and the place as though he was almost there.

And he would be.

Someday.

The boy looked down at the demon and the man as they smiled at each other in a sea of life and love.

"It... It's missing something..." he realized. Softly, he took his paintbrush again, and once more, returned to his artwork.

He returned to the picture that he was so focused on. With his paintbrush, the boy drew two shimmering gold circles above them, drew two final sets of wings spread out.

"Yes," he whispered, in awe, and in tears. "This is it..."

Placing the picture on his bedside cabinet ready to be pinned up on his wall, the boy grinned happily to himself, and closed his one eye, the other one covered by a brightly-coloured eyepatch. He lifted his hands, palms pressed together up to his chest, and bowed his head. The image was burned into his mind. He knew now what he wanted.

"Dear God…" he murmured softly, as he began to pray. "…Please help my daddy find you. And be really nice to him when he's up there with you, because he deserves so much more than anyone could ever give him down here. He was the best daddy in the world." The boy paused as though he was about to finish, but then went on. "And keep on loving all your creatures, as I know you will do, even when no-one else in the world loves them, love them even more than anyone else could, so that they can still be happy." The boy opened his eyes to slits, as if to check to see if He was watching. "…Amen…" he finished, then swung his legs over the edge of the bed, and pushed himself off.

Taking a last, excited glance at the picture on his bedside cabinet, the boy ran downstairs to get his mother, leaving it there to dry; a painting of the boy's father, and Mercury.

Each had wings and halos of their own, and were surrounded by a crowd of angels as they sang in greeting, welcoming the newcomers into their places, high in the sky.

In Heaven.

And despite all the emotion, despite all the anger and resentment, and despite the war that still raged and might always rage, one thing remained true.

A single promise that would always linger.

Thanks to the endless journey of everyone here, they would always be happy in some way.

Always.

The End